"She stepped aboard the *Aurora* as though she were stepping over an open grave and slipped past the assembled crew without a word or glance, passing so close to the man called Colin Hernandez he had to suppress an urge to touch her to make certain she was real and not a hologram. Five minutes later the *Aurora* eased into the harbor, and by noon the enchanted island of Saint Barthélemy was a lump of brown-green on the horizon. Stretched topless upon the foredeck, drink in hand, her flawless skin baking in the sun, was the most famous woman in the world. And one deck below, preparing an appetizer of tuna tartare, cucumber, and pineapple, was the man who was going to kill her."

Praise for *The English Spy*

An Amazon Best Book of July 2015

"Silva is a master craftsman, and his ability to keep Allon's story fresh after so many novels is to be deeply admired. Weaving in information from previous books while maintaining a propulsive pace, Silva has written a novel that longtime fans and first-time readers can enjoy with equal fervor."

Chris Schluep, Amazon Best Book citation

"A master storyteller . . . Silva has his finger on the pulse of modern events and has an uncanny ability to predict the future. . . . It is a world like no other told by an author like no other. If you are not yet a Silva/Allon fan, then you are missing out on one of the best series in modern literature."

Huffington Post

"Simply delicious. If you're a fan of perennial No. 1 best-selling author Daniel Silva, it's a must-read. If you're not a fan, you should be. . . . Highly recommended."

Minneapolis Star-Tribune

"This page-turner deepens Allon's legend and illuminates more of his shadowy world, all while cementing Silva's place among the top tier of spy thriller writers."

Kirkus Reviews

"A surefire blockbuster . . . The world needs more men like this Israeli agent. And more authors like Silva."

Bookreporter.com

By Daniel Silva

Daniel
Silva

The
English Spy

HarperCollins*Publishers*Ltd

Published by HarperCollins Publishers Ltd

First published in Canada by HarperCollins Publishers Ltd in an
original trade paperback edition: 2015
This HarperCollins Publishers Ltd mass market edition: 2016

HarperCollins books may be purchased for educational, business, or
sales promotional use through our Special Markets Department.

HarperCollins Publishers Ltd
2 Bloor Street East, 20th Floor
Toronto, Ontario, Canada
M4W 1A8

www.harpercollins.ca

Map designed by Nick Springer
Flag illustration © charnsitr/Shutterstock, Inc.

Library and Archives Canada Cataloguing in Publication information
is available upon request.

ISBN 978-1-44343-654-0

Printed and bound in The United States
RRD 9 8 7 6 5 4 3 2 1

For Betsy and Andy Lack.
And, as always, for my wife, Jamie,
and my children, Lily and Nicholas.

When a man rubs out a pencil mark, he should be careful to see that the line is quite obliterated. For if a secret is to be kept, no precautions are too great.

—GRAHAM GREENE, *THE MINISTRY OF FEAR*

No more tears now; I will think upon revenge.

—MARY, QUEEN OF SCOTS

PART ONE

DEATH OF A PRINCESS

GUSTAVIA, SAINT BARTHÉLEMY

NONE OF IT would have happened if Spider Barnes hadn't tied one on at Eddy's two nights before the *Aurora* was due to set sail. Spider was regarded as the finest waterborne chef in the entire Caribbean, irascible but altogether irreplaceable, a mad genius in a starched white jacket and apron. Spider, you see, was classically trained. Spider had done a stint in Paris. Spider had done London. Spider had done New York, San Francisco, and an unhappy layover in Miami before leaving the restaurant biz for good and taking to the freedom of the sea. He worked the big charters now, the kind of boats the film stars, rappers, moguls, and poseurs rented whenever they wanted to impress. And when Spider wasn't behind his stove, he was invariably propped atop one of the better bar stools on dry land. Eddy's was in his top five in the Caribbean Basin, perhaps his top five worldwide. He started at seven o'clock that evening with a few beers, blew a reefer in the shadowed garden at nine, and at ten was contemplating his first glass of vanilla rum. All seemed right with the world. Spider Barnes was buzzed and in paradise.

But then he spotted Veronica, and the evening took a dangerous turn. She was new to the island, a lost girl, a European of uncertain provenance who served drinks to day-trippers at the dive bar next door. She was pretty, though—pretty as a floral garnish, Spider remarked to his nameless drinking companion—and he lost his heart to her in ten seconds flat. He proposed marriage, which was Spider's favorite approach, and when she turned him down he suggested a roll in the sheets instead. Somehow it worked, and the two were seen teetering into a torrential downpour at midnight. And that was the last time anyone laid eyes on him, at 12:03 a.m. on a wet night in Gustavia, soaked to the skin, drunk and in love yet again.

The captain of the *Aurora*, a 154-foot luxury motor yacht based out of Nassau, was a man called Ogilvy—Reginald Ogilvy, ex–Royal Navy, a benevolent dictator who slept with a copy of the rulebook on his bedside table, along with his grandfather's King James Bible. He had never cared for Spider Barnes, never less so than at nine the next morning when Spider failed to appear at the regular meeting of the crew and cabin staff. It was no ordinary meeting, for the *Aurora* was being made ready for a very important guest. Only Ogilvy knew her identity. He also knew that her party would include a team of security men and that she was demanding, to say the least, which explained why he was alarmed by the absence of his renowned chef.

Ogilvy informed the Gustavia harbormaster of

the situation, and the harbormaster duly informed the local gendarmerie. A pair of officers knocked on the door of Veronica's little hillside cottage, but there was no sign of her either. Next they undertook a search of the various spots on the island where the drunken and brokenhearted typically washed ashore after a night of debauchery. A red-faced Swede at Le Select claimed to have bought Spider a Heineken that very morning. Someone else said he saw him stalking the beach at Colombier, and there was a report, never confirmed, of an inconsolable creature baying at the moon in the wilds of Toiny.

The gendarmes faithfully followed each lead. Then they scoured the island from north to south, stem to stern, all to no avail. A few minutes after sundown, Reginald Ogilvy informed the crew of the *Aurora* that Spider Barnes had vanished and that a suitable replacement would have to be found in short order. The crew fanned out across the island, from the waterside eateries of Gustavia to the beach shacks of the Grand Cul-de-Sac. And by nine that evening, in the unlikeliest of places, they had found their man.

He had arrived on the island at the height of hurricane season and settled into the clapboard cottage at the far end of the beach at Lorient. He had no possessions other than a canvas duffel bag, a stack of well-read books, a shortwave radio, and a rattletrap motor scooter that he'd acquired in Gustavia for a few grimy banknotes and a smile. The books were thick, weighty, and learned; the radio was of a quality rarely seen any longer. Late at night, when he sat on his sagging veranda reading by the light of his battery-powered lamp, the sound of music floated above the rustle of the palm fronds and the gentle slap and recession of the surf. Jazz and classical, mainly, sometimes a bit of reggae from the stations across the water. At the top of every hour he would lower his book and listen intently to the news on the BBC. Then, when the bulletin was over, he would search the airwaves for something to his liking, and the palm trees and the sea would once again dance to the rhythm of his music.

At first, it was unclear as to whether he was vacationing, passing through, hiding out, or planning to make the island his permanent address. Money seemed not to be an issue. In the morning, when he dropped by the boulangerie for his bread and coffee, he always tipped the girls generously. And in the afternoon, when he stopped at the little market near the cemetery for his German beer and American cigarettes, he never bothered to collect the loose change that came rattling out of the automatic dispenser. His French was reasonable but tinged with an accent no one could quite place. His Spanish, which he spoke to the Dominican who worked the counter at JoJo Burger, was much better, but still there was that accent. The girls at the boulangerie decided he was an Australian, but the boys at JoJo Burger reckoned he was an Afrikaner. They were all over the Caribbean, the Afrikaners. Decent folk for the most part, but a few of them had business interests that were less than legal.

His days, while shapeless, seemed not entirely

without purpose. He took his breakfast at the boulangerie, he stopped by the newsstand in Saint-Jean to collect a stack of day-old English and American papers, he did his rigorous exercises on the beach, he read his dense volumes of literature and history with a bucket hat pulled low over his eyes. And once he rented a whaler and spent the afternoon snorkeling on the islet of Tortu. But his idleness appeared forced rather than voluntary. He seemed like a wounded soldier longing to return to the battlefield, an exile dreaming of his lost homeland, wherever that homeland might be.

According to Jean-Marc, a customs officer at the airport, he had arrived on a flight from Guadeloupe in possession of a valid Venezuelan passport bearing the peculiar name Colin Hernandez. It seemed he was the product of a brief marriage between an Anglo-Irish mother and a Spanish father. The mother had fancied herself a poet; the father had done something shady with money. Colin had loathed the old man, but he spoke of the mother as though canonization were a mere formality. He carried her photograph in his billfold. The towheaded boy on her lap didn't look much like Colin, but time was like that.

The passport listed his age at thirty-eight, which seemed about right, and his occupation as "businessman," which could mean just about anything. The girls from the boulangerie reckoned he was a writer in search of inspiration. How else to explain the fact that he was almost never without a book? But the girls from the market conjured up a wild theory, wholly unsupported, that he had murdered a man

on Guadeloupe and was hiding out on Saint Barthélemy until the storm had passed. The Dominican
from JoJo Burger, who was in hiding himself, found
the hypothesis laughable. Colin Hernandez, he declared, was just another shiftless layabout living off
the trust fund of a father he hated. He would stay
until he grew bored, or until his finances grew thin.
Then he would fly off to somewhere else, and within
a day or two they would struggle to recall his name.

Finally, a month to the day after his arrival, there
was a slight change in his routine. After taking his
lunch at JoJo Burger, he went to the hair salon in
Saint-Jean, and when he emerged his shaggy black
mane was shorn, sculpted, and lustrously oiled.
Next morning, when he appeared at the boulangerie, he was freshly shaved and dressed in khaki
trousers and a crisp white shirt. He had his usual
breakfast—a large bowl of café crème and a loaf of
coarse country bread—and lingered over the previous day's London *Times*. Then, instead of returning
to his cottage, he mounted his motor scooter and
sped into Gustavia. And by noon that day, it was
finally clear why the man called Colin Hernandez
had come to Saint Barthélemy.

He went first to the stately old Hotel Carl Gustaf,
but the head chef, after learning he had no formal
training, refused to grant him an interview. The
owners of Maya's turned him politely away, as did
the management of the Wall House, Ocean, and
La Cantina. He tried La Plage, but La Plage wasn't
interested. Neither were the Eden Rock, the Gua-

nahani, La Crêperie, Le Jardin, or Le Grain de Sel, the lonely outpost overlooking the salt marshes of Saline. Even La Gloriette, founded by a political exile, wanted nothing to do with him.

Undeterred, he tried his luck at the undiscovered gems of the island: the airport snack bar, the Creole joint across the street, the little pizza-and-panini hut in the parking lot of L'Oasis supermarket. And it was there fortune finally smiled upon him, for he learned that the chef at Le Piment had stormed off the job after a long-simmering dispute over hours and salary. By four o'clock that afternoon, after demonstrating his skills in Le Piment's birdhouse of a kitchen, he was gainfully employed. He worked his first shift that same evening. The reviews were universally glowing.

In fact, it did not take long for word of his culinary prowess to make its way round the little island. Le Piment, once the province of locals and habitués, was soon overflowing with a newfound clientele, all of whom sang the praises of the mysterious new chef with the peculiar Anglo-Spanish name. The Carl Gustaf tried to poach him, as did the Eden Rock, the Guanahani, and La Plage, all without success. Therefore, Reginald Ogilvy, captain of the *Aurora*, was in a pessimistic mood when he appeared at Le Piment without a reservation the night after the disappearance of Spider Barnes. He was forced to cool his heels for thirty minutes at the bar before finally being granted a table. He ordered three appetizers and three entrées. Then, after sampling each, he requested a brief word with the chef. Ten minutes elapsed before his wish was granted.

"Hungry?" asked the man called Colin Hernandez, looking down at the plates of food.

"Not really."

"So why are you here?"

"I wanted to see if you were as good as everyone seems to think you are."

Ogilvy extended his hand and introduced himself—rank and name, followed by the name of his boat. The man called Colin Hernandez raised an eyebrow quizzically.

"The *Aurora* is Spider Barnes's boat, isn't it?"

"You know Spider?"

"I think I had a drink with him once."

"You weren't alone."

Ogilvy took stock of the figure standing before him. He was compact, hard, formidable. To the Englishman's sharp eye, he seemed like a man who had sailed in rough seas. His brow was dark and thick; his jaw was sturdy and resolute. It was a face, thought Ogilvy, that had been built to take a punch.

"You're Venezuelan," he said.

"Says who?"

"Says everyone who refused to hire you when you were looking for a job."

Ogilvy's eyes moved from the face to the hand resting on the back of the chair opposite. There was no evidence of tattooing, which he saw as a positive sign. Ogilvy regarded the modern culture of ink as a form of self-mutilation.

"Do you drink?" he asked.

"Not like Spider."

"Married?"

"Only once."

"Children?"

"God, no."

"Vices?"

"Coltrane and Monk."

"Ever killed anyone?"

"Not that I can recall."

He said this with a smile. Reginald Ogilvy smiled in return.

"I'm wondering whether I might tempt you away from all this," he said, glancing around the modest open-air dining room. "I'm prepared to pay you a generous salary. And when we're not at sea, you'll have plenty of free time to do whatever it is you like to do when you're not cooking."

"*How* generous?"

"Two thousand a week."

"How much was Spider making?"

"Three," replied Ogilvy after a moment's hesitation. "But Spider was with me for two seasons."

"He's not with you now, is he?"

Ogilvy made a show of deliberation. "Three it is," he said. "But I need you to start right away."

"When do you sail?"

"Tomorrow morning."

"In that case," said the man called Colin Hernandez, "I suppose you'll have to pay me four."

Reginald Ogilvy, captain of the *Aurora*, surveyed the plates of food before rising gravely to his feet. "Eight o'clock," he said. "Don't be late."

François, the quick-tempered Marseilles-born owner of Le Piment, did not take the news well.

There was a string of affronts delivered in the rapid-fire patois of the south. There were promises of reprisals. And then there was the bottle of rather good Bordeaux, empty, that shattered into a thousand shards of emerald when hurled against the wall of the tiny kitchen. Later, François would deny he had been aiming at his departing chef. But Isabelle, a waitress who witnessed the incident, would call into question his version of events. François, she swore, had flung the bottle dagger-like directly at the head of Monsieur Hernandez. And Monsieur Hernandez, she recalled, had evaded the object with a movement that was so small and swift it occurred in the blink of an eye. Afterward, he had glared coldly at François for a long moment as though deciding how best to break his neck. Then, calmly, he had removed his spotless white kitchen apron and climbed aboard his motor scooter.

He spent the remainder of that night on the veranda of his cottage, reading by the light of his hurricane lamp. And at the top of every hour, he lowered his book and listened to the news on the BBC as the waves slapped and receded on the beach and the palm fronds hissed in the night wind. In the morning, after an invigorating swim in the sea, he showered, dressed, and packed his belongings into his canvas duffel: his clothing, his books, his radio. In addition, he packed two items that had been left for him on the islet of Tortu: a Stechkin 9mm pistol with a silencer screwed into the barrel, and a rectangular parcel, twelve inches by twenty. The parcel weighed sixteen pounds exactly. He placed it in the center of the duffel so it would remain balanced when carried.

He left the beach at Lorient for the last time at half past seven and, with the duffel resting upon his knees, rode into Gustavia. The *Aurora* sparkled at the edge of the harbor. He boarded at ten minutes to eight and was shown to his cabin by his sous-chef, a thin English girl with the unlikely name Amelia List. He stowed his possessions in the cupboard—including the Stechkin pistol and the sixteen-pound parcel—and dressed in the chef's trousers and tunic that had been laid upon his berth. Amelia List was waiting in the corridor when he emerged. She escorted him to the galley and led him on a tour of the dry goods pantry, the walk-in refrigerator, and the storeroom filled with wine. It was there, in the cool darkness, that he had his first sexual thought about the English girl in the crisp white uniform. He did nothing to dispel it. He had been celibate for so many months that he could scarcely recall what it felt like to touch a woman's hair or caress the flesh of a defenseless breast.

A few minutes before ten o'clock there came an announcement over the ship's intercom instructing all members of the crew to report to the afterdeck. The man called Colin Hernandez followed Amelia List outside and was standing next to her when two black Range Rovers braked to a halt at *Aurora*'s stern. From the first emerged two giggling sunburned girls and a pale florid-faced man in his forties who was holding the straps of a pink beach bag in one hand and the neck of an open bottle of champagne in the other. Two athletic-looking men spilled from the second Rover, followed a moment later by a woman who looked to be suffering from a case of terminal melancholia. She wore a peach-colored dress that left the impression of partial nudity, a wide-brimmed hat that shadowed her slender shoulders, and large opaque sunglasses that concealed much of her porcelain face. Even so, she was instantly recognizable. Her profile betrayed her, the profile so admired by the fashion photographers and the paparazzi who stalked her every move. There were no paparazzi present that morning. For once she had eluded them.

She stepped aboard the *Aurora* as though she were stepping over an open grave and slipped past the assembled crew without a word or glance, passing so close to the man called Colin Hernandez he had to suppress an urge to touch her to make certain she was real and not a hologram. Five minutes later the *Aurora* eased into the harbor, and by noon the enchanted island of Saint Barthélemy was a lump of brown-green on the horizon. Stretched topless upon the foredeck, drink in hand, her flawless skin baking in the sun, was the most famous woman in the world. And one deck below, preparing an appetizer of tuna tartare, cucumber, and pineapple, was the man who was going to kill her.

2

OFF THE LEEWARD ISLANDS

EVERYONE KNEW THE STORY. And even those who pretended not to care, or expressed disdain over her worldwide cult of devotion, knew every sordid detail. She was the immensely shy and beautiful middle-class girl from Kent who had managed to find her way to Cambridge, and he was the handsome and slightly older future king of England. They had met at a campus debate having something to do with the environment, and, according to the legend, the future king was instantly smitten. A lengthy courtship followed, quiet and discreet. The girl was vetted by the future king's people; the future king, by hers. Finally, one of the naughtier tabloids managed to snap a photograph of the couple leaving the Duke of Rutland's annual summer ball at Belvoir Castle. Buckingham Palace released a bland piece of paper confirming the obvious, that the future king and the middle-class girl with no aristocratic blood in her veins were dating. Then, a month later, with the tabloids ablaze with rumors and speculation, the palace announced that the middle-class girl and the future king planned to marry.

They were wed at St. Paul's Cathedral on a morning in June when the skies of southern England poured with black rain. Later, when things fell apart, there were some in the British press who would write that they were doomed from the start. The girl, by temperament and breeding, was wholly unsuited for life in the royal fishbowl; and the future king, for all the same reasons, was equally unsuited for marriage. He had many lovers, too many to count, and the girl punished him by taking one of her security guards to her bed. The future king, when told of the affair, banished the guard to a lonely outpost in Scotland. Distraught, the girl attempted suicide by taking an overdose of sleeping tablets and was rushed to the emergency room at St. Anne's Hospital. Buckingham Palace announced she was suffering from dehydration caused by a bout of influenza. When asked to explain why her husband had not visited her in the hospital, the palace murmured something about a scheduling conflict. The statement raised far more questions than it answered.

Upon her release, it became obvious to royal watchers that all was not well with the future king's beautiful wife. Even so, she performed her marital duty by bearing him two heirs, a son and a daughter, both delivered after abbreviated and difficult pregnancies. The king showed his gratitude by returning to the bed of a woman to whom he had once proposed marriage, and the princess retaliated by attaining a global celebrity that eclipsed that of the king's sainted mother. She traveled the world in support of noble causes, a horde of reporters and photographers hanging on her every word and movement, and yet all the while no one seemed to notice she was sliding toward something like madness. Finally, with her blessing and quiet assistance, it all came spilling onto the pages of a tell-all book: her husband's infidelities, the bouts of depression, the suicide attempts, the eating disorder brought on by her constant exposure to the press and public. The future king, incensed, engineered a stream of retaliatory press leaks about his wife's erratic behavior. Then came the coup de grâce, the recording of a passionate telephone conversation between the princess and her favorite lover. By then, the Queen had had enough. With the monarchy in jeopardy, she asked the couple to divorce as quickly as possible. They did so a month later. Buckingham Palace, without a trace of irony, issued a statement declaring the termination of the royal marriage "amicable."

The princess was permitted to keep her apartments in Kensington Palace but was stripped of the title Her Royal Highness. The Queen offered her a second-tier honorific but she refused it, preferring instead to be called by her given name. She even shed her SO14 bodyguards, for she viewed them more as spies than protectors of her security. The palace quietly kept tabs on her movements and associations, as did British intelligence, which viewed her more as a nuisance than a threat to the realm.

In public, she was the radiant face of global compassion. But behind closed doors she drank too much and surrounded herself with an entourage that one royal adviser described as "Eurorubbish." On this trip, however, her retinue of companions was smaller than usual. The two sunburned women were childhood friends; the man who boarded *Aurora* with an open bottle of champagne was Simon Hastings-Clarke, the grotesquely wealthy viscount who supported her in the style to which she had become accustomed. It was Hastings-Clarke who flew her privately around the world on his fleet of jets, and Hastings-Clarke who footed the bill for her bodyguards. The two men who accompanied them to the Caribbean were employed by a private security firm in London. Before leaving Gustavia, they had subjected the *Aurora* and its crew to only a cursory inspection. Of the man called Colin Hernandez, they asked a single question: "What are we having for lunch?"

At the request of the former princess, it was a light buffet, though neither she nor her companions seemed terribly interested in it. They drank a great deal that afternoon, roasting their bodies in the harsh sun of the foredeck, until a rainstorm drove them laughing to their staterooms. They remained there until nine that evening, when they emerged dressed and groomed as though for a garden party in Somerset. They had cocktails and canapés on the afterdeck and then repaired to the main salon for dinner: salad with truffle-infused vinaigrette, followed by lobster risotto and rack of lamb with artichoke, lemon *forte*, courgette, and *piment d'argile*. The former princess and her companions declared the meal magnificent and demanded an appearance

by the chef. When finally he appeared, they sere-
naded him with childlike applause.

"What will you make us tomorrow night?" asked
the former princess.

"It's a surprise," he replied in his peculiar accent.

"Oh, good," she said, fixing him with the same
smile he had seen on countless magazine covers. "I
do like surprises."

They were a small crew, eight in all, and it was
the responsibility of the chef and his assistant to
see to the china, the stemware, the silver, the pots
and pans, and the cooking utensils. They stood side
by side at the basin long after the former princess
and her companions had turned in, their hands
occasionally touching beneath the warm soapy
water, her bony hip pressing against his thigh. And
once, as they squeezed past one another in the linen
cabinet, her firm nipples traced two lines across his
back, sending a charge of electricity and blood to
his groin. They retired to their cabins alone, but
a few minutes later he heard a butterfly tap at his
door. She took him without a sound. It was like
performing the act of love with a mute.

"Maybe this was a mistake," she whispered into
his ear when they had finished.

"Why would you say that?"

"Because we're going to be working together for
a long time."

"Not so long."

"You're not planning to stay?"

"That depends."

"On what?"

He said nothing more. She laid her head on his chest and closed her eyes.

"You can't stay here," he said.

"I know," she answered drowsily. "Just for a little while."

He lay motionless for a long time after, Amelia List sleeping on his chest, the *Aurora* rising and falling beneath him, his mind working through the details of what was to come. Finally, at three o'clock, he eased from the berth and padded naked across the cabin to the cupboard. Soundlessly, he dressed in black trousers, a woolen sweater, and a dark waterproof coat. Then he removed the wrapper from the parcel—the parcel measuring twelve inches by twenty and weighing sixteen pounds precisely— and engaged the power source and the timer on the detonator. He returned the parcel to the cupboard and was reaching for the Stechkin pistol when he heard the girl stir behind him. He turned slowly and stared at her in the darkness.

"What was that?" she asked.

"Go back to sleep."

"I saw a red light."

"It was my radio."

"Why are you listening to the radio at three in the morning?"

Before he could answer, the bedside lamp flared. Her eyes flashed across his dark clothing before settling on the silenced gun that was still in his hand. She opened her mouth to scream, but he placed his palm heavily across her face before any sound could escape. As she struggled to free herself from his grasp, he whispered soothingly into her ear. "Don't worry, my love," he was saying. "It will only hurt a little."

Her eyes widened in terror. Then he twisted her head violently to the left, severing her spinal cord, and held her gently as she died.

It was not the custom of Reginald Ogilvy to stand the lonely hours of the middle watch, but concern for the safety of his famous passenger drove him to the bridge of the *Aurora* early that morning. He was checking the weather forecast on an onboard computer, a fresh cup of coffee in his hand, when the man called Colin Hernandez appeared at the top of the companionway, dressed entirely in black. Ogilvy looked up sharply and asked, "What are you doing here?" But he received no reply other than two rounds from the silenced Stechkin that pierced the front of his uniform and mauled his heart.

The coffee cup clattered loudly to the floor; Ogilvy, instantly dead, thudded heavily next to it. His killer moved calmly to the console, made a slight adjustment to the ship's heading, and re-treated down the companionway. The main deck was deserted, no other crew members on duty. He lowered one of the Zodiac dinghies into the black sea, clambered aboard, and released the line.

Adrift, he bobbed beneath a canopy of diamond-white stars, watching the *Aurora* slicing eastward toward the shipping lanes of the Atlantic, pilotless, a ghost ship. He checked the luminous face of his wristwatch. Then, when the dial read zero, he looked up again. Fifteen additional seconds elapsed, enough time for him to consider the remote possibility that the bomb was somehow defective. Finally, there was a flash on the horizon—the blinding white flash of the high explosive, followed by the orange-yellow of the secondary explosions and fire.

The sound was like the rumble of distant thunder. Afterward, there was only the sea beating against the side of the Zodiac, and the wind. With the press of a button, he fired the outboard and watched as the *Aurora* started her journey to the bottom. Then he turned the Zodiac to the west and opened the throttle.

3

THE CARIBBEAN-LONDON

THE FIRST INDICATION of trouble came when Pegasus Global Charters of Nassau reported that a routine message to one of its vessels, the 154-foot luxury motor yacht *Aurora*, had received no reply. The Pegasus operations center immediately requested assistance from all commercial ships and pleasure craft in the vicinity of the Leeward Islands, and within minutes the crew of a Liberian-registered oil tanker reported that they had seen an unusual flash of light in the area at approximately 3:45 that morning. Shortly thereafter the crew of a container ship spotted one of the *Aurora*'s dinghies floating empty and adrift approximately one hundred miles south-southeast of Gustavia. Simultaneously, a private sailing vessel encountered life preservers and other floating debris a few miles to the west. Fearing the worst, Pegasus management phoned the British High Commission in Kingston and informed the honorary consul that the *Aurora* was missing and presumed lost. Management then sent along a copy of the passenger manifest, which included the given name of the former princess.

"Tell me it isn't her," the honorary consul said incredulously, but Pegasus management confirmed that the passenger was indeed the former wife of the future king. The consul immediately rang his superiors at the Foreign Office in London, and the superiors determined the situation was of sufficient gravity to wake Prime Minister Jonathan Lancaster, at which point the crisis truly began.

The prime minister broke the news to the future king by telephone at half past one, but waited until nine to inform the British people and the world. Standing outside the black door of 10 Downing Street, his face grim, he recounted the facts as they were known at that time. The former wife of the future king had traveled to the Caribbean in the company of Simon Hastings-Clarke and two other longtime friends. On the holiday island of Saint Barthélemy, the party had boarded the luxury motor yacht *Aurora* for a planned one-week cruise. All contact with the vessel had been lost; surface debris had been discovered. "We hope and pray the princess will be found alive," the prime minister said solemnly. "But we must prepare ourselves for the very worst."

The first day of the search produced no remains or survivors. Nor did the second day or the third. After conferring with the Queen, Prime Minister Lancaster announced that his government was operating under the assumption that the beloved princess was dead. In the Caribbean, the search teams focused their efforts on finding wreckage rather than the bodies. It would not be a long search. In fact, just forty-eight hours later, an unmanned submersible operated by the French navy discovered the *Aurora* lying beneath two thousand feet of seawater. One expert who viewed the video images said it was clear the vessel had suffered some type of cataclysmic failure, almost certainly an explosion. "The question is," he said, "was it an accident, or was it intentional?"

A majority of the country—reliable polling said it was so—refused to believe she was actually gone. They hung their hopes on the fact that only one of the *Aurora*'s two Zodiac dinghies had been found. Surely, they argued, she was adrift on the open seas or had washed ashore on a deserted island. One disreputable Web site went so far as to report that she had been spotted on Montserrat. Another said she was living quietly by the sea in Dorset. Conspiracy theorists of every stripe concocted lurid tales of a plot to kill the princess that was conceived by the Queen's Privy Council and carried out by Britain's Secret Intelligence Service, better known as MI6. Pressure mounted on its chief, Graham Seymour, to issue a full-throated denial of the allegations, but he steadfastly refused. "These aren't *allegations*," he told the foreign secretary during a tense meeting at the service's vast riverfront headquarters. "These are fairy tales spun by people with mental disorders, and I won't dignify them with a response."

Privately, however, Seymour had already reached the conclusion that the explosion aboard the *Aurora* was not an accident. So, too, had his counterpart at the DGSE, the highly capable French intelligence

service. A French analysis of the wreckage video had
determined that the *Aurora* was blown apart by a
bomb detonated belowdecks. But who had smuggled
the device aboard the vessel? And who had primed
the detonator? The DGSE's prime suspect was the
man who had been hired to replace the *Aurora*'s
missing head chef on the evening before the yacht
left port. The French forwarded to MI6 a grainy
video of his arrival at Gustavia's airport, along with
a few poor-quality still photos captured by private
storefront security cameras. They showed a man
who did not care to have his picture taken. "He
doesn't strike me as the sort of chap who would go
down with the ship," Seymour told a gathering of
his senior staff. "He's out there somewhere. Find
out who he really is and where he's hiding out, pref-
erably before the Frogs."

He was a whisper in a half-lit chapel, a loose
thread at the hem of a discarded garment. They
ran the photographs through the computers. And
when the computers failed to find a match, they
searched for him the old-fashioned way, with shoe
leather and envelopes filled with money—American
money, of course, for in the nether regions of the
espionage world, dollars remained the reserve currency. MI6's man in Caracas could find no trace
of him. Nor could he find any hint of an Anglo-
Irish mother with a poetic heart, or of a Spanish-
businessman father. The address on his passport
turned out to be a derelict lot in a Caracas slum; his
last known phone number was long deceased. A paid
asset inside the Venezuelan secret police said he'd
heard a rumor about a link to Castro, but a source

close to Cuban intelligence murmured something about the Colombian cartels. "Maybe once," said an incorruptible policeman in Bogotá, "but he parted company with the drug lords a long time ago. The last thing I heard, he was living in Panama with one of Noriega's former mistresses. He had several million stashed in a dirty Panamanian bank and a beach condo on the Playa Farallón." The former mistress denied all knowledge of him, and the manager of the bank in question, after accepting a bribe of ten thousand dollars, could find no record of any accounts bearing his name. As for the beach condo in Farallón, a neighbor could recall little of his appearance, only his voice. "He spoke with a peculiar accent," he said. "It sounded as though he was from Australia. Or was it South Africa?"

Graham Seymour monitored the search for the elusive suspect from the comfort of his office, the finest office in all spydom, with its English garden of an atrium, its enormous mahogany desk used by all the chiefs who had come before him, its towering windows overlooking the river Thames, and its stately old grandfather clock constructed by none other than Sir Mansfield Smith Cumming, the first "C" of the British Secret Service. The splendor of his surroundings made Seymour restless. In his distant past, he had been a field man of some repute—not for MI6 but for MI5, Britain's less glamorous internal security service, where he had served with distinction before making the short journey from Thames House to Vauxhall Cross. There were some in MI6 who resented the appointment of an outsider, but most saw "the crossing," as it became known in the trade, as a sort of homecoming. Seymour's father had been a legendary MI6 officer, a deceiver of the Nazis, a shaper of events in the Middle East. And now his son, in the prime of life, sat behind the desk before which Seymour the Elder had stood, cap in hand.

With power, however, there often comes a feeling of helplessness, and Seymour, the espiocrat, the boardroom spy, soon fell victim to it. As the search ground futilely on, and as pressure from Downing Street and the palace mounted, his mood grew brittle. He kept a photo of the target on his desk, next to the Victorian inkwell and the Parker fountain pen he used to mark his documents with his personal cipher. Something about the face was familiar. Seymour suspected that somewhere—on another battlefield, in another land—their paths had crossed. It didn't matter that the service databases said it wasn't so. Seymour trusted his own memory over the memory of any government computer.

And so, as the field hands chased down false leads and dug dry wells, Seymour conducted a search of his own from his gilded cage atop Vauxhall Cross. He began by scouring his prodigious memory, and when it failed him, he requested access to a stack of his old MI5 case files and searched those, too. Again he found no trace of his quarry. Finally, on the morning of the tenth day, the console telephone on Seymour's desk purred sedately. The distinctive ringtone told him the caller was Uzi Navot, the chief of Israel's vaunted secret intelligence service. Seymour hesitated, then cautiously lifted the receiver to his ear. As usual, the Israeli spymaster didn't bother with an exchange of pleasantries.

"I think we might have found the man you're looking for."

"Who is he?"

"An old friend."

"Of yours or ours?"

"Yours," said the Israeli. "We don't have any friends."

"Can you tell me his name?"

"Not on the phone."

"How soon can you be in London?"

The line went dead.

4

VAUXHALL CROSS, LONDON

UZI NAVOT ARRIVED AT Vauxhall Cross shortly before eleven that evening and was fired into the executive suite in a pneumatic tube of an elevator. He wore a gray suit that fit him tightly through his massive shoulders, a white shirt that lay open against his thick neck, and rimless spectacles that pinched the bridge of his pugilist's nose. At first glance, few assumed Navot to be an Israeli or even a Jew, a trait that had served him well during his career. Once upon a time he had been a *katsa*, the term used by his service to describe undercover field operatives. Armed with an array of languages and a pile of false passports, Navot had penetrated terror networks and recruited a chain of spies and informants scattered around the world. In London he had been known as Clyde Bridges, the European marketing director for an obscure business software firm. He had run several successful operations on British soil at a time when it was Seymour's responsibility to prevent such activity. Seymour held no grudge, for such was the nature of relationships between spies: adversaries one day, allies the next.

A frequent visitor to Vauxhall Cross, Navot did not remark on the beauty of Seymour's grand office. Nor did he engage in the usual round of professional gossip that preceded most encounters between inhabitants of the secret world. Seymour knew the reason for the Israeli's taciturn mood. Navot's first term as chief was nearing its end, and his prime minister had asked him to step aside for another man, a legendary officer with whom Seymour had worked on numerous occasions. There was talk that the legend had struck a deal to retain Navot's services. It was unorthodox, allowing one's predecessor to remain on the premises, but the legend rarely concerned himself with adherence to orthodoxy. His willingness to take chances was his greatest strength—and sometimes, thought Seymour, his undoing.

Dangling from Navot's powerful right hand was a stainless-steel attaché case with combination locks. From it he removed a slender file folder, which he placed on the mahogany desk. Inside was a document, one page in length; the Israelis prided themselves on the brevity of their cables. Seymour read the subject line. Then he glanced at the photograph lying next to his inkwell and swore softly. On the opposite side of the imposing desk, Uzi Navot permitted himself a brief smile. It wasn't often that one succeeded in telling the director-general of MI6 something he didn't already know.

"Who's the source of the information?" asked Seymour.

"It's possible he was an Iranian," replied Navot vaguely.

"Does MI6 have regular access to his product?"

"No," answered Navot. "He's ours exclusively."

MI6, the CIA, and Israeli intelligence had worked closely for more than a decade to delay the Iranian march toward a nuclear weapon. The three services had operated jointly against the Iranian nuclear supply chain and shared vast amounts of technical data and intelligence. It was agreed that the Israelis had the best human sources in Tehran, and, much to the annoyance of the Americans and the British, they protected them jealously. Judging from the wording of the report, Seymour suspected that Navot's spy worked for VEVAK, the Iranian intelligence service. VEVAK sources were notoriously difficult to handle. Sometimes the information they traded for Western cash was genuine. And sometimes it was in the service of *taqiyya*, the Persian practice of displaying one intention while harboring another.

"Do you believe him?" asked Seymour.

"I wouldn't be here otherwise." Navot paused, then added, "And something tells me you believe him, too."

When Seymour offered no reply, Navot drew a second document from his attaché case and laid it on the desktop next to the first. "It's a copy of a report we sent to MI6 three years ago," he explained. "We knew about his connection to the Iranians back then. We also knew he was working with Hezbollah, Hamas, al-Qaeda, and anyone else who would have him." Navot added, "Your friend isn't terribly discriminating about the company he keeps."

"It was before my time," Seymour intoned.

"But now it's your problem." Navot pointed toward a passage near the end of the document. "As you can see, we proposed an operation to take him out of circulation. We even volunteered to do the job. And how do you suppose your predecessor responded to our generous offer?"

"Obviously, he turned it down."

"With extreme prejudice. In fact, he told us in no uncertain terms that we weren't to lay a finger on him. He was afraid it would open a Pandora's box." Navot shook his head slowly. "And now here we are."

The room was silent except for the ticking of C's old grandfather clock. Finally, Navot asked quietly, "Where were you that day, Graham?"

"What day?"

"The fifteenth of August, nineteen ninety-eight."

"The day of the bombing?"

Navot nodded.

"You know damn well where I was," Seymour answered. "I was at Five."

"You were the head of counterterrorism."

"Yes."

"Which meant it was your responsibility."

Seymour said nothing.

"What happened, Graham? How did he get through?"

"Mistakes were made. Bad mistakes. Bad enough to ruin careers, even today." Seymour gathered up the two documents and returned them to Navot. "Did your Iranian source tell you why he did it?"

"It's possible he's returned to the old fight. It's also possible he was acting at the behest of others.

Either way, he needs to be dealt with, sooner rather than later."

Seymour made no response.

"Our offer still stands, Graham."

"What offer is that?"

"We'll take care of him," Navot answered. "And then we'll bury him in a hole so deep that none of the old problems will ever make it to the surface."

Seymour lapsed into a contemplative silence. "There's only one person I would trust with a job like this," he said at last.

"That might be difficult."

"The pregnancy?"

Navot nodded.

"When is she due?"

"I'm afraid that's classified."

Seymour managed a brief smile. "Do you suppose he might be persuaded to take the assignment?"

"Anything's possible," replied Navot noncommittally. "I'd be happy to make the approach on your behalf."

"No," said Seymour. "I'll do it."

"There is one other problem," said Navot after a moment.

"Only one?"

"He doesn't know much about that part of the world."

"I know someone who can serve as his guide."

"He won't work with someone he doesn't know."

"Actually, they're very well acquainted."

"Is he MI6?"

"No," replied Seymour. "Not yet."

5

FIUMICINO AIRPORT, ROME

W HY DO YOU suppose my flight is delayed?" asked Chiara.

"It could be a mechanical problem," replied Gabriel.

"It could be," she repeated without conviction.

They were seated in a quiet corner of a first-class departure lounge. It didn't matter the city, thought Gabriel, they were all the same. Unread newspapers, tepid bottles of suspect pinot grigio, CNN International playing silently on a large flat-panel television. By his own calculation, Gabriel had spent one-third of his career in places like this. Unlike his wife, he was extraordinarily good at waiting.

"Go ask that pretty girl at the information desk why my flight hasn't been called," she said.

"I don't want to talk to the pretty girl at the information desk."

"Why not?"

"Because she doesn't know anything, and she'll simply tell me something she thinks I want to hear."

"Why must you always be so fatalistic?"

"It prevents me from being disappointed later."

Chiara smiled and closed her eyes; Gabriel looked at the television. A British reporter in a helmet and flak jacket was talking about the latest airstrike on Gaza. Gabriel wondered why CNN had become so enamored with British reporters. He supposed it was the accent. The news always sounded more authoritative when delivered with a British accent, even if not a word of it was true.

"What's he saying?" asked Chiara.

"Do you really want to know?"

"It'll help pass the time."

Gabriel squinted to read the closed captioning. "He says an Israeli warplane attacked a school where several hundred Palestinians were sheltering from the fighting. He says at least fifteen people were killed and several dozen more seriously wounded."

"How many were women and children?"

"All of them, apparently."

"Was the school the real target of the air raid?"

Gabriel typed a brief message into his Black-Berry and fired it securely to King Saul Boulevard, the headquarters of Israel's foreign intelligence service. It had a long and deliberately misleading name that had very little to do with the true nature of its work. Employees referred to it as the Office and nothing else.

"The real target," he said, his eyes on the Black-Berry, "was a house across the street."

"Who lives in the house?"

"Muhammad Sarkis."

"*The* Muhammad Sarkis?"

Gabriel nodded.

"Is Muhammad still among the living?"

"I'm afraid not."

"What about the school?"

"It wasn't hit. The only casualties were Sarkis and members of his family."

"Maybe someone should tell that reporter the truth."

"What good would it do?"

"More fatalism," said Chiara.

"No disappointment."

"Please find out why my flight is delayed."

Gabriel typed another message into his Black-Berry. A moment later came the response.

"One of the Hamas rockets landed close to Ben-Gurion."

"How close?" asked Chiara.

"Too close for comfort."

"Do you think the pretty girl at the information desk knows my destination is under rocket fire?"

Gabriel was silent.

"Are you sure you want to go through with it?" asked Chiara.

"With what?"

"Don't make me say it aloud."

"Are you asking whether I still want to be the chief at a time like this?"

She nodded.

"At a time like this," he said, watching the images of combat and explosions flickering on the screen, "I wish I could go to Gaza and fight alongside our boys."

"I thought you hated the army."

"I did."

She tilted her head toward him and opened her

eyes. They were the color of caramel and flecked with gold. Time had left no marks on her beautiful face. Were it not for her swollen abdomen and the band of gold on her finger, she might have been the same young girl he had first encountered a lifetime ago, in the ancient ghetto of Venice.

"Fitting, isn't it?"

"What's that?"

"That the children of Gabriel Allon should be born in a time of war."

"With a bit of luck, the war will be over by the time they're born."

"I'm not so sure about that." Chiara glanced at the departure board. The status box for Flight 386 to Tel Aviv read DELAYED. "If my plane doesn't leave soon, they're going to be born here in Italy."

"Not a chance."

"What would be so wrong with that?"

"We had a plan. And we're sticking to the plan."

"Actually," she said archly, "the plan was for us to return to Israel together."

"True," said Gabriel, smiling. "But events intervened."

"They usually do."

Seventy-two hours earlier, in an ordinary parish church near Lake Como, Gabriel and Chiara had discovered one of the world's most famous stolen paintings: Caravaggio's *Nativity with St. Francis and St. Lawrence*. The badly damaged canvas was now at the Vatican, where it was awaiting restoration. It was Gabriel's intention to conduct the early stages himself. Such was his unique combination of talents. He was an art restorer, he was a master spy and assassin, a legend who had overseen some of the greatest operations in the history of Israeli intelligence. Soon he would be a father again, and then he would be the chief. They didn't write stories about chiefs, he thought. They wrote stories about the men whom chiefs sent into the field to do their dirty work.

"I don't know why you're being so stubborn about that painting," Chiara said.

"I found it, I want to restore it."

"Actually, *we* found it. But that doesn't change the fact that there's no possible way you can finish it before the children are born."

"It doesn't matter whether I can finish it or not. I just want to—"

"Leave your mark on it?"

He nodded slowly. "It might be the last painting I ever get to restore. Besides, I owe it to him."

"Who?"

He didn't answer; he was reading the closed captioning on the television.

"What's he talking about now?" Chiara asked.

"The princess."

"What about her?"

"It seems the explosion that sank the boat was an accident."

"Do you believe it?"

"No."

"So why would they say something like that?"

"I suppose they want to give themselves time and space."

"For what?"

"To find the man they're looking for."

Chiara closed her eyes and leaned her head

against his shoulder. Her dark hair, with its shimmering auburn and chestnut highlights, smelled richly of vanilla. Gabriel kissed her hair softly and inhaled its scent. Suddenly, he didn't want her to get on the airplane alone.

"What does the departure board say about my flight?" she asked.

"Delayed."

"Can't you do something to speed things up?"

"You overestimate my powers."

"False modesty doesn't suit you, darling."

Gabriel typed another brief message into his BlackBerry and sent it to King Saul Boulevard. A moment later the device vibrated softly with the reply.

"Well?" asked Chiara.

"Watch the board."

Chiara opened her eyes. The status box for El Al Flight 386 still read DELAYED. Thirty seconds later it changed to BOARDING.

"Too bad you can't stop the war so easily," Chiara said.

"Only Hamas can stop the war."

She gathered up her carry-on bag and a stack of glossy magazines and rose carefully to her feet. "Be a good boy," she said. "And if someone asks you for a favor, remember those three lovely words."

"Find someone else."

Chiara smiled. Then she kissed Gabriel with surprising urgency.

"Come home, Gabriel."

"Soon."

"No," she said. "Come home now."

"You'd better hurry, Chiara. Otherwise, you'll miss your flight."

She kissed him one last time. Then she turned away without another word and boarded the plane.

Gabriel waited until Chiara's flight was safely airborne before leaving the terminal and making his way to Fiumicino's chaotic parking garage. His anonymous German sedan was at the far end of the third deck, the front end facing out, lest he had reason to flee the garage in a hurry. As always, he searched the undercarriage for evidence of a concealed explosive before sliding behind the wheel and starting the engine. An Italian pop song blasted from the radio, one of those silly tunes Chiara was always singing to herself when she thought no one else was listening. Gabriel switched to the BBC, but it was filled with news about the war so he lowered the volume. There would be time enough for war later, he thought. For the next few weeks there would only be the Caravaggio.

He crossed the Tiber over the Ponte Cavour and made his way to the Via Gregoriana. The old Office safe flat was at the far end of the street, near the top of the Spanish Steps. He squeezed the sedan into an empty spot along the curb and retrieved his Beretta 9mm pistol from the glove box before climbing out. The chill night air smelled of frying garlic and faintly of wet leaves, the smell of Rome in autumn. Something about it always made Gabriel think of death.

He walked past the entrance of his building, past

the awnings of the Hassler Villa Medici Hotel, to the Church of the Trinità dei Monti. A moment later, after determining he was not being followed, he returned to his apartment building. A single energy-efficient bulb burned weakly in the foyer; he moved through its sphere of light and climbed the darkened staircase. As he stepped onto the third-floor landing, he froze. The door of the flat was ajar, and from within came the sound of drawers opening and closing. Calmly, he drew the Beretta from the small of his back and used the barrel to slowly push open the door. At first, he could see no sign of the intruder. Then the door yielded another inch and he glimpsed Graham Seymour standing at the kitchen counter, an unopened bottle of Gavi in one hand and a corkscrew in the other. Gabriel slipped the gun into his coat pocket and went inside. And in his head he was thinking of three lovely words.

Find someone else . . .

6

VIA GREGORIANA, ROME

PERHAPS YOU'D BETTER see to this, Gabriel. Otherwise, someone's liable to get hurt."

Seymour surrendered the bottle of wine and the corkscrew and leaned against the kitchen counter. He wore gray flannel trousers, a herringbone jacket, and a blue dress shirt with French cuffs. The absence of personal aides or a security detail suggested he had traveled to Rome using a pseudonymous passport. It was a bad sign. The chief of MI6 traveled clandestinely only when he had a serious problem.

"How did you get in here?" asked Gabriel.

Seymour fished a key from the pocket of his trousers. Attached was the simple black medallion so beloved by Housekeeping, the Office division that procured and managed safe properties.

"Where did you get that?"

"Uzi gave it to me yesterday in London."

"And the code for the alarm? I suppose he gave you that, too."

Seymour recited the eight-digit number.

"That's a violation of Office protocol."

"There were extenuating circumstances. Besides," added Seymour, "after all the operations we've done together, I'm practically a member of the family."

"Even family members knock before entering a room."

"You're one to talk."

Gabriel removed the cork from the bottle, poured out two glasses, and handed one to Seymour. The Englishman raised his glass a fraction of an inch and said, "To fatherhood."

"It's bad luck to drink to children who haven't been born yet, Graham."

"Then what shall we drink to?"

When Gabriel offered no answer, Seymour went into the sitting room. From its picture window it was possible to see the bell tower of the church and the top of the Spanish Steps. He stood there for a moment gazing out across the rooftops as though he were admiring the rolling hills of his country estate from the terrace of his manor house. With his pewter-colored locks and sturdy jaw, Graham Seymour was the archetypal British civil servant, a man who'd been born, bred, and educated to lead. He was handsome, but not too; he was tall, but not remarkably so. He made others feel inferior, especially Americans.

"You know," he said finally, "you really should find somewhere else to stay when you're in Rome. The entire world knows about this safe flat, which means it isn't a safe flat at all."

"I like the view."

"I can see why."

Seymour returned his gaze to the darkened rooftops. Gabriel sensed there was something troubling him. He would get around to it eventually. He always did.

"I hear your wife left town today," he said at last.

"What other privileged information did the chief of my service share with you?"

"He mentioned something about a painting."

"It's not just any painting, Graham. It's the—"

"Caravaggio," said Seymour, finishing Gabriel's sentence for him. Then he smiled and added, "You do have a knack for finding things, don't you?"

"Is that supposed to be a compliment?"

"I suppose it was."

Seymour drank. Gabriel asked why Uzi Navot had come to London.

"He had a piece of intelligence he wanted me to see. I have to admit," Seymour added, "he seemed in good spirits for a man in his position."

"What position is that?"

"Everyone in the business knows Uzi is on his way out," answered Seymour. "And he's leaving behind a terrible mess. The entire Middle East is in flames, and it's going to get a lot worse before it gets better."

"Uzi wasn't the one who made the mess."

"No," agreed Seymour, "the Americans did that. The president and his advisers were too quick to part ways with the Arab strongmen. Now the president's confronted with a world gone mad, and he doesn't have a clue as to what to do about it."

"And if you were advising the president, Graham?"

"I'd tell him to resurrect the strongmen. It worked before, it can work again."

"All the king's horses, and all the king's men."

"Your point?"

"The old order is broken, and it can't be put back together. Besides," added Gabriel, "the old order is what brought us Bin Laden and the jihadists in the first place."

"And when the jihadists try to evict the Jewish state from the House of Islam?"

"They *are* trying, Graham. And in case you haven't noticed, they don't have much use for the United Kingdom, either. Like it or not, we're in this together."

Gabriel's BlackBerry vibrated. He looked at the screen and frowned.

"What is it?" asked Seymour.

"Another cease-fire."

"How long will this one last?"

"I suppose until Hamas decides to break it." Gabriel placed the BlackBerry on the coffee table and regarded Seymour curiously. "You were about to tell me what you're doing in my apartment."

"I have a problem."

"What's his name?"

"Quinn," answered Seymour. "Eamon Quinn."

Gabriel ran the name through the database of his memory but found no match. "Irish?" he asked.

Seymour nodded.

"Republican?"

"Of the worst kind."

"So what's the problem?"

"A long time ago, I made a mistake and people died."

"And Quinn was responsible?"

"Quinn lit the fuse, but ultimately I was responsible. That's the wonderful thing about our business. Our mistakes always come back to haunt us, and eventually all debts come due." Seymour raised his glass toward Gabriel. "Can we drink to that?"

7

VIA GREGORIANA, ROME

THE SKIES HAD been threatening all after-noon. Finally, at half past ten, a torrential downpour briefly turned the Via Gregoriana into a Venetian canal. Graham Seymour stood at the window watching fat gobbets of rain hammering against the terrace, but in his thoughts it was the hopeful summer of 1998. The Soviet Union was a memory. The economies of Europe and America were roaring. The jihadists of al-Qaeda were the stuff of white papers and terminally boring seminars about future threats. "We fooled ourselves into thinking we had reached the end of history," he was saying. "There were some in Parliament who actually proposed disbanding the Security Service and MI6 and burning us all at the stake." He glanced over his shoulder. "They were days of wine and roses. They were days of delusion."

"Not for me, Graham. I was out of the business at the time."

"I remember." Seymour turned away from Gabriel and watched the rain beating against the glass. "You were living in Cornwall then, weren't you? In that little cottage on the Helford River. Your first wife was at the psychiatric hospital in Stafford, and you were supporting her by cleaning paintings for Julian Isherwood. And there was that boy who lived in the cottage next door. His name escapes me."

"Peel," said Gabriel. "His name was Timothy Peel."

"Ah, yes, young Master Peel. We could never figure out why you were spending so much time with him. And then we realized he was exactly the same age as the son you lost to the bomb in Vienna."

"I thought we were talking about you, Graham."

"We are," replied Seymour.

He then reminded Gabriel, needlessly, that in the summer of 1998 he was the chief of counterterrorism at MI5. As such, he was responsible for protecting the British homeland from the terrorists of the Irish Republican Army. And yet even in Ulster, scene of a centuries-old conflict between Protestants and Catholics, there were signs of hope. The voters of Northern Ireland had ratified the Good Friday peace accords, and the Provisional IRA was adhering to the terms of the cease-fire. Only the Real IRA, a small band of hard-line dissidents, carried on the armed struggle. Its leader was Michael McKevitt, the former quartermaster general of the IRA. His common-law wife, Bernadette Sands-McKevitt, ran the political wing: the 32 County Sovereignty Movement. She was the sister of Bobby Sands, the Provisional IRA member who starved himself to death in the Maze prison in 1981.

"And then," said Seymour, "there was Eamon

Quinn. Quinn planned the operations. Quinn built the bombs. Unfortunately, he was good. Very good."

A heavy thunderclap shook the building. Seymour gave an involuntary flinch before continuing.

"Quinn had a certain genius for building highly effective bombs and delivering them to their targets. But what he didn't know," Seymour added, "was that I had an agent watching over his shoulder."

"How long was he there?"

"My agent was a woman," answered Seymour. "And she was there from the beginning."

Managing the agent and her intelligence, Seymour continued, proved to be a delicate balancing act. Because the agent was highly placed within the organization, she often had advance knowledge of attacks, including the target, the time, and the size of the bomb.

"What were we to do?" asked Seymour. "Disrupt the attacks and put the agent at risk? Or allow the attacks to go forward and try to make sure no one gets killed in the process?"

"The latter," replied Gabriel.

"Spoken like a true spy."

"We're not policemen, Graham."

"Thank God for that."

For the most part, said Seymour, the strategy worked. Several large car bombs were defused, and several others exploded with minimal casualties, though one virtually leveled the High Street of Portadown, a loyalist stronghold, in February 1998. Then, six months later, MI5's spy reported the group was plotting a major attack. Something big, she warned. Something that would blow the Good Friday peace process to bits.

"What were we supposed to do?" asked Seymour.

Outside, the sky exploded with lightning. Seymour emptied his glass and told Gabriel the rest of it.

On the evening of August 13, 1998, a maroon Vauxhall Cavalier, registration number 91 DL 2554, vanished from a housing estate in Carrickmacross, in the Republic of Ireland. It was driven to an isolated farm along the border and fitted with a set of false Northern Ireland plates. Then Quinn fitted it with the bomb: five hundred pounds of fertilizer, a machine-tooled booster rod filled with high explosive, a detonator, a power source hidden in a plastic food container, an arming switch in the glove box. On the morning of Sunday, August 15, he drove the car across the border to Omagh and parked it outside the S.D. Kells department store on Lower Market Street.

"Obviously," said Seymour, "Quinn didn't deliver the bomb alone. There was another man in the Vauxhall, two more in a scout car, and another man who drove the getaway car. They communicated by cellular phone. And we were listening to every word."

"The Security Service?"

"No," replied Seymour. "Our ability to monitor phone calls didn't extend beyond the borders of the United Kingdom. The Omagh plot originated in the Irish Republic, so we had to rely on GCHQ to do the eavesdropping for us."

The Government Communications Headquarters, or GCHQ, was Britain's version of the NSA. At 2:20 p.m. it intercepted a call from a man who sounded like Eamon Quinn. He spoke six words: "The bricks are in the wall." MI5 knew from past experience that the phrase meant the bomb was in place. Twelve minutes later Ulster Television received an anonymous telephone warning: "There's a bomb, courthouse, Omagh, main street, five hundred pounds, explosion in thirty minutes." The Royal Ulster Constabulary began evacuating the streets around Omagh's courthouse and frantically looking for the bomb. What they didn't realize was that they were looking in the wrong place.

"The telephone warning was incorrect," said Gabriel.

Seymour nodded slowly. "The Vauxhall wasn't anywhere near the courthouse. It was several hundred yards farther down Lower Market Street. When the RUC began the evacuation, they unwittingly drove people *toward* the bomb rather than away from it." Seymour paused, then added, "But that's exactly what Quinn wanted. He wanted people to die, so he deliberately parked the car in the wrong place. He double-crossed his own organization."

At ten minutes past three the bomb detonated. Twenty-nine people were killed, another two hundred were wounded. It was the deadliest act of terrorism in the history of the conflict. So powerful was the revulsion that the Real IRA felt compelled to issue an apology. Somehow, the peace process held. After thirty years of blood and bombs, the people of Northern Ireland had finally had enough.

"And then the press and the families of the victims started to ask uncomfortable questions," said Seymour. "How did the Real IRA manage to plant a bomb in the middle of Omagh without the knowledge of the police and the security services? And why were there no arrests?"

"What did you do?"

"We did what we always do. We closed ranks, burned our files, and waited for the storm to pass."

Seymour rose, carried his glass into the kitchen, and removed the bottle of Gavi from the refrigerator. "Do you have anything stronger than this?"

"Like what?"

"Something distilled."

"I'd rather drink acetone than distilled spirits."

"Acetone with a twist might do the trick about now." Seymour dumped an inch of wine into his glass and placed the bottle on the counter.

"What happened to Quinn after Omagh?"

"Quinn went into private practice. Quinn went international."

"What kind of work did he do?"

"The usual," replied Seymour. "Security work for the thugs and potentates, bomb-making clinics for the revolutionaries and the religiously deranged. We caught a glimpse of him every now and again, but for the most part he flew beneath our radar. Then the chief of Iranian intelligence invited him to Tehran, at which point King Saul Boulevard entered the picture."

Seymour popped the latches on his briefcase, removed a single sheet of paper, and placed it on the coffee table. Gabriel looked at the document and frowned.

"Another violation of Office protocol."

"What's that?"

"Carrying a classified Office cable in an insecure briefcase."

Gabriel picked up the document and began to read. It stated that Eamon Quinn, former member of the Real IRA, mastermind of the Omagh terrorist outrage, had been retained by Iranian intelligence to develop highly lethal roadside bombs to be used against British and American forces in Iraq. The same Eamon Quinn had performed a similar service for Hezbollah in Lebanon and Hamas in the Gaza Strip. In addition, he had traveled to Yemen, where he had helped al-Qaeda in the Arabian Peninsula construct a small liquid bomb that could be slipped onto an American jetliner. He was, the report said in its concluding paragraph, one of the most dangerous men in the world and needed to be eliminated immediately.

"You should have taken Uzi up on his offer."

"Hindsight is twenty-twenty," replied Seymour. "But I wouldn't be so glib. After all, Uzi would have probably given the job to you."

Gabriel methodically tore the document to tiny shreds.

"That's not good enough," said Seymour.

"I'll burn it later."

"Do me a favor, and burn Eamon Quinn while you're at it."

Gabriel was silent for a moment. "My days in the field are over," he said finally. "I'm a deskman now, Graham, just like you. Besides, Northern Ireland was never my neck of the woods."

"Then I suppose we'll have to find you a partner. Someone who knows the turf. Someone who can pass for a local if need be. Someone who actually knows Eamon Quinn personally." Seymour paused, then added, "Do you happen to know anyone who fits that description?"

"No," said Gabriel pointedly.

"I do," replied Seymour. "But there's one small problem."

"What's that?"

Seymour smiled and said, "He's dead."

VIA GREGORIANA, ROME

O R IS HE?"
       Seymour retrieved two photographs
       from his briefcase and placed one on the
coffee table. It showed a man of medium height and
build walking through passport control at Heathrow Airport.

"Recognize him?" asked Seymour.

Gabriel said nothing.

"It's you, of course." Seymour pointed to the
time code at the bottom of the image. "It was taken
last winter during the Madeline Hart affair. You
slipped into the United Kingdom unannounced to
do a little digging."

"I was there, Graham. I remember it well."

"Then you'll also recall that you began your
search for Madeline Hart on the island of Corsica,
a logical starting place because that's where she
disappeared. Shortly after your arrival, you went to
see a man named Anton Orsati. Don Orsati runs
the island's most powerful organized crime family,
a family that specializes in murder for hire. He
gave you a valuable piece of information regarding

her kidnappers. He also allowed you to borrow his best assassin." Seymour smiled. "Does any of this ring a bell?"

"Obviously, you were watching me."

"From a discreet distance. After all, you were searching for the mistress of the British prime minister at my behest."

"She wasn't just his mistress, Graham. She was—"

"This Corsican assassin is an interesting fellow," Seymour interrupted. "In truth, he's not Corsican at all, though he certainly speaks like one. He's an Englishman, a former member of the Special Air Service who walked off the battlefield in western Iraq in January 1991 after an incident involving friendly fire. The British military believes he's dead. Sadly, so do his parents. But then, you already knew that."

Seymour placed the second photograph on the coffee table. Like the first, it showed a man walking through Heathrow Airport. He was several inches taller than Gabriel, with short blond hair, skin the color of saddle leather, and square, powerful shoulders.

"It was taken on the same day as the first photo, a few minutes later. Your friend entered the country on a false French passport, one of several he has in his possession. On that particular day he was Adrien Leblanc. His real name is—"

"You've made your point, Graham."

Seymour gathered up the photographs and offered them to Gabriel.

"What am I supposed to do with these?"

"Keep them as a memento of your friendship."

Gabriel tore the photographs in half and placed them next to the shreds of the Office memo. "How long have you known?"

"British intelligence heard rumors for years about an Englishman working in Europe as a professional assassin. We were never able to learn his name. And never in our wildest dreams did we imagine he might be a paid asset of the Office."

"He's not a paid asset."

"How would you describe him?"

"An old adversary who's now a friend."

"Adversary?"

"A consortium of Swiss bankers once hired him to kill me."

"Consider yourself fortunate," said Seymour. "Christopher Keller rarely fails to fulfill the terms of a contract. He's very good at what he does."

"He speaks highly of you, too, Graham."

Seymour sat silently while a siren rose and faded in the street below. "Keller and I were close," he said finally. "I fought the IRA from the comfort of my desk, and Keller was at the sharp end of my stick. He did the sort of things that were necessary to keep the British homeland safe. And in the end he paid a terrible price for it."

"What's his connection to Quinn?"

"I'll let Keller tell you that part of the story. I'm not sure I can do it justice."

A gust of wind hurled rain against the windows. The room lights flickered.

"I haven't agreed to anything yet, Graham."

"But you will. Otherwise," Seymour added, "I'm going to drag your friend back to Britain in chains and hand him over to Her Majesty's Government for prosecution."

"On what charges?"

"He's a deserter and a professional killer. I'm sure we'll think of something."

Gabriel only smiled. "A man in your position shouldn't make idle threats."

"I'm not."

"Christopher Keller knows far too much about the private life of the British prime minister for HMG to ever put him on trial for desertion or anything else. Besides," Gabriel added, "I suspect you have other plans for Keller."

Seymour said nothing. Gabriel asked, "What else have you got in your briefcase?"

"A thick file on the life and times of Eamon Quinn."

"What do you want us to do?"

"What we should have done years ago. Take him off the market as quickly as possible. And while you're at it, find out who ordered and financed the operation to murder the princess."

"Maybe Quinn's returned to the fight."

"The fight for a united Ireland?" Seymour shook his head. "That fight is over. If I had to guess, he killed her at the behest of one of his patrons. And we both know the cardinal rule when it comes to assassinations. It's not important who fires the shot. It's who pays for the bullet."

Another gust of wind slammed against the windows. The lights dimmed and then died. The two spies sat in darkness for several minutes, neither man speaking.

"Who said that?" Gabriel asked finally.

"Said what?"

"That business about the bullet."

"I believe it was Ambler."

There was silence.

"I have other plans, Graham."

"I know."

"My wife is pregnant. Very pregnant."

"So you'll have to work quickly."

"I suppose Uzi's already approved it."

"It was his idea."

"Remind me to give Uzi a lousy assignment the moment after I'm sworn in as chief."

A flash of lightning illuminated Seymour's Cheshire cat grin. Then the darkness returned.

"I think I saw some candles in the kitchen when I was looking for a corkscrew."

"I like the darkness," said Gabriel. "It clarifies my thinking."

"What are you thinking about?"

"I'm thinking about what I'm going to say to my wife."

"Anything else?"

"Yes," said Gabriel. "I'm wondering how Quinn knew the princess was going to be on that boat."

9

BERLIN-CORSICA

THE SAVOY HOTEL stood at the unfashion-
able end of one of Berlin's most fashionable
streets. A red carpet stretched from its entrance; red tables stood beneath red umbrellas along
its facade. The previous afternoon Keller had spotted a famous actor drinking coffee there, but now,
as he emerged from the hotel's entrance, the tables
were deserted. The clouds were low and leaden and
a cold wind was plucking the last leaves from the
trees lining the pavements. Berlin's brief autumn
was receding. Soon it would be winter again.

"Taxi, monsieur?"

"No, thank you."

Keller slipped a five-euro note into the valet's
outstretched hand and set out along the street. He
had registered at the hotel under a French alias—
management was under the impression he was a
freelance journalist who wrote about films—and
stayed only a single night. He had spent the previous evening at a modest hotel called the Seifert,
and before that he had passed a sleepless night in a
grim little pension called the Bella Berlin. All three

establishments had one thing in common: they were near the Kempinski Hotel, which was Keller's destination. He was going there to meet a man, a Libyan, a former close associate of Gaddafi who had fled to France after the revolution with two suitcases filled with cash and jewels. The Libyan had invested $2 million with a pair of French businessmen after receiving assurances of a substantial profit. The French businessmen were already weary of their association with the Libyan. They were worried, too, about his past reputation for violence, for it was said of the Libyan that he used to enjoy pounding spikes through the eyes of the regime's opponents. The French businessmen had turned to Don Anton Orsati for help, and the don had given the assignment to his most accomplished assassin. Keller had to admit he was looking forward to the fulfillment of the contract. He had never cared for the now-deceased Libyan dictator or the thugs who had kept his regime in power. Gaddafi had allowed terrorists of every stripe to train at his desert camps, including members of the Provisional Irish Republican Army. He had also supplied the IRA with arms and explosives. Indeed, nearly all the Semtex used in IRA bombs came directly from Libya.

Keller crossed the Kantstrasse and headed down the ramp of an underground parking garage. On the second level, in a part of the garage untouched by security cameras, was a black BMW that had been left for him by a member of the Orsati organization. In the trunk was a Heckler & Koch 9mm pistol with a suppressor; in the glove box was a card-key that would open the door of any guest room at the Kempinski Hotel. The key had been acquired for the price of five thousand euros from a Gambian who worked in the hotel's laundry department. The Gambian had assured the man from the Orsati organization that the cardkey would remain operational for another forty-eight hours. After that, the codes would undergo a routine change, and hotel security would issue new passkeys to all essential employees. Keller hoped the Gambian was telling the truth. Otherwise, there would soon be an opening in the Kempinski's laundry department.

Keller slipped the gun and the cardkey into his briefcase. Then he placed his overnight bag in the trunk of the BMW and headed up the ramp to the street. The Kempinski was a hundred meters farther along the Fasanenstrasse, a big hotel with Vegas-bright lights over the entrance and a Parisian-style café overlooking the Kurfürstendamm. At one of the tables sat the Libyan. He was accompanied by a man of perhaps sixty and a once-beautiful woman with coal-black hair and Cleopatra makeup. The man looked like an old comrade from the court of Gaddafi; the woman looked well cared for and very bored. Keller assumed she belonged to the Libyan's friend, for the Libyan liked his women blond, professional, and pricey.

Keller entered the hotel, aware of the fact that several surveillance cameras were now watching him. It didn't matter; he was wearing a dark wig and heavy false spectacles. Five hotel guests, new arrivals, judging by the look of them, were waiting for an elevator. Keller allowed them to board the first available carriage and then rode to the fifth floor alone, his head lowered in such a way that the surveillance camera could not clearly capture the features of his face. When the doors opened, he stepped out of the carriage with the air of a man who was not looking forward to returning to the loneliness of yet another hotel room. A single member of the housekeeping staff gave him a drowsy nod, but otherwise the corridor was empty. The cardkey was now in the breast pocket of his overcoat. He removed it as he approached Room 518 and inserted it into the slot. The green light shone, the electronic lock disengaged. The Gambian would live another day.

The room had been recently serviced. Even so, the stench of the Libyan's appalling cologne persisted. Keller moved to the window and looked into the street. The Libyan and his two companions were still at their table at the café, though the woman appeared restless. In the time since Keller had seen them last, their plates had been cleared and coffee had been served. Ten minutes, he reckoned. Maybe less.

He turned from the window and calmly surveyed the room. The Kempinski thought it superior, but it was really quite ordinary: a double bed, a writing desk, a television console, a royal-blue armchair. The walls were thick enough to smother all sound from the adjoining rooms, though not thick enough to withstand a normal bullet, even a bullet that had penetrated a human body. As a result, Keller's HK was loaded with 124-grain hollow-point rounds that would expand on impact. Any round that struck the intended target would remain there. And in the unlikely event Keller somehow missed, the round would lodge harmlessly in the wall with a dull thud.

He returned to the window and saw that the Libyan and his two companions were on their feet. The man of perhaps sixty was shaking the Libyan's hand; the once-beautiful woman with coal-black hair was gazing longingly at the parade of exclusive shops lining the Ku-Damm. Keller drew the heavy curtains, sat down in the royal-blue armchair, and removed the HK from his briefcase. From the corridor came the squeak of a housekeeper's trolley. Then all was silent. He glanced at his wristwatch and marked the time. Five minutes, he thought. Maybe less.

A benevolent sun shone brightly upon the island of Corsica as the overnight ferry from Marseilles eased into the port of Ajaccio. Keller filed off the vessel with the other passengers and made his way to the car park, where he had left his battered old Renault station wagon. A powdery dust covered the windows and the hood. Keller thought the dust a bad omen. In all likelihood the sirocco had carried it from North Africa. Instinctively, he touched the small red coral hand hanging around his neck by a strand of leather. The Corsicans believed the talisman had the power to ward off the *occhju*, the evil eye. Keller believed it, too, though the presence of North African dust on his car the morning after he had killed a Libyan suggested the talisman had failed to protect him. There was an old woman in his village, a *signadora*, who had the power to draw

the evil from his body. Keller was not looking forward to seeing her, for the old woman also had the
power to glimpse both the past and the future. She
was one of the few people on the island who knew
the truth about him. She knew his long litany of
sins and misdeeds, and even claimed to know the
time and circumstances of his death. It was the one
thing she refused to tell him. "It is not my place,"
she would whisper to him in her candlelit parlor.
"Besides, to know how life ends would only ruin
the story."

Keller climbed behind the wheel of the Renault
and set out down the island's rugged western coastline, the turquoise-blue sea to his right, the high
peaks of the interior to his left. To pass the time he
listened to the news on the radio. There was nothing about a dead Libyan at a luxury hotel in Berlin.
Keller doubted the body had even been discovered
yet. He had committed the act in silence and upon
leaving the room had hung the Do Not Disturb
sign on the latch. Eventually, the Kempinski's management would take it upon themselves to knock on
the door. And upon receiving no response, management would enter the room and find a valued guest
with two bullet holes over his heart and a third in
the center of his forehead. Management would immediately telephone the police, of course, and a
hasty search would commence for the dark-haired,
mustachioed man seen entering the room. They
would manage to track his movements immediately
after the killing, but the trail would go cold in the
wooded gloom of the Tiergarten. The police would
never establish his identity. Some would suspect

him of being a Libyan like his victim, but a few of the wiser veterans would speculate that he was the same high-priced professional who had been killing in Europe for years. And then they would wash their hands of it, for they knew that murders carried out by professional assassins were rarely solved.

Keller followed the coastline to the town of Porto and then turned inland. It was a Sunday; the roads were quiet, and in the hill towns church bells tolled. In the center of the island, near its highest point, was the small village of the Orsatis. It had been there, or so it was said, since the time of the Vandals, when people from the coasts took to the hills for safety. Time seemed to have stopped there. Children played in the streets at all hours because there were no predators. Nor were there any illegal narcotics, for no dealer would risk the wrath of the Orsatis by peddling drugs in their village. Nothing much happened there, and sometimes there was not enough work to be done. But it was clean and beautiful and safe, and the people who lived there seemed content to eat well, drink their wine, and enjoy time with their children and their elders. Keller always missed them when he was away from Corsica for long. He dressed like them, he spoke the Corsican dialect like them, and in the evening, when he played *boules* with the men in the village square, he gave the same disgusted shake of his head whenever someone spoke of the French or, heaven forbid, the Italians. Once the people of the village had called him "the Englishman." Now he was merely Christopher. He was one of them.

The historic estate of the Orsati clan lay just

beyond the village, in a small valley of olive trees that produced the island's finest oil. Two armed guards stood watch at the entrance; they touched their Corsican flat caps respectfully as Keller turned through the gate and started up the long drive toward the villa. Laricio pine shaded the forecourt, but in the walled garden bright sunlight shone upon the long table that had been laid for the family's traditional Sunday lunch. For now, the table was unoccupied. The clan was still at Mass, and the don, who no longer set foot in church, was upstairs in his office. He was seated at a large oaken table, peering into an open leather-bound ledger, when Keller entered. At his elbow was a decorative bottle of Orsati olive oil—olive oil being the legitimate business through which the don laundered the profits of death.

"How was Berlin?" he asked without looking up.

"Cold," said Keller. "But productive."

"Any complications?"

"No."

Orsati smiled. The only thing he disliked more than complications were the French. He closed the ledger and settled his dark eyes on Keller's face. As usual, Don Orsati was dressed in a crisp white shirt, loose-fitting trousers of pale cotton, and leather sandals that looked as though they had been purchased at the local outdoor market, which was indeed the case. His heavy mustache had been trimmed, and his head of bristly gray-black hair glistened with tonic. The don always took inordinate care with his grooming on Sunday. He no longer believed in God but insisted on keeping the Sabbath sacred. He refrained from foul language on the Lord's Day, he tried to think good thoughts, and, most important, he forbade his *taddunaghiu* from fulfilling contracts. Even Keller, who had been raised an Anglican and was therefore considered a heretic, was bound by the don's edicts. Recently, he had been forced to spend an additional night in Warsaw because Don Orsati would not grant him dispensation to kill the target, a Russian mobster, on the day of rest.

"You'll stay for lunch," the don was saying.

"Thank you, Don Orsati," Keller said formally, "but I wouldn't want to impose."

"You? Impose?" The Corsican waved his hand dismissively.

"I'm tired," said Keller. "It was a rough crossing."

"You didn't sleep on the ferry?"

"Evidently," said Keller, "you haven't been on a ferry recently."

It was true. Anton Orsati rarely ventured beyond the well-guarded walls of his estate. The world came to him with its problems, and he made them go away—for a substantial fee, of course. He picked up a thick manila envelope and placed it in front of Keller.

"What's that?"

"Consider it a Christmas bonus."

"It's October."

The don shrugged. Keller lifted the flap of the envelope and peered inside. It was packed with bundles of hundred-euro notes. He lowered the flap and pushed the envelope toward the center of the table.

"Here on Corsica," the don said with a frown, "it is impolite to refuse a gift."

"The gift isn't necessary."

"Take it, Christopher. You've earned it."

"You've made me rich, Don Orsati, richer than I ever dreamed possible."

"But?"

Keller sat silently.

"A closed mouth catches neither flies nor food," said the don, quoting from his seemingly bottomless supply of Corsican proverbs.

"Your point?"

"Speak, Christopher. Tell me what's bothering you."

Keller was staring at the money, consciously avoiding the don's gaze.

"Are you bored with your work?"

"It's not that."

"Maybe you should take a break. You could focus your energies on the legitimate side of the business. There's plenty of money to be made there."

"Olive oil isn't the answer, Don Orsati."

"So there *is* a problem."

"I didn't say that."

"You didn't have to." The don regarded Keller carefully. "When you pull a tooth, Christopher, it will stop hurting."

"Unless you have a bad dentist."

"The only thing worse than a bad dentist is a bad companion."

"It is better to be alone," said Keller philosophically, "than to have bad companions."

The don smiled. "You might have been born an Englishman, Christopher, but you have the soul of a Corsican."

Keller stood. The don pushed the envelope across the tabletop.

"Are you sure you won't stay for lunch?"

"I have plans."

"Whatever they are," the don said, "they'll have to wait."

"Why?"

"You have a visitor."

Keller didn't have to ask the visitor's name. There were only a handful of people in the world who knew he was still alive, and only one who would dare to call on him unannounced.

"When did he arrive?"

"Last night," answered the don.

"What does he want?"

"He wasn't at liberty to say." The don scrutinized Keller with the watchful eyes of a canine. "Is it my imagination," he asked finally, "or has your mood suddenly improved?"

Keller departed without answering. Don Orsati watched him go. Then he looked down at the tabletop and swore softly. The Englishman had forgotten to take the envelope.

10

CORSICA

CHRISTOPHER KELLER HAD always taken great care with his money. By his own calculation he had earned more than $20 million working for Don Anton Orsati and, through prudent investing, had made himself vastly wealthy. The bulk of his fortune was held by banks in Geneva and Zurich, but there were also accounts in Monaco, Liechtenstein, Brussels, Hong Kong, and the Cayman Islands. He even kept a small amount of money at a reputable bank in London. His British account manager believed him to be a reclusive resident of Corsica who, like Don Orsati, left the island infrequently. The government of France was of the same opinion. Keller paid taxes on his legitimate investment earnings and on the respectable salary he earned from the Orsati Olive Oil Company, where he served as director of central European sales. He voted in French elections, donated to French charities, rooted for French sports teams, and, on occasion, had been forced to utilize the services of the French national health care authority. He had never been charged with a crime of any sort, a noteworthy achievement for a man of the south, and his driving record was impeccable. All in all, with one significant exception, Christopher Keller was a model citizen.

An expert skier and climber, he had been quietly shopping for a chalet in the French Alps for some time. At present, he maintained a single residence, a villa of modest proportions located one valley over from the valley of the Orsatis. It had exterior walls of tawny brown, a red tile roof, a large blue swimming pool, and a wide terrace that received the sun in the morning and in the afternoon was shaded by pine. Inside, its large rooms were comfortably decorated in rustic furnishings covered in white, beige, and faded yellows. There were many shelves filled with serious books—Keller had briefly studied military history at Cambridge and was a voracious reader of politics and contemporary issues—and upon the walls hung a modest collection of modern and Impressionist paintings. The most valuable work was a small landscape by Monet, which Keller, through an intermediary, had acquired from Christie's auction house in Paris. Standing before it now, one hand resting on his chin, his head tilted to one side, was Gabriel. He licked the tip of his forefinger, rubbed it over the surface, and shook his head slowly.

"What's wrong?" asked the Englishman.

"It's covered in surface grime. You really should let me clean it for you. It will only take—"

"I like it the way it is."

Gabriel wiped his forefinger on the front of his jeans and turned to face Keller. The Englishman was ten years younger than Gabriel, four inches taller, and thirty pounds heavier, especially through the shoulders and arms, where he carried a lethal quantity of finely sculpted power and mass. His short hair was bleached blond from the sea; his skin was very dark from the sun. He had bright blue eyes, square cheekbones, and a thick chin with a chisel notch in the center of it. His mouth seemed permanently fixed in a mocking smile. Keller was a man without allegiance, without fear, and without morals, except when it came to matters of friendship and love. He had lived life on his own terms, and somehow he had won.

"I thought you were supposed to be in Rome," he said.

"I was," answered Gabriel. "But Graham Seymour dropped into town. He had something he wanted to show me."

"What was it?"

"A photograph of a man walking through Heathrow Airport."

Keller's half-smile evaporated, his blue eyes narrowed. "How much does he know?"

"Everything, Christopher."

"Am I in danger?"

"That depends."

"On what?"

"On whether you agree to do a job for him."

"What does he want?"

Gabriel smiled. "What you do best."

Outside, the sun still held dominion over Keller's terrace. They sat in a pair of comfortable garden chairs, a small wrought-iron table between them. On it lay Graham Seymour's thick file on the professional exploits of one Eamon Quinn. Keller had yet to open it or even look at it. He was listening spellbound to Gabriel's account of Quinn's role in the murder of the princess.

When Gabriel finished, Keller held up the photograph of his recent passage through Heathrow Airport. "You gave me your word," he said. "You swore that you would never tell Graham that we were working together."

"I didn't have to tell him. He already knew."

"How?"

Gabriel explained.

"Devious bastard," muttered Keller.

"He's British," said Gabriel. "It comes naturally."

Keller looked at Gabriel carefully for a moment. "It's funny," he said, "but you don't seem terribly upset about the situation."

"It does present you with an interesting opportunity, Christopher."

Beyond the rim of the valley a church bell tolled midday. Keller placed the photograph atop the file and lit a cigarette.

"Must you?" asked Gabriel, waving away the smoke.

"What choice do I have?"

"You can stop smoking and add several years to your life."

"About Graham," said Keller, exasperated.

"I suppose you can stay here in Corsica and hope he doesn't decide to tell the French about you."

"Or?"

"You can help me find Eamon Quinn."

"And then?"

"You can go home again, Christopher."

Keller raised his hand to the valley and said, "This is my home."

"It isn't real, Christopher. It's a fantasy. It's make-believe."

"So are you."

Gabriel smiled but said nothing. The church bell had fallen silent; the afternoon shadows were gathering at the edge of the terrace. Keller crushed out his cigarette and looked down at the unopened file.

"Interesting reading?" he asked.

"Quite."

"Recognize anyone?"

"An MI5 man named Graham Seymour," said Gabriel, "and an SAS officer who's referred to only by his code name."

"What is it?"

"Merchant."

"Catchy."

"I thought so, too."

"What does it say about him?"

"It says he operated undercover in West Belfast for approximately a year in the late eighties."

"Why did he stop?"

"His cover was blown. Apparently, there was a woman involved."

"Does it mention her name?" asked Keller.

"No."

"What happened next?"

"Merchant was kidnapped by the IRA and taken to a remote farmhouse for interrogation and execution. The farmhouse was in South Armagh. Quinn was there."

"How did it end?"

"Badly."

A gust of wind stirred the pine. Keller gazed upon his Corsican valley as though it were slipping from his grasp. Then he lit another cigarette and told Gabriel the rest of it.

11

CORSICA

I T WAS KELLER'S aptitude with language that set him apart—not foreign languages, but the various ways in which the English language is spoken on the streets of Belfast and the six counties of Northern Ireland. The subtleties of local accents made it virtually impossible for officers of the SAS to operate undetected within the small, tightly knit communities of the province. As a result, most SAS men were forced to utilize the services of a Fred—the Regiment's term for a local helper—when tracking IRA members or engaging in street surveillance. But not Keller. He developed the ability to mimic the various dialects of Ulster with the speed and confidence of a native. He could even shift accents at a moment's notice—a Catholic from Armagh one minute, a Protestant from Belfast's Shankill Road the next, then a Catholic from the Ballymurphy housing estates. His unique linguistic skills did not escape the notice of his superiors. Nor was it long before they came to the attention of an ambitious young intelligence officer who ran the Northern Ireland account for MI5.

"I assume," said Gabriel, "that the young MI5 officer was Graham Seymour."

Keller nodded. Then he explained that Seymour, in the late 1980s, was dissatisfied with the level of intelligence he was receiving from MI5's informants in Northern Ireland. He wanted to insert his own agent into the IRA badlands of West Belfast to report on the movements and associations of known IRA commanders and volunteers. It was not a job for an ordinary MI5 officer. The agent would have to know how to handle himself in a world where one false step, one wrong glance, could get a man killed. Keller met with Seymour at a safe house in London and agreed to take on the assignment. Two months later he was back in Belfast posing as a Catholic named Michael Connelly. He took a two-room flat in the Divis Tower apartment complex on the Falls Road. His neighbor was a member of the IRA's West Belfast Brigade. The British Army maintained an observation post on the roof and used the top two floors as barracks and office space. When the Troubles were at their worst, the soldiers came and went by helicopter. "It was madness," said Keller, shaking his head slowly. "Absolute madness."

While much of West Belfast was unemployed and on the dole, Keller soon found work as a deliveryman for a laundry service on the Falls Road. The job allowed him to move freely through the neighborhoods and enclaves of West Belfast without suspicion and gave him access to the homes and laundry of known IRA members. It was a remarkable achievement, but no accident. The laundry was owned and operated by British intelligence.

"It was one of our most closely held operations," said Keller. "Even the prime minister wasn't aware of it. We had a small fleet of vans, listening equipment, and a lab in the back. We tested every piece of laundry we could get our hands on for traces of explosives. And if we got a positive hit, we put the owner and his house under surveillance."

Gradually, Keller began forming friendships with members of the dysfunctional community around him. His IRA neighbor invited him for dinner, and once, in an IRA bar on the Falls Road, a recruiter made a not-so-subtle pass at him, which Keller politely deflected. He attended Mass regularly at St. Paul's Church—as part of his training he had learned the rituals and doctrines of Catholicism—and on a wet Sunday in Lent he met a beautiful young girl there named Elizabeth Conlin. Her father was Ronnie Conlin, an IRA field commander for Ballymurphy.

"A serious player," said Gabriel.

"As serious as it gets."

"You decided to pursue the relationship."

"I didn't have much choice in the matter."

"You were in love with her."

Keller nodded slowly.

"How did you see her?"

"I used to sneak into her bedroom. She would hang a violet scarf in the window if it was safe. It was a tiny pebble-dash terrace house with walls like paper. I could hear her father in the next room. It was—"

"Madness," said Gabriel.

Keller said nothing.

"Did Graham know?"

"Of course."

"You told him?"

"I didn't have to. I was under constant MI5 and SAS surveillance."

"I assume he told you to break it off."

"In no uncertain terms."

"What did you do?"

"I agreed," replied Keller. "With one condition."

"You wanted to see her one last time."

Keller lapsed into silence. And when finally he spoke again, his voice had changed. It had taken on the elongated vowels and rough edges of working-class West Belfast. He was no longer Christopher Keller; he was Michael Connelly, the laundry deliveryman from the Falls Road who had fallen in love with the beautiful daughter of an IRA chieftain from Ballymurphy. On his last night in Ulster, he left his van on the Springfield Road and scaled the garden wall of the Conlin house. The violet scarf was hanging in its usual place, but Elizabeth's room was darkened. Keller soundlessly raised the window, parted the gauzy curtains, and slipped inside. Instantly, he absorbed a blow to the side of his head, like the blow of an ax blade, and began to fade from consciousness. The last thing he remembered before blacking out was the face of Ronnie Conlin.

"He was speaking to me," said Keller. "He was telling me that I was about to die."

Keller was bound, gagged, hooded, and bundled into the boot of a car. It took him from the slums of West Belfast to a farmhouse in South Armagh. There he was taken to a barn and beaten severely.

Then he was tied to a chair for interrogation and trial. Four men from the IRA's notorious South Armagh Brigade would serve as the jury. Eamon Quinn would serve as the prosecutor, judge, and executioner. He planned to administer the sentence with a field knife he had taken from a dead British soldier. Quinn was the IRA's best bomb maker, a master technician, but when it came to personal killing he preferred the knife.

"He told me that if I cooperated, my death would be reasonable. If I didn't, he was going to cut me to pieces."

"What happened?"

"I got lucky," said Keller. "They did a lousy job with the bindings, and I cut *them* to pieces instead. I did it so quickly they never knew what hit them."

"How many?"

"Two," answered Keller. "Then I got my hands on one of their guns and shot two more."

"What happened to Quinn?"

"Quinn wisely fled the field of battle. Quinn lived to fight another day."

The following morning the British Army announced that four members of the South Armagh Brigade had been killed in a raid on a remote IRA safe house. The official account made no mention of a kidnapped undercover SAS officer named Christopher Keller. Nor did it mention a laundry service on the Falls Road secretly owned by British intelligence. Keller was flown back to the mainland for treatment; the laundry was quietly closed. It was a major blow to British efforts in Northern Ireland.

"And Elizabeth?" asked Gabriel.

"They found her body two days later. Her head had been shaved. Her throat was slit."

"Who did it?"

"I heard it was Quinn," said Keller. "Apparently, he insisted on doing it himself."

Upon his release from the hospital, Keller returned to SAS headquarters at Hereford for rest and recovery. He took long, punishing hikes on the Brecon Beacons and trained new recruits in the art of silent killing, but it was clear to his superiors that his experiences in Belfast had changed him. Then, in August 1990, Saddam Hussein invaded Kuwait. Keller rejoined his old Sabre squadron and was deployed to the Middle East. And on the evening of January 28, 1991, while searching for Scud missile launchers in Iraq's western desert, his unit came under attack by Coalition aircraft in a tragic case of friendly fire. Only Keller survived. Enraged, he walked off the battlefield and, disguised as an Arab, slipped across the border into Syria. From there, he hiked westward across Turkey, Greece, and Italy, until he finally washed ashore in Corsica, where he fell into the waiting arms of Don Anton Orsati.

"Did you ever look for him?"

"Quinn?"

Gabriel nodded.

"The don forbade it."

"But that didn't stop you, did it?"

"Let's just say I followed his career closely. I knew he went with the Real IRA after the Good Friday peace accords, and I knew he was the one who planted that bomb in the middle of Omagh."

"And when he fled Ireland?"

"I made polite inquiries as to his whereabouts. Impolite inquiries, too."

"Any of them bear fruit?"

"Most definitely."

"But you never tried to kill him?"

"No," said Keller, shaking his head. "The don forbade it."

"But now you've got your chance."

"With the blessing of Her Majesty's Secret Service." Keller gave a brief smile. "Rather ironic, don't you think?"

"What's that?"

"Quinn drove me out of the game, and now he's pulling me back in." Keller looked at Gabriel seriously for a moment. "Are you sure you want to be involved in this?"

"Why wouldn't I?"

"Because it's personal," replied Keller. "And when it's personal, it tends to get messy."

"I do personal all the time."

"Messy, too." The shadows had reclaimed the terrace. The wind made ripples upon the surface of Keller's blue swimming pool. "And if I do this?" he asked. "What then?"

"Graham will give you a new British identity. A job, too." Gabriel paused, then added, "If you're interested."

"A job doing what?"

"Use your imagination."

Keller frowned. "What would you do if you were me?"

"I'd take the deal."

"And give up all this?"

"It isn't real, Christopher."

Beyond the rim of the valley a church bell tolled one o'clock.

"What am I going to say to the don?" asked Keller.

"I'm afraid I can't help you with that."

"Why?"

"Because it's personal," replied Gabriel. "And when it's personal, it tends to get messy."

———————————————

There was a ferry leaving for Nice at six that evening. Gabriel boarded at half past five, drank a coffee in the café, and stepped onto the observation deck to wait for Keller. By 5:45 he had not arrived. Five additional minutes passed with no sign of him. Then Gabriel glimpsed a battered Renault turning into the car park and a moment later saw Keller trotting up the ramp with an overnight bag hanging from one powerful shoulder. They stood side by side at the railing and watched the lights of Ajaccio receding into the gloom. The gentle evening wind smelled of *macchia*, the dense undergrowth of scrub oak, rosemary, and lavender that covered much of the island. Keller drew the air deeply into his lungs before lighting a cigarette. The breeze carried his first exhalation of smoke across Gabriel's face.

"Must you?"

Keller said nothing.

"I was beginning to think you'd changed your mind."

"And let you go after Quinn alone?"

"You don't think I can handle him?"

"Did I say that?"

Keller smoked in silence for a moment.

"How did the don take it?"

"He recited many Corsican proverbs about the ingratitude of children. And then he agreed to let me go."

The lights of the island were growing dimmer; the wind smelled only of the sea. Keller reached into his coat pocket, removed a Corsican talisman, and held it out to Gabriel.

"A gift from the *signadora*."

"We don't believe in such things."

"I'd take it if I were you. The old woman implied it could get nasty."

"How nasty?"

Keller made no reply. Gabriel accepted the talisman and hung it around his neck. One by one the lights of the island went dark. And then it was gone.

12

DUBLIN

TECHNICALLY, THE OPERATION upon which Gabriel and Christopher Keller embarked the following day was a joint undertaking between the Office and MI6. The British role was so black, however, that only Graham Seymour knew of it. Therefore, it was the Office that saw to the travel arrangements, and the Office that rented the Škoda sedan that was waiting in the long-term parking lot at Dublin Airport. Gabriel searched the undercarriage before climbing behind the wheel. Keller slid into the passenger seat and, frowning, closed the door.

"Couldn't they have got something better than a Škoda?"

"It's one of Ireland's most popular cars, which means it won't stand out."

"What about guns?"

"Open the glove box."

Keller did. Inside was a Beretta 9mm, fully loaded, along with a spare magazine and a suppressor.

"Only one?"

"We're not going to war, Christopher."

"That's what you think."

Keller closed the glove box, Gabriel inserted the key into the ignition. The engine hesitated, coughed, and then finally turned over.

"Still think they should have rented a Škoda?" asked Keller.

Gabriel slipped the car into gear. "Where do we start?"

"Ballyfermot."

"Bally where?"

Keller pointed to the exit sign and said, "Bally that way."

The Republic of Ireland was once a land with almost no violent crime. Until the late 1960s Ireland's national police force, the Garda Síochána, numbered just seven thousand officers, and in Dublin there were only seven squad cars. Most crime was of the petty variety: burglaries, pickpocketing, the occasional strong-armed robbery. And when there was violence involved, it was usually fueled by passion, alcohol, or a combination of the two.

That changed with the outbreak of the Troubles across the border in Northern Ireland. Desperate for money and arms to fight the British Army, the Provisional IRA began robbing banks in the south. The low-level thieves from the impoverished slums and housing estates of Dublin learned from the Provos' tactics and began carrying out daring armed heists of their own. The Gardaí, understaffed and outmatched, were quickly overwhelmed by the twin threat of the IRA and the local crime lords. By 1970 Ireland was tranquil no more. It was a gangland where criminals and revolutionaries operated with impunity.

In 1979 two unlikely events far from Ireland's shores sped the country's descent into lawlessness and social chaos. The first was the Iranian revolution. The second was the Soviet invasion of Afghanistan. Both resulted in a flood of cheap heroin onto the streets of Western European cities. The drug poured into the slums of south Dublin in 1980. A year later it ravaged the ghettos of the north side. Lives were broken, families were shattered, and crime rates soared as desperate addicts tried to feed their habits. Entire communities became dystopian wastelands where junkies shot up openly in the streets and dealers were kings.

The economic miracle of the 1990s transformed Ireland from one of Europe's poorest countries into one of its richest, but with prosperity came an even greater appetite for narcotics, especially cocaine and Ecstasy. The old crime bosses gave way to a new breed of kingpins who waged bloody wars over turf and market share. Where once Irish mobsters used sawed-off shotguns to enforce their will, the new gangland warriors armed themselves with AK-47s and other heavy weaponry. Bullet-riddled bodies began to appear on the streets of the housing estates. According to a Garda estimate in 2012, twenty-five violent drug gangs now plied their deadly trade in Ireland. Several had established lucrative ties to foreign organized crime groups, including remnants of the Real IRA.

"I thought they were against drugs," said Gabriel.

"That might be true up there," said Keller, pointing toward the north, "but down here in the Republic it's a different story. For all intents and purposes, the Real IRA is just another drug gang. Sometimes they deal drugs directly. Sometimes they run protection rackets. Mainly, they extort money from the dealers."

"What does Liam Walsh do?"

"A little of everything."

Rain blurred the headlamps of the evening rush hour traffic. It was lighter than Gabriel had expected. He supposed it was the economy. Ireland's had fallen farther and faster than most. Even the drug dealers were hurting.

"Walsh has republicanism in his veins," Keller was saying. "His father was IRA, and so were his uncles and brothers. He went with the Real IRA after the great schism, and when the war effectively ended he came down to Dublin to make his fortune in the drug business."

"What's his connection to Quinn?"

"Omagh." Keller pointed to the right and said, "There's your turn."

Gabriel guided the car into Kennelsfort Road. It was lined on both sides by terraces of small two-story houses. Not quite the Irish miracle, but not a slum, either.

"Is this Ballyfermot?"

"Palmerstown."

"Which way?"

With a wave of his hand, Keller instructed Gabriel to continue straight. They skirted an indus-

trial park of low gray warehouses, and suddenly
they were on Ballyfermot Road. After a moment
they came upon a parade of sad little shops: a discount department store, a discount linen store, a
discount optician, a chip shop. Across the street was
a Tesco supermarket, and next to the supermarket
was a betting parlor. Sheltering in the entrance were
four men in black leather coats. Liam Walsh was the
smallest of the lot. He was smoking a cigarette; they
were all smoking cigarettes. Gabriel turned into the
Tesco car park and eased into an empty space. It had
a clear view of the betting parlor.

"Maybe you should leave the engine running,"
said Keller.

"Why?"

"It might not start again."

Gabriel killed the engine and doused the headlamps. Rain beat heavily against the windscreen.
After a few seconds Liam Walsh vanished in a
blurry kaleidoscope of light. Then Gabriel flicked
the wipers and Walsh reappeared. A long black
Mercedes sedan had pulled up outside the betting
parlor. It was the only Mercedes on the street, probably the only one in the neighborhood. Walsh was
talking to the driver through the open window.

"He looks like a real pillar of the community,"
said Gabriel quietly.

"That's how he likes to portray himself."

"So why is he standing outside a betting parlor?"

"He wants the other gangs to know that he's
watching his turf. A rival tried to kill him on that
very spot last year. If you look closely, you can see
the bullet holes in the wall."

The Mercedes moved off. Liam Walsh returned to the shelter of the entrance.

"Who are those nice-looking fellows with him?"

"The two on the left are his bodyguards. The other one is his second-in-command."

"Real IRA?"

"To the core."

"Armed?"

"Most definitely."

"So what do we do?"

"We wait for him to make a move."

"Here?"

Keller shook his head. "If they see us sitting in a parked car, they'll assume we're Garda or members of a rival gang. And if they assume that, we're dead."

"Then maybe we shouldn't sit here."

Keller nodded toward the chip shop on the other side of the road and climbed out. Gabriel followed after him. They stood side by side along the edge of the road, hands thrust into their pockets, heads bowed against the windblown rain, waiting for an opening in the traffic.

"They're watching us," said Keller.

"You noticed that, too?"

"Hard not to."

"Does Walsh know your face?"

"He does now."

The traffic broke; they crossed the road and headed toward the entrance of the chip shop. "It might be better if you don't speak," said Keller. "This isn't the sort of neighborhood that gets a lot of visitors from exotic lands."

"I speak perfect English."

"That's the problem."

Keller opened the door and went inside first. It was a narrow room with a cracked linoleum floor and peeling walls. The air was thick with grease, starch, and the faint smell of wet wool. There was a pretty young girl behind the counter and an empty table against the window. Gabriel sat with his back to the road while Keller went over to the counter and ordered in the accent of someone from south Dublin.

"Very impressive," murmured Gabriel when Keller joined him. "For a minute there I thought you were about to break into 'When Irish Eyes Are Smiling.'"

"As far as that pretty young lass is concerned, I'm as Irish as she is."

"Yes," said Gabriel doubtfully. "And I'm Oscar Wilde."

"You don't think I can pass for an Irishman?"

"Maybe one who's been on a very long vacation in the sun."

"That's my story."

"Where have you been?"

"Majorca," replied Keller. "The Irish love Majorca, especially Irish mobsters."

Gabriel glanced around the interior of the café. "I wonder why."

The girl walked over to the table and deposited a plate of chips and two Styrofoam cups of milky tea. As she was leaving, the door opened and two pale men in their mid-twenties hurried in out of the weather. A woman in a damp coat and downtown shoes entered a moment later. The two men took a table near Keller and Gabriel and began speaking in a dialect that Gabriel found almost impenetrable. The woman sat at the back of the shop. She had only tea to drink and was reading a worn paperback book.

"What's going on outside?" asked Gabriel.

"Four men standing in front of a betting parlor. One man looking like he's had enough of the rain."

"Where does he live?"

"Not far," answered Keller. "He likes to live among the people."

Gabriel drank some of the tea and made a face. Keller pushed the plate of chips across the table. "Eat some."

"No."

"Why not?"

"I want to live long enough to see my children born."

"Good idea." Keller smiled, then added, "Men of your age really should be careful about what they eat."

"Watch yourself."

"How old are you, exactly?"

"I can't remember."

"Problems with memory loss?"

Gabriel drank some of the tea. Keller nibbled at the chips.

"They're not as good as the fries in the south of France," he said.

"Did you get a receipt?"

"Why would I need a receipt?"

"I hear the bookkeepers at MI6 are very picky."

"Let's not get carried away about MI6 just yet. I haven't made any decisions."

"Sometimes our best decisions are made for us."

"You sound like the don." Keller ate another chip. "Is it true about MI6 bookkeepers?"

"I was just making conversation."

"Are yours tough?"

"The worst."

"But not with you."

"Not so much."

"So why didn't they get you something better than a Škoda?"

"The Škoda is fine."

"I hope he'll fit in the trunk."

"We'll slam the lid on him a few times if we have to."

"What about the safe house?"

"I'm sure it's lovely, Christopher."

Keller didn't appear convinced. He picked up another chip, thought better of it, and dropped it onto the plate.

"What's going on behind me?" he asked.

"Two lads speaking no known language. One woman reading."

"What's she reading?"

"I believe it's John Banville."

Keller nodded thoughtfully, his eyes on Ballyfermot Road.

"What do you see?" asked Gabriel.

"One man standing outside a betting parlor. Three men getting into a car."

"What kind of car?"

"Black Mercedes."

"Better than a Škoda."

"Much."

"So what do we do?"

"We leave the fries and take the tea."

"When?"

Keller rose to his feet.

13

BALLYFERMOT, DUBLIN

T HEY DROPPED THE Styrofoam cups into a rubbish bin in the Tesco parking lot and climbed into the Škoda. This time, Keller drove; it was his turf. He eased into Ballyfermot Road and worked his way through the traffic until there were two cars separating them from the Mercedes. He drove calmly, one hand balanced atop the steering wheel, the other resting on the automatic shift. His eyes were straight ahead. Gabriel had commandeered the side-view mirror and was watching the traffic behind them.

"Well?" asked Keller.

"You're very good, Christopher. You're going to make a fine MI6 officer."

"I was asking whether we're being followed."

"We're not."

Keller removed his hand from the shift and used it to extract a cigarette from his coat pocket. Gabriel tapped the black-and-yellow notice on the visor and said, "This is a no-smoking car."

Keller lit the cigarette. Gabriel lowered his window a few inches to vent the smoke.

"They're stopping," he said.

"I can see that."

The Mercedes turned into an angled parking space outside a newsagent. For a few seconds no one got out. Then Liam Walsh stepped from the rear passenger-side door and entered the shop. Keller drove about fifty meters farther along the road and parked outside a takeaway pizza parlor. He killed the lights but left the engine running.

"I suppose he needed to pick up a few things on his way home."

"Like what?"

"A *Herald*," suggested Keller.

"No one reads newspapers anymore, Christopher. Haven't you heard?"

Keller glanced toward the pizza parlor. "Maybe you should go inside and get us a couple of slices."

"How do I order without speaking?"

"You'll think of something."

"What kind of pizza do you like?"

"Go," said Keller.

Gabriel climbed out and entered the shop. There were three people in the queue in front of him. He stood there waiting as the smell of warm cheese and yeast washed over him. Then he heard a brief burst of a car horn and, turning, saw the black Mercedes speeding off along Ballyfermot Road. He went back outside and lowered himself into the passenger seat. Keller reversed out of the space, slipped the car into drive, and accelerated slowly.

"Did he buy anything?" asked Gabriel.

"Couple of papers and a pack of Winstons."

"How did he look when he came out?"

"Like he really didn't need newspapers or cigarettes."

"I assume the Garda watches him on a regular basis?"

"I certainly hope so."

"Which means he's used to being followed from time to time by men in unmarked sedans."

"One would think."

"He's turning," said Gabriel.

"I can see that."

The car had turned into a bleak, unlit street of small terraced houses. No traffic, no shops, no place where two outsiders might conceal themselves. Keller pulled to the curb and doused the headlamps. A hundred meters farther down the street, the Mercedes nosed into a drive. The lights of the car went dark. Four doors opened, four men climbed out.

"Chez Walsh?" asked Gabriel.

Keller nodded.

"Married?"

"Not anymore."

"Girlfriend?"

"Could be."

"What about a dog?"

"You have a problem with dogs?"

Gabriel didn't answer. Instead, he watched the four men approach the house and disappear through the front door.

"What do we do now?" he asked.

"I suppose we could spend the next several days waiting for a better opportunity."

"Or?"

"We take him now."

"There are four of them and two of us."

"One," said Keller. "You're not coming."

"Why not?"

"Because the future chief of the Office can't get mixed up in something like this. Besides," Keller added, patting the bulge beneath his jacket, "we only have one gun."

"Four against one," said Gabriel after a moment. "Not very good odds."

"Actually, given my history, I like my chances."

"How do you intend to play it?"

"The same way we used to play it in Northern Ireland," answered Keller. "Big boys' games, big boys' rules."

Keller climbed out without another word and soundlessly closed the door. Gabriel swung a leg over the center console and slid behind the wheel. He flicked the wipers and glimpsed Keller walking along the street, hands in his coat pockets, shoulders tilted into the wind. He checked his Black-Berry. It was 8:27 p.m. in Dublin, 10:27 p.m. in Jerusalem. He thought of his beautiful young wife sitting alone in their apartment in Narkiss Street, and of his two unborn children resting comfortably in her womb. And here he was on a desolate street in south Dublin, a sentinel on yet another night watch, waiting for a friend to settle an old score. The rain hammered against the windscreen, the bleak street became a watery dreamscape. Gabriel flicked the wipers a second time and saw Keller pass through a sphere of yellow sodium light. And when he flicked the wipers a third time, Keller was gone.

The house was located at 48 Rossmore Road. It had a gray pebble-dash exterior, with a white-framed window on the ground floor and two more on the second. The narrow drive had space enough for a single car. Next to the drive was a gated walkway, and next to the walkway was a patch of grass bordered by a low hedgerow. It was respectable in every way, save for the man who lived there.

Like all the houses at that end of the street, Number 48 had a garden in back, beyond which spread the sporting fields of a Catholic school for boys. The entrance to the school was around the corner on Le Fanu Road. The main gate was open; there seemed to be a gathering of the parent body in the assembly hall. Keller passed through the gate unnoticed and struck out across a blacktop lined for games of every sort. And suddenly he was back at the dreary school in Surrey where his parents had banished him at the age of ten. He was the boy of whom much was expected—a good family, an excellent student, a natural leader. The older boys never touched him because they feared him. The headmaster once let him off without a beating because secretly the headmaster feared him, too.

At the edge of the blacktop was a row of dripping trees. Keller passed beneath their bare limbs and set out across the darkened sporting fields. Along their northern edge rose a wall, approximately two meters in height, covered in vines. Beyond it were the rear gardens of the houses lining Rossmore Road. Keller went to the farthest corner of the field and paced off fifty-seven steps precisely. Then, silently, he scaled the wall and dropped toward the ground on the other side. By the time his shoes struck the damp earth, he had drawn the silenced Beretta and leveled it toward the back door of the house. Lights burned within; shadows moved against the drawn curtains. Keller held the gun tightly in his hands, watching, listening. Big boys' games, he thought. Big boys' rules.

At ten minutes past nine o'clock, Gabriel's BlackBerry vibrated softly. He raised it to his ear, listened, and then killed the connection. The rain had given way to a listless mist; Rossmore Road was empty of traffic and pedestrians. He drove to the house at Number 48, parked in the street, and switched off the engine. Again his BlackBerry vibrated, but this time he did not answer. Instead, he pulled on a pair of flesh-colored rubber gloves, climbed out, and opened the modest-sized trunk. Inside was a suitcase that had been left by the courier from Dublin Station. Gabriel removed it and carried it up the garden walk. The front door yielded to his touch; he stepped inside and closed it quietly behind him. Keller stood in the entrance hall, the Beretta in his hand. The air smelled of cordite and, faintly, of blood. It was a smell that was all too familiar to Gabriel. He walked past Keller without a word and entered the sitting room. A cloud of smoke hung on the air. Three men, each with a neat bullet hole in the center of his forehead, a fourth with a smashed nose and a jaw that looked as if it had been dislodged with a sledgehammer. Gabriel reached down and searched the neck for a pulse. Then, after finding one, he unzipped the suitcase and went to work.

The suitcase contained three rolls of heavy-duty duct tape, a dozen disposable flex cuffs, a nylon bag capable of holding a man six feet in height, a black hood, a blue-and-white tracksuit, espadrilles, two changes of undergarments, a first aid kit, earplugs, vials of sedative, syringes, rubbing alcohol, and a copy of the Koran. The Office referred to the contents of the suitcase as a mobile detainee pack. Among veteran field agents, however, it was known as a terrorist travel kit.

After determining that Walsh was in no danger of expiration, Gabriel mummified him in duct tape. He didn't bother with the plastic flex cuffs; in matters of art and physical restraint, he was a traditionalist by nature. As he was applying the last swaths of tape to Walsh's mouth and eyes, the Irishman began to regain consciousness. Gabriel quieted him with a dose of the sedative. Then, with Keller's help, he placed Walsh in the duffel bag and pulled the zipper closed.

The house had no garage, which meant they had no choice but to take Walsh out the front door, in plain view of the neighbors. Gabriel found the key to the Mercedes on the body of one of the dead men. He moved the car into the street and backed the Škoda into the drive. Keller carried Walsh outside alone and deposited him in the open trunk. Then he climbed into the passenger seat and allowed Gabriel to drive. It was for the best. In Gabriel's experience, it was unwise to allow a man who had just killed three people to operate a motor vehicle.

"Did you turn out the lights?"

Keller nodded.

"What about the doors?"

"They're locked."

Keller removed the suppressor and the magazine from the Beretta and placed all three in the glove box. Gabriel turned into the street and started back toward Ballyfermot Road.

"How many rounds did you fire?" he asked.

"Three," answered Keller.

"How long before the Garda finds those bodies?"

"It's not the Garda we should be worried about."

Keller flicked his cigarette into the darkness. Gabriel saw sparks explode in his rearview mirror.

"How do you feel?" he asked.

"Like I never left."

"That's the problem with revenge, Christopher. It never makes you feel better."

"That's true," said Keller, lighting another cigarette. "And I'm just getting started."

14

CLIFDEN, COUNTY GALWAY

THE COTTAGE STOOD on Doonen Road, perched atop a high rocky bluff overlooking the dark waters of Salt Lake. It had three bedrooms, a large kitchen with modern appliances, a formal dining room, a small library and study, and a cellar with walls of stone. The owner, a successful Dublin lawyer, had wanted a thousand euros for a week. Housekeeping had countered with fifteen hundred for two, and the lawyer, who rarely received offers in winter, accepted the deal. The money appeared in his bank account the next morning. It came from something called Taurus Global Entertainment, a television production company based in the Swiss city of Montreux. The lawyer was told the two men who would be staying in his cottage were Taurus executives who were coming to Ireland to work on a project that was sensitive in nature. That much, at least, was true.

The cottage was set back from Doonen Road by approximately a hundred meters. There was a flimsy aluminum gate that had to be opened and closed by hand and a gravel drive that wound its way steeply up the bluff through the gorse and the heather. On the highest point of the land stood three ancient trees bowed by the wind that blew from the North Atlantic and up the narrows of Clifden Bay. The wind was cold and without remorse. It rattled the windows of the cottage, clawed at the tiles of the roof, and prowled the rooms each time a door opened. The small terrace was uninhabitable, a no-man's-land. Even the gulls did not stay there long.

Doonen Road was not a real road but a narrow strip of pavement, scarcely wide enough for a single car, with a ribbon of green grass down the center. Holidaymakers traveled it occasionally, but mainly it served as the back door to Clifden village. It was a young town by Irish standards, founded in 1814 by a landowner and sheriff named John d'Arcy who wished to create an island of order within the violent and lawless wilds of Connemara. D'Arcy built a castle for himself, and for the villagers a lovely town with paved streets and squares and a pair of churches with steeples that could be seen for miles. The castle was now a ruin, but the village, once virtually depopulated by the Great Famine, was among the most vibrant in the west of Ireland.

One of the men staying in the rented cottage, the smaller of the two, hiked to the village each day, usually in late morning, dressed in a dark green oilskin coat with a rucksack over his shoulder and a flat cap pulled low over his brow. He would purchase a few things at the supermarket and snare a bottle or two from Ferguson Fine Wines, Italian usually, sometimes French. And then, having acquired his provisions, he would wander past the shop windows along Main Street with the air of a man who was preoccupied by weightier matters. On one occasion he popped into the Lavelle Art Gallery to have a quick peek at the stock. The proprietor would later recall that he seemed unusually knowledgeable about paintings. His accent was hard to place. Maybe German, maybe something else. It didn't matter; to the people of Connemara, everyone else had an accent.

On the fourth day his stroll along Main Street was more perfunctory than usual. He entered only a single shop, the newsagent, and purchased four packets of American cigarettes and a copy of the *Independent*. The front page was filled with the news from Dublin, where three members of the Real IRA had been found slain in a house in Ballyfermot. Another man was missing and presumed abducted. The Garda was searching for him. So, too, were elements of the Real IRA.

"Drug gangs," muttered the man behind the counter.

"Terrible," agreed the visitor with the accent no one could quite place.

He inserted the newspaper into his rucksack and, with some reluctance, the cigarettes. Then he hiked back to the cottage owned by the lawyer from Dublin, who, as it turned out, was deeply loathed by the full-time residents of Clifden. The other man, the one with skin like leather, was listening intently to the midday news on RTÉ.

"We're close," was all he said.

"When?"

"Maybe tonight."

The smaller of the two men went onto the terrace while the other man smoked. A black storm was pushing up Clifden Bay, and the wind felt as though it were filled with shrapnel. Five minutes was all he could stand. Then he went back inside, into the smoke and the tension of the wait. He felt no shame. Even the gulls did not stay on the terrace for long.

Throughout his long career, Gabriel had had the misfortune of meeting many terrorists: Palestinian terrorists, Egyptian terrorists, Saudi terrorists, terrorists motivated by faith, terrorists motivated by loss, terrorists who had been born in the worst slums of the Arab world, terrorists who had been raised in the material comfort of the West. Oftentimes, he imagined what these men might have achieved had they chosen another path. Many were highly intelligent, and in their unforgiving eyes he saw lifesaving cures never found, software never devised, music never composed, and poems never written. Liam Walsh, however, made no such impression. Walsh was a killer without remorse or proper education who had no ambition in life other than the destruction of life and property. In his case a career in terrorism, even by the reduced standards of the diehard Irish republicans, was about the best he could have hoped for.

He was without physical fear, however, and possessed a natural obduracy that made him difficult to break. For the first forty-eight hours he was left in total isolation in the damp chill of the cellar, blindfolded, gagged, deafened by earplugs, immobilized by duct tape. He was offered no food, only water, which he refused. Keller saw to his bathroom needs, which were minimal given his dietary restrictions. When necessary, he addressed Walsh in the accent of a Protestant of the working classes from East Belfast. The Irishman was offered no way out of his predicament, and he did not ask for one. Having seen three of his mates killed in the blink of an eye, he seemed resigned to his fate. Like the SAS, Irish terrorists and drug gangsters played by big boys' rules.

On the morning of the third day, maddened by thirst, he partook of a few ounces of room-temperature water. At midday he drank tea with milk and sugar, and in the evening he was given more tea and a single slice of toasted bread. It was then that Keller addressed him for the first time at any length. "You're in a shitload of trouble, Liam," he said in his East Belfast accent. "And the only way out is to tell me what I want to know."

"Who are you?" asked Walsh through the pain of his broken jaw.

"That depends entirely on you," replied Keller. "If you talk to me, I'll be your best friend in the world. If you don't, you're going to end up like your three friends."

"What do you want to know?"

"Omagh," was all Keller said.

On the morning of the fourth day, Keller removed the plugs from Walsh's ears and the gag from his mouth and elaborated on the situation in which the Irishman now found himself. Keller claimed to be a member of a small Protestant vigilante group

seeking justice for the victims of republican terrorism. He suggested it had ties to the Ulster Volunteer Force, the loyalist paramilitary group that had
killed at least five hundred people, mainly Roman
Catholic civilians, during the worst of the Troubles
in Northern Ireland. The UVF accepted a cease-
fire in 1994, but its murals, with their images of
armed masked men, still adorned walls in Protestant neighborhoods and towns in Ulster. Many of
the murals bore the same slogan: "Prepared for
peace, ready for war." The same could have been
said for Keller.

"I'm looking for the one who built the bomb," he
explained. "You know the bomb I'm talking about,
Liam. The bomb that killed twenty-nine innocent
people in Omagh. You were there that day. You were
in the car with him."

"I don't know what you're talking about."

"You were there, Liam," Keller repeated. "And
you were in contact with him after the movement
went to shit. He came down here to Dublin. You
looked after him until it got too hot."

"It's not true. None of it's true."

"He's back in circulation, Liam. Tell me where I
can find him."

Walsh said nothing for a moment. "And if I tell
you?" he asked finally.

"You'll spend some time in captivity, a long time,
but you'll live."

"Bullshit," spat Walsh.

"We're not interested in you, Liam," answered
Keller calmly. "Only him. Tell us where we can
find him, and we'll let you live. Play dumb, and I'm

going to kill you. And it won't be with a nice neat bullet to the head. It'll hurt, Liam. It'll hurt badly."

That afternoon a storm laid siege to the length and breadth of Connemara. Gabriel sat by the fire reading from a volume of Fitzgerald while Keller drove the windblown countryside looking for unusual Garda activity. Liam Walsh remained in isolation in the cellar, bound, gagged, blinded, deafened. He was given no liquid or food. By that evening he was so weakened by hunger and dehydration that Keller almost had to carry him to the toilet.

"How long?" asked Gabriel over dinner.

"We're close," said Keller.

"That's what you said earlier."

Keller was silent.

"Is there anything we can do to hurry things along? I'd like to be out of here before the Garda come knocking on the door."

"Or the Real IRA," added Keller.

"Well?"

"He's immune to pain at this point."

"What about water?"

"Water's always good."

"Does he know?"

"He knows."

"Do you need help?"

"No," said Keller, rising. "It's personal."

When Keller was gone, Gabriel went onto the terrace and stood in the ball-bearing rain. Five minutes was all it took. Even a hard man like Liam Walsh couldn't stand the water for long.

15

THAMES HOUSE, LONDON

Each Friday evening, usually at six o'clock but sometimes a bit later if London or the wider world were in crisis, Graham Seymour had drinks with Amanda Wallace, the director-general of MI5. It was, without doubt, his least favorite appointment of the week. Wallace was Seymour's former boss. They had entered MI5 the same year and had risen through the ranks along parallel tracks, Seymour in the counterterrorism department, Wallace in counterespionage. In the end it was Amanda who had won the race to the DG's suite. But now, quite unexpectedly and in the twilight of his career, Seymour had been handed the biggest prize of all. Amanda hated him for it, for he was now London's most powerful spy. Quietly, she worked to undermine him at every turn.

Like Seymour, Amanda Wallace had espionage in her DNA. Her mother had toiled in the file rooms of MI5's Registry during the war, and upon graduation from Cambridge, Amanda had considered no career other than intelligence. Their common lineage should have made them allies. Instead, Amanda had instantly cast Seymour in the role of rival. He was the handsome scoundrel to whom success came too easily, and she was the awkward, rather shy girl who would run him off his feet. They had known each other thirty years and together had reached the twin peaks of British intelligence, and yet the basic dynamics of their relationship had never changed.

On the previous Friday, Amanda had come to Vauxhall Cross, which meant that under the rules of their relationship it was Seymour's turn to travel. He saw it as no imposition; he always liked going back to Thames House. His official Jaguar was cleared into the underground car park at 5:55 p.m., and two minutes later Amanda's elevator deposited him on the uppermost floor. The main corridor was as quiet as a night ward. Seymour supposed the senior staff were mixing with the troops at one of the building's two private bars. As always, he stopped to have a look inside his old office. Miles Kent, his successor as deputy, was staring blankly into his computer terminal. He looked as though he hadn't slept in a week.

"How is she?" asked Seymour warily.

"Fit to be tied. But you'd better hurry," Kent added. "Mustn't keep the queen bee waiting."

Seymour continued along the corridor to the DG's suite. A member of Amanda's all-male staff greeted him in the anteroom and showed him immediately into her large office. She was standing contemplatively in a window overlooking the Houses of Parliament. Turning, she consulted her wristwatch. Amanda valued punctuality above all other attributes.

"Graham," she said evenly, as though she were reading his name from one of the dense briefing books her staff always prepared before an important meeting. Then she gave an efficient smile. It looked as though she had taught herself the gesture by practicing in front of a mirror. "So good of you to come."

A drinks tray had been left on Amanda's long, gleaming conference table. She prepared a gin and tonic for Seymour and for herself a bone-dry martini with olives and cocktail onions. She prided herself on her ability to hold her liquor, a skill that, in her opinion, was obligatory for a spy. It was one of her few endearing qualities.

"Cheers," said Seymour, raising his glass a fraction of an inch, but again Amanda only smiled. The BBC played silently on a large flat-panel television. A senior officer of the Garda Síochána was standing outside a small house in Ballyfermot where three men, all members of a Real IRA drug gang, had been found dead.

"Rather nasty," said Amanda.

"A turf war, apparently," murmured Seymour over the rim of his glass.

"Our friends in the Garda have their doubts about that."

"What have they got?"

"Nothing, actually, which is why they're concerned. The phones usually light up with chatter after a big gangland assassination, but not this time. And then," she added, "there's the manner in which they were killed. Usually, these mobsters hose down the entire room with automatic-weapons fire. But whoever did this was very precise. Three shots, three dead bodies. The Garda are convinced they're dealing with professionals."

"Do they have any idea where Liam Walsh is?"

"They're operating under the assumption he's somewhere in the Republic, but they haven't a clue where." She looked at Seymour and raised an eyebrow. "He's not strapped to a chair in some MI6 safe house, is he, Graham?"

"No such luck."

Seymour looked at the television. The BBC had moved on to the next story. Prime Minister Jonathan Lancaster was in Washington for a meeting with the American president. It had not gone as well as he had hoped. Britain was not terribly in vogue in Washington at the moment, at least not at the White House.

"Your friend," said Amanda coolly.

"The American president?"

"Jonathan."

"Yours, too," replied Seymour.

"My relationship with the prime minister is cordial," said Amanda deliberately, "but it's nothing like yours. You and Jonathan are thick as thieves."

It was clear Amanda wanted to say more about Seymour's unique bond with the prime minister. Instead, she freshened his drink while sharing a piece of naughty gossip about the wife of a certain ambassador from an oil-rich Arab emirate. Seymour reciprocated with a report he'd received about a man with a British accent who was shopping for shoulder-fired antiaircraft missiles at an arms bazaar in Libya. After that, with the ice having been broken, they fell into an easy conversation of the sort that only two senior spymasters could have. They shared, they divulged, they advised, and on two occasions they actually laughed. Indeed, for a few minutes it seemed their rivalry did not exist. They talked about the situation in Iraq and Syria, they talked about China, they talked about the global economy and its impact on security, and they talked about the American president, whom they blamed for many of the world's problems. Eventually, they talked about the Russians. These days, they always did.

"Their cyberwarriors," said Amanda, "are blasting away at our financial institutions with everything they've got in their nasty little toolbox. They're also targeting our government systems and the computer networks of our biggest defense contractors."

"Are they after something specific?"

"Actually," she replied, "they don't seem to be looking for much of anything. They're just trying to inflict as much damage as possible. There's a recklessness we've never seen before."

"Any change in their posture here in London?"

"D4 has noticed a distinct increase in activity at the London *rezidentura*. We're not sure what it means, but it's clear they're involved in something big."

"Bigger than planting a Russian illegal in the prime minister's bed?"

Amanda raised an eyebrow and traced an olive around the rim of her glass. The face of the princess appeared on the television. Her family had announced the creation of a fund to support causes she held dear. Jonathan Lancaster had been allowed to make the first donation.

"Hear anything new?" asked Amanda.

"About the princess?"

She nodded.

"Nothing. You?"

She set down her drink and considered Seymour for a moment in silence. Finally, she asked, "Why didn't you tell me it was Eamon Quinn?"

She tapped her nail on the arm of the chair while she awaited a response, never a good sign. Seymour decided he had no choice but to tell her the truth, or at least a version of it.

"I didn't tell you," he said at last, "because I didn't want to involve you."

"Because you don't trust me?"

"Because I don't want you to be tainted in any way."

"Why would I be tainted? After all, Graham, *you* were the head of counterterrorism at the time of the Omagh bombing, not me."

"Which is why you became the DG of the Security Service." He paused, then added, "And not me."

A strained silence fell between them. Seymour longed to leave but could not. The matter had to have some resolution.

"Was Quinn acting on behalf of the Real IRA," asked Amanda finally, "or someone else?"

"We should have an answer to that in a few hours."

"As soon as Liam Walsh breaks?"

Seymour offered no reply.

"Is it an authorized MI6 operation?"

"Off the books."

"Your specialty," said Amanda caustically. "I suppose you're working with the Israelis. After all, they wanted to take Quinn out of circulation a long time ago."

"And we should have taken them up on the offer."

"How much does Jonathan know?"

"Nothing."

She swore softly, something she rarely did. "I'm going to give you a great deal of latitude on this," she said finally. "Not for your sake, mind you, but for the sake of the Security Service. But I expect advance warning if your operation spills onto British soil. And if anything goes boom, I'll make certain it's your neck on the block, not mine." She smiled. "Just so there's no misunderstanding."

"I would have expected nothing else."

"Very well, then." She looked at her watch. "I'm afraid I've got to run, Graham. Next week at your place?"

"I'm looking forward to it." Seymour rose and extended his hand. "Always a pleasure, Amanda."

16

CLIFDEN, COUNTY GALWAY

THEY BROUGHT HIM upstairs from the cellar and, with his eyes still blinded by duct tape, allowed him to shower for the first time. Then they dressed him in the blue-and-white tracksuit and gave him a few bites of food and some sweet milky tea to drink. It did little for his appearance. With his swollen face, pale skin, and emaciated frame, he looked like a corpse risen from the mortuary slab.

The meal complete, Keller repeated his admonition. The Irishman would be treated well so long as he answered Keller's questions truthfully and in a normal speaking voice. If he lied, evaded, shouted, or made any foolish attempt to escape, he would be returned to the cellar and the conditions of his confinement would be far less pleasant than before. Gabriel did not speak but Walsh, with his auditory senses heightened by blindness and fear, was clearly aware of his presence. Gabriel preferred it that way. He did not want to leave Walsh with the mistaken impression that he was under the control of a single man, even if that man happened to be one of the deadliest in the world.

Keller had no formal training in the techniques of interrogation, but like all good interrogators he established in Walsh the habit of answering questions truthfully and without hesitation or evasion. They were simple questions at first, questions with answers that were easily verifiable. Date of birth. Place of birth. Names of his parents and siblings. The schools he had attended. His recruitment by the Irish Republican Army. Walsh stated that he was born in Ballybay, County Monaghan, on October 16, 1972. The place of his birth was significant in that it was two miles from Northern Ireland, in the tense Border Region. His birthday was significant, too; he shared it with Michael Collins, the Irish revolutionary leader. He attended Catholic schools until he was eighteen, when he joined the IRA. His recruiter made no attempt to glamorize the life Walsh had chosen. He would be poorly paid and would live on the knife's edge of danger. In all likelihood he would spend several years in prison. The chances were good he would die violently.

"And the recruiter's name?" asked Keller in his Ulsterman's accent.

"I'm not allowed to say."

"You are now."

"It was Seamus McNeil," Walsh said after a moment's hesitation. "He was—"

"A member of the South Armagh Brigade," Keller cut in. "He was killed in an ambush by British soldiers and buried with IRA honors, may he rest in peace."

"Actually," said Walsh, "he died during a shoot-out with the SAS."

"Only cowboys and gangsters do shoot-outs," replied Keller. "But you were about to tell me about your training."

Which Walsh did. He was sent to a remote camp in the Republic for small-arms training and lessons in the manufacture and delivery of bombs. He was told to quit drinking and to avoid socializing with non-IRA members. Finally, six months after his recruitment, he was assigned to an elite IRA active service unit. Its membership included a master bomb maker and operational planner named Eamon Quinn. Quinn was several years older than Walsh and already a legend. In the 1980s he had been sent to a desert camp in Libya for training. But in the end, said Walsh, it was Quinn, not the Libyans, who had done most of the instructing. In fact, Quinn was the one who gave the Libyans the design for the bomb that brought down Pan Am Flight 103 over Lockerbie, Scotland.

"Bullshit," said Keller.

"Whatever you say," replied Walsh.

"Who else was at the camp with him?"

"It was PLO, mainly, and a couple of lads from one of the splinter organizations."

"Which one?"

"I believe it was the Popular Front for the Liberation of Palestine."

"You know your Palestinian terror groups."

"We have a great deal in common with the Palestinians."

"How so?"

"We're both occupied by racist colonial powers."

Keller looked at Gabriel, who was gazing impassively at his hands. Walsh, still blindfolded, seemed to sense the tension in the room. Outside, the wind prowled at the doors and windows of the cottage, as if searching for a point of entry.

"Where am I?" asked Walsh.

"Hell," replied Keller.

"What do I have to do to get out?"

"Keep talking."

"What do you want to know?"

"The details of your first operation."

"It was 1993."

"What month?"

"April."

"Ulster or mainland?"

"Mainland."

"What city?"

"The only city that matters."

"London?"

"Yes."

"Bishopsgate?"

Walsh nodded. *Bishopsgate . . .*

The truck, a Ford Iveco tipper, vanished from Newcastle-under-Lyme, Staffordshire, in March. They took it to a rented warehouse and painted it dark blue. Then Quinn fitted it with the bomb, a one-ton ammonium nitrate/fuel oil device that he assembled in South Armagh and smuggled into England. On the morning of April 24, Walsh drove the truck to London and parked it outside 99 Bishopsgate, an office tower occupied solely by HSBC. The blast shattered more than five hundred tons of glass, collapsed a church, and killed a news photographer. The British government responded by surrounding London's financial district in a security cordon known as the "ring of steel." Undeterred, the IRA returned to London in February 1996 with another truck bomb designed and assembled by Eamon Quinn. This time, the target was Canary Wharf in the Docklands. The blast was so powerful it shook windows five miles away. The prime ministers of Britain and Ireland quickly announced the resumption of peace talks. Eighteen months later, in July 1997, the IRA accepted a cease-fire. "It was," said Liam Walsh, "a fucking disaster."

"And when the IRA fractured later that autumn," said Keller, "you went with McKevitt and Bernadette Sands?"

"No," replied Walsh. "I went with Eamon Quinn."

From the outset, Walsh continued, the Real IRA was riddled with informers reporting to MI5 and Crime and Security, a shadowy division of the Garda Síochána that operated out of unmarked offices in the Phoenix Park section of Dublin. Even so, the group managed to carry out a string of bombings, including a devastating attack on Banbridge on August 1, 1998. The bomb weighed five hundred pounds and was concealed inside a red Vauxhall Cavalier. The coded telephone warnings were imprecise—no location, no time of detonation. As a result, thirty-three people were seriously injured, including two officers of the Royal Ulster Constabulary. Pieces of the Vauxhall were found six hundred yards away. It was, said Walsh, a preview of coming attractions.

"Omagh," said Keller quietly.

Walsh said nothing.

"You were part of the operational team?"

Walsh nodded.

"Which car?" asked Keller. "Bomb, scout, or escape?"

"Bomb."

"Driver or passenger?"

"I was supposed to be the driver, but there was a change at the last minute."

"Who drove?"

Walsh hesitated, then said, "Quinn."

"Why the change?"

"He said he was more on edge than usual before an operation. He said the driving would help calm his nerves."

"But that wasn't the real reason, was it, Liam? Quinn wanted to take matters into his own hands. Quinn wanted to put a nail in the coffin of the peace process."

"A bullet in the head was how he described it."

"He was supposed to leave the bomb at the courthouse?"

"That was the plan."

"Did he even look for a parking space?"

"No," said Walsh, shaking his head. "He went straight to Lower Market Street and parked outside S.D. Kells."

"Why didn't you do something?"

"I tried to talk him out of it, but he wouldn't listen."

"You should have tried harder, Liam."

"You obviously don't know Eamon Quinn."

"Where was the escape car?"

"In the parking lot of the supermarket."

"And when you got inside?"

"The call went back to the other side of the border."

" 'The bricks are in the wall.' "

Walsh nodded.

"Why didn't you tell anyone the bomb was in the wrong place?"

"If I'd opened my mouth, Quinn would have killed me. Besides," Walsh added, "it was too late."

"And when the bomb went off?"

"It was shit city."

The death and devastation ignited revulsion on both sides of the border and around the world. The Real IRA issued an apology and announced a cease-fire, but it was too late; the movement had suffered irreparable damage. Walsh settled in Dublin to look after the Real IRA's interests in the burgeoning drug trade. Quinn went into hiding.

"Where?"

"Spain."

"What did he do?"

"He hung out on the beach until the money ran out."

"And then?"

"He called an old friend and said he wanted back in the game."

"Who was the friend?"

Walsh hesitated, then said, "Muammar Gaddafi."

17

CLIFDEN, COUNTY GALWAY

T WASN'T REALLY GADDAFI, Walsh added quickly. It was a close confidant from Libyan intelligence whom Quinn had befriended when he was at the desert terror training camp. Quinn requested sanctuary, and the man from Libyan intelligence, after consulting with the ruler, agreed to allow Quinn into the country. He lived in a walled villa in an upscale Tripoli neighborhood and did odd jobs for the Libyan security services. He was also a frequent visitor to Gaddafi's underground bunker, where he would regale the leader with stories of the fight against the British. In time, Gaddafi shared Quinn with some of his less savory regional allies. He developed contacts with every bad actor on the continent: dictators, warlords, mercenaries, diamond smugglers, Islamic militants of every stripe. He also made the acquaintance of a Russian arms dealer who was pouring weaponry and ammunition into every civil war and insurgency in sub-Saharan Africa. The arms dealer agreed to send a small container of AK-47s and plastic explosives to the Real IRA. Walsh took delivery of the shipment in Dublin.

"Do you remember the name of the man from Libyan intelligence?" asked Keller.

"He called himself Abu Muhammad."

Keller looked at Gabriel, who nodded slowly.

"And the Russian arms dealer?" asked Keller.

"It was Ivan Kharkov, the one who was killed in Saint-Tropez a few years ago."

"You're sure, Liam? You're sure it was Ivan?"

"Who else could it be? Ivan controlled the arms trade in Africa, and he killed anyone who tried to get in on the action."

"And the villa in Tripoli? Do you know where it was?"

"It was in the neighborhood they call al-Andalus."

"The street?"

"Via Canova. Number Twenty-Seven," Walsh added. "But don't waste your time. Quinn left Libya years ago."

"What happened?"

"Gaddafi decided to clean up his act. He gave up his weapons programs and told the Americans and the Europeans that he wanted to normalize relations. Tony Blair shook his hand in a tent outside Tripoli. BP got drilling rights on Libyan soil. Remember?"

"I remember, Liam."

Apparently, said Walsh, MI6 knew that Quinn was living secretly in Tripoli. The chief of MI6 prevailed upon Gaddafi to send Quinn packing, and Gaddafi agreed. He called a few of his friends in Africa, but no one would take Quinn in. Then he called one of his best friends in the world, and the deal was done. A week later Gaddafi gave Quinn a signed copy of his *Green Book* and put him on an airplane.

"And the friend who agreed to take Quinn?"

"Three guesses," said Walsh. "First two don't count."

The friend was Hugo Chavez, president of Venezuela, ally of Russia, Cuba, and the mullahs of Tehran, thorn in the side of America. Chavez saw himself as a leader of the world's revolutionary movement, and he operated a not-so-secret training camp for terrorists and leftist rebels on Margarita Island. Quinn soon became the star attraction. He worked with everyone from the Shining Path of Peru to Hamas and Hezbollah, sharing the deadly tricks of the trade he'd acquired during his long career matching wits with the British. Chavez, like Gaddafi before him, treated Quinn well. He gave him a villa by the sea and a diplomatic passport to travel the world. He even gave him a new face.

"Who did the work?"

"Gaddafi's doctor."

"The Brazilian?"

Walsh nodded. "He came to Caracas and performed the surgery in a hospital there. He gave Quinn a total reconstruction. The old pictures are useless now. Even I barely recognized him."

"You saw him when he was in Venezuela?"

"Twice."

"You went to the camp?"

"Never."

"Why not?"

"I wasn't cleared for the camp. I saw him on the mainland."

"Keep talking, Liam."

A year after Quinn arrived in Venezuela, a senior man from VEVAK, the Iranian intelligence service, paid a quiet visit to the island. He wasn't there to see his allies from Hezbollah; he was there to see Quinn. The man from VEVAK stayed on the island for a week. And when he went back to Tehran, Quinn went with him.

"Why?"

"The Iranians wanted Quinn to build a weapon."

"What kind of weapon?"

"A weapon that Hezbollah could use against Israeli tanks and armored vehicles in southern Lebanon."

Keller looked at Gabriel, who appeared to be contemplating a crack in the ceiling. Walsh, unaware of the true identity of his small audience, was still talking.

"The Iranians set Quinn up in a weapons factory in a Tehran suburb called Lavizan. He built a version of an antitank weapon that he'd been working on for years. It created a fireball that traveled a thousand feet per second and engulfed the advancing armor in flames. Hezbollah used it against the Israelis in the summer of 2006. The Israeli tanks went up like kindling. It was like the Holocaust."

Keller again cast a sidelong glance toward Gabriel, who was now staring directly at Liam Walsh.

"And when he finished designing the antitank weapon?" asked Keller.

"He went to Lebanon to work directly with Hezbollah."

"What kind of work?"

"Roadside bombs, mainly."

"And then?"

"The Iranians sent him to Yemen to work with al-Qaeda in the Arabian Peninsula."

"I didn't know there were ties between the Iranians and al-Qaeda."

"Whoever told you that?"

"Where is he now?"

"I haven't a clue."

"You're lying, Liam."

"I'm not. I swear I don't know where he is or who he's working for."

"When was the last time you saw him?"

"Six months ago."

"Where?"

"Spain."

"Spain is a big country, Liam."

"It was in the south, in Sotogrande."

"An Irish playground."

"It's like Dublin with the sun turned up."

"Where did you meet?"

"A little hotel down by the marina. Very quiet."

"What did he want?"

"He wanted me to deliver a package."

"What kind of package?"

"Money."

"Who was the money for?"

"His daughter."

"I never knew he was married."

"Most people don't."

"Where's the daughter?"

"In Belfast with her mother."

"Keep talking, Liam."

The combined services of British intelligence had assembled a mountain of material on the life and times of Eamon Quinn, but nowhere in their voluminous files was there any mention of a wife or a child. It was no accident, said Walsh. Quinn the operational planner had gone to great lengths to keep his family a secret. Walsh claimed to have attended the ceremony at which the two were wed, and later he helped to manage the family's financial affairs during the years Quinn was living abroad as a superstar of international terrorism. The package Quinn gave to Walsh in the Spanish resort of Sotogrande contained one hundred thousand pounds in used bills. It was the largest single payment Quinn had ever entrusted to his old friend.

"Why so much money?" asked Keller.

"He said it would be the last payment for a while."

"Did he say why?"

"No."

"And you didn't ask?"

"I knew better."

"And you delivered the payment in full?"

"Every single pound."

"You didn't keep a small service charge for yourself? After all, Quinn would have never known."

"You obviously don't know Eamon Quinn."

Keller asked whether Quinn had ever stolen into Belfast to see his family.

"Never."

"And they never traveled outside the country to see him?"

"He was afraid the British would follow them. Besides," Walsh added, "they wouldn't have recognized him. Quinn had a new face. Quinn was someone else."

Which returned them to the subject of Quinn's surgically altered appearance. Gabriel and Keller had in their possession the images that the French had captured in Saint Barthélemy—a few frames of airport video, a few grainy still photos captured by storefront security cameras—but in none was Quinn's face clearly visible. He was a mop of black hair and a beard, a man to glimpse once and quickly forget. Liam Walsh had the power to complete Quinn's portrait, for Walsh had sat across from him six months earlier, in a Spanish hotel room.

Gabriel had produced composite sketches under challenging circumstances, but never with a witness who was blindfolded. In fact, he was quite certain it was not possible. Keller explained how the process would work. There was another man present, he said, a man who was as good with a sketchpad and a pencil as he was with his fists and a gun. This man was neither Irish nor an Ulsterman. Walsh was to describe Quinn's appearance for him. He could look at the man's sketchpad, but under no circumstances was he to look at his face.

"What if I look accidentally?"

"Don't."

Keller removed the duct tape from Walsh's eyes. The Irishman blinked several times. Then he stared directly at the figure seated on the opposite side of the table behind a sketchpad and a box of colored pencils.

"You just violated the rules," said Gabriel calmly.

"Do you want to know what he looks like, or not?"

Gabriel picked up a pencil. "Let's start with his eyes."

"They're green," replied Walsh. "Like yours."

They worked without a break for the next two hours. Walsh described, Gabriel sketched, Walsh corrected, Gabriel revised. Finally, at midnight, the portrait was complete. The Brazilian plastic surgeon had done a fine job. He had given Quinn a face without character or a memorable feature. Still, it was a face Gabriel would recognize if it passed him on the street.

If Walsh was curious about the identity of the green-eyed man behind the sketchpad, he gave no sign of it. Nor did he resist when Keller covered his eyes with a blindfold of duct tape, or when Gabriel injected him with enough sedative to keep him quiet for a few hours. They zipped him unconscious into the duffel bag and wiped down every item and surface in the cottage that any of them had touched. Then they hoisted him into the trunk of the Škoda and climbed into the front seat. Keller drove. It was his turf.

The roads were empty, the rain was sporadic, a

torrential downpour one minute, a blustery mist the next. Keller smoked one cigarette after the next and listened to the news on the radio. Gabriel stared out the window at the black hills and the windswept moors and bogs. In his thoughts, however, there was only Eamon Quinn. Since fleeing Ireland, Quinn had worked with some of the most dangerous men in the world. It was possible he had been acting out of conscience or political belief, but Gabriel doubted it. Surely, he thought, Quinn was past all that. He had gone the way of Carlos and Abu Nidal before him. He was a terrorist for hire, killing at the behest of powerful patrons. But who had paid for Quinn's bullet? Who had commissioned him to kill a princess? Gabriel had a long list of potential suspects. For now, though, finding Quinn would take precedence. Liam Walsh had given them ample places to look, none more promising than a house in West Belfast. A part of Gabriel wanted to search elsewhere, for he regarded wives and children as off-limits. Quinn, however, had left them no other choice.

At the eastern end of Killary Harbor, Keller turned onto an unpaved track and followed it into a dense patch of heather and gorse. He stopped in a small clearing, killed the lights and the engine, and popped the interior trunk release. Gabriel reached for the latch, but Keller stopped him. "Stay," was all he said before opening the door and stepping into the rain.

By then, Walsh had regained consciousness. Gabriel listened as Keller explained what was about to transpire. Because Walsh had cooperated, he would

be released with no further harm. Under no circumstances was he to discuss his interrogation with
his associates. Nor was he to make any attempt to
pass a message of warning to Quinn. If he did, said
Keller, he was dead.

"Are we clear, Liam?"

Gabriel overheard Walsh murmuring something
in the affirmative. Then he felt the rear end of
the Škoda rise slightly as Keller helped the Irishman from the boot. The lid closed; Walsh shuffled
blindfolded into the heather, Keller clutching one
elbow. For a moment there was only the wind and
the rain. Then from deep in the heather came two
muted flashes of light.

Keller soon reappeared. He slid behind the
wheel, started the engine, and reversed back to the
road. Gabriel stared out the window as news from
a troubled world issued softly from the radio. This
time, he didn't bother to ask how Keller felt. It was
personal. He closed his eyes and slept. And when
he woke it was daylight and they were crossing the
border into Northern Ireland.

18

OMAGH, NORTHERN IRELAND

T HE FIRST TOWN on the other side of the border was Aughnacloy. Keller stopped for gas next to a pretty flint church and then followed the A5 north to Omagh, just as Quinn and Liam Walsh had done on the afternoon of August 15, 1998. It was a few minutes after nine when they breached the town's southern outskirts; the rain had ended and a bright orange sun shone through a slit in the clouds. They left the car near the courthouse and walked to a café on Lower Market Street. Keller ordered a traditional Irish breakfast but Gabriel asked for only tea and bread. He glimpsed his reflection in the window and was dismayed by his appearance. Keller, he decided, looked worse. His eyes were red-rimmed and bloodshot, and his face was sorely in need of a razor. Nowhere in his expression, however, was there any suggestion he had recently killed a man in a patch of heather and gorse in County Mayo.

"Why are we here?" asked Gabriel as he watched the first pedestrians of the morning, shopkeepers mainly, moving purposefully along the shimmering pavements.

"It's a nice place."

"You've been here before?"

"On several occasions, actually."

"What brought you to town?"

"I used to meet a source here."

"IRA?"

"More or less."

"Where's the source now?"

"Greenhill Cemetery."

"What happened?"

Keller fashioned his hand into the shape of a gun and placed the barrel against his temple.

"IRA?" asked Gabriel.

Keller shrugged. "More or less."

The food arrived. Keller devoured his as though he had not eaten in many days, but Gabriel picked at his bread without appetite. Outside, the clouds were playing tricks with the light. It was morning one minute, dusk the next. Gabriel imagined the street littered with shattered glass and human limbs. He looked at Keller and again asked why they had come to Omagh.

"In case you were having second thoughts."

"About what?"

Keller looked down at the remnants of his breakfast and said, "Liam Walsh."

Gabriel made no reply. On the opposite side of the street, a woman with one arm and burns on her face was attempting to unlock the door of a dress shop. Gabriel supposed she was one of the wounded. There were more than two hundred that day: men, women, teenagers, small children. The politicians and the press always seemed to focus on the dead after a bombing, but the wounded were soon forgotten—the ones with scorched flesh, the ones with memories so terrible that no amount of therapy or medication could put their minds at rest. Such were the accomplishments of a man like Eamon Quinn, a man who could make a ball of fire travel one thousand feet per second.

"Well?" asked Keller.

"No," said Gabriel. "No second thoughts."

A red Vauxhall sedan pulled to the curb outside the café and two men climbed out. Gabriel felt a rush of blood to his face as he watched the men move off down the street. Then he stared at the car as though he were waiting for the timer in the glove box to reach zero.

"What would you have done?" he asked suddenly.

"About what?"

"If you'd known where the bomb was that day."

"I would have tried to warn them."

"And if the bomb were about to explode? Would you have risked your life?"

The waitress placed the check on the table before Keller could answer. Gabriel paid the bill in cash, pocketed the receipt, and followed Keller into the street. The courthouse was to the right. Keller turned left instead and led Gabriel past the brightly colored shops and storefronts, to a tower of blue-green glass rising from the pavement like a gravestone. It was the memorial for the victims of the Omagh bombing, placed on the very spot where the car had exploded. Gabriel and Keller stood there for a moment, neither man speaking, as pedestrians hurried past. Most averted their eyes. On the opposite side of the street a woman with pale hair and sunglasses lifted a smartphone to her face, as if to take a photograph. Keller quickly turned his back to her. So did Gabriel.

"What would you have done, Christopher?"

"About the bomb?"

Gabriel nodded.

"I would have done everything in my power to move the people to safety."

"Even if you died?"

"Even if I died."

"How can you be so sure?"

"Because I wouldn't have been able to live with myself."

Gabriel was silent for a moment. Then he said quietly, "You're going to make a fine MI6 officer, Christopher."

"MI6 officers don't kill terrorists and leave their bodies in the countryside."

"No," said Gabriel. "Only the good ones."

He looked over his shoulder. The woman with the smartphone was gone.

Twenty-five years had passed since Christopher Keller last set foot in Belfast, and the city center had changed much in his absence. Indeed, were it not for a few landmarks like the Opera House and the Europa Hotel, he scarcely would have recognized it. There were no British soldiers patrolling the streets, no army surveillance posts atop the taller buildings, and no fear on the faces of the pedestrians walking along Great Victoria Street. The city's geography remained sharply divided along sectarian lines, and there were still paramilitary murals in some of the rougher neighborhoods. But for the most part, evidence of the long and bloody war had been erased. Belfast promoted itself as a tourist mecca. And for some reason, thought Keller, the tourists actually came.

One of the city's main attractions was a vibrant Celtic music scene that had reappeared in the absence of war. Most of the bars and pubs that featured live music were located in the streets around St. Anne's Cathedral. Tommy O'Boyle's was on Union Street, on the ground floor of an old redbrick Victorian factory. It was not yet noon, and the door was locked. Keller thumbed the button on the intercom and quickly turned his back to the security camera. Greeted by silence, he pressed the button a second time.

"We're closed," a voice said.

"I can read," Keller replied in his Belfast accent.

"What do you want?"

"A word with Billy Conway."

A few seconds of silence, then, "He's busy."

"I'm sure he can make time for me."

"What's your name?"

"Michael Connelly."

"Doesn't ring a bell."

"Tell him I used to work for the Sparkle Clean laundry service on the Road back in the day."

"That place closed down years ago."

"We're thinking about going back into business."

There was another silence. Then the voice said, "Be a good lad and let me have a look at your face."

Keller hesitated before glancing into the lens of the security camera. Ten seconds later the deadbolts of the door popped open.

"Come inside," the voice instructed.

"I prefer it out here."

"Suit yourself."

A wad of newsprint somersaulted along the shadowed pavement, driven by a cold wind from the River Lagan. Keller turned up his coat collar. He thought of his sunlit terrace overlooking his valley in Corsica. It seemed alien to him now, a place he had visited once in his childhood. He could no longer conjure the aroma of the hills or a clear image of the don's face. He was Christopher Keller again. He was back in the game.

He heard a rattle and, turning, saw the door of Tommy O'Boyle's opening slowly. Standing in the narrow breach was a small, thin man in his late fifties, with gray stubble on his face and a bit more on his head. He looked as though he had just seen a ghost. In a way, he had.

"Hello, Billy," said Keller genially. "Good to see you again."

"I thought you were dead."

"I am dead." Keller put a hand on the man's shoulder. "Take a walk with me, Billy. We need to talk."

19

GREAT VICTORIA STREET, BELFAST

THEY HAD TO go somewhere no one would recognize them. Billy Conway suggested an American doughnut shop on Great Victoria Street; no IRA man, he said, would ever be caught dead there. He ordered two large coffees and pounced on an empty table in the back corner, next to the fire exit. It was the Belfast disease. Don't sit too close to glass windows in case a bomb goes off in the street. Always leave yourself an escape route if the wrong sort comes through the front door. Keller sat with his back to the room. Conway eyed the other patrons over the rim of his cup.

"You should have called first," he said. "You nearly gave me a coronary."

"Would you have agreed to see me?"

"No," said Billy Conway. "I don't reckon I would've."

Keller smiled. "You were always honest, Billy."

"Too honest. I helped you put a lot of men into the Maze." Conway paused, then added, "Into the ground, too."

"It was a long time ago."

"Not that long." Conway's eyes flickered around the interior of the shop. "They gave me quite a going-over after you left town. They said you gave them my name in that farmhouse down in South Armagh."

"I didn't."

"I know," Conway said. "I wouldn't be alive if you'd given me up, would I?"

"Not a chance, Billy."

Conway's eyes were on the move again. He had helped to save countless lives and prevent untold millions in property damage. And his reward, thought Keller, was to spend the rest of his life waiting for an IRA bullet. The IRA was like an elephant. It never forgot. And it surely never forgave an informant.

"How's business?" asked Keller.

"Fine. You?"

Keller gave a noncommittal shrug of his shoulders.

"What business are you in these days, Michael Connelly?"

"It's not important."

"I assume that wasn't your real name."

Keller made a face to say that it wasn't.

"How did you learn to speak like that?"

"Like what?"

"Like one of us," said Conway.

"I suppose it's a gift."

"You've other gifts as well," said Conway. "It was four against one in that farmhouse, and even then it wasn't a fair fight."

"Actually," said Keller, "it was five against one."

"Who was the fifth?"

"Quinn."

A silence fell between them.

"You're a brave man to come back after all these years," Conway said after a moment. "If they find out you're in town, you're a dead man. Peace accord or no peace accord."

The door of the shop opened and several tourists—Danes or Swedes, Keller could not decide—came in from the street. Conway frowned and drank his coffee.

"The tour guides take them into the neighborhoods and show them where the worst atrocities happened. And then they bring them to Tommy O'Boyle's to hear the music."

"It's good for business."

"I suppose." He looked at Keller. "Is that why you came back? To take a tour of the Troubles?"

Keller watched the tourists file into the street. Then he looked at Conway and asked, "Who was the one who interrogated you after I left Belfast?"

"It was Quinn."

"Where'd he do it?"

"I'm not sure. I really don't remember much except for the knife. He told me he was going to cut out my eyes if I didn't admit to being a spy for the British."

"What did you tell him?"

"Obviously, I denied it. And I might have begged for my life a little, too. He seemed to like that. He was always a cruel bastard."

Keller nodded slowly, as though Conway had spoken words of great insight.

"You hear about Liam Walsh?" Conway asked.

"Hard not to."

"Who do you suppose was behind it?"

"The Garda says it was drugs."

"The Garda," said Conway, "are completely full of shit."

"What do you know?"

"I know that someone walked into Walsh's house in Dublin and killed three very hard men without breaking a sweat." Conway paused, then asked, "Sound familiar?"

Keller said nothing.

"Why'd you come back here?"

"Quinn."

"You're not going to find him in Belfast."

"Did you know he had a wife and daughter here?"

"I'd heard rumors to that effect, but I was never able to come up with a name."

"Maggie Donahue."

Conway lifted his eyes thoughtfully toward the ceiling. "Makes sense."

"Know her?"

"Everybody knows Maggie."

"Work?"

"Across the street at the Europa. In fact," Conway added with a glance at his watch, "she's probably there now."

"What about the kid?"

"Goes to school at Our Lady of Mercy. Must be sixteen by now."

"Know where they live?"

"Just off the Crumlin Road in the Ardoyne."

"I need the address, Billy."

"No problem."

20

THE ARDOYNE, WEST BELFAST

IT TOOK BILLY CONWAY less than thirty minutes to establish that Maggie Donahue lived at 8 Stratford Gardens with her only child, a daughter who was called Catherine, after Quinn's sainted mother. The neighbors were unaware of the source of the child's name, though most suspected that Maggie Donahue's absent husband, be he dead or alive, was an IRA man of some sort, quite possibly a dissident who had rejected the tenets of the Good Friday Agreement. Such sentiments ran deep in the Ardoyne. During the worst of the Troubles, the Royal Ulster Constabulary regarded the neighborhood as a no-go area, too dangerous to patrol or even enter. More than a decade after the peace accords, it was the scene of rioting and clashes between Catholics and Protestants.

To supplement the cash payments she received from her husband, Maggie Donahue worked as a waitress in the Lobby Bar of the Europa Hotel, the most bombed hotel in the world. That afternoon she had the misfortune of attending to the particular needs of a guest named Herr Johannes

Klemp. His hotel registration card listed a Munich address, but his work—apparently it had something to do with interior design—required him to spend a great deal of time away from home. Like many frequent travelers, he was somewhat difficult to please. His lunch, it seemed, was a catastrophe. His salad was too limp, his sandwich too cold, the milk for his coffee had gone bad. Worse still, he had taken a liking to the poor creature whose job it was to make him happy. She did not find his attempts at small talk appealing. Few women did.

"Long day?" he asked as she refilled his cup with coffee.

"Just beginning."

She smiled wearily. She had hair the color of a raven's wing, pale skin, and large blue eyes over wide cheekbones. She had been pretty once, but her face had taken on a hard edge. He supposed Belfast had aged her. Or perhaps, he thought, it was Quinn who had ruined her looks.

"You're from here?" he asked.

"Everyone's from here."

"East or West?"

"You ask a lot of questions."

"I'm just curious."

"About what?"

"Belfast," he said.

"Is that why you came here? Because you're curious?"

"Work, I'm afraid. But I have the rest of the day to myself, so I thought I'd see a bit of the city."

"Why don't you hire a tour guide? They're very knowledgeable."

"I'd rather slit my wrists."

"I know how you feel." Her irony seemed to bounce off him like a pebble thrown at a bullet train. "Is there anything else I can do for you?"

"You can take the rest of the day off and show me around the city."

"Can't," was all she said.

"What time do you get off work?"

"Eight."

"I'll stop by for a drink and tell you about my day."

She smiled sadly and said, "I'll be here."

He paid the bill in cash and headed out to Great Victoria Street, where Keller waited behind the wheel of the Škoda. Lying on the backseat, wrapped in clear cellophane, was a bouquet of flowers. The small envelope was neatly addressed *MAGGIE DONAHUE*.

"What time does she get off work?" asked Keller.

"She said eight o'clock, but she might have been trying to avoid me."

"I told you to play nice."

"It's not in my DNA to be nice to the wife of a terrorist."

"It's possible she doesn't know."

"Where did her husband get a hundred thousand pounds in used bills?"

Keller had no answer.

"What about the girl?" asked Gabriel.

"She's in class until three."

"And then?"

"A field hockey game against Belfast Model School."

"Protestant?"

"Mostly."

"Should be interesting."

Keller was silent.

"So what do we do?"

"We deliver some flowers to Eight Stratford Gardens."

"And then?"

"We have a look inside."

But first they decided to take a detour through Keller's violent past. There was the old Divis Tower, where he had lived among the IRA as Michael Connelly, and the abandoned cleaning service on the Falls Road, where the same Michael Connelly had tested the household laundry of the IRA for evidence of explosives. Farther down the Road was the iron gate of Milltown Cemetery, where Elizabeth Conlin, the woman Keller had loved in secret, lay buried in a grave that Eamon Quinn had dug for her.

"You've never been?" asked Gabriel.

"It's too dangerous," said Keller, shaking his head. "The IRA keep watch over the graves."

From Milltown they drove past the Ballymurphy housing estates to Springfield Road. Along its northern flank rose a barricade separating a Protestant enclave from a neighboring Catholic district. The first of the so-called peace lines appeared in

Belfast in 1969 as a temporary solution to the city's sectarian bloodletting. Now they were a permanent feature of its geography—indeed, their number, length, and scale had actually increased since the signing of the Good Friday accords. On Springfield Road the barricade was a transparent green fence about ten meters in height. But on Cupar Way, a particularly tense part of the Ardoyne, it was a Berlin Wall–like structure topped by razor wire. Residents on both sides had covered it in murals. One likened it to the separation fence between Israel and the West Bank.

"Does this look like peace to you?" asked Keller.

"No," answered Gabriel. "It looks like home."

Finally, at half past one, Keller turned into Stratford Gardens. Number 8, like its neighbors, was a two-level redbrick house with a white door and a single window on each floor. Weeds flourished in the forecourt; a green rubbish bin lay toppled by the wind. Keller pulled to the curb and switched off the engine.

"One wonders," said Gabriel, "why Quinn decided to live in a luxury villa in Venezuela instead of here."

"Did you get a look at the door?"

"A single lock, no deadbolt."

"How long will it take you to unbutton it?"

"Thirty seconds," said Gabriel. "Less than that if you let me leave those stupid flowers behind."

"You have to take the flowers."

"I'd rather take the gun."

"I'll keep the gun."

"What happens if I run into a couple of Quinn's friends in there?"

"Pretend to be a Catholic from West Belfast."

"I'm not sure they'll believe me."

"They'd better," said Keller. "Otherwise, you're dead."

"Any other helpful advice?"

"Five minutes, and not a minute more."

Gabriel opened the door and stepped into the street. Keller swore softly. The flowers were still in the backseat.

21

THE ARDOYNE, WEST BELFAST

A SMALL IRISH TRICOLOR hung limply from an oxidized mount in the door frame. Like the dream of a united Ireland, it was faded and tattered. Gabriel tried the latch and, as expected, found it was locked. Then he drew a thin metal tool from his pocket and, using the technique taught to him in his youth, worked it carefully in the mechanism. A few seconds was all it took for the lock to surrender. When he tried the latch a second time, it invited him to enter. He stepped inside and closed the door quietly behind him. No alarm sounded, no dog barked.

The morning post lay scattered across the bare floor. He gathered up the various envelopes, fliers, magazines, and advertising supplements and leafed quickly through them. Each was addressed to Maggie Donahue, except for a teen-oriented fashion magazine, which was addressed to her daughter. There appeared to be no private correspondence of any sort, only the customary commercial debris that clogs mail services the world over. Gabriel pocketed a credit card bill and returned the rest to the floor. Then he entered the sitting room.

It was a small room, a few meters square, scarcely enough space for the couch, the television console, and the pair of floral matching armchairs. On the coffee table was a stack of old magazines and Belfast newspapers, along with additional post, opened and unopened. One of the items was a newsletter and fund-raising appeal from the 32 County Sovereignty Movement, the political wing of the Real IRA. Gabriel wondered whether its senders realized the addressee was the secret spouse of the group's most accomplished maker of bombs and explosives.

He returned the letter to its envelope and the envelope to its place on the table. The walls of the room were bare except for a violent Irish seascape of flea-market quality hanging above the couch. On one of the end tables stood a framed photograph of a mother and child on the occasion of the child's First Communion at Holy Cross Church. Gabriel could find no trace of Quinn in the child's face. In that, if nothing else, she was fortunate.

He glanced at his wristwatch. Ninety seconds had elapsed since he had entered the house. He parted the thin curtains and peered out as a car rolled slowly past in the street. Inside were two men. They appeared to take careful note of Keller as they passed the parked Škoda. Then the car continued along Stratford Gardens and disappeared around the corner. Gabriel looked at the Škoda. The lights were still doused. Next he looked at his BlackBerry. No warning texts, no missed calls.

He released the curtain and entered the kitchen. A lipsticked coffee cup stood on the counter; dishes soaked in a pool of soapy water in the basin. He opened the refrigerator. It was packaged fare mainly, nothing green, no fruit, no beer, only a half-drunk bottle of supermarket Italian white from Tesco.

He released the door of the refrigerator and began opening and closing drawers. In one he found a blank cream-colored envelope, and in the envelope was a handwritten note from Quinn.

Deposit it in small amounts so it looks like tip money . . . Give my love to C . . .

Gabriel slipped the letter into his coat pocket next to the credit card bill and checked his watch. Two and a half minutes. He stepped from the kitchen and headed upstairs.

The car returned at 1:37. Again it cruised slowly past Number 8, but this time it stopped next to the Škoda. At first, Keller pretended not to notice. Then, indifferently, he lowered his window.

"What're you doing here?" asked the driver in a thick West Belfast accent.

"Waiting on a friend," replied Keller in the same dialect.

"What's the friend's name?"

"Maggie Donahue."

"And you?" asked the passenger in the car.

"Gerry Campbell."

"Where you from, Gerry Campbell?"

"Dublin."

"And before that?"

"Derry."

"When did you leave?"

"None of your fucking business."

Keller was no longer smiling. Neither were the two men in the other car. The window slid up; the car moved off along the quiet street and disappeared around the corner a second time. Keller wondered how long it would take them to establish that Maggie Donahue, the secret wife of Eamon Quinn, was at that moment working in the Lobby Bar of the Europa Hotel. Two minutes, he thought. Maybe less. He pulled out his mobile and dialed.

"The natives are starting to get restless."

"Try giving them the flowers."

The connection went dead. Keller started the engine and wrapped his hand around the grip of the Beretta. Then he stared into the rearview mirror and waited for the car to return.

At the top of the stairs was a pair of doors. Gabriel entered the room on the right. It was the larger of the two, though hardly a master suite. Clothing lay strewn across the floor and atop the unmade bed. The curtains were tightly drawn; there was no light other than the red digits of the alarm clock, which was set ten minutes fast. Gabriel opened the top drawer of the bedside table and illuminated its contents with the beam of his Maglite. Dried-out pens, dead batteries, an envelope containing several hundred pounds in well-used bills, another letter from Quinn. It seemed he wanted to see his daughter. There was no mention of where he was living or where a meeting might take place. Still, it suggested that Liam Walsh had been less than truthful when he claimed that Quinn had had no personal contact with his family since fleeing Ireland after the Omagh bombing.

Gabriel added the letter to his small collection of evidence and opened the closet door. He searched the clothing and found several items clearly belonging to a man. It was possible Maggie Donahue had taken a lover in her husband's long absence. It was possible, too, that the clothing belonged to Quinn. He removed one of the items, a pair of woolen trousers, and held them to his own frame. Quinn, he recalled, was five foot ten, not a big man but bigger than Gabriel. He searched the pockets for litter. In one he found three coins, euros, and a small blue-and-yellow ticket. It was torn, half of it missing. Gabriel could make out four numbers, 5846, but nothing more. On the back were a few centimeters of a magnetic data stripe.

Gabriel pocketed the ticket, returned the trousers to their original hanger, and entered the bathroom. In the medicine chest he found men's razors, men's aftershave, and men's deodorant. Then he crossed the hall and entered the second bedroom. In cleanliness, Quinn's daughter was the precise opposite of her mother. Her bed was smoothly made; her clothing hung neatly from the rod in her closet. Gabriel searched the drawers of her dresser. There were no drugs or cigarettes, no evidence at all of a life kept secret from her mother. Nor was there any trace of Eamon Quinn.

Gabriel checked the time. Five minutes had

elapsed. He moved to the window and watched the car with two men pass slowly in the street. When it was gone, Gabriel's BlackBerry vibrated. He lifted it to his ear and heard the voice of Christopher Keller.

"Time's up."

"Two more minutes."

"We don't have two minutes."

Keller rang off without another word. Gabriel looked around the room. He was used to searching the premises of professionals, not teenagers. Professionals were good at hiding things, teenagers not so. They assumed all adults were dolts, and their over-confidence was usually their undoing.

Gabriel returned to the closet and searched the insides of her shoes. Next he leafed through her fashion magazines, but they produced nothing other than subscription offers and fragrance samples. Finally, he thumbed through her small collection of books. It included a history of the Troubles written by an author sympathetic to the IRA and the cause of Irish nationalism. And it was there, wedged between two pages, that he found what he was looking for.

It was a photograph of a teenage girl and a man wearing a brimmed hat and sunglasses. They were posed on a street of faded old buildings, perhaps European, perhaps South American. The girl was Catherine Donahue. And the man at her side was her father, Eamon Quinn.

Stratford Gardens was quiet when Gabriel emerged from the house at Number 8. He slipped through the metal gate, walked over to the Škoda, and climbed into the passenger seat. Keller wound his way through the mean streets of the Catholic Ardoyne and returned to Crumlin Road. Then he made a quick right turn into Cambrai Street and eased off the throttle. Union Jacks fluttered from the lampposts. They had crossed one of Belfast's invisible borders. They were safely back on Protestant ground.

"Did you find anything?" asked Keller finally.

"I think so."

"What is it?"

Gabriel smiled and said, "Quinn."

22

WARRING STREET, BELFAST

"IT COULD BE ANYONE," said Keller.

"It could be," replied Gabriel. "But it isn't. It's Quinn."

They were in Keller's room at the Premiere Inn on Warring Street. It was around the corner from the Europa and far less luxurious. He had checked in as Adrien LeBlanc and had spoken French-accented English to the staff. Gabriel, during his brief journey across the drab lobby, had said nothing at all.

"Where do you suppose they are?" asked Keller, still studying the photograph.

"Good question."

"There are no signs on the buildings or cars on the street. It's almost as if—"

"He chose the spot with great care."

"Maybe it's Caracas."

"Or maybe it's Santiago or Buenos Aires."

"Ever been?"

"Where?"

"Buenos Aires," said Keller.

"Several times, actually."

"Business or pleasure?"

"I don't do pleasure."

Keller smiled and looked at the photo again. "It looks a bit like the old center of Bogotá to me."

"I'll have to take your word on that one."

"Or maybe it's Madrid."

"Maybe."

"Let me see that ticket stub."

Gabriel handed it over. Keller scrutinized the front side carefully. Then he turned it over and ran his finger along the portion of the magnetic stripe.

"A few years ago," he said at last, "the don accepted a contract on a gentleman who'd stolen a great deal of money from people who don't care to have their money stolen. The gentleman was in hiding in a city like the one in this photograph. It was an old city of faded beauty, a city of hills and streetcars."

"What was the gentleman's name?"

"I'd rather not say."

"Where was he hiding?"

"I'm getting to that."

Keller was studying the front of the ticket again. "Because this gentleman had no car, he was by necessity a dedicated user of public transport. I followed him for a week before the hit, which meant that I had to be a dedicated user of public transport, too."

"Do you recognize the ticket, Christopher?"

"I might."

Keller picked up Gabriel's BlackBerry, opened Google, and typed several characters into the search box. When the results appeared, he clicked one and smiled.

"Find it?" asked Gabriel.

Keller turned the BlackBerry around so Gabriel could see the screen. On it was a complete version of the ticket he had found in the home of Maggie Donahue.

"Where's it from?" asked Gabriel.

"A city of hills and streetcars."

"I take it you're not referring to San Francisco."

"No," said Keller. "It's Lisbon."

"That doesn't prove the photo was taken there," Gabriel said after a moment.

"Agreed," answered Keller. "But if we can prove that Catherine Donahue was there . . ."

Gabriel said nothing.

"You didn't happen to see her passport when you were in that house, did you?"

"No such luck."

"Then I suppose we'll have to think of some other way to have a look at it."

Gabriel picked up his BlackBerry and keyed in a brief message to Graham Seymour in London, requesting information on any and all foreign travel by Catherine Donahue of 8 Stratford Gardens, Belfast, Northern Ireland. One hour later, as darkness fell hard upon the city, they had their answer.

The British Foreign and Commonwealth Office issued the passport on November 10, 2013. One week later she boarded a British Airways flight in Belfast and flew to London's Heathrow Airport where, ninety minutes later, she transferred to a second British Airways flight, bound for Lisbon. According to Portuguese immigration authorities, she remained in the country for just three days. It was her one and only foreign trip.

"None of which proves Quinn was living there at the time," Keller pointed out.

"Why bring her to Lisbon of all places? Why not Monaco or Cannes or St. Moritz?"

"Maybé Quinn was on a budget."

"Or maybe he keeps an apartment there, something in a charming old building in the kind of neighborhood where no one would notice a foreigner coming and going."

"Know any places like that?"

"I've spent my life living in places like that."

Keller was silent for a moment. "What now?" he asked finally.

"I suppose we could take the photo and my composite sketch to Lisbon and start knocking on doors."

"Or?"

"We retain the services of someone who specializes in finding those who would rather not be found."

"Any candidates?"

"Just one."

Gabriel picked up his BlackBerry and dialed Eli Lavon.

23

BELFAST–LISBON

THEY DECIDED TO TAKE the long way down to Lisbon. Better to not hit town too quickly, said Gabriel. Better to take care with their travel arrangements and their tail. For the first time, Quinn was in their sights. He was no longer just a rumor. He was a man on a street, with a daughter at his side. He had flesh on his bones, blood in his veins. He could be found. And then he could be put out of his misery.

And so they left Belfast as they had entered it, quietly and under false pretenses. Monsieur Le-Blanc told the clerk at the Premiere that he had a small personal crisis to attend to; Herr Klemp spun a similar tale at the Europa. Passing through the lobby he saw Maggie Donahue, secret wife of the murderer, serving a very large whiskey to an inebriated businessman. She avoided Herr Klemp's gaze, and Herr Klemp avoided hers.

They drove to Dublin, abandoned the car at the airport, and checked into a pair of rooms at the Radisson. In the morning they ate breakfast like strangers in the hotel's restaurant and then boarded separate flights to Paris, Gabriel on Aer Lingus, Keller on Air France. Gabriel's flight arrived first. He collected a clean Citroën from the car park and was waiting in the arrivals lane as Keller emerged from the terminal.

They spent that night in Biarritz, where Gabriel had once taken a life in vengeance, and the next night in the Spanish city of Vitoria, where Keller, at the behest of Don Anton Orsati, had once killed a member of the Basque separatist group ETA. Gabriel could see that Keller's ties to his old life were beginning to fray, that Keller, with each passing day, was growing more comfortable with the prospect of working for Graham Seymour at MI6. Quinn had unleashed the chain of events that had broken Keller's bonds with England. And now, twenty-five years later, Quinn was leading Keller back home.

From Vitoria they moved on to Madrid, and from Madrid they drove to Badajoz along the Portuguese border. Keller was anxious to push on to Lisbon, but at Gabriel's insistence they headed farther west and caught the season's last faint rays of sun at Estoril. They stayed in separate hotels along the beach and led the separate lives of men without wives, without children, without care or responsibility. Gabriel spent several hours each day making certain they were not under surveillance. He was tempted to send a message to Chiara in Jerusalem but did not. Nor did he make contact with Eli Lavon. Lavon was one of the most experienced man-trackers in the world. In his youth he had hunted down the members of Black September, perpetrators of the 1972 Munich Olympics massacre. Then, after leaving the Office, he had gone into private practice, tracking looted Holocaust assets and the occasional Nazi war criminal. If there were any trace of Quinn in Lisbon—a residence, an alias, another wife or child—Lavon would find it.

But when two more days passed without word, even Gabriel began to have doubts, not in Lavon's ability but in his faith that Quinn was somehow linked to Lisbon. Perhaps Catherine Donahue had traveled to the city with friends or as part of a school trip. Perhaps the trousers Gabriel had found in Maggie Donahue's closet had belonged to another man, as had the torn ticket for Lisbon's streetcar system. They would have to search for him elsewhere, he thought—in Iran, or Lebanon, or Yemen, or Venezuela, or in any of the countless other places where Quinn had plied his deadly trade. Quinn was a man of the underworld. Quinn could be anywhere.

But on the third morning of their stay, Gabriel received a brief but promising message from Eli Lavon suggesting that the man in question was thought to be a frequent visitor to the city of interest. By midday Lavon was certain of it, and by late afternoon he had uncovered an address. Gabriel rang Keller at his hotel and told him they were ready to move. They left Estoril as they had entered it, quietly and under false pretenses, and headed for Lisbon.

"He calls himself Alvarez."

"Portuguese or Spanish spelling?"

"That depends on his mood."

Eli Lavon smiled. They were seated at a table in Café Brasileira, in the Chiado district of Lisbon. It was half past nine and the café was very crowded. No one seemed to take much notice of the two men of late middle age hunched over cups of coffee in the corner. They conversed in quiet German, one of several languages they had in common. Gabriel spoke in the Berlin accent of his mother, but Lavon's German was decidedly Viennese. He wore a cardigan sweater beneath his crumpled tweed jacket and an ascot at his throat. His hair was wispy and unkempt; the features of his face were bland and easily forgotten. It was one of his greatest assets. Eli Lavon appeared to be one of life's downtrodden. In truth, he was a natural predator who could follow a highly trained intelligence officer or hardened terrorist down any street in the world without attracting a flicker of interest.

"First name?" asked Gabriel.

"Sometimes José. Other times he's Jorge."

"Nationality?"

"Sometimes Venezuelan, sometimes Ecuadorian." Lavon smiled. "Are you beginning to see a pattern?"

"But he never tries to pass himself off as Portuguese?"

"He doesn't have the language for it. Even his Spanish is on the rough side. Apparently, he has quite an accent."

Someone at the bar must have said something funny, because a sonic boom of laughter reverberated off the checkered tile floor and died out high in the ceiling, where the chandeliers emitted a gauzy golden glow. Gabriel looked past Lavon's shoulder and imagined that Quinn was sitting at the next table. But it wasn't Quinn; it was Christopher Keller. He was holding a cup of coffee in his right hand. The right hand meant they were clean, the left meant trouble. Gabriel looked at Lavon again and asked about the location of Quinn's apartment. Lavon inclined his head in the direction of the Bairro Alto.

"What's the building like?"

Lavon made a gesture with his hand to indicate it fell somewhere between acceptable and condemnable.

"Concierge?"

"In the Bairro Alto?"

"What floor?"

"Second."

"Can we get inside?"

"I'm surprised you'd even ask. The question is," Lavon continued, "do we *want* to get inside?"

"Do we?"

Lavon shook his head. "When one is fortunate enough to find the pied-à-terre of a man like Eamon Quinn, one doesn't risk throwing it away by rushing through the front door. One acquires a fixed observation post and waits patiently for the target to appear."

"Unless there are other factors to consider."

"Such as?"

"The possibility another bomb might explode."

"Or that one's wife is about to give birth to twins."

Gabriel frowned but said nothing.

"In case you're wondering," said Lavon, "she's doing well."

"Is she angry?"

"She's seven and a half months pregnant, and her husband is sitting in a café in Lisbon. How do you think she feels?"

"How's her security?"

"Narkiss Street is quite possibly the safest street in all Jerusalem. Uzi keeps a security team outside the door all hours." Lavon hesitated, then added, "But all the bodyguards in the world are no substitute for a husband."

Gabriel made no reply.

"May I make a suggestion?"

"If you must."

"Go back to Jerusalem for a few days. Your friend and I can keep watch on the apartment. If Quinn shows up, you'll be the first to know."

"If I go to Jerusalem," replied Gabriel, "I'll never want to leave."

"Which is why I suggested it." Lavon cleared his throat gently. It was a warning of an impending intimacy. "Your wife would like you to know that in one month's time, perhaps less, you will be a father again. She'd like you to be present for the occasion. Otherwise, your life won't be worth living."

"Did she say anything else?"

"She might have mentioned something about Eamon Quinn."

"What was that?"

"Apparently, Uzi's briefed her on the operation. Your wife doesn't take kindly to men who blow up innocent women and children. She'd like you to find Quinn before you come home. And then," Lavon added, "she'd like you to kill him."

Gabriel glanced at Keller and said, "That won't be necessary."

"Yes," said Lavon. "Lucky you."

Gabriel smiled and drank some of his coffee. Lavon reached into his coat pocket and withdrew a silver thumb drive. He placed it on the table and pushed it toward Gabriel.

"As requested, the complete Office file on Tariq al-Hourani, born in Palestine during the great Arab catastrophe, shot to death in the stairwell of a Manhattan apartment building shortly before the Twin Towers came tumbling down." Lavon paused, then added, "I believe you were there at the time. Somehow, I wasn't invited."

Gabriel stared at the thumb drive in silence. There were portions of the file he would not force himself to read again—for it was Tariq al-Hourani who, on a snowy January night in 1991, had planted a bomb beneath Gabriel's car in Vienna. The explosion had killed Gabriel's son Dani and maimed Leah, his first wife. She lived now in a psychiatric hospital atop Mount Herzl, trapped in a prison of memory and a body destroyed by fire. During a recent visit, Gabriel had told her he would soon be a father again.

"I would have thought," said Lavon quietly, "that you knew his file by heart."

"I do," said Gabriel. "But I'd like to refresh my memory about one particular part of his career."

"What's that?"

"The time he spent in Libya."

"You have a hunch?"

"Maybe."

"Is there anything else you want to tell me?"

"I'm glad you're here, Eli."

Lavon stirred his coffee slowly. "That makes one of us."

They emerged from Brasileira's famous green door into a tiled square where Fernando Pessoa sat bronzed for all eternity, his punishment for being Portugal's most famous poet and man of letters. A cold wind from the Tagus swirled in an amphitheater of graceful yellow buildings; a tram clattered past in the Largo Chiado. Gabriel imagined Quinn sitting in a seat in the window, Quinn of the surgically altered face and merciless heart, Quinn the prostitute of death. Lavon was heading up the slope of the hill, slowly, in the manner of a flâneur. Gabriel fell in beside him and together they wound their way through a labyrinth of darkened streets. Lavon never paused to take his bearings or consult a map. He was speaking in German about a discovery he'd made recently on a dig beneath the Old City of Jerusalem. When he wasn't working for the Office, he served as an adjunct professor of biblical archaeology at Hebrew University. Indeed, owing to a monumental find he had made beneath the Temple Mount, Eli Lavon was regarded as Israel's answer to Indiana Jones.

He stopped suddenly and asked, "Recognize it?"

"Recognize what?"

"This spot." Greeted by silence, Lavon turned. "How about now?"

Gabriel turned, too. There were no lights burning anywhere in the street. The darkness had rendered the buildings shapeless, without character or detail.

"This is where they were standing." Lavon walked a few paces up the cobbled street. "And the person who snapped the photograph was standing here."

"I wonder who it was."

"It could have been someone who passed in the street."

"Quinn doesn't strike me as the sort who would let a complete stranger take a photo of him."

Lavon set off again without another word and climbed higher into the district. He made several more turns, left and right, until Gabriel had lost all sense of direction. His only point of orientation was the Tagus, which appeared sporadically through gaps in the buildings, its surface shining like the scales of a fish. Finally, Lavon slowed to a stop and nodded once toward the entrance of an apartment house. It was slightly taller than most buildings in the Bairro Alto, four floors instead of three, and defaced at street level by graffiti. A shutter on the second floor hung aslant on one hinge; a flowering vine dripped from the rusted balcony. Gabriel walked over to the doorway and inspected the intercom. The nameplate for 2B was empty. He placed his thumb atop the button and the buzzer sounded clearly, as if through an open window or walls of paper. Then he placed his hand lightly upon the latch.

"Do you know how long it would take me to open this?"

"About fifteen seconds," answered Lavon. "But good things come to those who wait."

Gabriel peered down the slope of the street. On the corner was a matchbox of a restaurant where Keller was indifferently studying the menu at a streetside table. Directly opposite the building was a pair of stubby sugar-cube dwellings, and a few paces farther along was another four-level apartment house with a facade the color of a canary. Taped to its entrance, curled like a cold cut left too long in the sun, was a flier explaining in Portuguese and English that an apartment in the building was available to let.

Gabriel tore away the flier and slipped it into his pocket. Then, with Lavon at his side, he walked past Keller without a word or glance and headed down the hill toward the river. In the morning, while taking coffee at Café Brasileira, he rang the number printed on the flier. And by midday, after paying six months' rent and a security deposit in advance, the apartment was his.

24

BAIRRO ALTO, LISBON

GABRIEL MOVED INTO the apartment at dusk with the air of a man whose wife could no longer tolerate his company. He had no possessions other than a well-traveled overnight bag, and wore no expression other than a scowl that said he would prefer to be left to his own devices. Eli Lavon arrived an hour later bearing two bags of groceries—the makings, or so it seemed, of a meal of consolation. Keller came last. He stole into the building with the silence of a night thief and settled in front of a window as though he were digging into a hide in the Bandit Country of South Armagh. And thus commenced the long watch.

The apartment was furnished, but barely. The small gathering of mismatched chairs in the sitting room looked as if they had been acquired at a neighborhood flea market; the two bedrooms were like the cells of ascetic monks. The shortage of accommodations was of no consequence, for one man kept watch at the window always. Invariably, it was Keller. He had waited a long time for Quinn to rise from his cellar and wanted the honor of being the first to clap eyes upon the prize. Gabriel hung the composite sketch of Quinn on the wall like a family portrait, and Keller consulted it each time a man of appropriate age and height—mid-forties, perhaps five foot ten—passed in the narrow street. At sunrise on the third morning, he was convinced he saw Quinn approaching from the direction of the shuttered café. It was Quinn's face, he told Lavon in an excited whisper. More important, he said, it was Quinn's walk. But it wasn't Quinn; it was a Portuguese man who, they discovered later, worked in a shop a few streets away. Lavon, a scholar of physical surveillance, explained that the mistake was one of the dangers of a long vigil. Sometimes the watcher sees what he wants to see. And sometimes the prize is standing right in front of him and the watcher is too blinded by fatigue or ambition to even realize it.

The landlord believed Gabriel to be the apartment's sole occupant, so only Gabriel showed his face in public. He was a man with a damaged heart, a man with too much time on his hands. He wandered the hilly streets of the Bairro Alto, he rode trams seemingly without destination, he visited the Museu do Chiado, he took his afternoon coffee at Café Brasileira. And in a green park along the banks of the Tagus, he met an Office courier who gave him a case filled with the tools of a field outpost: a tripod-mounted camera with a night-vision telephoto lens, a parabolic microphone, secure radios, a concealable miniature transmitter, and a laptop computer with a secure satellite link to King Saul Boulevard. In addition, there was a note from the chief of Operations gently chiding Gabriel for acquiring a safe property on his own rather than through the auspices of Housekeeping. There was also a handwritten letter from Chiara. Gabriel read it twice before burning it in the bathroom sink. Afterward, his mood was as dark as the ashes he washed ritually down the drain.

"My offer still stands," said Lavon.

"What's that?"

"I'll stay here with Keller. You go home to be with your wife."

Gabriel's answer was the same as before, and Lavon never raised the subject again—even late at night, when the tables of the corner restaurant had been packed away and rain baptized the silent street. They dimmed the lights of the apartment so their shadows would not be visible from without, and in the darkness the years faded from their faces. They might have been the same boys of twenty whom the Office had dispatched in the autumn of 1972 to hunt down the perpetrators of the Munich Olympics massacre. The operation had been code-named Wrath of God. In the Hebrew-based lexicon of the team, Lavon had been an *ayin*, a tracker. Gabriel was an *aleph*, an assassin. For three years they stalked their prey across Europe, killing in darkness and in broad daylight, living in fear that at any moment they might be arrested and charged as murderers. They had spent endless nights in shabby rooms watching doorways and men, secretly inhabiting the lives of others. Stress and visions of blood robbed them both of the ability to sleep. A transistor radio was their only link to the real world. It told them about wars won and lost, about an American president who resigned in disgrace, and some-times, on warm summer nights, it played music for them—the same music that normal boys of twenty were listening to, boys who had not been sent forth by their country to serve as executioners, angels of vengeance for eleven murdered Jews.

Sleeplessness was soon epidemic in the little apartment in the Bairro Alto. They had planned to serve rotating two-hour shifts at the outpost by the window, but as the days wore on, and the mutual insomnia took hold, the three veteran op-eratives stood something like a joint permanent watch. All those who passed beneath their window were photographed, regardless of their age, gender, or national origin. Those who entered the target building received additional scrutiny, as did its resi-dents. Gradually, their secrets came spilling into the observation post. Such was the nature of any long-term watch. More often than not, it was the venal sins of the innocent that were exposed.

The apartment contained a television with a sat-ellite dish that lost hold of its signal each time rain fell from the sky or a modest exhalation of wind blew through the street. It served as their link to a world that with each passing day seemed to be spin-ning further out of control. It was the world Gabriel would inherit the moment he swore his oath as the next chief of the Office. And it would be Keller's world, too, should he choose it. Keller was Gabri-el's last restoration. His dirty varnish had been re-moved, his canvas had been relined and retouched. He was no longer the English assassin. Soon he would be the English spy.

Like all good watchers, Keller was blessed with a natural forbearance. But seven days into the vigil, his patience abandoned him. Lavon suggested a walk along the river or a drive up the coast, anything to break the monotony of the watch, but Keller refused to leave the apartment or surrender his post in the window. He photographed the faces that passed beneath his feet—the old acquaintances, the new arrivals, the passersby—and he waited for a man in his mid-forties, approximately five feet ten inches in height, to alight at the entrance of the apartment house on the opposite side of the thin street. To Lavon, it seemed as if Keller were keeping watch on Lower Market Street in Omagh, waiting for a red Vauxhall Cavalier riding low on its rear axle to pull to the curb, waiting for two men, Quinn and Walsh, to climb out. Walsh had been punished for his sins. Quinn would be next.

But when another day passed with no sign of him, Keller suggested they take the search elsewhere. South America, he said, was the logical place. They could slip into Caracas and start kicking down doors until they found Quinn's. Gabriel appeared to give the idea serious consideration. In reality, he was watching the woman of perhaps thirty sitting alone at the restaurant at the end of the street. She had placed her handbag on the chair next to her. It was a large handbag, large enough to accommodate toiletries, even a change of clothing. The zipper was open, and the bag was turned in a way that made the contents easily accessible. A female Office field agent would have left her bag in the same place, thought Gabriel, especially if the bag contained a gun.

"Are you listening to me?" asked Keller.

"Hanging on every word," lied Gabriel.

The last light of dusk was fading; the woman of perhaps thirty was still wearing sunglasses. Gabriel trained the telephoto lens upon her face, zoomed in, and stole her photograph. He examined it carefully in the viewfinder of the camera. It was a good face, he thought, a face worthy of painting. The cheekbones were wide, the chin was small and delicate, the skin was flawless and white. The sunglasses rendered her eyes invisible, but Gabriel would have guessed they were blue. Her hair was shoulder length and very black. He doubted the color was natural.

At the moment Gabriel had taken her photograph, the woman had been looking at the menu. Now she was gazing up the length of the street. It was not the preferred view. Most patrons of the restaurant faced the opposite direction, which had a better vista of the city. A waiter appeared. Too late, Gabriel seized the parabolic microphone and trained it on the table. He heard the waiter say "Thank you" in English, followed by a burst of dance music. It was the ringer of her mobile. She dismissed the call with the press of a button, returned the phone to the handbag, and withdrew a Lisbon guidebook. Gabriel again placed his eye to the viewfinder and zoomed in, not on the woman's face but on the guidebook she held in her hand. It was Frommer's, English-language. She lowered it after a few seconds and resumed her study of the street.

"What are you looking at?" asked Keller.

"I'm not sure."

Keller moved closer to the window and followed Gabriel's gaze. "Pretty," he said.

"Maybe."

"Newcomer or habitué?"

"Tourist, apparently."

"Why would a pretty young tourist eat alone?"

"Good question."

The waiter reappeared bearing a glass of white wine, which he placed on the table next to the Lisbon guidebook. He opened his order pad, but the woman said something that made him withdraw without writing anything down. He returned a moment later with a check. He placed it on the table and departed. No words were exchanged.

"What just happened?" asked Keller.

"It seems the pretty young tourist had a change of heart."

"I wonder why."

"Maybe it had something to do with the phone call she didn't pick up."

The woman's hand was now delving into the open handbag. When it reappeared, it was holding a single banknote. She placed it atop the check, weighted it with the wineglass, and rose.

"I guess she didn't like it," said Gabriel.

"Maybe she has a headache."

The woman was now reaching for the bag. She placed the strap over her shoulder and took one final look up the length of the street. Then she turned in the opposite direction, rounded the corner, and was gone.

"Too bad," said Keller.

"We'll see," said Gabriel.

He was watching the waiter collect the money. But in his thoughts he was calculating how long it would be before he saw her again. Two minutes, he reckoned; that's how long it would take her to make her way back to her destination along a parallel street. He marked the time on his wristwatch, and when ninety seconds had passed he placed his eye to the viewfinder and began counting slowly. When he reached twenty, he saw her emerge from the half-light, the bag over her shoulder, the sunglasses over her eyes. She stopped at the entrance of the target building, inserted a key into the lock, and pushed open the door. As she entered the foyer, another tenant, a man in his mid-twenties, was coming out. He glanced over his shoulder at her; whether it was in admiration or curiosity, Gabriel could not tell. He snapped the tenant's photograph, then looked toward the darkened windows on the second floor. Ten seconds later light blossomed behind the blinds.

25

BAIRRO ALTO, LISBON

THEY DID NOT see her again until half past eight the following morning when she appeared on the balcony wearing only a bathrobe—Quinn's bathrobe, thought Gabriel, for it was far too large for her slender frame. She held a cigarette thoughtfully to her lips and surveyed the street in the steel dawn light. Her eyes were uncovered, and as Gabriel suspected they were blue. Blue as weather. Vermeer blue. He snapped several photographs and forwarded them to King Saul Boulevard. Then he watched the woman withdraw from the balcony and disappear behind the French doors.

For twenty additional minutes light burned in her window. Then the light was extinguished, and a moment later she stepped from the entrance of the building. Her bag hung from one shoulder, her right, and her hands were jammed into the pockets of her coat. It was a schoolgirl toggle coat, not the urban-tough leather jacket she had worn the night before. Her step was brisk; her boots clattered loudly against the paving stones. The sound rose as she flowed beneath the window of the observation post and then receded as she passed the shuttered restaurant and disappeared.

The Citroën that Gabriel had collected in Paris was parked around the corner from the observation post, on a street wide enough to accommodate cars. Keller retrieved it while Gabriel followed the woman on foot down another cobbled alleyway lined with shops and cafés. At the end of the street was a broader boulevard that flowed down the hill like a tributary of the Tagus. The woman entered a coffee shop, ordered at the bar, and sat at the counter along the window. Gabriel entered a café on the opposite side of the boulevard and did the same. Keller waited curbside until a police officer nudged him onward.

For fifteen minutes their positions remained unchanged: the woman in her café, Gabriel in his, Keller behind the wheel of the Citroën. The woman stared into her mobile phone while she drank her coffee and appeared to make at least one call. Then, at half past nine, she slipped the phone into her handbag and went into the street again. She walked south toward the river for several paces before stopping abruptly and waving down a taxi headed in the opposite direction. Gabriel quickly left the café and climbed into the passenger seat of the Citroën. Keller swung a U-turn and put his foot to the floor.

Thirty seconds elapsed before they were able to reestablish contact with the taxi. It plunged northward through the morning traffic, slicing in and out of the trucks, the buses, the shiny German-made sedans of the newly rich and the wheezing rattle-traps of Lisbon's less fortunate. Gabriel had operated infrequently in Lisbon, and his knowledge of the city's geography was rudimentary. Even so, he had an idea of where the taxi was headed. The route it was following pointed toward Lisbon Airport like the needle of a compass.

They entered a modern quarter of the city and flowed in a river of traffic to a large circle at the edge of a green park. From there they tacked to the northeast to another circle, which spat them onto the Avenida da República. Near the end of the avenue they began to see the first signs for the airport. The taxi followed each one and eventually braked to a halt outside the departure level of Terminal 1. The woman stepped out and headed quickly toward the entrance, as though she were running late for her flight. Gabriel instructed Keller to ditch the Citroën in short-term parking with the gun in the trunk and the keys in the magnetic caddy above the left rear wheel. Then he climbed out and followed the woman into the terminal.

She paused briefly inside the doors to take her bearings and scrutinize the large departure board hanging above the gleaming modern hall. Then she headed directly to the British Airways counter and joined the short queue at first class. It was a piece of good fortune; British Airways flew to only a single destination from Lisbon. Flight 501 departed in an hour. The next flight wasn't until seven that evening.

Gabriel drew his BlackBerry from his coat pocket and sent a message to the Travel department at King

Saul Boulevard requesting two first-class tickets on
BA Flight 501—one ticket for Johannes Klemp,
the other for Adrien LeBlanc. Travel quickly confirmed receipt of the message and asked Gabriel to
stand by. Two minutes later the reservation numbers appeared. Only one first-class seat was available; Travel, in its infinite wisdom, reserved it for
Gabriel. Monsieur LeBlanc was booked into one of
the few remaining seats in economy. It was in the
rear of the aircraft, in the zone of wailing children
and toilet odors.

Gabriel sent another message to King Saul Boulevard, requesting a car on a hot standby at Heathrow. Then he returned the BlackBerry to his pocket
and watched the woman heading ticket in hand
toward security. Keller waited until she was gone
before walking over to Gabriel's side.

"Where are we going?" he asked.

Gabriel smiled and said, "Home."

They checked in separately: no luggage, no carry-
ons of any kind. A Portuguese border policeman
stamped their false passports; an airport security
officer waved them through the screeners. They
had forty-five minutes to kill before the flight, so
they dawdled in the perfumed halls of duty-free and
snagged some reading material from a newsstand
so they wouldn't board the plane empty-handed.
The woman was at the gate when they arrived, her
sky-blue eyes fixed on the screen of her mobile. Gabriel sat behind her and waited for the flight to be
called. The first announcement was in Portuguese,

the second in English. The woman waited for the second before rising. She dropped the mobile into her handbag and cruised onto the Jetway through the first-class lane. Gabriel did the same a moment later. While holding his ticket out to the gate attendant, he glanced at Keller, who was standing miserably among the overpacked huddled masses. Keller scratched his nose with his middle finger and frowned at the swaddled infant who would soon be his tormentor.

By the time Gabriel entered the aircraft, the woman had settled into her seat and been handed a glass of complimentary champagne. She was next to the window in the second row, on the left side of the fuselage. Her bag was at her feet, not quite properly stowed. An in-flight magazine lay on her thighs. She had yet to open it.

She paid Gabriel no heed as he squeezed past an overweight pensioner and dropped into his seat: fourth row, aisle, right side of the aircraft. An overly made-up flight attendant pressed a glass of champagne into Gabriel's hand. There was a reason it was complimentary; it tasted like sparkling turpentine. He placed the glass carefully on the center console and nodded to his seatmate, a British businessman with a Yorkshire accent who was shouting something about a missing shipment into his mobile phone.

Gabriel withdrew his own device and keyed in another message to King Saul Boulevard, this time asking for an identity check of a woman of perhaps thirty who was at that moment occupying Seat 2A of British Airways Flight 501. The response came five minutes later, as Keller was shuffling past Gabriel like a prisoner being marched out for a work detail. The passenger in question was Anna Huber, thirty-two years of age, German citizen, last known address Lessingstrasse 11, Frankfurt.

Gabriel powered off the BlackBerry and studied the woman on the other side of the aisle. Who are you? he thought. And what are you doing on this airplane?

26

HEATHROW AIRPORT, LONDON

T HE FLIGHT WAS two hours and forty-six
minutes in duration. The woman called
Anna Huber passed the journey foodless and
with no drink other than the champagne. Thirty
minutes before they were due to land, she carried
her handbag into the toilet and deadbolted the door.
Gabriel thought about Quinn's visit to Yemen,
where he worked with al-Qaeda on a bomb capable
of bringing down an airliner. Perhaps this is how
it would end, he thought. He would plunge to his
death in a green English field, strapped to a seat
with a businessman from Yorkshire. Then suddenly
the lavatory door squeaked open and the woman
reappeared. She had run a brush through her dark
hair and added a hint of color to her pale cheeks.
Her blue eyes passed over Gabriel with no trace of
recognition as she reclaimed her seat.

The plane emerged from the bottom of a cloud
and dropped onto the runway with a heavy thud that
opened a few of the overhead luggage bins. It was
a few minutes after one, but outside it looked like
nightfall. The businessman was soon blaring into

his mobile; it seemed the crisis in his affairs had not resolved itself. Gabriel powered on his BlackBerry and learned that a silver Volkswagen Passat would be waiting outside Terminal 3. He sent a message of confirmation, and when the seatbelt light died, he rose slowly and joined the queue of passengers waiting to exit the aircraft. The woman called Anna Huber was trapped against the window, hunched over, burdened by the handbag. When the cabin doors opened, Gabriel waited for her to step into the aisle. She gave him a terse nod of gratitude—again there was no suggestion of recognition—and filed onto the Jetway.

Her German passport allowed her to enter the United Kingdom through the express EU lane. Gabriel was standing directly behind her when the British immigration officer asked about the nature of her visit. Her response was inaudible to Gabriel, though clearly it pleased the immigration officer, who rewarded her with a warm smile. Gabriel received no such welcome. The immigration officer stamped his passport with thinly restrained violence and returned it without eye contact.

"Enjoy your stay," he said.

"Thank you," replied Gabriel, and set off after the woman.

He caught up with her in the cattle chute that herded passengers into the arrivals hall. A low-level operative from London Station was standing along the railing, next to a pair of black-veiled women. He was holding a paper sign that read ASHTON and wearing an expression of profound boredom. He jammed the sign into his pocket and fell in next to

Gabriel as he threaded his way through a tearful family reunion.

"Where's the car?"

The operative nodded toward the left-most door.

"Go back to the rail and hold up your sign. Another man will be along in a few minutes."

The operative dropped away. Outside, a line of taxis and airport shuttles waited in the early-afternoon gloom. The woman threaded her way through the traffic and headed for the short-stay car park. It was the one scenario for which Gabriel had not accounted. He drew his BlackBerry and called Keller.

"Where are you?"

"Passport control."

"There's a man in the arrivals hall holding a sign that says Ashton. Tell him to take you to the car."

Gabriel rang off without another word and followed the woman into the car park. Her vehicle was on the second level, a blue BMW sedan, British registration. She fished the key from her handbag, popped the locks with the remote, and lowered herself into the driver's seat. Gabriel rang Keller a second time.

"Where are you now?"

"Behind the wheel of a silver Passat."

"Meet me at the exit of short-term parking."

"Easier said than done."

"If you're not there in two minutes, we're going to lose her."

Gabriel killed the call and concealed himself behind a concrete pillar as the BMW passed. Then he headed down the ramp at a trot and returned to

the arrivals level of the terminal. The BMW was
nosing from the exit. It slid past Gabriel's position and disappeared from sight. Gabriel started
to dial Keller a third time but stopped when he
saw the flashing headlamps of a rapidly approaching Volkswagen. He swung into the passenger seat
and waved Keller forward. They caught up with
the BMW as it was turning onto the A4, bound for
West London. Keller eased off the throttle and lit
a cigarette. Gabriel lowered his window and rang
Graham Seymour.

The call arrived during a brief lull between a meeting of his senior staff and a visit by the chief of
Jordanian intelligence, a man whom Seymour secretly loathed. Seymour jotted down the key details.
Later, he wished he had not. A woman named Anna
Huber, German passport, Frankfurt address, had
just arrived in London via Lisbon, where she had
passed a single night in an apartment connected
to Eamon Quinn. At Heathrow Airport she had
collected a blue BMW, British registration AG62
VDR, from the short-stay car park. The car was
now headed toward London, followed by the future
chief of Israeli intelligence and an SAS deserter
turned professional assassin.

Seymour had taken the call on a device reserved
for his private communications. Next to it was his
direct line to Amanda Wallace at Thames House.
He hesitated for a few seconds, then lifted the receiver to his ear. It rang without dialing. Amanda's
voice came instantly on the line.

"Graham," she said genially. "What can I do for you?"

"I'm afraid that operation of mine has touched British soil."

"In what form?"

"A car headed toward the center of London."

After hanging up, Amanda Wallace boarded her private elevator and rode down to the operations center. She settled into her usual chair on the top deck and snatched up a telephone that reconnected her to Graham Seymour.

"Where are they?" she asked.

Ten tense seconds elapsed before Seymour answered. The BMW was approaching the Hammersmith flyover. Amanda Wallace ordered one of the techs to feed the CCTV image into the center video screen. Twenty seconds later she saw the blue BMW speed past in a blur of wet traffic.

"What kind of car does Allon have?"

Seymour answered as the Passat flowed through the shot, three cars behind the BMW. Amanda ordered the op center techs to track the movements of the two vehicles. Then she rang the chief of A4, MI5's covert surveillance and operational arm, and ordered him to put the cars under physical watch.

Other senior staff were now rushing into the op center, including Miles Kent, the deputy director. Amanda asked him to run a check of the BMW's registration. In less than a minute, Kent had an answer. There was no record of AG62 VDR in the database. The registration plates were false.

"Find out if any blue BMWs have been reported stolen," snapped Amanda.

This search took longer than the first, nearly three minutes. A BMW of the same make and model had gone missing four days earlier in the seaside town of Margate. But it was gray, not blue.

"They must have painted it," said Amanda. "Find out when it was left at Heathrow, and get me the video."

She looked at the center screen. The BMW was passing through the intersection of West Cromwell Road and Earl's Court Road. The Passat was three cars behind. Gabriel Allon, whom Amanda had met just once, was clearly visible in the passenger seat. So was the man behind the wheel.

"Who's the driver of the chase car?" she asked Graham Seymour.

"It's a long story."

"I'm sure it is."

The BMW was approaching the Natural History Museum. The surrounding pavements were crowded with schoolchildren. Amanda squeezed the telephone so tightly the blood drained from her knuckles. When she spoke, though, she managed to sound calm and assured.

"I'm not prepared to allow this to continue much longer, Graham."

"I'll support whatever decision you make."

"That's very good of you." Her voice contained a knife's edge of contempt. She was still watching the center screen. "Tell Allon to back off. We'll take it from here."

She listened as Seymour relayed the message.

Then she picked up the receiver of a dedicated line to the commissioner of the Metropolitan Police Service. The commissioner came on instantly.

"There's a dark blue BMW sedan headed east on Cromwell Road. UK registration AG62 VDR. The registration plates are known to be false, the car is almost certainly stolen, and the woman driving it is connected to a known terrorist."

"What do you recommend?"

Amanda Wallace stared at the video screen. The BMW was on Brompton Road heading toward Hyde Park Corner. And three cars behind it, traveling at the same rate of speed, was the silver Passat.

At the edge of Brompton Square, a London policeman sat astride a motorbike. He paid the BMW no heed as it sped past him. Nor did his head turn at the approach of a silver Passat. Gabriel lifted the BlackBerry to his ear.

"What's going on?" he asked Graham Seymour.

"Amanda has ordered the Met to intervene and take the woman into custody."

"Where are they?"

"One team is coming down Park Lane. A second is approaching Hyde Park Corner from Piccadilly."

A row of exclusive shops slid past Gabriel's rain-spattered window. An art gallery, a home-design showroom, a real estate broker, an open-air café where tourists swilled drinks beneath the shelter of a green awning. In the distance a siren cried. To Gabriel, it sounded like a child calling for its mother.

Keller slammed suddenly on the brakes. Ahead,

a red light had halted the traffic. Two cars—a taxi and a private vehicle—separated Gabriel and Keller from the BMW. Brompton Road stretched before them. On the right side of the street rose the gingerbread turrets of the Harrods department store. The sirens were growing louder, but the police were not yet in sight.

The signal switched to green, the traffic shot forward. They passed Montpelier Street and another row of shops and cafés. Then the BMW lurched into a lane reserved for buses and came to a stop outside a branch of the HSBC bank. The front door swung open; the woman climbed out and walked calmly away. In an instant she vanished beneath the canopy of umbrellas bobbing like mushrooms along the pavement.

Gabriel stared at the blue car parked along the curb, and at the throngs of tourists and pedestrians rushing through the rain, and at the dreamlike facade of the iconic department store rising on the opposite side of the street. Then, finally, he looked down at his BlackBerry, which was vibrating silently in his palm. It was a text message from an unidentified sender, six words in length.

THE BRICKS ARE IN THE WALL . . .

27

BROMPTON ROAD, LONDON

THEY LEAPT FROM the car in a blur, flailing their arms like madmen, each shouting the same single word over the wail of the approaching sirens. For a few seconds no one reacted. Then Gabriel drew a Beretta from the glove box of the car and the pedestrians recoiled in fear. It proved to be an effective tool, the fear. He drove the crowd away from the BMW, helping the fallen to their feet, while Keller desperately tried to evacuate a double-decker bus. Terrified passengers jammed the doorways front and rear. Keller tore them free and hurled them into the street like rag dolls.

Motorists traveling in both directions along Brompton Road had stopped to watch the commotion. Gabriel beat his fists on the windscreens of the cars and waved the drivers onward, but it was no use. The traffic was hopelessly snarled. In the back of a white Ford compact, a curly-haired boy of two was strapped tightly into a car seat. Gabriel clawed at the latch, but the door was locked and the child's terrified mother, apparently thinking him a madman, refused to open it. "There's a bomb!"

he shouted through the glass. "Get away!" But the woman only stared back, uncomprehending and mute, as the child began to cry.

Keller had completed the evacuation of the bus and was hammering wildly on the windows of the HSBC bank. Gabriel lifted his eyes from the child and stared over the roofs of the motionless cars toward the opposite pavement. A crowd of by-standers had gathered outside Harrods. Gabriel ran toward them, shouting, waving his gun, and the crowd dispersed in terror. In the stampede a preg-nant woman fell to the pavement. Gabriel rushed to her side and hoisted her to her feet.

"Can you walk?"

"I think so."

"Hurry!" he shouted at her. "For your child."

He thrust her toward safety and in his thoughts began to calculate how much time had elapsed since the text message had appeared on his BlackBerry. Twenty seconds, he thought, thirty at most. In that brief span of time, they had managed to move more than a hundred people from what would soon be the immediate blast zone, but cars still jammed the street, including the white Ford compact.

Shoppers were now streaming from the entrance of Harrods. Gun in hand, Gabriel herded them back into the lobby, shouting at them to take shelter deep within the building. Returning to the street, he saw that the traffic had not moved. The white Ford compact waved to him like a flag of surrender. The woman was still behind the wheel, paralyzed by in-decision, unaware of what was about to happen. In the backseat the child screamed inconsolably.

The Beretta slipped from his hand, and suddenly he was running, tearing at the air with his hands, as though trying to propel his way there faster. As he reached for the car door, a flash of brilliant white light blinded him, like the light of a thousand suns. He rose on a blast of scorching wind and tumbled helplessly backward into a storm of glass and blood. A child's hand reached for him; he seized it briefly but it slipped through his grasp. Then a darkness fell over him, silent and still, and there was nothing at all.

PART TWO

DEATH OF
A SPY

LATER, THE METROPOLITAN Police would determine that it was forty-seven seconds—forty-seven seconds from the time the woman abandoned the car on Brompton Road to the instant the bomb contained in its trunk detonated. It weighed five hundred pounds and was of expert construction. Of Quinn they expected nothing less.

Initially, however, the Met did not know it was Quinn. All that would come later, after the shouting matches, the threats of resignation and reprisal, and the inevitable orgy of bloodletting. The Met knew only what they had been told by Amanda Wallace, chief of MI5, in the minutes before disaster struck. A thirty-two-year-old woman with a German passport had collected a stolen late-model BMW from the short-stay car park at Heathrow's Terminal 3 and was driving alone toward central London. MI6 had been told by a senior foreign intelligence operative—the operative was not identified—that the woman was connected to a known terrorist mastermind and bomb maker. Amanda Wallace recommended to the Met commissioner that he take any and all appropriate measures to impede the car's progress and take the woman into custody. The commissioner had responded by dispatching units of the SCO19, the Met's tactical firearms division. The first armed response vehicle arrived at the scene at the instant of detonation. Both officers were among the dead.

Nothing remained of the blue BMW, only a crater, twenty meters wide and ten meters deep, on the spot where it once stood. A portion of the roof was later found floating in the Serpentine, a distance of more than half a kilometer away. Cars and buses burned like embers in the street; a geyser spewed from a fractured water main, cleansing the severed limbs of the dead and wounded. Curiously, the buildings on the north side of the street, the side closest to the car, suffered only moderate structural damage. It was Harrods that bore the brunt of the bomb's rage. The blast ripped away the building's facade, exposing its interior like the floors of a doll's house—bed and bath, furniture and home accessories, fine jewelry and perfume, women's wear. For a long time afterward, dazed patrons of the Georgian Restaurant stood staring into the shattered street below. The famed tearoom was popular among wealthy women from the oil-rich emirates of the Gulf. Cloaked in their black veils, they looked like ravens perched upon a wire.

The number of casualties proved difficult to calculate. By nightfall the dead would number fifty-two, with more than four hundred wounded, many critically. Several television experts expressed relief—even shock—that the numbers were not far higher. Survivors spoke of two men who had engaged in a desperate attempt to move passersby to safety in the seconds before the bomb exploded. Their efforts were clearly visible in a videotape that found its way onto the BBC. One man, armed, herded pedestrians along the pavement, while the other ripped passengers from a London bus. There was confusion over their identity. Their car, like the bomb car, had been blown to pieces, and neither man came forward, at least not to the public. The Met disowned them; MI5 and the Secret Intelligence Service chose not to comment. The CCTV video showed one of the men taking shelter seconds before the bomb detonated, but the second man was last seen running toward a white Ford Fiesta trapped in the snarled traffic along Brompton Road. The occupants of the car, a mother and her young son, were incinerated in the fireball. The man was presumed to be among the dead, too, though his body was never found.

The initial shock and revulsion quickly gave way to anger and an intense search for the perpetrators. Atop the list of possible suspects was ISIS, the extreme jihadist group that had terrorized and beheaded its way to an Islamic caliphate stretching from Aleppo nearly to the gates of Baghdad. The group had vowed to attack the West, and its ranks included several hundred residents of the United Kingdom who had retained their precious British passports. Surely, declared the television experts, ISIS had both the motive and the capability to strike in the heart of London. But an ISIS spokesman denied the group had been involved, as did several other elements in the global Islamic conglomerate of death known as al-Qaeda. A remote Palestinian faction did claim responsibility, as did something called the Martyrs of the Two Holy Mosques. Neither claim was taken seriously.

The one person who could answer the question of responsibility was the woman who had delivered the bomb to its target: Anna Huber, thirty-two years of age, German citizen, last known address Lessingstrasse 11, Frankfurt. But forty-eight hours after the attack, her whereabouts remained a mystery. Attempts to track her movements electronically proved useless. CCTV briefly showed her walking along Brompton Road toward Knightsbridge. But after the detonation, as smoke, debris, and panicked crowds poured into the street, the cameras lost sight of her. No one named Anna Huber had left the country via plane or rail; no one named Anna Huber had crossed another European frontier. Units of the German Bundespolizei raided her apartment and found four uninhabited rooms containing no trace of the person who might have once lived there. Neighbors described her as quiet and introspective. One said she was an international aid worker who spent a great deal of time in Africa. Another said she did something in the travel industry. Or was it journalism?

Responsibility for protecting the British homeland from terrorist attack fell primarily to MI5 and the Joint Terrorism Analysis Center. As a result, public and political anger over the Brompton Road bombing was directed largely at Amanda Wallace. The word *embattled* began to appear before her name in print or whenever it was mentioned on television or radio. Unnamed sources at the Met complained that the Security Service had been "less than forthcoming" with intelligence related to the attack. One senior investigator likened the flow of information from Thames House to Scotland Yard to the advance of a glacier. Later, he clarified his statement, calling cooperation between the two organizations "nonexistent."

Subsequently, there appeared in the press unflattering accounts of Amanda's management style. Underlings were said to fear her; numerous senior staff were said to be searching for greener pastures elsewhere at a time when Britain could least afford it. It was written of Amanda that she had a difficult relationship with Graham Seymour, her counterpart at MI6. It was said the two were scarcely speaking, that during one crisis meeting at Number Ten they had refused even to acknowledge each other's presence. One notable former spook said that relations between Britain's two intelligence services were at their lowest point in a generation. A respected journalist who covered security issues for the *Guardian* wrote that "British intelligence was in the midst of a force-ten crisis," and for once the journalist was correct.

At which point a deathwatch commenced outside Thames House, with Amanda Wallace as its target. It did not last long—two days, three at most. Then Amanda put an end to it. Her weapon of choice was the same esteemed correspondent from the *Guardian*, a man whom she had cultivated for years. His story began not with the bombing on Brompton

Road but with the death of the princess, and it got worse from there. Quinn's name was featured prominently. So, too, was Graham Seymour's. It was, said one political commentator, the finest example of murder by press leak he had ever seen.

By midmorning a new deathwatch had commenced. This time, the target was the chief of Her Majesty's Secret Intelligence Service. He issued no statement and adhered to his schedule as normal until half past eleven, when his official Jaguar, with its blacked-out windows, was spotted sliding through the gates of Downing Street. He remained inside Number Ten for less than an hour. Later, Simon Hewitt, the prime minister's director of communications, refused to confirm that the spymaster had set foot there. Shortly after two o'clock his Jaguar was seen turning into the underground parking garage of Vauxhall Cross, but as it turned out, Graham Seymour was not in it. He was sitting in the back of an unmarked panel van, and by then the van was already far from London.

29

DARTMOOR, DEVON

THE ROAD HAD no name and appeared on no map. Viewed from space, it looked like a scratch in the moorland, perhaps the remnant of a brook that had run over the land in the days when men erected circles of stone. At its entrance was a sign, weathered and rusted, warning that the road was private. And at its end was a gate that whispered quiet authority.

The grounds beyond the gate were barren and bleak, an acquired taste. The man who built the cottage there had made his money in shipping. He had bequeathed it to his only son, and the son, who had no heirs, had entrusted it to the Secret Intelligence Service, where he had worked for the better part of a half-century. He had served in many distant corners of the empire, under many different names, but mainly he was known as Wormwood. The service named the cottage in his honor. Those who stayed there found the name appropriate.

It was set upon a swell in the land and was fashioned of Devon stone that had darkened with age and neglect. Behind it, across a broken courtyard, was a converted barn with offices and living quarters for the staff. When Wormwood Cottage was unoccupied, a single caretaker called Parish kept watch over it. But when a guest was present—guests were always referred to as "company"—the staff could number as many as ten. Much depended on the nature of the guest and the men from whom he was hiding. A "friendly" with few enemies might be given the run of the place. A defector from Iran or Russia would be treated almost as a prisoner.

The two men who arrived on the evening of the Brompton Road bombing fell somewhere in between. They had appeared with only a few minutes' warning, accompanied by an acolyte of the chiefs who went by the work name Davies and a doctor who treated the wounds of the untreatable. The doctor had spent the rest of the night putting the older of the two men back together again. The younger one had watched over his every move.

He was an Englishman, the younger one, an expatriate, a man who had lived in another land, spoken another language. The older of the two was the legend. Two members of the staff had looked after him once before, after an incident in Hyde Park involving the daughter of the American ambassador. He was a gentleman, an artist by nature, a bit on the quiet side, a touch temperamental, but many of his ilk were. They would watch over him, tend to his wounds, and then send him on his way. And not once would they speak his name, for as far as they were concerned he did not exist. He was a man without a past or future. He was a blank page. He was dead.

For the first forty-eight hours of his stay, he was quieter than normal. He spoke only to the doctor who treated his wounds and to the Englishman. To the staff he said nothing at all, only a deflated "Thank you" whenever they brought him meals or clean clothing. He kept to his small room overlooking the empty moorland, with only the television and the London papers for company. He made just one request; he wanted his BlackBerry. Parish the permanent caretaker patiently explained that company, even company of his exalted stature, weren't permitted the use of private communications devices in Wormwood Cottage or on its grounds.

"I need to know their names," the injured man said on the third morning of his stay, when Parish personally delivered his tea and toast.

"Whose names, sir?"

"The woman and the child. The police haven't released their names."

"I'm afraid it's not my place, sir. I'm just the caretaker."

"Get me their names," he said again, and Parish, wishing to remove himself from the room, promised to do his utmost.

"What about my BlackBerry?"

"Sorry," said Parish. "House rules."

By the fourth day he was strong enough to leave his room. He was sitting in the garden at midday when the Englishman set off on a hike across the moor, and was there at sunset when the Englishman returned, dragging a pair of broken bodyguards in his wake. The Englishman walked every afternoon regardless of the weather—even on the fifth day, when a gale blew hard across the moors. On that day he insisted on carrying a rucksack weighted down with whatever debris the staff could find. The two bodyguards were half-dead by the time they stumbled back to the cottage. That night, in the living quarters of the converted barn, they spoke with hushed reverence of a man with almost super-human strength and endurance. One of the body-guards was former SAS and thought he recognized the mark of the Regiment. It was in his step, he said, and in the way his eyes took in the contour of the land. Sometimes it seemed as if he were viewing it for the first time. Other times it appeared as though he were wondering how he ever could have left it. The bodyguards had looked after all kinds at the cottage—defectors, spies, blown field agents, frauds in search of a taxpayer-funded payday—but this one was different. He was special. He was dangerous. He had a dark past. And, perhaps, a bright future.

On the sixth day—the day of the *Guardian* ar-ticle, the day that would later be remembered as the day British intelligence tore itself asunder—the younger of the two men set off toward the tor, a hike of ten miles, twenty if the bloody fool insisted on walking both ways. Five miles into the journey, while crossing a windswept highland, he paused suddenly, as if alerted to the presence of danger. His head rose and snapped to the left with an animal swiftness. Then he stood motionless, his eyes fixed on the target.

It was an unmarked panel van bumping along the road from Postbridge. He watched it turn into the road without a name. Watched it shoot into the hedgerows like a steel ball in a maze. Then he lowered his head and set off again. He walked with a heavy pack on his back and at a pace the bodyguards found hard to match. He walked like he was running away from something. He walked like he was coming home.

The gate was open by the time the van reached the end of the road. Only Parish was there to greet it. A dreadful sight, he thought, watching the chief of Her Majesty's Secret Service crawling from the back of an ordinary van—*crawling*, he told the others that night, like some jihadi who'd been plucked from the battlefield and subjected to God knows what. Parish respectfully shook the chief's hand while the wind played havoc with his plentiful gray locks.

"Where is he?" he asked.

"Which one, sir?"

"Our friend from Israel."

"In his room, sir."

"And the other one?"

"Out there," said Parish to the moorland.

"How long until he returns?"

"Hard to say, sir. Sometimes I'm not sure he's coming back at all. He strikes me as the sort of chap who could walk a very long way if he set his mind to it."

The chief gave the faintest trace of a smile.

"Shall I tell the security team to bring him home, sir?"

"No," said Graham Seymour as he entered the cottage. "I'll see to that."

30

WORMWOOD COTTAGE, DARTMOOR

THE WALLS OF Wormwood Cottage contained a sophisticated audio-and-video surveillance system capable of recording every word and deed of its guests. Graham Seymour ordered Parish to switch off the system and to remove all staff save for Miss Coventry, the cook, who served them a pot of Earl Grey tea and freshly baked scones with Devonshire clotted cream. They sat at the small table in the kitchen, which was set in a snug alcove with windows all around. Spread on one chair like an uninvited guest was a copy of the *Guardian*. Seymour looked at it with an expression as bleak as the moors.

"I see you've been keeping up with the news."

"I didn't have much else to do."

"It was for your own good."

"Yours, too."

Seymour drank his tea but said nothing.

"Will you survive?"

"I should think so. After all, the prime minister and I are rather close."

"He owes you his political life, not to mention his marriage."

"Actually, you were the one who saved Jonathan's career. I was only your secret enabler." Seymour picked up the newspaper and frowned at the headline.

"It's remarkably accurate," said Gabriel.

"It should be. He had a good source."

"You seem to be taking it all quite well."

"What choice do I have? Besides, it wasn't personal. It was an act of self-defense. Amanda wasn't about to take the fall."

"The result is still the same."

"Yes," said Seymour darkly. "British intelligence is a shambles. And as far as the public are concerned, I'm squarely to blame."

"Funny how it all worked out that way."

A silence fell between them.

"Are there any more surprises to come?" asked Seymour.

"A dead body in County Mayo."

"Liam Walsh?"

Gabriel nodded.

"I suppose he deserved it."

"He did."

Seymour picked thoughtfully at a scone. "I'm sorry I got you mixed up in all this. I should have left you in Rome to finish your Caravaggio."

"And I should have told you that a woman who'd just spent the night in Eamon Quinn's secret Lisbon apartment had boarded a flight for London."

"Would it have made a difference?"

"It might have."

"We aren't policemen, Gabriel."

"Your point?"

"My instincts would have been the same as yours. I wouldn't have detained her at Heathrow. I would have let her run and hoped she led me to the prize."

Seymour returned the newspaper to the empty chair. "I must admit," he said after a moment, "you don't look bad for a man who just came face-to-face with a five-hundred-pound bomb. Perhaps you truly are an archangel after all."

"If I were an archangel, I would have found a way to save them all."

"You saved a great many, though, at least a hundred by our estimate. And you would have come through it without a scratch if you'd had the sense to take cover inside Harrods."

Gabriel made no reply.

"Why did you do it?" asked Seymour. "Why did you go running back into the street?"

"I saw them."

"Who?"

"The woman and the child who were in that car. I tried to warn her, but she didn't understand. She wouldn't—"

"It wasn't your fault," said Seymour, cutting him off.

"Do you know their names?"

Seymour stared out the window. The descending sun had set fire to the moors.

"The woman was Charlotte Harris. She was from Shepherd's Bush."

"And the boy?"

"He was called Peter, after his grandfather."

"How old was he?"

"Two years, four months." Seymour paused and

considered Gabriel carefully. "About the same age as your son, wasn't he?"

"It doesn't matter."

"Of course it does."

"Dani was a few months older."

"And strapped to a car seat when the bomb exploded."

"Are you finished, Graham?"

"No." Seymour allowed a silence to creep into the room. "You're about to be a father again. A chief, too. And fathers and chiefs don't go face-to-face with five-hundred-pound bombs."

Outside, the sun was balanced atop a distant hill. The fire was draining from the moors.

"How much does my service know?" asked Gabriel.

"They know you were close to the bomb when it exploded."

"How?"

"Your wife recognized you in the CCTV video. As you might expect, she's rather anxious to have you home. So is Uzi. He threatened to fly to London and bring you back personally."

"Why didn't he?"

"Shamron convinced him to stay away. He thought it best to let the dust settle."

"Wise move."

"Would you have expected anything else?"

"Not from Shamron."

Ari Shamron was the twice-former director-general of the Office, the chief of chiefs, the eternal one. He had formed the Office in his likeness, written its language, handed down its commandments, imparted its soul. Even now, in old age and failing health, he guarded his creation jealously. It was because of Shamron that Gabriel would soon succeed his friend as chief of the Office. And it was because of Shamron, too, that he had hurled himself like a madman toward a white Ford car with a child strapped into the rear seat.

"Where's my phone?" he asked.

"In our lab."

"Are your techs having a good time pulling apart our software?"

"Ours is better."

"Then I suppose they've managed to figure out where Quinn was when he sent that text."

"GCHQ thinks it came from a mobile in London. The question is," he continued, "how did he get your private number?"

"I suppose he got it from the same people who hired him to kill me."

"Any suspects?"

"Only one."

31

WORMWOOD COTTAGE, DARTMOOR

T HERE WERE BARBOUR jackets hanging in the hall closet and Wellington boots lined against the wall of the mudroom. Miss Coventry prevailed upon them to take a torch—night fell suddenly on the moor, she explained, and even experienced hikers sometimes became disoriented in the featureless landscape. The torch was military-issue and had a beam like a searchlight. If they became lost, quipped Gabriel as he dressed, they could use it to signal a passing airliner.

By the time they left the cottage, the sun was a memory. Ribbons of orange light lay low upon the horizon, but a fingernail moon floated overhead and a spray of stars shone cold and hard in the east. Gabriel, weakened, his body aching from a thousand bruises, moved hesitantly along the footpath, the unlit torch in his hand. Seymour, taller, for the moment fitter, hovered at his side, his brow deeply furrowed in concentration as he listened to Gabriel explain what had transpired and, more important, why it had come to pass. The plot had its genesis, he said, at a house in a birch forest, on the shore of a frozen lake. Gabriel had committed an unforgivable act there against a man like himself—a made man, a man protected by a vengeful service—and for that Gabriel had been sentenced to die. But not just Gabriel; another would die with him. And a third man who had been complicit in the affair would be punished, too. The man would be disgraced, his service weakened by scandal.

"Me?" asked Seymour.

"You," said Gabriel.

The men behind the plot, he continued, had not acted in haste. They had planned with great care, with their political master looking over their shoulders every step of the way. Quinn was their weapon. Quinn was their perfect bait. The men behind the plot had no established links to the bomb maker, but surely their paths had crossed. They had flown him to their headquarters, treated him like a conquering hero, showered him with toys and money. And then they had sent him into the world to commit an act of murder—a murder that would shock a nation and set the rest of the plot in motion.

"The princess?"

Gabriel nodded.

"You can't prove a word of it."

"No," said Gabriel. "Not yet."

For several days after her murder, he continued, British intelligence had been unaware of Quinn's involvement. Then Uzi Navot came to London with a piece of intelligence from an important Iranian source. Seymour traveled to Rome; Gabriel, to Corsica. Then, with Keller as his guide, he went trolling through Quinn's murderous past. They found a secret family in West Belfast and a small apartment in the hills of Lisbon, where a woman called Anna Huber spent a single night, watched over by three men. Two of the men boarded an airplane with her, and the next act of the plot commenced. A blue BMW, stolen, repainted, fitted with false license plates, was left at Heathrow Airport. The woman collected the car and drove it to Brompton Road. She parked across the street from a London landmark, armed the bomb, and melted into the crowd while the two men tried desperately to save as many lives as possible. They knew the bomb was about to explode because Quinn had told them so. With a cryptic text message, Quinn had signed his name. And all the while, the men who had hired him were watching. Perhaps, added Gabriel, they still were.

"You think my service has been penetrated?" asked Seymour.

"Your service was penetrated a long time ago."

Seymour paused and looked over his shoulder at the fading lights of Wormwood Cottage. "Is it safe for you here?"

"You tell me."

"Parish knew my father. He's as loyal as they come. Even so," Seymour added, "we should probably move you soon, just to be on the safe side."

"I'm afraid it's too late for that, Graham."

"Why?"

"Because I'm already dead."

Seymour stared at Gabriel for a moment, bewildered. And then he understood.

"I want you to contact Uzi over your usual link," said Gabriel. "Tell him I've succumbed to my injuries. Express your deepest condolences. Tell him to send Shamron to collect the body. I can't do this without Shamron."

"Do what?"

"I'm going to kill Eamon Quinn," said Gabriel coldly. "And then I'm going to kill the man who paid for the bullet."

"Leave Quinn to me."

"No," said Gabriel. "Quinn is mine."

"You're in no shape to go chasing after anyone, let alone one of the world's most dangerous terrorists."

"Then I suppose I'll need someone to carry my bags. He should probably be someone from MI6," Gabriel added quickly. "Someone to look after British interests."

"Do you have someone in mind?"

"I do," replied Gabriel. "But there's one problem."

"What's that?"

"He's not MI6."

"No," said Seymour. "Not yet."

Seymour followed Gabriel's gaze into the blackened landscape. At first there was nothing. Then three figures rose slowly from the darkness. Two appeared to be laboring with fatigue, but the third was pounding along the footpath as though he had many miles to go. He paused briefly and, looking up, gave a single stiff-armed wave. Then suddenly he was standing before them. Smiling, he extended a hand toward Seymour.

"Graham," he said amiably. "Long time no see. Are you staying for supper? I hear Miss Coventry is making her famous cottage pie."

Then he turned and set off into the darkness. And a moment later he was gone.

32

WORMWOOD COTTAGE, DARTMOOR

G RAHAM SEYMOUR DID indeed stay at Wormwood Cottage for supper that night, and for a long time afterward, too. Miss Coventry served them the cottage pie and a decent claret at the kitchen table and then left them to a warm fire in the sitting room and to the past. Gabriel remained largely a spectator to the proceedings, a witness, a taker of notes. Keller did most of the talking. He spoke of his undercover work in Belfast, of the death of Elizabeth Conlin, and of Quinn. And he spoke, too, of the night in January 1991 when his Sabre squadron came under Coalition air attack in western Iraq, and of his long walk into the waiting arms of Don Anton Orsati. Seymour listened largely without interruption and without judgment, even when Keller described some of the many assassinations he'd carried out at the don's behest. Seymour wasn't interested in passing judgment. He was interested only in Keller.

And so he cracked a bottle of Wormwood Cottage's finest single malt, added a log to the pile of embers in the grate, and proposed an arrangement that would result in Keller's repatriation. He would be given a job at MI6. With it would come a new name and identity. Christopher Keller would remain dead to everyone but his immediate family and his service. He would handle cases that suited his particular skill set. Under no circumstances would he be drafting white papers at a desk in Vauxhall Cross. MI6 had plenty of analysts to do that.

"And if I bump into an old chum on the street?"

"Tell the old chum he's mistaken and keep walking."

"Where will I live?"

"Anywhere you want, so long as it's in London."

"What about my villa in Corsica?"

"We'll see."

From his outpost next to the fire, Gabriel treated himself to a brief smile. Keller's questions resumed.

"Who will I work for?"

"Me."

"Doing what?"

"Whatever I need."

"And when you're gone?"

"I'm not going anywhere."

"That's not what I read in the newspapers."

"One of the things you'll soon learn working at MI6 is that the newspapers are almost always wrong." Seymour raised his glass and examined the color of the whisky by the light of the fire.

"What are we going to say to Personnel?" asked Keller.

"As little as possible."

"There's no way I can survive a traditional vetting."

"I should think not."

"What about my money?"

"How much is there?"

Keller answered truthfully. Seymour raised an eyebrow.

"We'll have to work out something with the lawyers."

"I don't like lawyers."

"Well, you can't keep it hidden in secret bank accounts."

"Why not?"

"Because, for obvious reasons, MI6 officers aren't allowed to keep them."

"I won't be a normal MI6 officer."

"You still have to play by the rules."

"I never have before."

"Yes," said Seymour. "That's why you're here."

And on it went, long past midnight, until finally the deal was done and Seymour crawled laboriously into the back of his undignified unmarked van. He left behind a notebook computer incapable of making contact with the outside world, and a password-protected thumb drive containing two videos. The first was an edited montage of CCTV images showing the delivery of the blue BMW to Heathrow Airport. The car had appeared on CCTV for the first time near Bristol, several hours before the bombing. The driver headed directly toward London along the M4. He wore a hat and sunglasses, rendering his features invisible to the cameras. He stopped once for fuel, paid in cash, and said nothing to the clerk during the exchange. Nor did he address anyone in the car park at Heathrow's Terminal 3, where he deposited the BMW at 11:30 a.m., half an hour after British Airways Flight 501 departed Lisbon. After retrieving a suitcase from the backseat, he entered the terminal and boarded the Heathrow Express train to London's Paddington Station, where a motorcycle was waiting. One hour later the bike slipped out of CCTV coverage on a country lane south of Luton. The motorcycle remained unaccounted for. The car's point of origin on the day of the bombing was never determined.

The second video was devoted entirely to the woman. It began with her passage through Heathrow Airport and ended with her disappearance in the smoke and chaos that she had unleashed on London's Brompton Road. To it, Gabriel added several minutes of footage from his own memory. There was a woman sitting alone at a street-side restaurant, and a woman abruptly hailing a taxi on a busy boulevard, and a woman on an airplane staring directly into his face without a trace of recognition. She was good, he thought, a worthy opponent. She had known that dangerous men were following her, and yet she had never once shown fear or even apprehension. It was possible she was someone whom Quinn had met during his travels through the nether regions of global terrorism, but Gabriel doubted it. She was a professional, an elite professional. She was of a higher caliber, a better class.

Gabriel watched the video again from the beginning, watched the BMW slide into the bus-only lane outside the HSBC bank, watched the woman climb out and walk calmly away. Then he saw two men leap from a silver Passat—one armed with a gun, one with only brute strength—and begin herding the crowds to safety. At forty-five seconds the street went deathly still and quiet. Then a man could be seen running wildly toward a white Ford compact trapped in the stalled traffic. The bomb obliterated the shot. It should have obliterated the man, too. Perhaps Graham Seymour was right. Perhaps Gabriel was an archangel after all.

It was nearly dawn by the time he powered off the computer. As instructed, he returned it to Parish the caretaker at breakfast, along with a handwritten note to be delivered personally to Graham Seymour at Vauxhall Cross. In it, Gabriel requested permission to conduct two meetings—one with London's most prominent political journalist, the other with the world's most famous defector. Seymour agreed to both requests and dispatched an unmarked service van to Wormwood Cottage. By late that afternoon it was speeding along the cliffs of the Lizard Peninsula in West Cornwall. Keller, it seemed, was not alone. The late Gabriel Allon was going home, too.

33

GUNWALLOE COVE, CORNWALL

H E HAD SEEN it for the first time from the deck of a ketch a mile out to sea, the small cottage at the southern end of Gunwalloe Cove, perched atop the cliffs in the manner of Monet's *Customs Officer's Cabin at Pourville*. Below it was a crescent of beaten sand where an old shipwreck slept beneath the treacherous surf. Behind it, beyond the purple thrift and red fescue of the cliff tops, rose a sloping green field crisscrossed by hedgerows. At that moment, Gabriel saw none of it, for he was hunched like a refugee in the back of the service van. He knew they were close, though; the road told him so. He knew every bend and straightaway, every dip and pothole, the bark of every watchdog, the sweet bovine aroma of every pasture. And so, when the van made the hard right turn at the Lamb and Flag pub and started the final downhill run toward the beach, he straightened slightly in anticipation. The van slowed, probably to avoid a fisherman coming up from the cove, and then made another sharp turn, a left, into the private drive. Suddenly, the rear door of the van was swinging open and an

MI6 security man was welcoming him to his own home, as though he were a stranger setting foot in Cornwall for the first time. "Mr. Carlyle," he bellowed over the wind. "Welcome to Gunwalloe. I hope you had a good trip, sir. The traffic can be positively brutal this time of day."

The air was crisp and salty, the late-afternoon light was brilliant orange, the sea was aflame and flecked with whitecaps. Gabriel stood for a moment in the drive, feeling hollowed out with longing, until the security man nudged him politely toward the entrance—because the security man was under strict orders not to allow him to remain visible to a world that would soon believe him dead. Looking up, he imagined Chiara standing reproachfully in the doorway, her riotous hair tumbling about her shoulders, her arms folded across her childless womb. But as he climbed the three front steps, she slipped away from him. Automatically, he hung his oilskin coat on the hook in the entrance hall and ran a hand over the old suede flat cap he used to wear during his sojourns along the cliffs. Then, turning, he saw Chiara for a second time. She was removing a heavy earthenware pot from the oven, and when she lifted its lid the savor of veal, wine, and sage filled the cottage. Photographs of a missing Rembrandt portrait lay scattered across the kitchen counter where she worked. Gabriel had just agreed to find the painting for an art dealer named Julian Isherwood, not knowing his search would lead directly into the heart of Iran's nuclear program. He had managed to locate and destroy four secret uranium enrichment facilities, a stunning achievement that significantly slowed Iran's march toward a nuclear weapon. The Iranians surely did not view Gabriel's accomplishment in the same flattering light. In fact, they wanted him dead just as badly as the men who had hired Eamon Quinn.

The vision of Chiara was gone. He opened the French doors and for an instant he imagined he could hear the church bells of Lyonesse, the mythical submerged City of Lions, tolling beneath the surface of the sea. A single fisherman stood waist-deep in the breakers; the beach was deserted except for a woman walking along the water's edge, trailed a few feet by a man in a nylon sailing jacket. She was headed north, which meant she presented him with her long back. A gust of cold wind blew from the sea, cold enough to chill Gabriel, and in his thoughts he was watching her walk along a frozen street in St. Petersburg. Then, as now, he had viewed her from above; he had been standing at the parapet of a church dome. The woman had known he was there but had not looked up. She was a professional, an elite professional. She was of a higher caliber, a better class.

By now, she had reached the northernmost end of the beach. She pirouetted and the man in the nylon jacket turned with her. The sea spray added a dreamlike quality to the image. She paused to watch the fisherman lift a struggling bass from the breakers and, laughing at something the man had said, plucked a stone from the tide line and flung it into the sea. Turning, she paused again, apparently distracted by something unexpected she had seen. Perhaps it was the man standing at the railing of the terrace, in the manner of the man who had been standing on the parapet of a church tower in St. Petersburg. She cast another stone into the turbulent sea, lowered her head, and kept walking. Now, as then, Madeline Hart did not look up.

It had started as an affair between Prime Minister Jonathan Lancaster and a young woman who worked at his party's headquarters. But the woman was no ordinary woman—she was a Russian sleeper agent who had been planted in England as a child—and the affair was no ordinary affair. It was part of an elaborate Russian plot designed to pressure the prime minister into signing over lucrative North Sea drilling rights to a Kremlin-owned energy company called Volgatek Oil & Gas. Gabriel had learned the truth from the man who had run the operation, an SVR officer named Pavel Zhirov. Afterward, Gabriel and his team of Office operatives had plucked Madeline Hart from St. Petersburg and smuggled her out of the country. The scandal that accompanied her defection was the worst in British history. Jonathan Lancaster, personally humiliated and politically wounded, responded by canceling the North Sea deal and freezing Russian money held by British banks. By one estimate, the Russian president personally lost several billion dollars. Frankly, thought Gabriel, it was a wonder he had waited so long to retaliate.

It had been the intention of the KGB to turn Madeline Hart into an English girl, and through years of training and manipulation they had succeeded. Her grasp of the Russian language was limited, and she felt no allegiance to the land she had left as a child. It had been her wish upon her return to Britain to resume her old life, but political and security considerations had made that impossible. Gabriel had given her the use of his beloved cottage in Cornwall. He knew she would find the setting to her liking. She had been raised in government-funded deprivation, in a council house in Basildon, England. She wanted nothing more in life than a room with a view.

"How did you find me?" she asked as she climbed the steps to the terrace. And then she smiled. It was the same question she had posed to Gabriel that afternoon in St. Petersburg. Her eyes were the same blue-gray and were wide with excitement. Now they narrowed with concern as she scrutinized the damage to his face.

"You look positively dreadful," she said in her English accent. It was a combination of London and Essex but without a trace of Moscow. "What happened?"

"It was a skiing accident."

"You don't strike me as the sort to ski."

"It was my first time."

A faintly awkward moment followed as she invited him to enter his own home. She hung her coat on the hook next to his and went into the kitchen to make tea. She filled the electric kettle with bottled water and pulled down an old box of Harney & Sons from the cupboard. Gabriel had picked it up a hundred years ago at the Morrisons in Marazion. He sat on his favorite stool and watched another woman inhabit the space usually occupied by his wife. The London newspapers lay on the countertop, unread. All featured lurid coverage of the Brompton Road bombing and the infighting between Britain's intelligence services. He looked at Madeline. The cold sea air had added color to her pale cheeks. She seemed content, happy even, not at all like the broken woman he had found in St. Petersburg. Suddenly, he hadn't the heart to tell her she was the cause of all that had happened.

"I was beginning to think I'd never see you again," she said. "It's been—"

"Too long," said Gabriel, cutting her off. "When was the last time you were in the UK?"

"I was here this summer."

"Business or pleasure?"

He hesitated before answering. For a long time after her defection, he had refused even to tell Madeline his real name. Defectors had a way of becoming homesick.

"It was a business venture," he said at last.

"Successful, I hope."

He had to think about it. "Yes," he said after a moment. "I suppose it was."

Madeline lifted the kettle from its base and poured the steaming water into a chubby white teapot that Chiara had picked out from a shop in Penzance. Watching her, Gabriel asked, "Are you happy here, Madeline?"

"I live in fear you're going to evict me."

"Why would you think such a thing?"

"I've never had a home of my own before," she said. "No mother, no father, only the KGB. I became the person I wanted to be. And then they took that away from me, too."

"You can stay here as long as you want."

She opened the refrigerator, removed a container of milk, and poured a measure into Chiara's little beehive jug.

"Warm or cold?" she asked.

"Cold."

"Sugar?"

"Heavens, no."

"There might be a tube of McVitie's in the pantry."

"I ate." Gabriel poured milk into the bottom of his cup and poured the tea on top of it. "Are my neighbors behaving?"

"They're a bit nosy."

"You don't say."

"It seems you made quite an impression on them."

"It wasn't me."

"No," she said. "It was Giovanni Rossi, the great Italian art restorer."

"Not so great."

"That's not what Vera Hobbs says."

"How are her scones these days?"

"Almost as good as the scones at the café atop Lizard Point."

His smile must have betrayed how much he missed it here.

"I don't know how you could have left this place," she said.

"Nor do I."

She eyed him thoughtfully over the rim of her teacup. "Are you the chief of your service yet?"

"Not yet."

"How much longer?"

"A few months, maybe less."

"Will I read about it in the newspapers?"

"We now publicize the name of our chief, just like MI6."

"Poor Graham," she said with a glance toward the papers.

"Yes," said Gabriel vaguely.

"Do you think Jonathan will sack him?"

It was odd to hear her refer to the prime minister by his Christian name. He wondered what she had called him on those nights at Downing Street when Diana Lancaster was away.

"No," he said after a moment. "I don't think so."

"Graham knows too much."

"There's that."

"And Jonathan is very loyal."

"To everyone but his wife."

The remark wounded her.

"I'm sorry, Madeline. I shouldn't—"

"It's all right," she said quickly. "I deserved it."

Her long, sinewy hands were suddenly restless. She calmed them by removing the teabags from the pot, adding a splash of hot water, and replacing the lid.

"Is everything as you remember it?" she asked.

"The woman behind the counter is different. Otherwise, everything is the same."

She smiled uneasily but said nothing.

"Have you been rummaging through my things?" he asked.

"Constantly."

"Find anything interesting?"

"Regrettably, no. It's almost as if the man who lived here didn't exist."

"Just like Madeline Hart."

He saw dismay in her eyes. They moved slowly around the room, her room with a view.

"Are you ever going to tell me why you look so dreadful?"

"I was on Brompton Road when the bomb exploded."

"Why?"

Gabriel answered truthfully.

"So you're the foreign intelligence operative."

"I'm afraid so."

"And you were the one who tried to move the people to safety."

He said nothing.

"Who was the other man?"

"It's not important."

"You always say that."

"Only when it really is."

"And the woman?" she asked.

"Her passport said she was—"

"Yes," she interrupted him. "I read that in the newspaper."

"Did you see the CCTV video?"

"Nothing much to see, really. A woman gets out of a car, a woman walks calmly away, a street goes boom."

"Very professional."

"Very," she agreed.

"Did you see the still photo of her from Heathrow?"

"Pretty grainy."

"Think she's German?"

"Half, I'd say."

"And the other half?"

Madeline stared at the sea.

34

GUNWALLOE COVE, CORNWALL

THERE WERE FOUR photographs in all: the single shot that Gabriel had taken of the woman sitting alone at the restaurant and three more he had snapped as she stood on Quinn's rusted balcony. He arranged them on the counter-top, where he had once laid the photographs of the stolen Rembrandt for Chiara, and felt a tug of guilt as Madeline bent at the waist to scrutinize them.

"Who took these?"

"It's not important."

"You have a good eye."

"Almost as good as Giovanni Rossi."

She picked up the first photograph, a woman in dark sunglasses alone at a streetside table, seated in a direction that afforded her an inferior view of the city.

"She didn't zip up her handbag."

"You noticed that, too."

"A normal tourist would zip up her bag because of thieves and pickpockets."

"She would."

She returned the photograph to its place on the

counter and lifted another. It showed a woman standing alone at the balustrade of a balcony, a flowering vine spilling from her feet. The woman was holding a cigarette to her lips in a manner that exposed the underside of her right arm. Madeline leaned closer and knitted her brow thoughtfully.

"Do you see that?" she asked.

"What?"

She held up the photograph. "She has a scar."

"It could be a flaw in the image."

"It could be, but it isn't. It's a flaw in the girl."

"How can you be sure?"

"Because," said Madeline, "I was there when it happened."

"Do you know her?"

"No," she said, staring at the photograph. "But I know the girl she used to be."

35

GUNWALLOE COVE, CORNWALL

GABRIEL HAD HEARD the story the first time on the shore of a frozen Russian lake, from the mouth of a man called Pavel Zhirov. Now, in a cottage by the sea, he heard it again from the woman who had become Madeline Hart. She did not know her real name; of her biological parents she knew little. Her father had been a senior general in the KGB, perhaps the head of the all-powerful First Chief Directorate. Her mother, a KGB typist of no more than twenty, had not survived long after the birth. An overdose of sleeping pills and vodka had taken her life, or so Madeline had been told.

She had been placed in an orphanage. Not a real orphanage, but a KGB orphanage where, as she liked to say, she had been raised by wolves. At a certain point—she could not recall when—her caretakers had stopped speaking to her in Russian. For a time she was raised in total silence, until the last traces of the Russian language had leaked from her memory. Then she was placed in the care of a unit that spoke to her only in English. She watched videos of British children's programs and read British children's books. The limited exposure to British culture did little for her accent. She spoke English, she said, like a newsreader for Radio Moscow.

The facility where she lived was in suburban Moscow, not far from the headquarters of the First Chief Directorate in Yasenevo, which the KGB referred to as Moscow Center. Eventually she was moved to a KGB training camp deep in the Russian interior, near a closed city that had no name, only a number. The camp contained a small English town, with high street shops, a park, a bus with an English-speaking driver, and a terrace of brick houses where the trainees lived together as families. In a separate part of the camp was a small American town with a theater that played popular American movies. And a short distance from the American town was a German village. It was run in concert with the East German Stasi. The food was flown in weekly from East Berlin: German sausage, beer, fresh German ham. Everyone agreed the German-speaking train-ees had it best.

For the most part the trainees kept to their sepa-rate false worlds. Madeline lived with the man and woman who would eventually resettle with her in Britain. She attended a stern English school, had tea and crumpets in a little English shop, and played in an English park that was invariably buried beneath several inches of Russian snow. On occasion, how-ever, she was allowed to watch an American movie in the American town, or to have dinner in the beer garden of the German village. It was on one such outing that she met Katerina.

"I assume she wasn't living in the American village," said Gabriel.

"No," answered Madeline. "Katerina was a German girl."

She was several years older than Madeline, an adolescent on the doorstep of womanhood. She was already beautiful, but not as beautiful as she would become. She spoke a bit of English—the trainees in the German program were taught to be bilingual—and she enjoyed practicing with Madeline, whose English, while oddly accented, was perfect. As a rule, friendships between trainees from different schools were discouraged, but in the case of Madeline and Katerina the trainers made an exception. Katerina had been depressed for some time. Her trainers were not at all convinced she was suited for life in the West as an illegal.

"How did she end up in the illegals program?" asked Gabriel.

"In much the same way I did."

"Her father was KGB?"

"Her mother, actually."

"And the father?"

"He was a German intelligence officer who'd been targeted for sexual entrapment. Katerina was the offspring of the relationship."

"Why didn't the mother have an abortion?"

"She wanted the baby. They took it from her. And then they took her life."

"And the scar?"

Madeline didn't answer. Instead, she picked up the photograph again—the photograph of the girl she had known as Katerina standing on a balcony in Lisbon.

"What was she doing there?" she asked. "And why did she leave a bomb on Brompton Road?"

"She was in Lisbon because her controllers knew we were watching the apartment."

"And the bomb?"

"It was meant for me."

She looked up sharply. "Why were they trying to kill you?"

Gabriel hesitated, and then said, "Because of you, Madeline."

A silence fell between them.

"What did you think would happen," she said finally, "if you killed a KGB officer on Russian soil and then helped me to defect to the West?"

"I thought the Russian president would be angry. But I didn't think he would set off a bomb on Brompton Road."

"You underestimate the Russian president."

"Never," replied Gabriel. "The Russian president and I have a long history."

"He's tried to kill you before?"

"Yes," said Gabriel. "But this is the first time he's ever succeeded."

Her blue-gray eyes flashed over him quizzically. And then she understood.

"When did you die?" she asked.

"Several hours ago, at a British military hospital. I fought hard, but it was no use. My injuries were too severe."

"Who else knows?"

"My service, of course, and my wife has been quietly notified of my passing."

"What about Moscow Center?"

"If, as I suspect, they've been reading MI6's mail, they're already raising glasses of vodka to my demise. But just to make sure, I'm going to make it abundantly clear."

"Is there anything I can do?"

"Say nice things about me at my funeral. And take more than one bodyguard when you go walking on the beach."

"There were two, actually."

"The fisherman?"

"We're having roast sea bass for dinner." She smiled and asked, "What are you going to do with all your free time now that you're dead?"

"I'm going to find the men who killed me."

Madeline picked up the photograph of Katerina on the balcony. "What about her?" she asked.

Gabriel was silent for a moment. Then he said, "You never told me about the scar on her arm."

"It happened during a training exercise."

"What kind of training?"

"Silent killing." She looked at Gabriel and added darkly, "The KGB starts early."

"You?"

"I was too young," she said, shaking her head. "But Katerina was older and they had other plans for her. Her instructor handed her a knife one day and told her to kill him. Katerina obeyed. Katerina always obeyed."

"Go on."

"Even after he disarmed her, she kept coming at him. Eventually, she cut herself on her own weapon. She's lucky she didn't bleed to death." Madeline looked down at the photograph. "Where do you think she is now?"

"I suppose she's somewhere in Russia."

"In a town without a name." Madeline returned the photograph to Gabriel. "Let's hope she stays there."

When Gabriel returned to Wormwood Cottage, he climbed the stairs to his room and fell exhausted into his bed. He longed to telephone his wife but didn't dare. Surely, his enemies were prowling the grid for traces of his voice. Dead men didn't make phone calls.

When sleep finally claimed him, he was made restless by dreams. In one he was crossing the nave of a cathedral in Vienna, carrying a wooden case filled with his restoration supplies. A German girl waited in the doorway to engage him in conversation, as she had done that night, but in his dream she was Katerina and blood flowed freely from a deep wound to her arm. "Can you repair it?" she asked, showing him the wound, but he slipped past her without a word and made his way through quiet Viennese streets, to a square in the old Jewish Quarter. The square was blanketed with snow and jammed with London buses. A woman was trying to start the engine of a Mercedes sedan but the engine wouldn't turn over because the bomb was pulling power from the battery. His son was strapped into his car seat in the back, but the woman behind the wheel was not his wife. It was Madeline Hart. "How did you find me?" she asked through the broken glass of her window. And then the bomb exploded.

He must have called out in his sleep because Keller was standing in the doorway of his room when he woke. Miss Coventry served them breakfast in the kitchen and then saw them into the cold foggy morning as they set off for a hike across the moor. Gabriel's legs were weak with inactivity, but Keller took mercy on him. They passed the first mile at a moderate pace that increased gradually as Gabriel spoke of Madeline and the offspring of a KGB honey trap named Katerina. They were going to find her, said Gabriel. And then they were going to send a message to the Kremlin that needed no translation.

"Don't forget Quinn," said Keller.

"Maybe there was no Quinn. Maybe Quinn was just a name and a track record. Maybe he was just a piece of bait they tossed into the water to lure us to the surface."

"You don't really believe that, do you?"

"It's crossed my mind."

"Quinn murdered the princess."

"According to a source inside Iranian intelligence," said Gabriel pointedly.

"How soon can we move?"

"After my funeral."

Returning to Wormwood Cottage, he found a change of clothing lying folded at the foot of his bed. He showered, dressed, and climbed once more into the back of the paneled van. This time, it bore him eastward to a safe house in Highgate. The house was familiar to him; he had operated there before. Entering, he tossed his coat over the back of a chair in the sitting room and climbed the stairs to a small study on the second floor. It had an arrow slit of a window overlooking the cul-de-sac, a dead man's view. Rain gurgled in the gutters, pigeons wept in the eaves. Thirty minutes passed, long enough for darkness to fall and a row of streetlamps to flicker hesitantly to life. Then a gray car came crawling up the slope of the hill, driven with what appeared to be inordinate care. It parked in front of the safe house and the driver, a young, harmless-looking man, climbed out. A woman climbed out, too—the woman who would inform the world of his tragic death. He looked at his watch and smiled. She was late. She always was.

36

HIGHGATE, LONDON

A BSOLUTELY NOT," said Samantha Cooke. "Not now, not ever. Not in a million bloody years."

"Why not?"

"Shall I count the reasons?"

She was standing in the middle of the sitting room, one hand suspended, the palm upturned, the inquisitor awaiting her answer. Upon entering, she had dropped her handbag onto the seat of a faded wing chair, but she had yet to remove her sodden coat. Her hair was ash blond and shoulder length, her eyes were blue and naturally probing. At present, they were fixed incredulously on Gabriel's face. A year earlier he had given Samantha Cooke and her newspaper, the *Telegraph*, one of the biggest exclusives in the history of British journalism—an interview with Madeline Hart, the Russian spy who had been the prime minister's secret lover. Now he was asking for a favor in return. Another exclusive, this one concerning his death.

"For starters," she was saying, "it wouldn't be ethical. Not by a mile."

"I do love it when British journalists talk about ethics."

"I don't work for a tabloid. I work for a quality broadsheet."

"Which is why I need you. If the story appears in the *Telegraph*, people will think it's true. If it appears in the—"

"You've made your point." She shed her coat and tossed it atop her handbag. "I think I need a drink."

Gabriel nodded toward the trolley.

"Join me?"

"It's a bit early in the day for me, Samantha."

"Me, too. I have a story to write."

"What's it about?"

"Jonathan Lancaster's newest plan to fix the National Health Service. Truly riveting stuff."

"I have a better story."

"I'm sure you do." She picked up a bottle of Beefeater, hesitated, and went for the Dewar's instead: two fingers in a cut-glass tumbler, ice, enough water to keep her wits about her. "Who does this house belong to?"

"It's been in the family for many years."

"I never realized you were an English Jew." She lifted a decorative bowl from an end table and turned it over.

"What are you looking for?"

"Bugs."

"The pest control people came last week."

"I was referring to listening devices."

"Oh."

She peered into a lampshade.

"Don't bother."

She lifted her eyes to him but said nothing.

"Have you never published a story that turned out to be wrong?"

"Not intentionally."

"Really?"

"Not of this magnitude," she elaborated.

"I see."

"On occasion," she said, the glass hovering beneath her lips, "I have found it necessary to put an incomplete story into print so that the target of the story feels compelled to finish it."

"Interrogators do the same thing."

"But I don't waterboard my subjects or pull out their fingernails."

"You should. You'd get better stories."

She smiled in spite of herself. "Why?" she asked. "Why do you want me to kill you in print?"

"I'm afraid I can't tell you that."

"But you have to tell me. Otherwise, there's no story." She was right, and she knew it. "Let's start with the basics, shall we? When did you die?"

"Yesterday afternoon."

"Where?"

"A British military hospital."

"Which one?"

"Can't say."

"Long illness?"

"Actually, I was severely injured in a bombing."

Her smile evaporated. She placed her drink carefully on the end table. "Where do the lies end and the truth begin?"

"Not lies, Samantha. Deception."

"Where?" she asked again.

"I was the operative who warned British intelligence about the bomb on Brompton Road. I was one of the men who tried to move the pedestrians to safety before it exploded." He paused, then added, "And I was the target."

"Can you prove it?"

"Look at the CCTV video."

"I've seen it. It could be anyone."

"But it isn't anyone, Samantha. It was Gabriel Allon. And now he's dead."

She finished her drink and made another: more Dewar's, less water.

"I'd have to tell my editor."

"Impossible."

"I'd trust my editor with my life."

"But it's not your life we're talking about. It's mine."

"You don't have a life anymore, remember? You're dead."

Gabriel stared at the ceiling and exhaled slowly. He was growing weary of the fencing match.

"I'm sorry I brought you all the way here," he said after a moment. "Mr. Davies will run you back to your office. Let's pretend this never happened."

"But I haven't finished my drink."

"What about your piece on Jonathan Lancaster's plan to save the NHS?"

"It's rubbish."

"The plan or the piece?"

"Both." She walked over to the drinks trolley and used the silver tongs to lift a lump of ice from the bucket. "You've already given me a rather good story, you know."

"Trust me, Samantha. There's more."

"How did you know there was a bomb in that car?"

"I can't tell you that yet."

"Who was the woman?"

"She wasn't Anna Huber. And she wasn't from Germany."

"Where was she from?"

"A bit farther to the east."

Samantha Cooke allowed the ice to fall into her drink and then laid the tongs thoughtfully upon the trolley. Her back was turned to Gabriel. Even so, he could see that she was engaged in a profound struggle with her journalistic conscience.

"She's Russian? Is that what you're saying?"

Gabriel didn't respond.

"I'll take your silence as a yes. The question is, why would a Russian leave a car bomb on Brompton Road?"

"You tell me."

She made a show of thought. "I suppose they wanted to send a message to Jonathan Lancaster."

"And the nature of the message?"

"Don't fuck with us," she said coldly. "Especially when it comes to matters of money. Those drilling rights in the North Sea would have been worth billions to the Kremlin. And Lancaster snatched them away."

"Actually, I was the one who snatched them away. Which is why the Russian president and his henchmen wanted me dead."

"And now you want to make them think they succeeded?"

He nodded.

"Why?"

"Because it will make my job easier."

"What job?"

He said nothing.

"I see," she said softly. She sat down and drank some of her whisky. "If it were ever to become public that I—"

"I think you know me better than that."

"How would you want it sourced?"

"British intelligence."

"Another lie."

"Deception," he corrected her gently.

"And if I call your service?"

"They won't answer. But if you call this number," he said, handing her a slip of paper, "a rather taciturn gentleman will confirm my untimely passing."

"Does he have a name?"

"Uzi Navot."

"The chief of the Office?"

Gabriel nodded. "Call him on an open line. And whatever you do, don't mention the fact that you spoke to the decedent recently. Moscow Center will be listening."

"I'll need a British source. A real one."

He handed her another slip of paper. Another telephone number. "It's his private line. Don't abuse the privilege."

She tucked both numbers into her handbag.

"How quickly can you get it into print?"

"If I crash it, I can do it for tomorrow's paper."

"What time will it appear on the Web site?"

"Midnight or so."

A silence fell between them. She raised the drink to her lips but stopped. She had a long night ahead of her.

"What happens when the world discovers you're not dead?" she asked.

"Who says they will?"

"You don't intend to stay dead, do you?"

"There's one major advantage," he said.

"What's that?"

"No one will ever try to kill me again."

She placed her drink on the end table and rose. "Is there anything special you want me to say about you?"

"Say that I loved my country and my people. And say that I was very fond of England, too."

Gabriel helped her into her coat. She slung her handbag over her shoulder and extended her hand. "It was a pleasure almost getting to know you," she said. "I think I'm going to miss you."

"No more tears now, Samantha."

"No," she said. "We will think upon revenge."

37

WORMWOOD COTTAGE, DARTMOOR

WHEN GABRIEL RETURNED TO Wormwood Cottage that evening, he found
an official-looking sedan parked in the
drive. In the kitchen Miss Coventry was clearing
dinner from the table, and in the study two men
were hunched over a heated game of chess. Both
combatants were smoking. The pieces looked like
soldiers lost in the fog of war.

"Who's winning?" asked Gabriel.

"Who do you think?" replied Ari Shamron. He
looked at Keller and asked, "Are you ever going to
move?"

Keller did. Shamron exhaled sadly and added
Keller's second knight to his tiny prisoner-of-war
camp. The pieces stood in two neat rows next to
the ashtray. Shamron had always imposed a certain
discipline on those unfortunate enough to fall into
his hands.

"Eat something," he said to Gabriel. "This won't
take long."

Miss Coventry had left a plate of lamb and peas in
a warm oven. He ate alone at the kitchen table and

listened to the game unfolding in the next room. The click of the chess pieces, the snap of Shamron's old Zippo lighter: it was oddly comforting. From Keller's agonized silence he inferred the battle was not going well. He washed his plate and cutlery, placed them on the rack to dry, and returned to the sitting room. Shamron was warming his hands against the coal-and-wood fire in the grate. He wore pressed khaki trousers, a white oxford cloth shirt, and an old leather bomber jacket with a tear in the left shoulder. Firelight reflected in the lenses of his ugly steel spectacles.

"Well?" asked Gabriel.

"He fought hard, but to no avail."

"How's his game?"

"Courageous, skillful, but lacking in strategic vision. He takes great pleasure in killing, but hasn't the sense to realize that sometimes it's better to let an enemy live than put him to the sword." Shamron glanced at Gabriel and smiled. "He's an operator, not a planner."

Shamron returned his gaze to the fire. "Is this how you imagined it would be?"

"What's that?"

"Your last night on earth."

"Yes," said Gabriel. "This is exactly how I imagined it would be."

"Trapped in a safe house with me. A British safe house," Shamron added with disdain. He looked around at the walls and ceiling. "Are they listening?"

"They say they're not."

"Do you trust them?"

"Yes."

"You shouldn't. In fact," Shamron said, "you should never have got mixed up in this quest for Quinn in the first place. For the record, I was against it. Uzi overruled me."

"Since when do you listen to Uzi?"

Shamron shrugged, conceding the point. "I've had an empty box next to Eamon Quinn's name for quite some time," he said. "I wanted you and your friend to put a check in it before another plane fell out of the sky."

"The box is still empty."

"Not for long." Shamron's lighter flared. The acrid smell of Turkish tobacco mixed with the scent of English wood and coal.

"And what about you?" asked Gabriel. "Did you think it would end this way?"

"With your death?"

Gabriel nodded.

"Too many times to count."

"There was that night in the Empty Quarter," said Gabriel.

"What about Harwich?"

"And Moscow."

"Yes," said Shamron. "We'll always have Moscow. Moscow is why we're here."

He smoked in silence for a moment. Normally, Gabriel would have pleaded with him to stop, but not now. Shamron was grieving. He was about to lose a son.

"Your friend from the *Telegraph* just got off the phone with Uzi."

"How did it go?"

"Apparently, he spoke quite well of you. A towering talent, a great loss to the country. It seems Israel is less safe tonight." Shamron paused, then added, "I think he actually enjoyed it."

"Which part?"

"All of it. After all," Shamron said, "if you're dead, you can't become the next chief."

Gabriel smiled.

"Don't get any ideas," said Shamron. "As soon as this is over, you're going home to Jerusalem, where you will experience a miraculous resurrection."

"Just like—"

Shamron held up a hand. He had been raised in a village in eastern Poland where there had been regular pogroms. He had yet to make his peace with Christianity.

"I'm surprised you didn't come to England with an extraction team," said Gabriel.

"The thought crossed my mind."

"But?"

"It's important we send a message to the Russians that they will pay a heavy price if they assassinate our chief in waiting. The irony of it is that the message will be delivered by you."

"Do you think Russians understand irony?"

"Tolstoy did. But the tsar only understands force."

"What about the Iranians?"

Shamron considered the question before answering. "They have less to lose," he said finally. "Therefore they will have to be handled more carefully."

He dropped the end of his cigarette into the fire and coaxed another from his crumpled packet.

"The man you're looking for is in Vienna. He's staying at the InterContinental Hotel. Housekeeping has arranged accommodations for you and Keller. You'll find two old friends there as well. Use them as you see fit."

"What about Eli?"

"He's still sitting in that dump in Lisbon."

"Get him to Vienna."

"Do you want to keep the Lisbon apartment under watch?"

"No," said Gabriel. "Quinn will never set foot there again. Lisbon has served its purpose."

Shamron nodded his head slowly in agreement. "As far as your communications," he said, "we'll have to do it old school, the way we did during Wrath of God."

"It's hard to go old school in the modern world."

"You have the ability to make a four-hundred-year-old painting look new again. I'm sure you'll think of something." Shamron consulted his wristwatch. "I wish you could make one last phone call to your wife, but I'm afraid it's not possible under the circumstances."

"How's she taking word of my death?"

"As well as can be expected." Shamron glanced at Gabriel. "You're a lucky man. There aren't many women who would let their husbands go to war against the Kremlin in the final weeks of a pregnancy."

"It's part of the deal."

"That's what I thought, too. I devoted my life to my people and my country. And in the process I drove away everyone I ever held dear." Shamron paused, then added, "Everyone but you."

Outside, it was beginning to rain again, a sudden

onslaught that sent fat drops hissing onto the grate. Shamron seemed not to notice; he was staring at his wristwatch. Time had always been his enemy, never more so than now.

"How much longer?" he asked.

"Not long," replied Gabriel.

Shamron smoked in silence as the raindrops sacrificed themselves upon the red-hot grate.

"Is this how you imagined it would be?" he asked.

"It's exactly how I pictured it."

"A terrible thing, isn't it?"

"What's that, Ari?"

"For the child to die before the parent. It upends the natural order of things." He dropped his cigarette into the fire. "One can't grieve properly. One can only think of vengeance."

Ari Shamron, like Gabriel, had reached only limited accommodation with the modern world. He carried a mobile cellular device grudgingly, for he knew better than most the degree to which such contraptions could be turned against their users. Presently, it was resting in the wooden box on Parish's desk reserved for the prohibited possessions of "company." Parish was not ashamed to admit that he did not care for the old man. *The smoking! My word, the smoking.* Worse than the young Englishman who was always walking the moors. The old man smelled like an ashtray. Looked like death warmed over. *And the teeth!* Had a smile like a steel trap and just about as pleasant.

It was unclear whether the old man planned to

spend the night. He had given no indication of his plans, and Parish had received no guidance from Vauxhall Cross, save for a curious note regarding the Web site of the *Telegraph* newspaper. Parish was to check it regularly beginning at midnight. A story would appear there that would be of interest to the two men from Israel. Vauxhall Cross didn't bother to say *why* it would be of interest. Apparently, it would be self-evident. Parish was to print out the story and deliver it to the two men without comment and with appropriate solemnity, whatever that meant. Parish had worked for MI6 for nearly thirty years in one capacity or another. He was used to strange instructions from headquarters. In his experience, they went hand-in-hand with important operations.

And so he remained at his desk late that night, long after Miss Coventry had been driven home to her dreary Devon village, and long after the security guards, worn thin after a day of chasing the young Englishman across the moors, had turned in for the night. The installation had gone electronic, which meant that it was being protected by machines rather than men. Parish read a few pages of P. D. James, bless her soul, and listened to a bit of Handel on the radio. Mainly he listened to the rain. Another dirty night. When would it ever end?

Finally, at the stroke of midnight, he opened the Web browser on his computer and keyed in the address for the *Telegraph*. It was the usual drivel: a Westminster row over the NHS, a bombing in Baghdad, something about a pop star's love life that Parish found deeply repellent. There was nothing, however, that looked as though it would be remotely of interest to the "company" from the Holy Land. Oh, there was some faint glimmer of hope regarding the Iran nuclear negotiations, but surely they didn't need Parish to tell them about that.

So he returned to his P. D. James and his Handel until five minutes past, when he clicked REFRESH and saw the same rubbish as before. At ten past nothing had changed. But when he refreshed the page at twelve fifteen it froze like a block of ice. Parish was no expert in cybermatters, but he knew that Web sites often became unresponsive during periods of transition or heavy traffic. He knew, too, that no amount of clicking or tapping would speed the process, so he allowed a few more lines of the novel to flow past his eyes while the Web page wriggled free of its digital restraints.

It happened at 12:17 precisely. The page rolled over, three words appeared at the top. Big typeface, big as Dartmoor. Parish took the Lord's name in vain, immediately regretted it, and clicked PRINT. Then he shoved the pages into his coat pocket and struck out across the courtyard to the back door of the cottage. And all the while he was turning over the curious instructions he had received from Vauxhall Cross. *Appropriate solemnity, indeed!* But how exactly was one supposed to tell a man he was dead?

38

LONDON–THE KREMLIN

T LAY THERE for the better part of an hour, unreported by the rest of the media, perhaps unnoticed. Then a producer from the BBC World Service, prompted by a phone call from a *Telegraph* editor, inserted the story into the one o'clock news bulletin. Israel Radio was listening, and within a few minutes phones were ringing and reporters were being roused from their beds. So, too, were members of the country's influential security and intelligence services, past and present. On the record, no one would go near it. Off the record, they suggested it was probably true. The Ministry of Foreign Affairs said only that it was looking into the report; the prime minister's office said it hoped there was some mistake. Nevertheless, as the first rays of sun fell upon Jerusalem that morning, somber music filled the airwaves. Gabriel Allon, Israel's avenging angel, next in line to be the chief of the Office, was dead.

In London, however, the news of Allon's death was an occasion for controversy rather than sorrow. He'd had a long history on British soil, some of which was known to the public, most of which thankfully was not. There were his operations against Zizi al-Bakari, the Saudi financier of terror, and Ivan Kharkov, the Kremlin's favorite arms dealer. There was his dramatic rescue of Elizabeth Halton, the daughter of the American ambassador, outside Westminster Abbey, and there was the nightmare in Covent Garden. But why had he been following the bomb car along Brompton Road? And why had he made a headlong dash toward a white Ford trapped in the stalled traffic? Was he working in concert with MI6, or had he returned to London of his own accord? Was Israel's notorious intelligence service somehow to blame for the tragedy? British intelligence refused all comment, as did the Metropolitan Police. Prime Minister Lancaster, while touring a distressed state school in London's East End, ignored a reporter's question about the matter, which the rest of the British media took as proof the story was true. The leader of the opposition demanded a parliamentary inquiry, but the imam of London's most radical mosque could scarcely contain his joy. He called Allon's death "long overdue and a welcome gift from Allah to the Palestinian people and the Islamic world at large." The Archbishop of Canterbury gently criticized the remarks as "unhelpful."

At Green's Restaurant and Oyster Bar, an elegant watering hole in St. James's frequented by inhabitants of London's art world, the mood was decidedly funereal. They had known Gabriel Allon not as an intelligence operative but as one of the finest art restorers of his generation—though some had been unwittingly drawn into his operations, and a few had been willing accomplices. Julian Isherwood, the noted dealer who had employed Allon for longer than he cared to remember, was inconsolable with grief. Even tubby Oliver Dimbleby, the lecherous dealer from Bury Street who was thought to be incapable of tears, was seen sobbing over a glass of Montrachet he'd poached from Roddy Hutchinson. Jeremy Crabbe, the director of Old Master paintings at the venerable Bonhams auction house, called Allon "one of the greats, truly." Not to be outdone, Simon Mendenhall, the permanently suntanned chief auctioneer from Christie's, said the art world would never be the same. Simon had never laid eyes on Gabriel Allon and probably couldn't pick him out of a police lineup. And yet somehow he had spoken words of undeniable truth, something he rarely did.

There was sadness, too, across the pond in America. A former president for whom Allon had run many secret errands said the Israeli intelligence officer had played a crucial role in keeping the U.S. homeland safe from another 9/11-style terror spectacular. Adrian Carter, the longtime chief of the CIA's National Clandestine Service, called him "a partner, a friend, perhaps the bravest man I have ever known." Zoe Reed, an anchor on CNBC, faltered while reading a scripted account of Allon's death. Sarah Bancroft, a special curator at New York's Museum of Modern Art, inexplicably canceled her appointments for the day. A few hours later she told her secretary she would be taking the remainder of the week off. Those who witnessed her abrupt departure from the museum described her as distraught.

It was no secret that Allon had been fond of Italy, and for the most part Italy had been fond of him, too. At the Vatican, His Holiness Pope Paul VII repaired to his private chapel upon hearing the news, while his powerful private secretary, Monsignor Luigi Donati, made several urgent phone calls, trying to determine whether it was true. One of the calls was to General Cesare Ferrari, chief of the Carabinieri's famed Art Squad. The general had nothing to report. Nor did Francesco Tiepolo, the owner of a prominent Venetian restoration firm who had retained Allon to secretly restore several of the city's most prominent altarpieces. Allon's wife was from the ancient Jewish ghetto, and his father-in-law was the chief rabbi of the city. Donati placed several calls to the rabbi's office and home. All went unanswered, leaving the papal private secretary no choice but to assume the worst.

In several other places around the world, however, the reaction to Allon's death was far different—especially inside the complex of heavily guarded buildings located in the southwestern Moscow suburb of Yasenevo. The complex had once been the headquarters of the KGB's First Chief Directorate. Now it belonged to the SVR. Even so, most of those who worked there still referred to it by its old KGB name, which was Moscow Center.

In most parts of the complex, life went on normally that day. But not in the third-floor office of Colonel Alexei Rozanov. He had arrived at Yasenevo

at three a.m. in a blinding snowstorm and had spent
the remainder of the morning in a tense exchange
of cables with the SVR's *resident* in London, a close
friend named Dmitry Ulyanin. The cables were
protected by the SVR's latest encryption and transmitted over the service's most secure link. Nevertheless, Rozanov and Ulyanin discussed the matter
as though it were a routine problem involving the
visa request of a British businessman. By one that
afternoon, Ulyanin and his well-staffed London
rezidentura had seen enough to convince them that
the *Telegraph* report was true. Rozanov, a cynic by
nature, remained skeptical, however. Finally, at two
o'clock, he snatched up the receiver of his secure
phone and dialed Ulyanin directly. Ulyanin had encouraging news.

"We spotted the old man leaving the big building
on the Thames about an hour ago."

The big building on the Thames was the headquarters of MI6, and the old man was Ari Shamron. The London *rezidentura* had been following
Shamron on and off since his arrival in the United
Kingdom.

"Where did he go next?"

"He went to Heathrow and boarded an El Al
flight to Ben-Gurion. By the way, Alexei, the flight
was delayed by several minutes."

"Why?"

"It seemed the ground crew had to load one final
item into the cargo hold."

"What was that?"

"A coffin."

The secure line crackled and hissed during the

ten long seconds during which Alexei Rozanov did not speak.

"Are you sure it was a coffin?" he asked finally.

"Alexei, please."

"Maybe it was a recently deceased British Jew who wished to be buried in the Promised Land."

"It wasn't," said Ulyanin. "The old man stood at attention on the tarmac while the coffin was being loaded."

Rozanov killed the connection, hesitated, and then dialed the most important number in Russia. A male voice answered. Rozanov recognized it. Inside the Kremlin the man was known only as the Gatekeeper.

"I need to see the Boss," Rozanov said.

"The Boss is tied up all afternoon."

"It's important."

"So is our relationship with Germany."

Rozanov swore softly. He'd forgotten that the German chancellor was in town.

"It will only take a few minutes," he said.

"There's a short break between the last meeting and the dinner. I might be able to squeeze you in."

"Tell him I have good news."

"You'd better," the Gatekeeper said, "because the chancellor is giving him quite an earful about Ukraine."

"What time should I be there?"

"Five o'clock," said the Gatekeeper, and the line went dead. Alexei Rozanov replaced the receiver and watched the snow falling on the grounds of Yasenevo. Then he thought about a coffin being loaded onto an Israeli jetliner at Heathrow Airport while an old man stood at attention on the tarmac, and for the first time in almost a year he actually smiled.

In point of fact, it had been ten months to the day. Ten months since Alexei Rozanov had learned that his old friend and comrade Pavel Zhirov had been found in a birch forest in Tver Oblast, frozen solid, two bullets in his brain. Ten months since he had been summoned to the Kremlin for a meeting with the federal president himself. The Boss wanted Rozanov to undertake a mission of vengeance. A series of messy killings wouldn't do. The Boss wanted to punish his enemies in a way that would sow discord among their ranks and make them think twice about ever interfering in Russia's affairs again. More than anything, though, the Boss wanted to make certain that Gabriel Allon never became chief of Israel's secret intelligence service. The Boss had big plans. He wanted to restore Russia's faded glory, reclaim its lost empire. And Gabriel Allon, an intelligence operative from a minuscule country, was one of his most meddlesome opponents.

Rozanov had thought long and hard about his plan, had plotted it with care and assembled the necessary pieces. Then, with the blessing of the federal president, he had ordered the killing that had set the operational wheels turning. Graham Seymour, the chief of MI6, had reacted the way Rozanov had expected he would. So had Allon. Now his body lay in the belly of a jetliner bound for Ben-Gurion Airport. Rozanov supposed they would bury him on the Mount of Olives, next to the grave of his son.

He didn't really much care. He cared only that Allon was no longer among the living.

He opened the bottom drawer of his desk. It contained a bottle, a glass, and a packet of Dunhills, a taste for which he had acquired while working in London before the collapse of the Soviet Union— the great catastrophe, as Rozanov referred to it. He had touched neither alcohol nor tobacco in ten months. Now he poured himself a generous measure of vodka and tapped loose one of the Dunhills. Something made him hesitate before lighting it. He reached for the phone again, stopped, and inserted a DVD into his computer instead. The disk whirred; Brompton Road appeared on his screen. He watched it all from the beginning. Then he watched the man running headlong toward the white car. As the image turned to hash, Alexei Rozanov smiled a second time. "The fool," he said softly, and he struck a match.

Rozanov ordered a car from the motor pool for four o'clock. Because he was going against Moscow's nightmarish traffic, it took only forty minutes to reach the Kremlin's Borovitskaya Tower. He entered the Grand Presidential Palace and, escorted by a waiting aide, made his way upstairs to the federal president's office. The Gatekeeper was at his desk in the anteroom. His dour expression was identical to the one usually worn by the president himself.

"You're early, Alexei."

"Better than late."

"Have a seat."

Rozanov sat. Five o'clock came and went. So
did six. Finally, at half past, the Gatekeeper came
for him.

"He can give you two minutes."

"Two minutes are all I need."

The Gatekeeper led Rozanov along a marble hall
to a pair of heavy golden doors. A guard opened
one, Rozanov entered alone. The office was a cav-
ernous space, darkened except for a sphere of light
that illuminated the desk where the Boss sat. He
was looking down at a stack of papers and continued
to do so long after Rozanov arrived. The SVR man
stood before the desk in silence, his hands clasped
protectively over his genitals.

"Well?" asked the Boss finally. "Is it true or not?"

"The London *rezident* says it is."

"I'm not asking the London *rezident*. I'm asking
you."

"It's true, sir."

The Boss looked up. "You're sure?"

Rozanov nodded.

"Say it, Alexei."

"He's dead, sir."

The Boss looked down at his documents again.
"Remind me how much we owe the Irishman."

"Under our agreement," Rozanov said judiciously,
"he was to receive ten million on completion of the
first phase of the operation and another ten million
for the second."

"Where is he now?"

"In an SVR safe house."

"*Where*, Alexei?"

"Budapest."

"And the woman?"

"Here in Moscow," answered Rozanov, "awaiting a departure order."

A silence dropped between them, like the silence of a cemetery at night. Rozanov was relieved when the Boss finally spoke.

"I'd like to make a small change," he said.

"What sort of change?"

"Tell the Irishman he'll receive all twenty million on completion of *both* phases of the operation."

"That could be a problem."

"No, it won't."

The Boss pushed a file folder across his massive desk. Rozanov lifted the cover and looked inside. Death solves all problems, he thought. No man, no problem.

39

LONDON–VIENNA

BUT GABRIEL ALLON was not dead, of course. In fact, at the very moment Alexei Rozanov was entering the Kremlin, he was boarding a British Airways flight at London's Heathrow Airport. His hair had been tinted silver; his eyes were no longer green. In his coat pocket was a worn British passport and several credit cards in the same name, a gift from Graham Seymour, given with the approval of the prime minister himself. His seat was in first class, third row, next to the window. As he dropped into it, a flight attendant offered him a drink and a selection of newspapers. He chose the *Telegraph* and read of his death as the redbrick western suburbs of London sank away beneath him.

The flight from Heathrow to Vienna was two hours in duration. He pretended to read, he pretended to sleep, he picked at his plastic in-flight meal, he rebuffed a kindly attempt at conversation by his seatmate. Dead men, it seemed, did not talk on airplanes. Nor did they carry cellular devices.

When the plane touched down at Vienna's Schwechat Airport, he was the only passenger in first class who did not automatically reach for a mobile phone. Yes, he thought as he removed his bag from the overhead bin, death had its advantages.

In the concourse he followed the signs to passport control, pausing now and again to take his bearings, despite the fact that he could find his way there blindfolded. The eyes of the young immigration officer lingered on his face a moment too long.

"Mr. Stewart?" he asked, looking at the passport now.

"Yes," replied Gabriel in a neutral accent.

"Your first time in Austria?"

"No."

The border policeman thumbed through the pages of the passport and found proof of previous visits.

"What brings you here this time?"

"Music."

The Austrian stamped the passport and returned it without comment. Gabriel walked to the arrivals hall, where Christopher Keller was standing next to a currency-exchange kiosk. He followed Gabriel outside to the short-term parking lot. A car had been left there, an Audi A6, slate gray.

"Better than a Škoda," said Keller.

Gabriel pried the key loose from the left rear wheel well and searched the undercarriage for a bomb. Then he unlocked the doors, tossed his bag into the backseat, and climbed behind the wheel.

"Maybe I should drive," said Keller.

"No," replied Gabriel as he started the engine. It was his turf.

He had no need of a map or navigation device; his memory served as his guide. He followed the Ost Autobahn to the Danaukanal and then headed west through the apartment blocks of Landstrasse to the Stadtpark. The InterContinental Hotel stood on the southern flank of the park, on the Johannes-gasse. There were an unusual number of uniformed police in the surrounding streets and more in the hotel's drive.

"The nuclear talks," explained a valet as Gabriel stepped from the car and removed his bag from the backseat.

"Which delegation is staying here?" he asked, but the valet hoisted an insincere smile and said, "Enjoy your stay, Herr Stewart."

There were more police in the lobby, uniformed and plainclothes, and a few tieless thugs who looked like Iranian security. Gabriel and Keller walked past them to Reception, checked into their rooms, and rode the elevator to the fourth floor. Keller had been assigned 428. Gabriel was in 409. He swiped his cardkey and hesitated briefly before twisting the latch. Inside, Mozart issued softly from the bedside radio. He switched it off, searched the room thoroughly, and hung his clothing neatly in the closet for the benefit of the housekeeping staff. Then he picked up the telephone and dialed the hotel operator.

"Feliks Adler, please."

"My pleasure."

The phone rang twice. Then Eli Lavon came on the line.

"What room are you in, Herr Adler?"

"Seven twelve."

Gabriel hung up the phone and headed upstairs.

40

INTERCONTINENTAL HOTEL, VIENNA

Eli Lavon unchained the door to him and drew him hastily inside. Lavon was not the only one present. Yaakov Rossman was peering through a slit in the curtains, and stretched upon the double bed, his eyes fixed dully on a Premier League football match, was Mikhail Abramov. Neither man seemed particularly relieved to see Gabriel still among the living, especially Mikhail. Mikhail should have died a couple of times himself.

"Good news from home," said Lavon. "Your body arrived safely. It's on its way to Jerusalem now."

"How far are we taking this?"

"Just far enough so that the Russians notice."

"And my wife?"

"She's grieving, of course, but she's surrounded by friends."

Gabriel plucked the remote from Mikhail's fingers and surfed the news channels. Apparently, his fifteen minutes were over, for even the BBC had moved on. He paused on CNN, where a reporter was standing outside the headquarters of the International Atomic Energy Agency, site of the negotiations between the United States, its European allies, and the Islamic Republic of Iran. Unfortunately for Israel and the Sunni Arab states of the Middle East, the two sides were close to a deal that would leave Iran as a threshold nuclear power.

"It seems your death couldn't have come at a worse time," said Lavon.

"I did the best I could." Gabriel glanced around at the other occupants of the room and added, "We all did."

"Yes," agreed Lavon. "But so did the Iranians."

Gabriel was looking at the television screen again. "Is our friend in there?"

Lavon nodded. "He doesn't sit at the table with the negotiators, but he's part of the Iranian support staff."

"Have we had any contact with him since he arrived in Vienna?"

"Why don't you ask his case officer?"

Gabriel looked at Yaakov Rossman, who was still peering into the street below. He had short black hair and a pockmarked face. Yaakov had spent his career running agents in some of the most dangerous places in the world—the West Bank, the Gaza Strip, Lebanon, Syria, and now Iran. He lied to his agents as a matter of course and knew that on occasion they lied to him, too. Some lies were an acceptable part of the bargain, but not the lie he had been told by his prized Iranian source. It had been part of a plot to assassinate the future chief of Yaakov's service, and for that the Iranian would have to be punished. Not immediately, though. First he would be given a chance to atone for his sins.

"I usually pop into town," Yaakov explained, "whenever the two sides are negotiating. The Americans aren't always so forthcoming in their readouts of what's going on at the table. Reza fills in the pieces for us."

"So he won't be surprised to hear from you?"

"Not at all. In fact," added Yaakov, "he's probably wondering why I haven't made contact already."

"He probably thinks you're sitting shiva for me in Jerusalem."

"Let's hope so."

"Where's the family?"

"They crossed the border a couple of hours ago."

"Any problems?"

Yaakov shook his head.

"And Reza doesn't know anything?"

Yaakov smiled. "Not yet."

He resumed his surveillance of the street. Gabriel looked at Lavon and asked, "What room is he staying in?"

Lavon nodded toward the wall.

"How did you manage that?"

"We hacked into the system and got his room number."

"Been inside?"

"Whenever we feel like it."

The wizards in the Office's Technology department had developed a magic cardkey capable of opening any electronic hotel room door in the world. The first swipe stole the code. The second opened the deadbolt.

"And we left a little something behind," said Lavon.

He reached down and raised the volume on a laptop computer. A Bach concerto was playing on the bedside radio in the next room.

"What's the coverage?" asked Gabriel.

"Room only. We didn't bother with the phone. He never uses it for outside calls."

"Anything unusual?"

"He talks in his sleep, and he's a secret drinker. Other than that, nothing."

Lavon lowered the volume on the laptop; Gabriel looked at the television screen. This time, a reporter was standing on a balcony overlooking the Old City of Jerusalem.

"I hear he was about to be a father," said Mikhail.

"Really?" asked Gabriel.

"Twins."

"You don't say."

Mikhail, affecting boredom, switched back to the football game. Gabriel returned to his room and waited for the phone to ring.

The gleaming headquarters of the International Atomic Energy Agency was located on the opposite bank of the river Danube, in a district of Vienna known as the International City. The talks between the Americans and the Iranians continued there until eight p.m., when both sides, in a rare show of accord, agreed it was time to break for the night. The chief American negotiator appeared briefly before reporters to say that progress had been made. Her Iranian counterpart was less sanguine. He muttered something about American intransigence and climbed into the back of his official limousine.

It was half past eight by the time the Iranian motorcade arrived at the InterContinental Hotel. The delegation crossed the lobby under heavy security and boarded several elevators that had been held for their convenience, much to the annoyance of the hotel's other guests. Only one member of the delegation, Reza Nazari, a veteran VEVAK officer who was posing as an Iranian diplomat, was staying on the seventh floor. He made his way along the empty corridor to Room 710, inserted his cardkey into the slot, and entered. The sound of the door closing was audible in the next room, where only one man, Yaakov Rossman, remained. Owing to the transmitter concealed beneath the Iranian's bed, Yaakov heard other sounds as well. A coat tossed across a chair, shoes hitting the floor, a call to room service, a toilet flushing. Yaakov lowered the volume on the laptop computer, lifted the receiver of the room phone, and dialed. Two rings, then the voice of Reza Nazari. In English, Yaakov explained what he wanted.

"It's not possible, my friend," said Nazari. "Not tonight."

"All things are possible, Reza. Especially tonight."

The Iranian hesitated, then asked, "When?"

"Five minutes."

"Where?"

Yaakov told the Iranian what to do, hung up the phone, and raised the volume on the laptop. A man canceling his room service order, a man pulling on

his shoes and overcoat, a door closing, footsteps in
the hall. Yaakov reached for the phone again and
dialed Room 409. Two rings, then the voice of a
dead man. The dead man sounded pleased by the
news. All things were possible, thought Yaakov as
he hung up the phone. Especially tonight.

Three floors below, Gabriel rose from his bed and
walked calmly to the window. And in his thoughts
he was calculating how long it would be before the
man who had conspired to kill him appeared in the
hotel's floodlit forecourt. Forty-five seconds was all
it took before he shot from the entrance. Viewed
from above, he was an unthreatening figure, a speck
in the night, a nothing man. He made his way to the
street, waited for the sparse evening traffic to pass,
and then crossed into the Stadtpark, a rhombus of
darkness in an otherwise illuminated city. No one
from the Iranian delegation followed him, only a
small man in a neat fedora who was registered at the
hotel under the name Feliks Adler.

Gabriel went to the phone and made two calls,
one to the guest in Room 428, the other to the valet
to request his car. Then he shoved a Beretta into the
waistband of his jeans, pulled on a leather jacket,
and tugged a flat cap low over the face that had appeared on far too many television screens that day.
The corridor outside his room was empty, as was
the elevator that bore him to the lobby. He passed
unnoticed through the security men and police
officers and headed into the cold night. The Audi
waited in the drive; Keller was already behind the

wheel. Gabriel directed him to the eastern edge of
the Stadtpark, and they were idling curbside when
Reza Nazari emerged into the lamplight. A Mercedes waited there, headlamps doused, two men
inside. Nazari slid into the backseat and the car accelerated rapidly away. The Iranian did not know it
then, but he had just made the second biggest mistake of his life.

Gabriel watched the taillights of the car disappear down the graceful Viennese street. Then he
saw Herr Adler emerge from the park. He removed
his hat, the signal the Iranian was clean, and started
back to the hotel. Herr Adler had requested permission to skip that evening's festivities. Herr Adler
had never been one for the rough stuff.

41

LOWER AUSTRIA

W HERE ARE WE GOING?"
"Somewhere quiet."
"I can't be away from the hotel for long."
"Don't worry, Reza. No one's going to be turning into a pumpkin tonight."

Yaakov took a long look over his shoulder. Vienna was a smudge of yellow light on the horizon. Before them lay the rolling cropland and vineyards of Lower Austria. Mikhail was driving a few kilometers over the speed limit. He was holding the wheel with one hand and with the other was tapping a nervous rhythm on the shift. It seemed to annoy Reza Nazari.

"Who's your friend?" he asked Yaakov.

"You may refer to him as Isaac."

"Son of Abraham, poor kid. Good thing the archangel appeared. Otherwise . . ." His voice trailed off. He was staring out the window at the black fields. "Why aren't we meeting in our usual place?"

"A change of scenery."

"Why?"

"Did you happen to see the news today?"

"Allon?"

Yaakov nodded.

"My condolences," said the Iranian.

"Spare me, Reza."

"He was going to be the chief, was he not?"

"One heard rumors to that effect."

"So now I suppose Uzi will keep his job. He's a good man, Uzi, but he's no Gabriel Allon. Uzi got all the credit for blowing up our enrichment facilities, but everyone knows it was Allon who inserted those sabotaged centrifuges into our supply chain."

"What centrifuges?"

Reza Nazari smiled. It was a professional smile, careful, discreet. He was a small, slight man with deeply set brown eyes and a closely trimmed beard, a man of the desk rather than the field, a man of moderation—or so he had claimed when he made his initial approach to the Office two years earlier, during a working visit to Istanbul. He said he wanted to spare his country another disastrous war, that he wanted to serve as a bridge between the Office and forward-thinking men like himself inside VEVAK. The bridge had not come cheap. Nazari had been paid more than a million dollars, a staggering sum by Office standards. In exchange, he had supplied a steady stream of high-grade intelligence that had given Israel's politicians and military leaders an unprecedented window on Iranian intentions. Nazari was so valuable that the Office had created a bolt-hole for his family in the event his treachery were ever discovered. Unbeknownst to Nazari, the escape procedures had been activated earlier that day.

"We were closer to a weapon than you realized,"

Nazari was saying. "If Allon hadn't blown up those four enrichment facilities, we could have had a weapon within a year. But we rebuilt those facilities and added a few more. And now . . ."

"You're close again."

Nazari nodded. "But that doesn't seem to bother your friends in America. The president wants his deal. It's legacy time, as they say."

"The president's legacy is of no concern to the Office."

"But you share his conclusion that a nuclear Iran is inevitable. Uzi has no appetite for a military confrontation. Allon was another story, though. He would have flattened us if he had the chance." The Iranian shook his head slowly. "One wonders why he was following that car in London."

"Yes," said Yaakov. "One wonders."

A road sign floated past Nazari's window: CZECH REPUBLIC 42 KM. He looked at his watch again.

"Why didn't we meet in our usual place?"

"We have a little surprise for you, Reza."

"What kind of surprise?"

"Something to show our appreciation for everything you've done."

"How much farther?"

"Not far."

"I have to be back at my hotel by midnight at the latest."

"Don't worry, Reza. No pumpkins."

Yaakov Rossman had been entirely honest in two important respects. He did indeed have a surprise for his prized agent, and they were not far from their destination. It was a villa located about five kilometers west of the town of Eibesthal, a quaint, tidy dwelling bordered on one side by a vineyard and on the other by a dormant field. The exterior of the villa was a pleasing Italianate yellow; its windows were framed in white. It was unthreatening in every way except for its isolation. More than a kilometer separated the house from its nearest neighbor. A cry for help would go unanswered. The crack of an un-suppressed gunshot would die in the rolling terrain.

The villa was set about fifty meters from the road and reached by an unpaved drive lined with pine trees. Parked outside was an Audi A6, its engine block ticking softly, its hood warm to the touch. Mikhail pulled in next to it, killed the engine, killed the lights. Yaakov looked at Nazari and smiled hospitably.

"You didn't bring anything stupid tonight, did you, Reza?"

"Like what?"

"Like a gun."

"No gun," answered the Iranian. "Only a suicide vest."

Yaakov's smile dimmed. "Open your coat," he said.

"How long have we been working together?"

"Two years," answered Yaakov, "but tonight is different."

"Why?"

"You'll see in a minute."

"Who's in there?"

"Open your coat, Reza."

The Iranian did as he was told. Yaakov gave him a quick but thorough search. He found nothing but a billfold, a mobile phone, a packet of French cigarettes, a lighter, and a key to a room in the Vienna InterContinental. He stuffed all the items into the seat pocket and nodded into the rearview mirror. Mikhail climbed from behind the wheel and opened Nazari's door. In the sudden light Yaakov saw the first trace of something more than just apprehension in the Iranian's face.

"Something wrong, Reza?"

"You're an Israeli, I'm an Iranian. Why should I be nervous?"

"You're our most important asset, Reza. Someday they're going to write a book about us."

"May it be published long after we're dead."

Nazari stepped out of the car and with Mikhail at his side started toward the entrance of the villa. It was a walk of twenty paces, long enough for Yaakov to extract himself from the backseat and draw his weapon from his hip holster. He slipped the gun into his coat pocket and was a step behind his agent when they reached the door. It yielded to Mikhail's touch. Nazari hesitated, then, nudged by Yaakov, followed Mikhail inside.

The entrance hall was in semidarkness, but light glowed from within and wood smoke hung on the air. Mikhail led the way into the sitting room, where a large fire burned in the open hearth. Gabriel and Keller stood before it, their backs to the room, seemingly lost in thought. Seeing the two men, Nazari froze and then recoiled. Yaakov seized one arm, Mikhail the other. Together they lifted Nazari slightly so that his shoes could gain no purchase on the bare wooden floor.

Gabriel and Keller exchanged a look, a smile, a private unspoken joke at their visitor's expense. Then Gabriel turned slowly, as if until that moment he had been unaware of the commotion behind him. Nazari was wriggling, a fish on a line, his sunken eyes wide with terror. Gabriel considered him calmly, his head cocked slightly to one side, a hand resting against his chin.

"Something wrong, Reza?" he asked finally.

"You're—"

"Dead?" Gabriel smiled. "Sorry, Reza, but it appears you missed."

On the coffee table was a .45-caliber Glock, a man stopper, a weapon of mass destruction. Gabriel reached down, picked up the gun by the grip, pondered its weight and balance. He offered the gun to Keller, who held up a hand defensively, as though he were being offered an ember from the fire. Then Gabriel approached Nazari slowly and stopped three feet away from him. The gun was in Gabriel's right hand. With his left hand he reached out with the speed of a striking snake and seized Nazari's throat. Instantly, the Iranian's face took on the color of a ripened plum.

"Is there anything you wish to say to me?" asked Gabriel.

"I'm sorry," the Iranian gasped.

"So am I, Reza. But I'm afraid it's too late for that."

Gabriel squeezed harder until he could feel cartilage beginning to crack. Then he placed the barrel of the gun against Nazari's forehead and pulled the trigger. As the gun exploded, Keller turned away and looked into the fire. It was personal, he was thinking. And when it's personal, it tends to get messy.

42

LOWER AUSTRIA

THE .45-CALIBER ROUND that Gabriel fired at Reza Nazari contained no projectile, but its powder loading was sufficient to produce a report of ear-shattering volume and a muzzle flash that left a small round burn in the center of his forehead, like the prayer mark of a devout Muslim. It was also sufficient to drop Nazari to the floor like a stone. For several seconds he did not stir or appear to draw a breath. Then Yaakov knelt and gave him a backhanded slap across the face that brought him back to consciousness. "You bastard," he gasped. "You fucking bastard."

"I'd watch my mouth if I were you, Reza. Otherwise, the next round I fire will be real."

There are some men who go catatonic with fear and others who respond with useless displays of false bravery. Reza Nazari chose the second, perhaps in reaction to his training, perhaps because he feared he had nothing to lose. He gave a wild flailing kick that Gabriel evaded easily, then latched onto Mikhail's leg in an attempt to topple him. A brutal blow beneath the shoulder blades was enough to staunch the attack. Then Mikhail stepped aside to allow Yaakov to finish the job. For two years Yaakov had cared for his agent, flattered him, paid him an exorbitant sum of money. Now, for two awful minutes, he administered a beating befitting Nazari's transgressions. He avoided striking the Iranian's face, however. It was critical Nazari remained presentable.

Keller had not participated in the beating of Reza Nazari. Instead, he had quietly placed a chair, wooden and armless, before the fire. Nazari tumbled into it limply and offered no further resistance as Yaakov and Mikhail bound his torso to the back with duct tape. Next they secured his legs while Gabriel calmly reloaded the Glock. He showed each round to Nazari before thumbing it into the magazine. There were no more blanks. The weapon was loaded with live ammunition.

"You have a simple choice," said Gabriel after snapping the magazine into the grip and chambering the first round. "You can live, or you can become a martyr." He placed the tip of the barrel between Nazari's eyes. "Which will it be, Reza?"

The Iranian stared at the gun in silence. Finally, he said, "I would like to live."

"Wise choice." Gabriel lowered the gun. "But I'm afraid you don't get to live for free, Reza. You have to pay a toll."

"How much?"

"First, you're going to tell me how you and your Russian friends conspired to kill me."

"And then?"

"You're going to help me find them."

"I wouldn't advise that, Allon."

"Why not?"

"Because the man who ordered your death is far too important to be killed."

"Who was it?"

"You tell me."

"The chief of the SVR?"

"Don't be silly," Nazari said incredulously. "No SVR chief would go after you without approval. The order came from the top."

"The Russian president?"

"Of course."

"How do you know?"

"Trust me, Allon, I know."

"This might come as a surprise to you, Reza, but you're the last person in the world that I trust right now."

"I can assure you," Nazari said, staring at the gun, "the feeling is mutual."

He requested to be cut free and to be treated with a modicum of dignity. Gabriel refused both, though he did grant Nazari's wish for water, if only to clear the annoying debris from his injured throat. Yaakov held the glass to his agent's lips while he drank and afterward dabbed a few stray droplets from the front of his suit jacket. The gesture did not go unnoticed by the Iranian.

"May I have a cigarette?" he asked.

"No," replied Gabriel.

Nazari smiled. "So it's true after all. The great Gabriel Allon doesn't like tobacco smoke." Still smiling, he looked at Yaakov. "But not my friend here. I remember our first meeting in that hotel room in Istanbul. I thought we were going to set off the smoke alarm."

It seemed as good a place as any to start, so Gabriel began his interrogation there—the autumn day, two years earlier, when Reza Nazari came to Istanbul for a round of meetings with Turkish intelligence. During a break in the proceedings, he walked to a small hotel on the Bosporus and in a room upstairs had his first meeting with a man he would know only as "Mr. Taylor." He told Mr. Taylor that he wanted to betray his country, and as proof of his bona fides handed over a flash drive filled with high-grade intelligence, including documents related to Iran's nuclear program.

"Were the documents genuine?"

"Of course."

"Did you steal them?"

"I didn't have to."

"Who gave them to you?"

"My superiors at the Ministry of Intelligence."

"You were bad from the beginning?"

Nazari nodded.

"Who was your control officer?"

"I'd rather not say."

"And I'd rather not splatter your brains over the wall, but I will if I have to."

"It was Esfahani."

Mohsen Esfahani was deputy chief of VEVAK.

"What was the goal of the operation?" asked Gabriel.

"To influence the Office's thinking regarding Iranian capabilities and intentions."

"*Taqiyya.*"

"Call it what you will, Allon. We Persians have been at this a long time. Even longer than the Jews."

"If I were you, Reza, I'd keep the boasting to a minimum. Otherwise, I'm going to let Mr. Taylor have his way with you."

The Iranian fell silent. Gabriel asked about the million dollars that the Office had placed in a private bank in Luxembourg for Nazari's use.

"We assumed you were watching the money," the Iranian replied, "so Esfahani instructed me to spend some of it. I bought gifts for my children and a strand of pearls for my wife."

"Nothing for Esfahani?"

"A gold watch, but he made me return it. Mohsen is a true believer. He's like you, Allon. He's totally incorruptible."

"Wherever did you hear something like that?"

"Our file on you is very thick." Nazari paused, then added, "Almost as thick as Moscow Center's. But then, I suppose that's understandable. You've never set foot on Iranian soil, at least not that we're aware of. Russia, though . . ." He smiled. "Well, let's just say you have a lot of enemies there, Allon."

Among the many things the Office did not know about their prized agent was that he served as VE-VAK's primary liaison to the SVR. The reason was quite simple, he explained. Nazari had studied Russian history at university, spoke Russian fluently, and had operated in Afghanistan during the Soviet occupation. In Kabul he had met many KGB officers, including a young man who seemed destined for promotion. That turned out to be the case; the man was now one of Moscow Center's most powerful players. Nazari met regularly with him on issues ranging from Iran's nuclear program to the civil war in Syria, where VEVAK and the SVR had worked tirelessly to ensure the survival of their embattled client regime.

"His name?" asked Gabriel.

"Like you," replied Nazari, "he uses many different names. But if I had to guess, I'd say his real name is Rozanov."

"First name?"

"Alexei."

"Describe him."

The Iranian offered a somewhat vague description of a man who was approximately six feet tall and had thinning gray-blond hair that he combed in the manner of the Russian president.

"Age?"

"Could be fifty."

"Languages?"

"He can speak any language he sets his mind to."

"How often do you meet?"

"Once every two or three months, more often if necessary."

"Where?"

"Sometimes I travel to Moscow. Usually, we meet on neutral ground in Europe."

"What kind of neutral ground?"

"Safe houses, restaurants." He shrugged. "The usual."

"When was the last time?"

"A month ago."

"Where?"

"Copenhagen."

"Where in Copenhagen?"

"A little restaurant in the New Harbor."

"Did you talk about nukes and Syria that night?"

"Actually," said Nazari, "there was only one item on the agenda."

"What was that?"

"You."

43

LOWER AUSTRIA

B
UT THEY WERE getting ahead of themselves, because Copenhagen was not the first time that Reza Nazari and Alexei Rozanov had dwelt long and hard on the subject of Gabriel Allon. The name had featured prominently in many of their previous meetings, but never with more urgency or anger than during a dinner ten months earlier in the old town of Zurich. The SVR was in crisis. The body of Pavel Zhirov had just been found frozen solid in Tver Oblast, Madeline Hart had defected to Britain, and a Russian energy company owned by the Kremlin had just been stripped of the rights to drill for oil in the North Sea.

"And the cause of it all," said Nazari, "was you."

"Says who?"

"Says the only person who matters in Russia. Says the Boss."

"I assume the Boss wanted me dead."

"Not just dead," replied Nazari. "He wanted it done in such a way that Russia couldn't be implicated. He also wanted to punish the British. Graham Seymour, in particular."

"Which is why the Russians chose Eamon Quinn."

Nazari said nothing.

"I take it you were familiar with Quinn's name."

"I considered him a friend."

"Because you were the one who retained Quinn to build antitank weapons for Hezbollah."

Nazari nodded.

"A weapon that could make a ball of fire travel a thousand feet per second."

"They were very effective, as the IDF discovered."

Yaakov reached for Nazari in anger, but Gabriel stopped him and continued with his questioning.

"What did Rozanov want from you?"

"At that point, only an introduction."

"And you agreed?"

"When it came to you," said Nazari, "our interests intersected with those of the Russians."

At that time, Nazari resumed, Quinn was living in Venezuela under the protection of a dying Hugo Chavez. His future was uncertain. It was not at all clear that Chavez's successor would allow him to remain in the country or have use of a Venezuelan passport. Cuba was a possibility, but Quinn wasn't interested in living under the thumb of the Castro brothers. He needed a new home, a new sponsor.

"The timing," said Nazari, "couldn't have been better."

"Where did you meet?"

"In a hotel in downtown Caracas."

"Was there anyone else there?"

"Rozanov brought a woman."

Gabriel held up a photograph of Katerina standing on Quinn's balcony in Lisbon. Nazari nodded.

"What was her role in the operation?"

"I wasn't privy to all the details. At that point, I was just the conduit to Quinn."

"How much was he paid?"

"Ten million."

"In advance?"

"On completion of the assignment."

"My death?"

Nazari glanced at Keller and said, "His, too."

Which brought them back to Copenhagen. Alexei Rozanov was on edge that night, but excited. The first target had been chosen. All Rozanov needed was someone to whisper Quinn's name into the ear of Israeli and British intelligence. He asked Nazari to be his messenger, and Nazari promptly turned him down.

"Why?"

"Because I didn't want to do anything that might endanger my position with Mr. Taylor."

"What changed your mind?"

Nazari was silent.

"How much did he pay you, Reza?"

"Two million."

"Where's the money?"

"He wanted to deposit it in a Moscow bank, but I insisted on Switzerland."

Gabriel asked Nazari for the name of the bank, the account number, and any passwords. Nazari supplied the information. The bank was in Geneva. Recently, the Office had found it necessary to examine the institution's balance sheet. Getting access to

Nazari's funds wouldn't pose much of a challenge.

"I don't suppose you mentioned any of this to Mohsen Esfahani."

"No," Nazari answered after a moment's hesitation. "Mohsen knows nothing."

"And your wife?" asked Gabriel. "Did you mention it to her?"

"Why would you ask such a thing?"

"Because I'm curious by nature."

"No," said Nazari, again after a hesitation. "My wife knows nothing."

"Maybe you should tell her."

Gabriel accepted a mobile phone from Mikhail and offered it to Nazari. The Iranian stared at the device, uncomprehending.

"Go ahead, Reza. Call her."

"What have you done?"

"We've pulled the fire alarm."

"What does that mean?"

It was Yaakov who explained. "Do you remember the bolt-hole we created for you and your family, Reza? The bolt-hole that wasn't necessary because you were never the real thing?"

Panic spread like wildfire across the Iranian's face.

"But you never mentioned any of that to your wife," Yaakov continued. "In fact, you left the bolt-hole in place, just in case things went sideways for you at VEVAK and you needed a port in the storm. All we had to do was pull the fire alarm and they—"

"Where are they?" Nazari interrupted.

"I can tell you where they *aren't*, Reza, and that's the Islamic Republic of Iran."

A dangerous calm settled into Nazari's sunken eyes. They moved slowly from Yaakov to Gabriel.

"You just made a mistake, my friend. A man such as yourself knows well the hazards in targeting innocent family members."

"That's one of the great things about being dead, Reza. I'm no longer bound by a guilty conscience." Gabriel paused, then added, "It clarifies my thinking." He withdrew the mobile phone. "The question is," he asked, "have I clarified your thinking, too?"

Nazari's gaze moved from Gabriel's face to the fire. The dangerous calm was gone. It had been replaced by hopelessness, a realization he had no choice but to place himself at the mercy of a mortal enemy.

"What do you want from me?" he asked finally.

"I want you to save your family. And yourself."

"And how might I do that?"

"By helping me find Eamon Quinn and Alexei Rozanov."

"It's not possible, Allon."

"Says who?"

"Says the Boss."

"I'm the boss now," said Gabriel. "And you're working for me."

They spent the next hour going over everything again from the beginning. Particular attention was paid to the details of the bank account in Geneva and the circumstances of Nazari's last meeting with Alexei Rozanov in Copenhagen. The precise date, the name of the restaurant, the time and manner of their arrival, the names of the hotels where they had stayed.

"And your next meeting?" asked Gabriel.

"We have nothing planned."

"Who usually initiates contact?"

"That depends on the state of play. If Alexei has something to discuss, he makes contact and suggests a venue. And if I need to see him—"

"How do you make contact with him?"

"In a way that you and the NSA can't monitor."

"You drop a chatty e-mail to a harmless-looking account?"

"Sometimes," said Nazari, "the simple ways are best."

"What's Rozanov's address?"

"He uses several."

Nazari then recited four addresses from memory. They were all random combinations of letters and numerals. It was an impressive feat of recall.

By then, it was approaching eleven. There was just enough time to return Nazari to the Inter-Continental by his deadline. Gabriel warned the Iranian of the consequences of any breach of their hastily drawn contract. Then he cut him loose from the chair. Nazari looked surprisingly well for a man who had been subjected to a thrashing and a mock execution. The only visible evidence of his ordeal was the small burn in the center of his forehead. "Put some ice on it when you get back to your room," said Yaakov as he shoved Nazari into the car. "We want you to look your best for the negotiations tomorrow."

They dropped him at the eastern edge of the

Stadtpark, and Mikhail trailed him back to the hotel. The lobby was deserted; Nazari boarded an elevator alone and rode it to the seventh floor, where his compromised room awaited him. Hunched over a laptop computer in the room next door, Eli Lavon listened to what came next. A man being violently sick into the toilet, a man weeping uncontrollably after a phone call to his home in Tehran went un-answered. Lavon lowered the volume and gave his quarry a modicum of privacy. Big boys' games, he was thinking. Big boys' rules.

44

SPARROW HILLS, MOSCOW

KATERINA AKULOVA'S DREAM unfolded the way it always did. She was walking through a birch forest near her old training camp when the trees parted like a curtain and a lake of crystalline blue appeared. She had no need to disrobe; in her dreams she was always unclothed, no matter the situation. She slid beneath the calm flat surface and swam through the streets of her ersatz German village. Then the water turned to blood, and she realized she was drowning in it. Starved of oxygen, her heart banging against her ribs, she kicked wildly toward a pinprick of light. But each time she breached the surface, a hand pushed her down again. It was a woman's hand, smooth, flawless. Though Katerina had never felt its touch, she knew it to be the hand of her mother.

Finally, she sat upright in bed, gasping for air as though she had not drawn a breath in several minutes. Her hair was damp and limp, her hands were shaking with fear. She reached out for her cigarettes, lit one with difficulty, and drew the smoke deeply into her lungs. The nicotine calmed her, as it always did. She looked at the clock and saw it was approaching noon. Somehow, she'd slept nearly twelve hours. Outside, the previous night's snow had moved on and a white disk of a sun blazed low in the pale sky. Moscow, it seemed, had been granted a few hours' reprieve from winter.

She swung her feet to the floor, padded into the kitchen, and brewed a cup of coffee in the automatic maker. She drank it while standing over the machine and immediately prepared another. Her SVR-issue mobile phone was lying on the counter. She picked it up and frowned at the screen. There was still no departure order from Alexei. She was convinced it was not oversight on Alexei's part. Alexei had his reasons. He always did.

She checked the weather forecast. It was a few degrees above freezing, rare for Moscow at that time of year, and the clouds were expected to stay away for the remainder of the afternoon. It had been a long time since she'd had any exercise, and she decided a run would do her good. She carried her coffee into the bedroom and dressed: a base layer top and bottom, a cold-weather tracksuit, a pair of new running shoes—genuine American shoes, not the cheap, threadbare knockoffs that came out of Russian factories. Better to run barefoot than in Russian trainers. Next she pulled on a pair of heavy gloves and stuffed her hair beneath a woolen cap. All that remained was her gun, a Makarov 9mm that she hated to carry when she was running. Besides, if some vodka-soaked pervert were foolish enough to try something, she was more than capable of looking after herself. She had once beaten a groper unconscious on the footpaths of Gorky Park. Alexei had finished the job—at least that was the rumor at Moscow Center. Katerina had never bothered to inquire about the man's fate. He had deserved it, whatever it was.

She stretched for a few minutes while smoking her second cigarette and drinking her third cup of black coffee. Then she rode the elevator down to the lobby and, ignoring the hungover greeting of the unshaven concierge, stepped into the street. The pavements had been cleared of snow; she set out at an easy pace westward to Michurinsky Prospekt. It bordered Moscow State University, the school Katerina might have attended if she had been a normal child and not the daughter of a KGB officer who'd forgotten to take her birth control while setting a honey trap.

At the bottom of the hill she turned right onto the gentle sweep of Kosygina Street. In the median was a paved footpath lined on both sides by bare-limbed trees. Her legs were beginning to warm; she could feel the first beads of perspiration forming beneath her jacket. She lengthened her stride, increased her pace. She passed a pretty green-and-white church and the Sparrow Hills observation point, where two smiling newlyweds were posed for photographs against the backdrop of the city. It was a tradition for Russian couples, one that Katerina would never experience. In the unlikely event she were to marry, the SVR would have to approve of her spouse. The wedding would take place in secret, and no photographers would be present. No family, either. Not a problem for Katerina, for she had none.

It was her intention to run to the Russian Academy of Sciences and then start toward home along the embankment of the Moscow River. But as she was passing the garish entrance of the Korston Hotel, she became aware of the fact that she was being followed by a Range Rover with blacked-out windows. She had seen it for the first time on Michurinsky Prospekt and a second time at the Sparrow Hills observation point, where one of the occupants, a man in a leather jacket, had been pretending to admire the view. Now the vehicle was parked outside the Korston, and the man in the leather jacket was walking toward Katerina through the trees. He was over six feet tall, well over two hundred pounds, and walked with the rolling arm-swinging stride of a man who spent a great deal of time in the gym.

It went against Katerina's training to turn her back to a potential threat, so she continued toward the man at the same pace, her eyes straight ahead, as though only vaguely aware of his presence. His hands were stuffed into the pockets of his leather coat. As she tried to pass, he removed one, his right, and grabbed her by the bicep. It was like being seized by the claw of a mechanical digger. Her feet skidded from beneath her. She would have fallen to the pavement if the hand had not kept her upright.

"Let go!" she snapped.

"*Nyet*," he said coldly.

She tried to pull away, more as a warning than a true attempt to escape, but he tightened his grip further still. Her next moves flowed by instinct. She stamped hard on the instep of his right foot and blinded him with a stiletto-like finger to each eye. As his grip relaxed, she pivoted and raised a knee into his groin. Then she pivoted again and delivered a vicious elbow to the temple that dropped him to the ground. She was preparing to do permanent damage to his exposed throat but stopped when she heard laughter on the path behind her. She placed her hands on her knees and fought hard for breath in the frigid air. Her mouth tasted of blood. She imagined it was the blood of her dreams.

―――――――――――

"Why did you do that?"

"I wanted to make sure you were ready to go back into the field."

"I'm always ready."

"You made that quite obvious." Alexei Rozanov shook his head slowly. "That poor devil will never need to bother with a condom again. I suppose he's lucky in a way."

They were in the back of Rozanov's SVR car, which was stuck in traffic along Kosygina Street. Apparently, there was an accident somewhere ahead. There usually was.

"Who was he?" Katerina asked.

"The young man you nearly killed?"

She nodded.

"He's a recent graduate of the Red Banner Institute. Until today, I had high hopes for him."

"What were you planning to use him for?"

"Muscle work," said Rozanov without a trace of irony.

The car crept forward at a walking pace. Rozanov withdrew his packet of Dunhills from the breast pocket of his overcoat and extracted one thoughtfully.

"When you return to your apartment," he said after a moment, "you'll find a suitcase waiting in the entrance hall, along with a passport and your travel documents. You leave first thing in the morning."

"For where?"

"You'll spend one night in Warsaw to establish your identity. Then you'll make your way across Europe to Rotterdam. We've booked a room for you at a hotel near the ferry terminal. A car will be waiting for you on the other side."

"What kind of car?"

"A Renault. The key will be concealed in the usual place. The weapons will be hidden in the back. We got you a Skorpion." Rozanov smiled. "You always liked the Skorpion, didn't you, Katerina?"

"What about Quinn?" she asked.

"He'll meet you at your hotel." Rozanov paused, then added, "I wouldn't expect him to be in a good mood."

"What's wrong?"

"The president has decided to withhold payment of Quinn's money until he completes the second phase of the operation."

"Why would the president do something like that?"

"To provide Quinn with an incentive," answered Rozanov. "Our Irish friend has a long history of taking matters into his own hands. That text message he insisted on sending to Allon almost destroyed a perfectly planned operation."

"You should never have given him Allon's number."

"I had no choice. Quinn was very specific in his demands. He wanted Allon to know there was a bomb in that car. And he wanted him to know who put it there."

They had managed to inch their way back to the Sparrow Hills observation point. The newlyweds were gone; a new couple had taken their place. Posed with them was a child, a girl of six or seven in a white dress, with flowers in her hair.

"Pretty girl," said Rozanov.

"Yes," said Katerina distantly.

Rozanov scrutinized her for a moment. "Is it my imagination," he asked at last, "or are you reluctant to return to the field?"

"It's your imagination, Alexei."

"Because if you're not capable of performing your duties, I need to know."

"Ask your new castrati whether I'm capable."

"I know you were—"

"It's not a problem," she said, cutting him off.

"I was hoping that would be your answer."

"You knew it would be."

They had arrived at the source of the traffic jam. It was an old babushka lying dead in the street. Her drawstring *avoska* lay next to her; apples were scattered across the asphalt. A few car horns sounded in protest. New or old, it didn't matter. Life was cheap in Russia.

"My God," said Rozanov softly as the old woman's smashed body slid past his window.

"It's not like you to be upset by the sight of a little blood."

"I'm not like you, Katerina. I kill with a pen and paper."

"So do I, if there's nothing else available."

Rozanov smiled. "It's good to know you still have your sense of humor."

"One has to have a sense of humor in this line of work."

"I couldn't agree more." Rozanov drew a file folder from his attaché case.

"What's that?"

"The president has one more job he'd like you to handle before you return to Russia."

Katerina accepted the file and stared at the photograph on the first page. New or old, she thought, it didn't matter. Life was cheap in Russia. Hers included.

45

COPENHAGEN, DENMARK

'M SORRY," SAID Lars Mortensen, "but I didn't catch your name."

"Merchant," replied Christopher Keller.

"Israeli, are you?"

"Afraid so."

"And the accent?"

"Born in London."

"I see."

Mortensen was the chief of the PET, Denmark's small but efficient internal security and intelligence service. Officially, it was a branch of the Danish national police and operated under the authority of the Ministry of Justice. Its headquarters was located in an anonymous office north of the Tivoli Gardens. Mortensen's office was on the top floor. Its furnishings were solid, pale, and Danish. So was Mortensen.

"As you might expect," Mortensen was saying, "Allon's death came as a terrible shock to me. I considered him a friend. We worked together on a case a few years back. Things went bad in a house up north. I took care of it for him."

"I remember."

"You worked on that case, too?"

"No."

Mortensen tapped the tip of a silver pen against the contents of an open file. "Allon struck me as the sort of man who would be difficult to kill. It's hard to imagine he's really gone."

"We feel the same way."

"And this request of yours—it has something to do with Allon's death?"

"I'd rather not say."

"And I'd rather not be having this meeting," Mortensen said coolly. "But when a friend requests a favor, I try to be accommodating."

"Our service has experienced a terrible loss," said Keller after a moment. "As you can imagine, we're focused on nothing else."

It was thin gruel, but good enough for the Danish secret policeman. "What will we be looking for in the video?"

"Two men."

"Where did they meet?"

"A restaurant called Ved Kajen."

"In the New Harbor?"

Keller nodded. Mortensen asked for the date and the time. Keller supplied both.

"And the two men?" asked Mortensen.

Keller handed over a photograph.

"Who is he?"

"Reza Nazari."

"Iranian?"

Keller nodded.

"VEVAK?"

"Absolutely."

"And the other man?"

"He's an SVR hood named Alexei Rozanov."

"Do you have a photograph?"

"That's why I'm here."

Mortensen laid the photograph of the Iranian thoughtfully on his desktop. "We are a small country," he said after a moment. "A peaceful country, except for a few thousand hotheaded Muslim fanatics. Do you understand what I'm saying?"

"I believe I do."

"I don't want any trouble with the Persian Empire. Or the Russians, for that matter."

"Not to worry, Lars."

Mortensen glanced at his watch. "This might take a few hours. Where are you staying?"

"The d'Angleterre."

"What's the best way to reach you?"

"Hotel phone."

"What's the name?"

"LeBlanc."

"I thought you said your name was Merchant."

"I did."

Keller left the PET's headquarters on foot and walked as far as the Tivoli Gardens—far enough to confirm that Mortensen had assigned two teams of watchers to follow him. The skies above Copenhagen were the color of granite, and a few gritty flakes of snow were swirling in the light of the streetlamps. Keller crossed the Rådhuspladsen and loitered in the Strøget, Copenhagen's main pedestrian shop-

ping street, before returning to the stately Hotel
d'Angleterre. Upstairs in his room, he killed an hour
watching the news. Then he rang the hotel operator and in French-accented English told her he was
heading down to the Balthazar champagne bar for a
drink. He spent another hour at a corner table nurs-
ing a glass of brut alone. It was, he thought glumly,
a glimpse of the life that awaited him at MI6. The
great Gabriel Allon, may he rest in peace, had once
described the life of a professional spy as one of constant travel and mind-numbing boredom broken by
interludes of sheer terror.

Finally, a few minutes after seven, a waitress wan-
dered over and informed Keller that he had a call.
He took it on a house phone in the lobby. It was Lars
Mortensen.

"I think we might have found the picture you're
looking for," he said. "There's a car waiting outside."

It wasn't hard to spot the PET sedan. It was occupied by two of the same men who had followed him
earlier. They ferried him across the city and deposited him in a room at PET headquarters equipped
with a large video screen. On it was a still image of
a Persian-looking man crossing a narrow cobbled
street. The date and time code matched the information the Iranian had supplied during his interrogation outside Vienna.

"Nazari?" asked Lars Mortensen.

When Keller nodded, Mortensen tapped a few
keys on an open laptop and a new image appeared
on the screen. A tall man, wide cheekbones, fair hair
thinning on top. A Moscow Center hood, if ever
there was one.

"Is that the man you're looking for?"

"I'd say he's the one."

"I've got a few more pictures and a bit of video, but that's definitely the best." Mortensen ejected a disk from the computer, placed it in a case, and held it up for Keller to see. "Compliments of the Danish people," he said. "No charge."

"Were you able to find anything on their travel?"

"The Iranian left Copenhagen the next morning on a flight to Frankfurt. He was scheduled to fly on to Tehran."

"And the Russian?"

"We're still working on that." Mortensen handed Keller the disk. "By the way, the bill for dinner was more than four hundred euros. The Russian paid in cash."

"It was a special occasion."

"What were they celebrating?"

Keller slipped the disk into his coat pocket.

"I see," said Mortensen.

The next morning Christopher Keller flew to London. He was met at Heathrow Airport by an MI6 reception team and driven at an unusually high rate of speed to a safe house on Bishop's Road in Fulham. Graham Seymour was seated at the linoleum table in the kitchen, his Chesterfield coat tossed over the back of a chair. With a movement of his eyes, he instructed Keller to sit. Then he pushed a single sheet of paper across the tabletop and laid a silver pen upon it.

"Sign it."

"What is it?"

"It's for your new phone. If you're working for us, you can't use your old one any longer."

Keller picked up the document. "Minutes? Data plan? That sort of thing?"

"Just sign it."

"What name should I use?"

"Your given name."

"When do I get my new name?"

"We're working on that."

"Do I get a say?"

"No."

"Hardly seems fair."

"Our parents don't allow us to choose our names, and neither does MI6."

"If you try to name me Francis, I'm going back to Corsica."

Keller scribbled something illegible on the signature line of the document. Seymour handed him a new BlackBerry and recited an eight-digit number for the MI6 encryption.

"Recite the number back to me," he said.

Keller did.

"Whatever you do," said Seymour, "don't write it down."

"Why would I do something as foolish as that?"

Seymour placed another document in front of Keller. "This one allows you to handle MI6 documents. You're a member of the club now, Christopher. You're one of us."

Keller's pen hovered over the page.

"Something wrong?" asked Seymour.

"I'm just wondering whether you really want me to sign this."

"Why wouldn't I?"

"Because if I get a shot at Eamon Quinn—"

"Then I expect you to take it." Seymour paused, then added, "Just like when you were in Ulster."

Keller signed the document. Seymour handed him a flash drive.

"What's this?"

"Alexei Rozanov."

"Funny," said Keller, "but he looked taller in the photos."

Keller returned to Heathrow in time to make the early-afternoon British Airways flight to Vienna. He arrived a few minutes after four and took a taxi to an address just beyond the Ringstrasse. It was a fine old Biedermeier apartment building, with a coffeehouse at street level. Keller thumbed the bell push, was admitted into the foyer, and found his way to the flat on the third floor. The door hung slightly ajar. A dead man waited anxiously inside.

THE PHOTOGRAPHS FROM Copenhagen proved that Reza Nazari had met with a Russian-looking man at the time and place specified during his interrogation. And the file from MI6 proved the Russian-looking man was indeed Alexei Rozanov. He had worked in London under diplomatic cover in the 1990s. Both MI5 and MI6 knew him well.

"His full name is Alexei Antonovich." Keller inserted the flash drive into Gabriel's laptop, typed in the encryption password, and opened the file. "He ran a string of mid-level SVR assets at embassies all over town. Made a run at a couple of MI5 officers, too. Frankly, MI5 never thought much of him. Neither did MI6. But when Alexei returned to Moscow Center, his star was suddenly in ascent."

"Do we know why?"

"It probably had something to do with his friendship with the Russian president. Alexei is part of the tsar's inner circle. A very big fish indeed."

Gabriel scrolled through the MI6 file until he came to a photograph. It showed a man walking along a damp London street—Kensington High Street, according to the attached watch report. The subject had just left a luncheon meeting with a diplomat from the Canadian Embassy. The year was 1995. The Soviet Union was dead, the Cold War was over, and at Moscow Center nothing much had changed. The SVR regarded the United States, Great Britain, and the other members of the Western alliance as mortal enemies, and officers such as Alexei Antonovich Rozanov were ordered to spy the living daylights out of them. Gabriel compared the photograph to one of the shots from Copenhagen. The hairline was a bit higher, the face a bit fleshier and more decadent, but they were clearly the same man.

"The question is," said Keller, "can we get him out in the open?"

"We don't have to," replied Gabriel. "Nazari is going to do it for us."

"Another meeting?"

Gabriel nodded. Keller appeared dubious.

"Something wrong?"

"The negotiations between the United States and Iran are supposed to last another week."

"Yes," said Gabriel, tapping a copy of the *Times* of London. "I think I read something about that in the papers this morning."

"And when the talks adjourn," said Keller pointedly, "Reza will no doubt go back to Tehran."

"Unless he has pressing business elsewhere."

"A meeting with Alexei Rozanov?"

"Exactly."

Just then, a message flashed on the computer

screen. It stated that the Iranian delegation had just returned to the InterContinental. Gabriel raised the volume and a moment later heard Reza Nazari prowling his hotel room.

"Doesn't sound like a happy man to me," said Keller.

Gabriel made no reply.

"There's something else you haven't considered," Keller said after a moment. "There's a good chance Alexei Rozanov won't be interested in meeting with his co-conspirator."

"Actually, I think Alexei is going to be relieved just to hear the sound of Reza's voice."

"How are you going to pull that off?"

Gabriel smiled and said, "*Taqiyya*."

At half past seven the phone in Reza Nazari's room bleated softly. He lifted the receiver to his ear, listened to the instructions, and rang off without a word. His overcoat lay on the floor where he had let it fall earlier that evening. He pulled it on and rode an empty elevator down to the lobby. An Iranian security man nodded as Nazari passed. He didn't ask why the senior VEVAK man was leaving the hotel alone. He didn't dare.

Nazari crossed the street and entered the Stadtpark. As he walked along the banks of the Vienna River, he realized he was being followed. It was the small one, the one with a forgettable face who dressed like a pile of dirty laundry. The car was waiting in the same place, at the eastern edge of the park. The Israeli whom Nazari knew as Mr. Taylor was seated in back. As usual, he did not look pleased. He searched Nazari thoroughly and then nodded into the rearview mirror. The same one was behind the wheel, the one with bloodless skin and eyes like ice. He eased into the evening traffic and smoothly brought the car up to speed.

"Where are we going?" Nazari asked as Vienna slid gracefully past his window.

"The boss would like a word in private."

"About what?"

"Your future."

"I didn't realize I had one."

"A very bright one, if you do as you're told."

"I can't be late."

"Don't worry, Reza. No pumpkins."

THEY SAID HE was a seer, a visionary, a prophet. He was almost never wrong—and even if he was, it was only because enough time had not passed to prove him right. He had the power to move markets, to raise alert levels, to influence policy. He was undeniable, he was infallible. He was a burning bush.

His identity was not known, and even his nationality was a bit of a mystery. He was widely assumed to be an Australian—the Web site was hosted there—though many believed he was of Middle Eastern origin, for his insights into the region's tangled politics were thought to be far too subtle to be the product of a non-Oriental mind. And still others were convinced he was in fact a woman. A gender analysis of his writing style said it was at least a possibility.

Though influential, his blog was not read by the masses. Most of his readers were business elites, executives from private security firms, policymakers, and journalists who focused on matters related to international terrorism and the crisis facing Islam and the Middle East. It was one such journalist, a respected investigative reporter from an American television network, who noticed the brief item that appeared early the next morning. The reporter rang one of his sources—a retired CIA agent who had a blog of his own—and the retired agent said the item passed the smell test. That was good enough for the respected investigative reporter, who immediately posted a few lines of copy on his social media feed. And thus an international crisis was born.

The Americans were skeptical at first, the British less so. Indeed, one proliferation expert from MI6 called it the nightmare scenario come true: one hundred pounds of highly radioactive nuclear material, enough to produce one large dirty bomb or several smaller devices that would be capable of rendering major city centers uninhabitable for years. The radioactive material—its precise nature was not specified—had been stolen from a secret Iranian laboratory near the sacred city of Qom and sold on the black market to a smuggler linked to Chechen Islamic terrorists. The whereabouts of the Chechen and the material were unknown, though the Iranians were said to be searching frantically for both. For reasons that were not clear, they had chosen not to inform their Russian friends about the situation.

The Iranians denounced the report as a Western provocation and a Zionist lie. The laboratory named in the report did not exist, they said, and all nuclear material in the country was safe and accounted for. Even so, by the end of that day, it was all anyone was talking about in Vienna. The chief American negotiator said the report, regardless of its veracity, demonstrated the importance of reaching an agreement. Her Iranian counterpart appeared less convinced. He left the talks without addressing reporters and slipped into the back of his official car. At his side was Reza Nazari.

They traveled to the Iranian Embassy and remained there until ten that evening, when finally they returned to the InterContinental Hotel. Reza Nazari went to his room long enough to shed his coat and attaché case and then knocked on the door of his neighbor. Mikhail Abramov drew him quickly inside. Yaakov Rossman poured him a scotch from the minibar.

"It is forbidden," said Nazari.

"Take it, Reza. You deserve it."

The Iranian accepted the drink and raised it slightly in salutation. "My congratulations," he said. "You and your friends managed to create quite a stir today."

"What's the view from Tehran?"

"They're skeptical of the timing, to say the least. They assume the report was part of an Office plot designed to sabotage the talks and prevent an agreement."

"Did Allon's name come up?"

"How could it? Allon is dead."

Yaakov smiled. "And the Russians?" he asked.

"Deeply concerned," replied Nazari. "And that's putting it mildly."

"Did you volunteer to reassure them?"

"I didn't have to. Mohsen Esfahani instructed me to make contact and arrange a meeting."

"Will Alexei agree to see you?"

"I can't guarantee it."

"Then perhaps we should promise him something a bit more interesting than a mutual hand-holding session."

Nazari was silent.

"Did you bring your VEVAK BlackBerry?"

The Iranian held it up for Yaakov to see.

"Send a message to Alexei. Tell him you'd like to discuss recent developments here in Vienna. Tell him Russia has nothing at all to be concerned about."

Nazari quickly composed the e-mail, showed the text to Yaakov, and then pressed SEND.

"Very good." Yaakov pointed at his open laptop and said, "Now send him that one."

Nazari walked over and looked at the screen:

My government is lying to you about the seriousness of the situation. It is urgent I see you at once.

Nazari typed in the address and clicked SEND.

"That should get his attention," said Yaakov.

"Yes," said Nazari. "One would think."

48

VIENNA

THEY DID NOT hear from Alexei Rozanov that first night, nor was there any response the following morning. Reza Nazari left the hotel at eight thirty along with the rest of the Iranian delegation and twenty minutes after that disappeared down the black hole of the nuclear negotiations. At which point Gabriel, trapped in the Vienna safe flat with Christopher Keller, allowed himself to ponder at length all the reasons why his operation was doomed even before it had left port. It was possible, of course, that Reza Nazari had gone on the record with his service in the hours immediately following his brutal interrogation. It was possible, too, he had then told Alexei Rozanov that the man he had conspired to kill so spectacularly was very much alive and out for vengeance. Or perhaps there was no Alexei Rozanov. Perhaps he was nothing more than a figment of Nazari's fevered imagination, a clever piece of *taqiyya* designed to make himself useful to Gabriel and thus save his own life.

"Clearly," said Keller, "you've lost your mind."

"It happens to dead people." Gabriel picked up a photograph of Rozanov walking along a cobbled street in Copenhagen. "Maybe he won't come. Maybe his superiors at the SVR have decided to put him on ice for a while. Maybe he'll ask his old friend Reza to pop over to Moscow for a night of vodka and girls."

"Then we'll pop over to Moscow, too. And we'll kill him there."

No, said Gabriel, shaking his head slowly, they would not be going back to Moscow. Moscow was their forbidden city. They had been lucky to survive their last visit. They would not be going back for a return engagement.

At one that afternoon the negotiators broke for lunch. The morning session had been particularly unproductive because both sides were still in a panic over Gabriel's missing radioactive material. Reza Nazari slipped away from his delegation long enough to telephone Yaakov Rossman at the Inter-Continental. Yaakov then rang Keller at the safe flat and repeated the message.

"Radio silence from Moscow. No word from Alexei."

By then, it was approaching two o'clock. The skies were low and leaden; a few flakes of snow were blowing sideways beyond the windows of the safe flat. Except for Nazari's interrogation, Gabriel had been a prisoner of its rooms, hidden from view, shielded from the memories lurking just outside his door. It was Keller who suggested a walk. He helped Gabriel into his coat, wrapped a scarf around his neck, and pulled a hat low over his brow. Then he gave him a gun, a .45-caliber Glock, a man stopper, a weapon of mass destruction.

"What am I supposed to do with this?"

"Shoot any Russian who asks you for directions."

"What if I run into an Iranian?"

"Go," said Keller.

By the time Gabriel stepped from the building, the snow was dropping from the sky straight and steady, and the pavements looked like sugar-dusted Viennese cakes. He walked blindly for a few moments, not bothering to check whether he was being followed. Vienna had long ago made a mockery of his tradecraft. He loved its beauty, he hated its history. He was envious of it. He pitied it.

The safe flat was located in Vienna's Second District. Before the war it had been so heavily Jewish that the Viennese derisively referred to it as the Mazzesinsel, or the Matzo Island. Gabriel crossed the Ringstrasse, leaving the Second District for the First, and paused outside Café Central, where he had once encountered a man named Erich Radek, a former SS officer who had been ordered by Adolf Eichmann to conceal evidence of the Holocaust. Then he walked the short distance to Radek's stately old mansion, from which a team of Office agents had plucked the war criminal and started him on the first leg of a journey that would end in an Israeli jail cell. Gabriel stood alone at the gate as the snow whitened his shoulders. The exterior of the house was worn and cracked, and the curtains hanging in the unwashed windows appeared threadbare. It seemed no one wanted to reside in the home of the murderer. Perhaps, thought Gabriel, there was hope for them after all.

From Radek's fading mansion, he made his way through the Jewish Quarter to the Stadttempel. Two years earlier, in the narrow street outside the synagogue's entrance, he and Mikhail Abramov had killed a team of Hezbollah terrorists who were planning to carry out a Sabbath-night massacre. The rest of the world had been led to believe that two members of EKO Cobra, Austria's elite tactical police unit, had killed the terrorists. There was even a plaque outside the synagogue commemorating their bravery. Reading it, Gabriel smiled in spite of himself. It was as it should be, he thought. In both intelligence work and restoration, his goal was the same. He wished to come and go without being seen, to leave no trace of himself. For better or worse, it had not always worked out that way. And now he was dead.

After leaving the synagogue, Gabriel walked to a nearby building that had once housed a small investigative organization called Wartime Claims and Inquiries. The man who had run it, one Eli Lavon, had fled Vienna several years earlier, after a bomb destroyed the office and killed his two young female assistants. As Gabriel set off again, he noticed that Lavon was following him. He paused in the street and with a nearly imperceptible movement of his head instructed Lavon to join him. The watcher appeared sheepish. He didn't like being spotted by his target, even if the target had known him since he was a boy.

"What are you doing?" Gabriel asked Lavon in German.

"I heard a silly rumor," replied Lavon in the same language, "that the future chief of the Office was walking around Vienna without a bodyguard."

"Where did you hear something like that?"

"Keller told me. I've been following you since you left the safe flat."

"Yes, I know."

"No, you don't." Lavon smiled. "You really should be more careful, you know. You have a lot to live for."

They walked along the quiet street, the snow muffling the sound of their footfalls, until they came to a small square. Gabriel's heart tolled like an iron bell in his chest, and his legs seemed suddenly like deadweight. He tried to walk on, but the memories pulled him to a stop. He recalled struggling with the straps of his son's car seat, and the faint taste of wine on his wife's lips. And he could hear an engine hesitate because a bomb was pulling power from the battery. Too late, he had tried to warn her not to turn the key a second time. Then, in a flash of brilliant white, his world had been destroyed. Now, finally, his restoration was nearly complete. He thought of Chiara, and for an instant he hoped that Alexei Rozanov would not rise to the bait. Lavon seemed to know what Gabriel was thinking. He usually did.

"My offer still stands," he said quietly.

"What offer is that?"

"Leave Alexei to us," answered Lavon. "It's time for you to go home now."

Gabriel moved slowly forward and stopped on the very spot where the car had burned down to a blackened skeletal ruin. Despite the bomb's compact size, it had produced an unusually intense explosion and fire.

"Have you had a chance to look at Quinn's file?" he asked.

"Interesting reading," replied Lavon.

"Quinn was at Ras al Helal in the mid-eighties. You remember Ras al Helal, don't you, Eli? It was that camp in eastern Libya, the one near the sea. The Palestinians trained there, too." Gabriel peered over his shoulder. "Tariq was there."

Lavon said nothing. Gabriel stared at the snow-covered cobbles. "He arrived in eighty-five. Or was it eighty-six? He'd been having trouble with his bombs. Detonation failures, problems with his fuses and his timers. But when he emerged from Libya again . . ."

Gabriel's voice trailed off.

"It was a bloodbath," said Lavon.

Gabriel was silent for a moment. "Do you suppose they knew each other?" he asked finally.

"Quinn and Tariq?"

"Yes, Eli."

"I can't imagine they didn't."

"Maybe it was Quinn who helped Tariq solve the problems he was having." Gabriel paused, then added, "Maybe it was Quinn who designed the bomb that destroyed my family."

"You settled that account a long time ago."

Gabriel glanced over his shoulder at Lavon, but

Lavon was no longer listening. He was staring at the screen of his BlackBerry.

"What does it say?" asked Gabriel.

"It seems Alexei Rozanov would like to have a word with Nazari after all."

"When?"

"Day after tomorrow."

"Where?"

Lavon held up the BlackBerry. Gabriel peered at the screen and then tilted his face to the falling snow. Isn't it beautiful? he thought. The snow absolves Vienna of its sins. The snow falls on Vienna while the missiles rain down on Tel Aviv.

49

ROTTERDAM, THE NETHERLANDS

I T WAS A few minutes after eleven in the morning when Katerina Akulova stepped from Rotterdam's central train station. She entered a waiting taxi and in rather good Dutch instructed the driver to take her to the Hotel Nordzee. The street upon which it stood was more residential than commercial, and the hotel had the air of a run-down sea cottage that had been put to more prosperous use. Katerina went to the reception desk. The clerk, a young Dutch woman, seemed surprised to see her.

"Gertrude Berger," said Katerina. "My friend checked in yesterday. Mr. McGinnis."

The woman frowned at her computer terminal. "Actually," she said, "your room is unoccupied."

"Are you sure?"

The woman gave the serene smile she reserved for the most inane questions. "But a gentleman did leave something for you earlier this morning." She handed over a letter-size envelope with the Hotel Nordzee insignia in the upper left corner.

"Do you know what time he left it?"

"About nine, if I remember correctly."

"Do you recall what he looked like?"

The Dutch woman proceeded to describe a man approximately five feet ten inches in height, with dark hair and eyes.

"Was he Irish?"

"I couldn't say. His accent was rather hard to place."

Katerina placed a credit card on the desk. "I'll only need the room for a few hours."

The woman swiped the credit card and then handed over a key. "Do you need any help with your bag?"

"I can manage, thank you."

Katerina climbed the stairs to the second floor. Her room was at the end of a hallway lined with floral wallpaper and prints of bucolic canal scenes and Dutch landscapes. There were no security cameras visible, so she ran her hand around the door frame before inserting the key into the lock. She left her bag at the foot of the bed and searched the interior of the room for hidden cameras or listening devices. The air smelled of lime and stale cigarettes. It was a singularly male aroma.

She opened the bathroom window to dispel the odor, returned to the bedroom, and picked up the envelope she had been given by the girl at reception. She checked the seal to make certain it hadn't been tampered with and then tore away the flap. Inside was a single sheet of paper, neatly folded in thirds. On it, in block lettering, was a brief explanation for Quinn's absence. "You bastard," whispered Katerina. Then she burned the note in the bathroom sink.

Alexei Rozanov had ordered Katerina to proceed to the target country with no communication between herself and Moscow Center. The note, however, changed everything. It stated that Quinn would not be traveling with her as planned. Instead, he would meet her at the next stop on their itinerary, a small seaside hotel on England's Norfolk Coast. Under the SVR's strict operational rules, Katerina could not continue without the approval of her controller. And the only way to obtain that approval was to risk a contact.

She fished her phone from her handbag and composed a brief e-mail to an address with a German-based domain. The address was an SVR front that automatically encrypted the e-mail and forwarded it through a circuitous route of nodes and servers to Moscow Center. Alexei's reply arrived ten minutes later. It was blandly worded but clear in its intentions. She was to play it Quinn's way, at least for now.

By then, it was a few minutes after noon. Katerina reclined on the bed and dozed intermittently until half past three, when she checked out of the hotel and took a taxi to the P&O Ferries terminal. The *Pride of Rotterdam*, a 705-foot ferry capable of carrying 250 cars and more than a thousand passengers, was in the process of boarding. The SVR had reserved first-class accommodations for Katerina under the name Gertrude Berger. She left her suitcase in her assigned cabin, locked the door, and went upstairs to one of the bars. It was already packed with passengers, many of whom were in search of a little warm company to ease the loneliness of the ten-hour overnight passage. Katerina ordered a glass of wine and took a table on the vessel's port side.

It did not take long for the men in the bar to notice the attractive young woman sitting alone with no company other than her phone. Eventually, one came over, two drinks in hand, and asked in English whether he could join her. Katerina could tell by his accent he was German. He was in his mid-forties, thinning hair, well dressed. It was possible he was employed by one of the European security services. Nevertheless, she reckoned it was better to fence with him over a drink than to give him the cold shoulder. She accepted the glass of wine and with a glance invited him to sit.

As it turned out, he worked as an account manager for a firm in Bremen that manufactured high-quality machine tools—not exciting work, he said, but stable. It seemed his firm did a great deal of business in the north of England, which explained his presence on the Rotterdam-to-Hull ferry. He preferred the ferry to airplanes because it gave him much-needed time away from his marriage, which, not surprisingly, was in a less than optimal state. For two hours Katerina flirted with him in her impeccable German, occasionally delving into such arcane matters as deflation in the euro zone or the debt crisis in Greece. The businessman was obviously smitten. His only disappointment came at the end of the evening when she declined his offer to return to his cabin.

"I'd be careful if I were you," he said, rising slowly in defeat. "It seems you have a secret admirer."

"Who?"

He nodded toward the opposite side of the bar, where a man sat alone at a table. "He's been staring at you since the minute I sat down."

"Really?"

"Know him?"

"No," she said. "I've never seen him before."

The German man moved off in search of a more promising target. Katerina rose and went outside to the empty observation deck to smoke a cigarette. Quinn joined her a moment later.

"Who's your friend?" he asked.

"A salesman with hopes of glory."

"You sure about that?"

"I'm sure." She turned to look at him. He wore a businessman's gray suit, a tan raincoat, and black-rimmed spectacles that seemed to alter the shape of his face. The transformation was remarkable. Even Katerina scarcely recognized him. It was no wonder he had managed to survive all these years.

"Why weren't you at the hotel?" she asked.

"You're a smart girl. You tell me."

She turned to face the sea again. "You weren't there," she said after a moment of thought, "because you were afraid Alexei was going to kill you."

"And why would I be afraid of that?"

"Because he's refusing to pay you the money he owes you. And you're convinced the second phase

of the operation is actually a plot to get rid of
you so there will be no links between you and the
SVR."

"Is it?"

"Get a grip, Quinn."

His gaze was moving over her, back and forth, up
and down. "Are you armed?" he asked finally.

"No."

"Mind if I check for myself?"

Before she could answer, he had pulled her close
in a seemingly romantic embrace and was running
a hand over her body. It took him only a second or
two to find the Makarov pistol concealed beneath
her sweater. He slipped it into his coat pocket. Then
he opened her handbag and plucked out the mobile
phone. He powered it on and searched through the
e-mail in-box.

"You're wasting your time," she said.

"When was your last contact with Alexei?"

"Midday."

"What were his instructions?"

"Proceed as planned."

"Who was the man who bought you a drink in
the bar?"

"I told you—"

"Was he SVR?"

"You're paranoid."

"True," said Quinn. "Which is why I'm still
alive."

He powered down the phone and, smiling, held it
out to her. Then, with a flick of his wrist, he sent it
hurtling toward the sea.

"You bastard," said Katerina.

"Luck of the Irish," said Quinn.

<hr />

Quinn's cabin was on the same level as Katerina's, a few doors closer to the prow. He forced her inside and immediately dumped out the contents of her handbag on the bed. There was nothing outwardly electronic, only a wallet containing her German passport and credit cards and a bit of makeup. There was also a suppressor for the Makarov. Quinn slipped it into his pocket and instructed Katerina to remove her clothing.

"In your dreams," she said.

"It's not as if I haven't seen you—"

"The only reason I ever slept with you is because Alexei ordered me to."

"He ordered me to do the same thing. Now take off your clothes." When she remained motionless, Quinn screwed the suppressor into the end of the Makarov's barrel and pointed it at her face. "Let's start with the coat, shall we?"

She hesitated before removing her coat and handing it to Quinn. He searched the pockets and the lining but found nothing other than her cigarettes and her lighter. The lighter was large enough to contain a tracking beacon. He pocketed it for later disposal.

"Now the sweater and the jeans."

Again Katerina hesitated. Then she pulled the sweater over her head and wriggled out of the jeans. Quinn searched both articles of clothing, then, with a nod, instructed her to keep going.

"You're playing a very dangerous game, Quinn."

"Very," he agreed.

"What are you trying to accomplish?"

"It's quite simple, really. I want my money. And you're going to make certain I get it."

Quinn traced a finger along the curve of her breast while staring directly into her eyes. Her nipple firmed instantly to his touch. Her face, however, remained defiant.

"What did you expect would happen if you agreed to work for the SVR?"

"I expected Alexei to live up to his word."

"How naive of you."

"We had a deal. Promises were made."

"When dealing with Russians," she said, "promises mean nothing."

"I realize that now," said Quinn with a glance toward the Makarov.

"And if you get your money? Where will you go?"

"I'll find a place. I always do."

"Not even the Iranians would have you now."

"Then I'll go back to Lebanon. Or Syria." He paused, then added, "Or maybe I'll go home."

"To Ireland?" she asked. "Your war is over, Quinn. The SVR is all you have left."

"Yes," he said, slipping the strap of Katerina's bra from her shoulder. "And the SVR ordered you to kill me."

Katerina said nothing.

"You don't deny it?"

She folded her arms over her breasts. "What now?"

"I'm going to propose a simple deal. Twenty million dollars in exchange for one of the SVR's most valuable agents. I'm quite confident Alexei will pay."

"And where do you intend to hold me while you conduct the negotiations?"

"Somewhere Alexei and his goons will never find you. And in case you're wondering," he added, "the arrangements for your travel and indefinite confinement have already been made." He smiled. "Alexei seems to have forgotten that I've done this sort of thing a time or two."

Quinn offered Katerina her sweater, but she refused to accept it. Instead, she reached behind her back, loosened the clasp on her bra, and allowed it to fall from her body. She was perfect, thought Quinn—perfect except for the scar on the underside of her right wrist. He removed the magazine from the Makarov and switched off the light.

50

VIENNA–HAMBURG

THE MESSAGE FROM Alexei Rozanov could not have been more concise. A restaurant, a city, a time. The restaurant was Die Bank, a seafood brasserie in the Neustadt section of Hamburg. The time was nine p.m. on Thursday. It meant that Gabriel would have just forty-eight hours to plan the operation and move the necessary assets into place. He commenced work immediately after returning to the Vienna safe flat with Eli Lavon—and by midnight they had obtained the lodging, cars, weaponry, and secure communications equipment required for such an undertaking. They had also acquired additional personnel from Barak, Gabriel's fabled team of field operatives. The only item that eluded them was a second reservation at the restaurant. It seemed the Russian had secured the last available table for Thursday evening. Keller suggested hacking into the restaurant's computer and killing off a few tables—metaphorically, of course— but Gabriel overruled him. He knew Die Bank well. There was a large noisy bar where a pair of operatives could spend an hour or two without attracting notice.

The Office was not alone in its preparations. VEVAK, defenders of the Islamic revolution, arch-enemy of Israel and the West, was preparing, too. The service's secret travel department booked Reza Nazari a seat on Austrian Airlines Flight 171, which departed Vienna at five thirty p.m. and arrived in Hamburg at seven. Gabriel would have preferred a slightly earlier flight, but Nazari's late arrival meant there would be less time for Iranian or Russian mischief. VEVAK's choice of a hotel—a discount dump near the airport—was a problem, however. Gabriel asked Nazari to switch to the Marriott in the Neustadt instead. It was a short distance from the restaurant, and several members of the Israeli team were already booked there. Nazari requested an upgrade, and Tehran readily complied—thus making it, said Gabriel, the first joint Office-VEVAK operation in history. Reza Nazari did not find the observation humorous. That evening, when he came to Yaakov's room at the InterContinental for a final briefing, he was sweating with nerves. Gabriel began the session by presenting the Iranian with a gold pen.

"A token of your esteem?" asked Nazari.

"I thought about getting you a tie clip, but you Iranians don't wear ties."

"You Israelis aren't terribly fond of them, either." Nazari examined the pen carefully. "What's the range?"

"None of your business."

"Battery life?"

"Twenty-four hours, but don't get greedy. Turn the cap to the right when it's time to engage the power. If we lose transmission at any point during dinner, I'm going to assume that you switched it off intentionally. And that would be bad for your health."

Nazari made no reply.

"Keep it in the breast pocket of your suit jacket," Gabriel continued. "The microphone is sensitive, so sit naturally. If you suddenly try to sit in Alexei's lap, he might get the wrong impression."

Nazari placed the pen into his coat pocket. "What else?"

"We have to go over your script for the evening."

"Script?"

"I have no wish to interrogate Alexei Rozanov. Therefore, I'll need you to do it for me. Politely, of course."

"What are you looking for?"

"Quinn," said Gabriel.

Nazari was silent. Gabriel held up a single sheet of paper.

"Memorize the questions, make them your own. But be sure to use a light touch. If you sound like a prosecuting attorney, Alexei will be suspicious."

Gabriel offered the questions to Nazari. "Touch a match to it when you're finished tonight. We'll give you a refresher during the flight to Hamburg if you need one."

"That won't be necessary. I'm a professional, Allon. Like you."

Nazari accepted the list.

"What language will you be speaking?" asked Gabriel.

"He made the reservation under the name Alexei Romanov, so I assume it will be Russian."

"No winking or little hand signals," said Gabriel. "And don't try to slip him something under the table. We'll have eyes on you the entire time. Don't give me a reason to kill you. It won't take much."

"What happens after dinner?"

"That depends on how well you do your job."

"You're going to kill him, yes?"

"I'd worry about myself if I were you."

"I am." Nazari fell silent. "If you kill Alexei in Hamburg tomorrow night," he said after a moment, "the Russians will suspect my involvement. And then they'll kill *me*."

"Then I suggest you lock yourself in a secure room in Tehran and never come out again." Gabriel smiled. "Look on the bright side, Reza. You get to keep your family and your life, not to mention the two million in blood money the SVR stashed in Geneva for you. All in all, I'd say you made out quite well."

Gabriel rose to his feet. Reza Nazari did the same and extended his hand, but Gabriel only stared at it in anger.

"Be a good boy and do your homework. Because if you blow your lines in Hamburg tomorrow night, I'm going to personally blow your brains out." Gabriel wrapped his hand around Nazari's and squeezed until he could feel the bones beginning to crack. "Welcome to the new world order, Reza."

Not surprisingly, Reza Nazari did not sleep well that last night in Vienna, and neither did Gabriel. He passed it in the safe flat in the Second District, in the company of Christopher Keller and Eli Lavon. Lisbon was never far from his thoughts: the dreary little apartment in the Bairro Alto, the vines spilling from Quinn's balcony, the attractive woman of perhaps thirty whom he followed to London's Brompton Road. Lisbon had been a master performance staged for his benefit, and Gabriel had responded by crafting a story of his own—a story of radioactive material gone missing and of a legendary spy gone to an early grave. The final act would play out tomorrow night in Hamburg, and the star of the show would be Reza Nazari. It was a great deal of responsibility to place upon the shoulders of a mortal enemy, but Gabriel had no other choice. Nazari was the road that led to Alexei Rozanov, ally of the Russian president, patron of Eamon Quinn. The man who could make a ball of fire travel a thousand feet per second. The man who had been at a terrorist training camp in Libya with Tariq al-Hourani. No, he thought as he watched snow falling gently over Vienna, he would not sleep tonight.

The computer was his only companion. He reread the British dossier on Alexei Rozanov and reviewed the photos from Copenhagen. The Russian had arrived a few minutes late that evening, which, according to Nazari, was his custom. Two SVR bodyguards had surreptitiously followed him into the restaurant, and a third had remained with the car. It was a local acquisition, a big Mercedes sedan, Danish registration. The driver had waited on a quiet side street until Alexei Rozanov summoned him with a phone call at the end of the meal. The Russian had left the restaurant alone in order to preserve the illusion that he was not a man under full-time physical protection.

Dawn arrived late that last morning in Vienna, and it never got properly light outside. Gabriel and Keller left the safe flat a few minutes after eight o'clock and took a taxi to the airport. They checked in separately for the morning flight to Hamburg and upon arrival rode in a pair of taxis to the same spot on the Mönckebergstrasse, Hamburg's main shopping street. From there they walked together from the old city to the new—and from somewhere in the depths of his memory, Gabriel recalled that Hamburg had more canals and bridges than Amsterdam and Venice combined.

"What about St. Petersburg?" asked Keller.

"I wouldn't know," said Gabriel with a tense smile.

The street called Hohe Bleichen stretched from the Marriott Hotel to the fringes of the busy Axel-Springer-Platz. It was part Bond Street and part Rodeo Drive; it was modern Germany at its prosperous best. Ralph Lauren occupied a wedding cake of a building at the northern end. Prada and Dibbern china stood shoulder to shoulder a little farther to the south. And next to the luxury shoemaker Ludwig Reiter was Die Bank, the marble temple of dining so beloved by Hamburg's financial and commercial elite. Red banners with the restaurant's scribble of an insignia hung from the facade. Sculpted pillars guarded its entrance.

By then, it was a few minutes after one p.m., and the running battle of the lunch rush was at its most pitched. Gabriel entered alone and found a place at the gold-plated bar. He forced himself to drink a glass of rosé while he reacquainted himself with the sight lines of the restaurant's interior. Then he paid his bill in cash and went into the street again. It was narrow, with only a handful of parking spaces. The traffic flow was north to south. Directly opposite the restaurant was a tiny triangular esplanade where Keller sat on the edge of a concrete planter. Gabriel joined him.

"Well?" he asked.

"Nice place," answered Keller.

"For what?"

"Anything you decide." Keller looked up the length of the street. "These exclusive shops all close early. At nine o'clock this place will be very quiet. At eleven it'll be dead." He glanced at Gabriel and added, "No pun intended."

Gabriel was silent.

"It's five steps from the entrance of the restaurant to the curb," said Keller. "I could put him down from right here and be gone before his body hit the concrete."

"So could I," answered Gabriel. "But it's possible I might need to go over a couple of small points with him first."

"Quinn?"

Gabriel rose without another word and led Keller

southward across the Neustadt to St. Michael's Church. In the shadow of its soaring clock tower was a green park surrounded by stubby apartment houses. They entered one, a modern building with a smoked-glass atrium, and rode the elevator to the fourth floor. Gabriel knocked lightly on the door of 4D, and a tall academic-looking man named Yossi Gavish admitted them. Rimona Stern and Dina Sarid were peering into the screens of laptop computers at the dining room table, and in the sitting room Mordecai and Oded, a pair of all-purpose field hands, were leaning over a large-scale map of Hamburg. Dina looked up and smiled, but otherwise no one acknowledged Gabriel's presence as he entered. He removed his coat and went to the window. The clock tower of St. Michael's told him it was ten minutes past two o'clock. It was good to be home again, he thought. It was good to be alive.

51

PICCADILLY, LONDON

N LONDON IT was ten minutes past one, and Yuri Volkov was running a few minutes behind schedule. Officially, Volkov held a low-level post in the consular section of the Russian Embassy. In reality, he was a senior operative at the SVR's London *rezidentura*, second only to the *rezident* himself, Dmitry Ulyanin. British intelligence knew the true nature of his work, and he was the target of regular physical surveillance by MI5. For the better part of an hour, Volkov had been attempting to shake a two-person team from A4, a man and a woman posing as husband and wife. Now, as he moved along the crowded pavements of Piccadilly, he was confident he was finally alone.

The Russian crossed Regent Street and ducked into the Piccadilly Circus Underground station. The station sat astride both the Piccadilly and Bakerloo lines. Volkov fed a prepaid fare card through the scanner and made his way down the escalator to the Bakerloo platform. And there he spotted the asset, a weak-chinned balding man in his late forties wearing a department-store suit and a mackintosh

coat. He was the sort of man that young women instinctively avoided on the Underground. And with
good reason, thought Volkov, for young girls were
his vice. The SVR had found one for him, a child of
thirteen from some shithole in Siberia, and they'd
fed her to him on a plate. And now they owned
him. He was a mere cog in the vast machine of intelligence, but important matters routinely crossed
his desk. He had requested a crash meeting, which
meant that in all likelihood he had an important
piece of intelligence to pass along.

An overhead sign flashed to indicate the approach
of a northbound train. The man in the mackintosh
moved to the edge of the platform and Volkov, ten
paces to the left, did the same. They stared straight
ahead, each into a private space, as the train eased
into the station and expelled a crowd of passengers.
Then both men entered the same carriage through
different doors. The man in the mackintosh sat, but
Volkov remained standing. He moved to within five
feet of the man, an appropriate distance for secure
transmission, and seized hold of a handrail. As the
train lurched forward, the man in the mackintosh
removed a smart phone, thumbed the touchscreen
a few times, and then returned the phone to his
pocket. Ten seconds later the device in Volkov's
breast pocket pulsated three times, which meant the
information had been transmitted successfully. And
then it was done. No dead drops, no face-to-face
meetings, and it was all entirely secure. Even if MI5
managed to capture the spy's phone, there would be
no trace of the activity.

The train entered Regent's Park station, took on and disgorged a few more passengers, and started moving again. Two minutes later it arrived at Baker Street, where the man in the mackintosh departed. Yuri Volkov remained on the train until Paddington Station. From there it was a short walk back to the Russian Embassy.

It stood at the northern edge of Kensington Palace Gardens, behind a cordon of British security. Volkov entered the building and made his way down to the *rezidentura*, where he slipped into the secure communications vault. He removed the device from his coat pocket. It was about three inches by five, the size of an average external hard drive. He plugged it into a computer and typed in the necessary password. Instantly, the device began to whir, and the file it contained flowed into the computer. Fifteen seconds elapsed while the material was decrypted. Then it appeared *en clair* on the screen. "My God," was all Volkov said. Then he printed out a copy of the message and went in search of Dmitry Ulyanin.

Ulyanin was in his office, a phone to his ear, when Volkov entered without knocking and dropped the message on the desk. The *rezident* stared at it for a moment in disbelief before absently hanging up.

"I thought you saw Shamron at Vauxhall Cross."

"I did."

"What about the coffin they put on that plane?"

"It must have been empty."

Ulyanin slammed his fist onto the desktop, spilling his afternoon tea. He held up the printout and asked, "Do you know what's going to happen when this arrives in Moscow?"

"Alexei Rozanov is going to be very angry."

"Alexei's not the one I'm worried about." Ulyanin flicked the printout across his desk. "Cable Yasenevo right away. It was Alexei's operation, not mine. Let him clean up the mess."

Volkov returned to the communications vault and drafted the cable. He showed the draft to Ulyanin for approval, and after a brief argument it was Ulyanin who pushed the button that fired the news securely to Moscow Center. He returned to his office while Volkov waited for confirmation that the cable had been received. It took fifteen minutes to arrive.

"What did he say?" asked Ulyanin.

"Nothing."

"What are you talking about?"

"Alexei's not in Moscow."

"Where is he?"

"On an airplane bound for Hamburg."

"Why Hamburg?"

"A meeting. Something big, apparently."

"Let's just hope he checks his messages soon, because Gabriel Allon didn't fake his death for no reason." Ulyanin looked down at the sodden papers on his desk and shook his head slowly. "This is what happens when you send an Irishman to do a Russian's job."

52

FLEETWOOD, ENGLAND

QUINN OPENED ONE eye slowly, then the other. He saw his bare arm draped over the breasts of a woman, and his hand wrapped around the grip of a Makarov pistol, a finger resting alertly on the trigger guard. The room was in semidarkness; an open window admitted the sharp smell of the sea. In the instant between sleep and consciousness, Quinn struggled to place his whereabouts. Was he in his villa on Margarita Island? Or perhaps he was back at Ras al Helal, the seaside terror training camp in Libya. He recalled his time at the camp with fondness. He had made a friend there, a Palestinian bomb maker. Quinn had helped the Palestinian overcome a simple problem he was having with his design. In return, he had given Quinn an expensive Swiss wristwatch, paid for by Yasir Arafat himself. The engraving read *NO MORE TIMER FAILURES* . . .

Quinn raised the watch to his eyes now and saw that it was half past four in the afternoon. Through the open window came the sound of two men conversing in a Lancashire accent. He was not on Margarita Island or at the camp on the Libyan coast. He was in Fleetwood, England, in a hotel along the Esplanade, and the woman sleeping beneath his arm was Katerina. It was not an embrace of affection. Quinn had held her tightly against his body so he could get some much-needed rest. He had slept more than six hours, enough to see him through to the next phase of the operation.

Quinn lifted his arm and slipped from the bed, gently, so as not to wake Katerina. A complimentary coffee-and-tea service stood on a table near the window. Quinn filled the electric kettle, dropped a bag of Twinings into the aluminum pot, and peered out the window. The Renault was parked in the street. A duffel bag containing the weapons was still in the storage compartment. Quinn thought it better to leave the bag in the car rather than bring it into the hotel. It meant there would be fewer firearms within reach of the SVR's top female assassin.

Quinn carried the Makarov into the bathroom and showered quickly, leaving the curtain open so he could watch Katerina in the next room. She was still sleeping when he emerged. He prepared the tea and poured two cups, one with milk, the other with sugar. Then he woke Katerina and handed her the cup with the sugar.

"Get dressed," he said coldly. "It's time to let Moscow Center know you're still alive."

Katerina spent a long time in the shower and took inordinate care with her appearance while dressing. Finally, she pulled on her coat and followed

Quinn downstairs to the lobby, where a gray-haired woman of sixty sat in an alcove doing needlepoint. Quinn poked his head through the window and asked where he might find an Internet café.

"Lord Street, luv. Opposite the chippy."

It was a walk of five minutes, which they passed in silence. Lord Street was long and straight and lined with shops on both sides. The fish-and-chips shop was at the midway point; the Internet café, as promised, was directly opposite. Quinn purchased thirty minutes of time and led Katerina to a terminal in the corner. She addressed a new e-mail to the same SVR address and looked to Quinn for guidance.

"Tell Alexei that your phone is on the bottom of the North Sea and that you're under my control. Tell him to deposit twenty million dollars into my account in Zurich. Otherwise, I'm going to cancel the second phase of the operation and hold you as collateral until I receive payment in full."

Katerina began to type.

"In English," Quinn said.

"It doesn't fit my legend."

"I don't care."

Katerina deleted the German text and began again in English. She managed to make Quinn's demands sound like a mundane business dispute between two firms working on the same project.

"Lovely," said Quinn. "Now send it."

She clicked the SEND icon and immediately deleted the e-mail from her out-box.

"How long will it take them to reply?"

"Not long," she answered. "But why don't you go over to the bar and get us something to drink, so we don't look like a couple of assassins waiting for word from headquarters?"

Quinn handed her a ten-pound note. "Milk, no sugar."

Katerina rose and walked over to the bar. Quinn placed his chin in his palm and stared at the computer screen.

Their thirty minutes of computer time expired with no reply from Moscow. Quinn sent Katerina over to the counter to purchase additional time, and another fifteen minutes passed before an e-mail finally appeared in her in-box. The text was written in German. Katerina's expression darkened as she read it.

"What does it say?" asked Quinn.

"It says we have a problem."

"What's wrong?"

"They're still alive."

"Who?"

"Allon and the Englishman." She turned away from the screen and looked at Quinn seriously. "Apparently, that story about Allon's death was a lie. Moscow Center assumes they're searching for us."

Quinn felt his face flush with anger. "Did Alexei agree to deposit my money?"

"Perhaps you weren't listening. You failed to fulfill the terms of your contract, which means there is no money. Alexei suggests you let me leave the country at once. Otherwise, you're going to spend the rest of your life hiding from people like me."

"What about the second phase of the operation?"

"There is no operation, Quinn. Not anymore. Alexei has ordered us to abort."

Quinn stared at the screen for a moment. "Tell Alexei I didn't do all this for nothing," he said finally. "Tell him we're going to carry out the second phase. Tell him to confirm the location."

"He won't agree."

"Tell him," said Quinn through gritted teeth.

Katerina dispatched a second e-mail, again in English. This time, they had to wait only ten minutes for a reply. It came in the form of an address. Katerina pasted it into a search engine and hit the ENTER key. Quinn smiled.

53

THAMES HOUSE, LONDON

MILES KENT WAS the only person at Thames House who could penetrate the battlements of Amanda Wallace's office without an appointment. He entered at half past six that evening as she was preparing to leave for a long weekend in Somerset with her husband Charles, a wealthy Etonian who did something with money in the City. Amanda adored Charles and seemed completely oblivious to the fact he was carrying on a torrid affair with his young secretary. Kent had thought often about bringing the affair to Amanda's attention—it was a potential security risk, after all—but had decided such a move could be ruinous. Amanda could be ruthlessly vindictive, especially toward those whom she regarded as threats to her power. Charles would suffer no sanction for his indiscretion, but Kent might very well find himself turfed out of the service in the prime of his career. And then what? He'd have to take a job at a private security firm, the last port of call for dried-up spies and secret policemen.

"I hope this won't take long, Miles. Charles is on his way."

"It won't," said Kent as he lowered himself into one of the chairs in front of Amanda's desk.

"What have you got?"

"Yuri Volkov."

"What about him?"

"He was a busy boy today."

"How so?"

"He left the embassy on foot at midday. An A4 team followed him for about an hour. And then they misplaced him."

"Lost him? Is that what you mean?"

"It happens, Amanda."

"It's been happening too much lately." She placed some weekend reading material into her briefcase. "Where was the last place the team had eyes on the target?"

"Oxford Street. They came back to Thames House and spent the rest of the afternoon piecing together Volkov's subsequent movements using CCTV."

"And?"

"He took a stroll down Piccadilly to make sure he was clean. Then he ducked into the tube at the Circus and boarded a train."

"Piccadilly or Bakerloo?"

"Bakerloo. He rode it to Paddington Station and then returned to the embassy on foot."

"Did he meet with anyone?"

"No."

"Kill anyone?"

"Not that we're aware of," said Kent with a smile.

"What about when he was on the train?"

"He just stood there."

Amanda added another file to her briefcase. "It sounds to me, Miles, as though Yuri Volkov took a walk."

"Russian spies don't take a walk for no reason. They take a walk because they're spying. That's what they do."

"Where is he now?"

"Inside the embassy."

"Anything unusual?"

"GCHQ picked up a burst of high-priority message traffic not long after he returned, all heavily encrypted with stuff they haven't been able to unbutton."

"And you find the timing suspicious?"

"To say the least." Miles Kent was silent for a moment. "I have a bad feeling about this, Amanda."

"I can't do anything with bad feelings, Miles. I need actionable intelligence."

"It was the same bad feeling I had before that bomb exploded on Brompton Road."

Amanda closed her briefcase and retook her seat. "What do you propose?"

"I'm worried about the train ride."

"I thought you said he didn't make contact with anyone."

"There was no physical contact or communication, but that doesn't mean anything. I'd like authorization to run down every person who was on that carriage with him."

"We can't possibly spare the resources, Miles. Not now."

"What if we don't have a choice?"

Amanda made a show of thought. "Done," she said. "But D4 will have to shoulder the burden. I won't have you drawing assets from any of the other branches."

"Agreed."

"What else?"

"It might be a good idea for you to have a word with our friends across the river," said Kent, nodding toward the white facade of Vauxhall Cross. "We don't want to be blindsided again."

Kent rose to his feet and withdrew. Alone, Amanda picked up her phone and speed-dialed her husband's mobile, but there was no answer. She left a brief message saying she was going to be delayed and killed the connection. Then she picked up the receiver of a phone connected directly to Vauxhall Cross.

"I know it's only Thursday, but I wonder if I might tempt you with a drink."

"Hemlock?" asked Graham Seymour.

"Gin," said Amanda.

"My place or yours?"

LORD STREET, FLEETWOOD

QUINN AND KATERINA left the Internet café on Lord Street and started back to their hotel. Quinn moved calmly past the storefronts, but Katerina was jumpy and on edge. Her eyes moved restlessly about the street, and once, when a pair of teenage boys overtook them, she gouged her nails painfully into Quinn's bicep.

"Something bothering you?" asked Quinn.

"Two things, actually. Gabriel Allon and Christopher Keller." She gave him a sidelong glance. "That was a very expensive text message you sent to Allon. Alexei will never pay you now."

"Unless I fulfill the terms of the contract."

"How do you intend to do that?"

"By killing Allon and Keller, of course."

Katerina's lighter flared. "You only get one shot at men like that," she said, exhaling a cloud of smoke into the cold night air. "You'll never be able to find them again."

"I don't have to find them."

"Then how do you intend to kill them?"

"By bringing them to me."

"With what?"

"The last target," said Quinn.

Katerina stared at him incredulously. "You're mad," she said. "You'll never be able to pull it off alone."

"I won't be alone. You're going to help me."

"I have no interest in helping you."

"I'm afraid you don't have much of a choice."

They arrived back at the hotel. Katerina dropped her cigarette to the pavement and followed Quinn inside. The gray-haired woman was still working on her needlepoint in the alcove. Quinn informed her that they would be leaving in a few minutes.

"So soon?" she asked.

"Sorry," said Quinn, "but something's come up."

55

HAMBURG

A T THAT SAME moment Austrian Airlines
Flight 171 from Vienna touched down in
Hamburg and started toward its gate. Unbeknownst to the carrier, the passengers included
an Iranian intelligence officer and his Israeli han-
dler. The two men were seated several rows apart
and did not communicate during the flight. Nor
did they speak as they hiked through the terminal toward passport control. There they joined the
same line and both were admitted into Germany
after only a cursory inspection of their travel documents. In the Hamburg safe flat, Gabriel celebrated
his first small victory. Crossing borders was always
tricky for Iranians, even Iranians with diplomatic
passports in their pockets.

VEVAK's travel department had arranged a car
for Reza Nazari through the Iranian consulate. It
collected him at the arrivals level of the terminal
and took him directly to the Marriott Hotel in the
Neustadt. He arrived at 7:45 p.m., checked in, and
went upstairs to his room, leaving the Do Not Dis-

turb sign on the latch before entering. Two minutes later there was a knock at the door. He opened it and Yaakov Rossman came inside.

"Any last questions?" he asked.

"No questions," replied Nazari. "Just a demand."

"You're in no position to be making demands, Reza."

Nazari managed a weak smile. "Alexei always calls me before we meet. If I don't pick up, he won't come. It's as simple as that."

"Why didn't you mention this before?"

"It must have slipped my mind."

"You're lying."

"Whatever you say."

The Iranian was still smiling. Yaakov was staring at the ceiling in anger.

"How much is it going to cost me to make you answer the phone?" he asked.

"I want to hear the sound of my wife's voice."

"It's not possible. Not now."

"All things are possible, Mr. Taylor. Especially tonight."

Until that moment, Reza Nazari had been a model prisoner. Even so, Gabriel had been anticipating one final act of defiance. Only in movies, Shamron always said, did the condemned man accept the noose without a struggle—and only in operational planning rooms did coerced assets face their moment of ultimate betrayal without a last ultimatum. Nazari could have made any number of demands. That he insisted only on speaking to his wife elevated him, however slightly, in the eyes of those who held his fate in their hands. Indeed, it might very well have saved his life.

The arrangements for an emergency contact between Nazari and his wife had been made shortly after his initial interrogation in Austria. Yaakov had only to dial a number in Tel Aviv, and the call would be routed securely to the villa in eastern Turkey where an Office team was babysitting Nazari's wife and children. The conversation would be recorded at King Saul Boulevard, and a Persian speaker would be listening for any irregularities. The only danger was that the Russians and the Iranians might be listening, too.

With Gabriel's approval, Yaakov dialed the number at 8:05. By 8:10 Nazari's wife was on the line, and the translator was in place at King Saul Boulevard. Yaakov held out the phone toward Nazari.

"No tears, no good-byes. Just ask her about her day, and do your best to sound normal."

Nazari took the phone and lifted it to his ear. "Tala, my darling," he said, closing his eyes with relief. "It's so good to hear your voice."

The conversation was slightly more than five minutes in duration, longer than Gabriel would have preferred. He had not wanted to risk a direct live feed to Hamburg, so he had to wait several additional minutes to learn the call had gone off without a problem. Outside his window, the clock of St. Michael's Church read 8:20. With a few clicks on his computer keyboard, he moved his team into place. The evening's first crisis had been averted. All he needed now was Alexei Rozanov.

56

NEUSTADT, HAMBURG

OUR HUNDRED TRANQUIL feet separated the Marriott Hotel from Die Bank restaurant—a walk of perhaps three minutes, two if one were running late for a reservation. The guests who departed the hotel at 8:37 p.m. were in no particular hurry because like many in Hamburg that evening they had been unable to secure a coveted table. Their names were Yossi Gavish and Rimona Stern, though both were registered at the hotel under operational aliases. Yossi was a senior analyst in the Office's Research division who happened to have a flair for the dramatic and was good on his feet in the field. Rimona was the chief of the Office unit that spied on Iran's nuclear program. As such, she had been the primary recipient of Reza Nazari's false intelligence. She had never met the Iranian spy personally and was not looking forward to being in the same room with him tonight. In fact, earlier that evening, she had stated her preference for sending Nazari back to Tehran in a pine box. Her anger had come as no surprise to Gabriel. Rimona was the niece of Ari Shamron, and like her

famous uncle she did not take betrayal lightly, especially where Iranians were involved.

She was an analyst by training and experience,
but she shared Yossi's natural instincts in the
field. As she moved along the elegant street, a bag
in the window of Prada seemed to catch her eye.
She paused there for a moment while a car overtook them and while Yossi, playing the role of an-
noyed spouse, glared at his wristwatch. It was 8:41
when they passed through the imposing entrance
of Die Bank. The maître d' informed them there
were no tables available, so they moped off to the
bar to await a cancellation. Rimona sat facing the
entrance, Yossi the dining room. From the breast
pocket of his jacket he removed a gold pen identical
to the one Gabriel had given to Reza Nazari. Yossi
twisted the cap to the right and then returned the
pen to his pocket. Two minutes later a text message
appeared on his secure mobile. The transmitter
was working, the signal was strong and clear. Yossi
snared a passing waitress and ordered drinks. It was
8:44 p.m.

In the streets surrounding Die Bank, the rest of
Gabriel's team was moving quietly into place. On
the Poststrasse, Dina Sarid was easing a Volkswagen sedan into an empty space outside a Vodafone
outlet. Mordecai sat next to her in the front passenger seat, and in the back Oded was doing a few
deep-breathing exercises to slow his racing heart
rate. Fifty meters farther along the street, Mikhail
Abramov sat astride a parked motorbike, watching the pedestrians with an expression of profound
boredom on his face. Keller sat next to him atop a

motorbike of his own. He was peering at the screen of his mobile. The message told him the man of the hour had not yet surfaced. It was 8:48 p.m.

At 8:50 Alexei Rozanov had still not made contact with Reza Nazari. Gabriel stood in the window of the safe flat watching the clock atop St. Michael's Church as two more minutes passed without a call. Eli Lavon stood next to him, a consoling presence, a fellow mourner at the grave of an old friend.

"You have to send him, Gabriel. Otherwise, he's going to be late."

"What if he's not supposed to go to the restaurant until he hears from Alexei?"

"We'll have him make up an excuse."

"Maybe Alexei won't buy it." Gabriel paused, then added, "Or maybe he isn't coming."

"You're jumping at shadows."

"A five-hundred-pound bomb exploded in my face two weeks ago. I'm entitled."

Another minute passed with no call. Gabriel walked over to the laptop, keyed in a message, and clicked SEND. Then he returned to the window and stood at the side of his oldest friend in the world.

"Have you decided what you're going to do?" asked Lavon.

"About what?"

"Alexei."

"I'm going to give him a chance to sign my death certificate."

"And if he does?"

Gabriel turned away from the clock and looked at Lavon. "I want my face to be the last one he ever sees."

"Chiefs don't kill KGB officers."

"It's called the SVR now, Eli. And I'm not the chief yet."

———

"Give me your phone," said Yaakov.

"Why?"

"Just give me the damn thing. We don't have much time."

Reza Nazari surrendered his mobile. Yaakov removed the SIM card and inserted it into an identical device. Nazari hesitated before accepting it.

"A bomb?" he asked.

"Your phone for the evening."

"Should I assume it's compromised?"

"In every way imaginable."

Nazari slipped the phone into his coat pocket, next to the pen. "What happens at the end of dinner?"

"Whatever you do," Yaakov said, "don't walk out the door with him at the same time. I'll pick you up in front of the restaurant once Alexei is gone."

"Gone?"

Yaakov said nothing more. Reza Nazari pulled on his overcoat and headed down to the lobby.

It was 8:57 p.m.

———

Because the Marriott was an American hotel, its forecourt contained stainless-steel posts and ugly concrete flowerpots to protect the building against terrorist attack. Reza Nazari, servant of the world's largest state sponsor of international terrorism, navigated the defenses under the watchful gaze of Yaakov and turned into the street. It was empty of traffic, and the pavements were deserted. Nothing in the shop windows slowed Nazari's progress, though he did seem to take note of the two men on motorcycles in the little esplanade across the street from Die Bank. He entered the restaurant at nine precisely and presented himself to the maître d'. "Romanov," said the Iranian, and the maître d' ran a manicured finger along his reservations list. "Ah, yes, here it is. Romanov."

Nazari shed his overcoat and was shown into the high-ceilinged dining room. Passing the bar, he noticed a woman with sandstone-colored hair watching him. The man seated next to her was typing something into his mobile—confirmation of the asset's safe arrival, thought Nazari. The table was in the corner of the room, beneath an unnerving black-and-white photograph of a maniacal-looking bald man. Nazari took the seat facing the room. It would upset Alexei, but at that point Alexei's feelings were the least of his concerns. He was thinking only of his wife and children and the list of questions that Allon wanted answered. A waiter filled his glass with water; a sommelier offered him a wine list. Then, at 9:07, he felt the new mobile phone vibrate against his heart with an unfamiliar pattern. He didn't recognize the number. Even so, he accepted the call.

"Where are you?" asked a voice in Russian.

"In the restaurant," replied Nazari in the same language. Then he asked, "Where are *you*?"

"Running a few minutes behind schedule. But I'm close."

"Should I order you a drink?"

"Actually, we need to make a small change."

"How small?"

Rozanov explained what he wanted Nazari to do. Then he said, "Two minutes. Do you understand me?"

Before Nazari could answer, the connection was lost. Nazari quickly dialed the man he knew as Mr. Taylor.

"Did you hear that?"

"Every word."

"What do you want me to do?"

"If I were you, Reza, I'd be standing outside the restaurant in two minutes."

"But—"

"Two minutes, Reza. Or the deal's off."

The car was an S-Class Mercedes, Hamburg registration, black as a hearse. It appeared at the top of the street as Reza Nazari was rising to his feet and slid sedately past the darkened shops before stopping outside Die Bank. A valet approached, but the man in the front passenger seat waved him away. The driver was clinging to the wheel with both hands as though he had a gun to his head, and in the backseat a man held a mobile phone tensely to his ear. From the esplanade across the street, Keller could see him clearly. Wide cheekbones, fair hair thinning on top. A Moscow Center hood, if ever there was one.

"It's him," said Keller into the microphone of his secure radio. "Tell Reza to stay inside the restaurant. Let us put him down now and be done with it."

"No," snapped Gabriel.

"Why not?"

"Because I want to know why he changed the plan. And I want Quinn."

The radio crackled as Gabriel keyed out. Then the door of the restaurant swung open and Reza Nazari stepped into the street. Keller frowned. The best-laid plans, he thought.

Alexei Rozanov was still on the phone when Nazari lowered himself into the backseat. As the car shot forward, he glanced toward the esplanade where the two men sat astride their motorbikes. They made no attempt to follow, at least not one that Nazari could detect. He seized the armrest as the car rounded a corner at speed. Then he looked at Alexei Rozanov as the Russian terminated his phone call.

"What the hell is going on?" asked Nazari.

"I didn't think it was a good idea for you to be sitting in a restaurant in Hamburg."

"Why not?"

"Because we have a problem, Reza. A very serious problem."

W HAT DO YOU MEAN, he's still alive?"
        "I mean," replied Alexei Rozanov
        pointedly, "that Gabriel Allon is still
walking the face of the earth."

"His death was in the newspapers. The Office confirmed it."

"The newspapers know nothing. And the Office," added Rozanov, "was obviously lying."

"Has your service seen him?"

"No."

"Heard his voice?"

Rozanov shook his head.

"Then how do you know?"

"Our information comes from a human source. We've been told that Allon survived the explosion with only superficial injuries and was taken to an MI6 safe house."

"Where is he now?"

"Our source doesn't know."

"When did you learn about this?"

"A few minutes after my plane landed in Hamburg. Moscow Center advised me to cancel our meeting."

"Why?"

"Because there's only one reason why Gabriel Allon would fake his own death."

"He intends to kill us?"

The Russian was silent.

"You're not really worried, are you, Alexei?"

"Ask Ivan Kharkov whether I should be worried about Gabriel Allon's penchant for revenge." Rozanov glanced over his shoulder. "The only reason I came here tonight is because the Kremlin is nervous about the prospect of radioactive material in the hands of Chechen terrorists."

"The Kremlin has good reason to be worried."

"So it's true, then?"

"Absolutely."

"I'm relieved, Reza."

"Why would you be relieved about the Chechens being able to make a dirty bomb?"

"Because the timing of this whole thing was rather interesting, don't you think?" Rozanov stared out his window. "First, Allon fakes his own death. Then a hundred pounds of highly radioactive waste material goes missing from an Iranian lab." He paused, then added, "And now here we are in Hamburg together."

"What are you suggesting, Alexei?"

"Neither the SVR nor the FSB has uncovered any intelligence to suggest the Chechens have acquired Iranian nuclear waste material. I wouldn't be here if it wasn't for your e-mail."

"I sent you that e-mail because the reports are true."

"Or maybe you sent it because Allon told you to."

This time, it was Nazari who stared out his window. "You're starting to make me nervous, Alexei."

"That was my intention." The Russian was silent for a moment. "You're the only one who could have given Allon my name, Reza."

"You're forgetting Quinn."

Rozanov lit a Dunhill thoughtfully, as though he were moving pieces around a mental chessboard.

"Where is he?" asked Nazari.

"Quinn?"

Nazari nodded.

"Why would you ask such a question?"

"He was our asset."

"That's true, Reza. But now he belongs to us. And his whereabouts are none of your concern."

Nazari reached inside his overcoat for his cigarettes, but Rozanov seized his wrist with surprising strength.

"What are you doing?" the Russian asked.

"I was hoping to have a cigarette."

"You didn't bring a gun tonight, did you, Reza?"

"Of course not."

"You should have." Rozanov smiled coldly. "That was another mistake on your part."

The Mercedes was headed west on the Feldstrasse, a busy street linking the Neustadt to the quarter of St. Pauli. Two men on motorbikes followed, along with two cars, each containing three seasoned operatives of the Israeli secret intelligence service. None was aware of what had transpired between Alexei Rozanov and Reza Nazari. Only Gabriel and Eli Lavon, hunched over a laptop computer in the safe flat, were privy to the tense confrontation. The pen in the Iranian's pocket was no longer relevant—it was well out of range of the receiver—but Nazari's mobile phone was providing clear audio coverage.

For the moment the audio feed had gone quiet, never a good sign. No one in the car was speaking. No one, it seemed, was breathing. Gabriel tried to picture the scene inside. Two men in front, two in back, one a hostage. Perhaps Alexei had drawn a gun. Or perhaps, thought Gabriel, a display of weaponry was unnecessary. Perhaps Nazari, worn down by days of fear, had already signaled his guilt.

Gabriel looked at the winking light on his computer screen and asked, "What's Alexei doing?"

"I can think of several possibilities," replied Lavon. "None of them good."

"Why no evasive action? Why no countersurveillance moves?"

"Maybe Alexei doesn't quite believe it himself."

"Believe what?"

"That you were able to find him so quickly."

"He underestimates me? Is that what you're saying, Eli?"

"Hard to believe, but—"

Lavon fell silent as the sound of Rozanov's voice came over the feed. He was speaking in Russian.

"What's he saying?"

"He's giving the driver directions."

"Where are they headed?"

"Unclear. But I suspect it's someplace where they can give him a good going-over."

"I wouldn't mind listening to the questions."

"Could get ugly." Lavon paused, then added, "Terminally ugly."

Gabriel watched the winking light moving across the computer screen. The car was turning onto the Stresemannstrasse, a wider road, faster traffic.

"It's not a bad spot," said Gabriel.

"Doesn't get much better, actually."

Gabriel raised the radio to his lips and gave the order. Within seconds, two additional blinking lights appeared on the screen. One was Mikhail. The other was Keller.

"Killings are always cleaner than snatches," said Lavon quietly.

"Yes, Eli, I realize that."

"So why not end it here and now?"

"I've added another question to my list."

"What's that?"

"I want to know the name of the man who told the Russians I was alive."

The lights of Mikhail and Keller were moving closer. The Mercedes was still traveling at the same rate of speed.

"Let's hope there's no collateral damage," said Lavon.

Yes, thought Gabriel, as he heard gunshots. Let us hope.

There are quarters of Hamburg where the Germans hide behind a dowdy English facade. The spot

where the black Mercedes eventually ran aground
was just such a place—a triangular common, small
and grassy, bordered on one side by the street and
on the other two by terraces of redbrick houses
where one might have assumed the occupants were
drinking tea and watching the *News at Ten* on the
BBC. To reach it, the car had to first careen rudder-
less across two lanes of oncoming traffic. Along the
way it toppled a lamppost and smashed a small side-
walk billboard before finally coming to rest against
a slender young elm. Later, the neighborhood would
go to great lengths to save the tree, but to no avail.

The two men in the front seat of the car were
dead long before it shuddered to a halt. It was not
the crash that killed them but the bullets that were
fired expertly into their heads at close range while
the car was still moving. Witnesses would tell of
two men on motorcycles, one tall and lanky, the
other more powerfully built. Each fired two shots
only, and the shots were so perfectly synchronized
that the reports were scarcely distinguishable. Surveillance video would later confirm the accounts.
One Hamburg detective called it the most beautiful assassination he had ever seen, a rather tasteless
remark that would earn him a stern rebuke from his
superior. Dead bodies on German soil were never
beautiful, the senior man would say. Especially dead
Russians. It didn't matter that they were a couple of
Moscow Center gorillas. It was still an outrage.

The two motorcyclists quickly fled and were
never seen again. Nor did the authorities ever locate
the Volkswagen sedan that appeared within seconds of the crash. A stout troll-like man emerged

from the back and flung open the rear passenger-side door of the Mercedes as though it were made of papier-mâché. One witness would speak of a brief but severe beating, though others would take issue with that account. Regardless of what transpired, the tall Slavic-looking passenger who emerged from the Mercedes was dazed and bleeding. How he found his way into the Volkswagen was again a matter of some controversy. Some said he climbed into the Volkswagen willingly. Others said he was compelled to enter the car because the troll-like man was at that instant breaking his arm. The entire maneuver took just ten seconds. Then the Volkswagen and the unfortunate man of Slavic appearance were gone. The same Hamburg policeman saw no artistry in the troll's handiwork, but was no less impressed. Any fool can pull a trigger, he told colleagues, but only a real pro can snatch a Moscow Center hood like he was plucking an apple from a tree.

Which left only the passenger who had been seated behind the ill-fated driver. All the witnesses stated that he climbed out of the car under his own power, and all suggested he was undoubtedly something other than a Russian—an Arab maybe, perhaps a Turk, but not a Russian. Not in a million years. For a few seconds he appeared confused as to his whereabouts and current predicament. Then he noticed a man with pockmarked cheeks waving to him from the open window of yet another car. As he stumbled gratefully toward it, he was calling out the same word over and over again. The word was "Tala." On that the witnesses were in complete agreement.

THERE IS A strict routine to vacating an Office safe property, rules to follow, rituals to observe. They are prescribed by God and chiseled into stone. They are inviolable, even when a pair of Russians sit dead in a grassy common. And even when the operation's brass ring lies bound and gagged in the back of an escape car. Gabriel and Eli Lavon engaged in the ceremonial purification of the safe flat now, silently and automatically, but with the devotion of zealots. Like their enemies, they were true believers.

At half past nine they locked the door and went down to the street. Another ritual ensued, the close inspection of the car for a bomb. Finding nothing out of the ordinary, they climbed inside. Gabriel allowed Lavon to drive. He was a pavement artist by instinct, not a wheelman, but his natural caution when operating a motor vehicle was at that moment an operational asset.

From Hamburg they drove south to a town called Döhle. Beyond it was a stand of dense trees accessed by only a rutted track with a sign that read PRIVAT.

Mikhail had found it a day earlier, along with three
suitable backup sites. The backups weren't necessary; the woods were deserted. Lavon doused the
headlights as he entered and navigated with only the
yellow glow of the parking lamps. The trees were a
mixture of evergreen and deciduous. Gabriel would
have preferred birch trees, but birch forests weren't
common in the west of Germany. Only in the east.

Finally, the parking lamps illuminated a Volkswagen sedan waiting in a small clearing. Mikhail
was leaning against the front fender, arms crossed,
Keller next to him smoking a cigarette. At their feet
lay Alexei Rozanov. His mouth was bound by duct
tape, as were his hands. Not that restraint was necessary. The SVR officer was hovering somewhere
between consciousness and coma.

"Has he said anything?"

"He didn't have much of a chance," replied Keller.

"Did he see your face?"

"I suppose so, but I doubt he remembers it."

"Bring him back. I need to have a word with him."

Keller fetched a liter bottle of mineral water from
the back of the car and poured it over Rozanov's
face until the Russian stirred.

"Put him on his feet," said Gabriel.

"I doubt he'll stay there."

"Do it."

Keller and Mikhail each seized one of Rozanov's
arms and lifted him upright. As predicted, the Russian didn't remain vertical for long. They raised him
again but this time kept their grip on his arms. His
head had fallen forward, his chin was on his chest.
He was taller than he had appeared in the surveil-

lance photographs, and heavier—more than two hundred pounds of formerly toned muscle that was going to fat. He had run a good operation, but Gabriel had run a better one. He removed the Glock from the waistband of his trousers and used the barrel to raise Rozanov's chin. It took a few seconds for the Russian's swollen eyes to focus. When they did, there was no trace of fear or recognition. He was good, thought Gabriel. He tore the tape from the Russian's mouth.

"You don't seem terribly surprised to see me, Alexei."

"Have we met?" murmured the Russian.

Gabriel gave a humorless smile. "No," he said after a moment, "I haven't had the displeasure until now. But I know your work well. Very well, in fact. Chapter and verse. There are just a few small details I need to clear up."

"What are you offering, Allon?"

"Nothing."

"Then you'll get nothing in return."

Gabriel pointed the gun toward Rozanov's right foot and pulled the trigger. The crack of the gunshot echoed among the trees. So did the Russian's screams.

"Are you beginning to get a sense of the gravity of your situation, Alexei?"

Rozanov was at that moment incapable of speech, so Gabriel spoke for him.

"You and your service left a bomb on Brompton Road in London. It was meant for my friend and me, but it killed fifty-two innocent people. You killed Charlotte Harris of Shepherd's Bush. You killed her son, who was called Peter after his grandfather. It's because of them that you're here tonight." Gabriel pointed the Glock at Rozanov's face. "How do you plead, Alexei?"

"Eamon Quinn planted that bomb," gasped Rozanov. "Not us."

"You paid him to do it, Alexei. And you gave him a helper named Katerina."

Rozanov looked up sharply and stared at Gabriel through a haze of pain.

"Where's Quinn?" asked Gabriel.

"I don't know where he is."

"Where?" asked Gabriel again.

"I'm telling you, Allon. I don't know where he is."

Gabriel aimed the gun at Rozanov's left foot and pulled the trigger.

"Jesus! Please stop!"

The Russian was no longer screaming in pain. He was weeping like a child—weeping, thought Gabriel, like the limbless survivors of one of Quinn's bombs. Quinn who could make a ball of fire travel a thousand feet per second. Quinn who was at a camp in Libya with a Palestinian named Tariq al-Hourani.

Do you suppose they knew each other?

I can't imagine they didn't.

"Let's start with something simple," said Gabriel calmly. "How did you get the number for my mobile phone?"

"It happened while you were in Omagh," said the Russian. "At the memorial. A woman was following you. She pretended to take your picture."

"I remember her."

"She wirelessly attacked your BlackBerry. We were never able to decrypt any of your files, but we *were* able to get your number."

"Which you gave to Quinn."

"Yes."

"It was Quinn who sent me that text message in London."

"'The bricks are in the wall.'"

"Where was he when he sent it?"

"Brompton Road," said the Russian. "Safely out of the blast zone."

"Why did you let him do it?"

"He wanted you to know it was him."

"Professional pride?"

"Apparently, it had something to do with a man named Tariq."

Gabriel felt his heart give a sideways lurch. "Tariq al-Hourani?"

"Yes, that's him. The Palestinian."

"What about Tariq?"

"Quinn said he wanted to repay an old debt."

"By killing me?"

Rozanov nodded. "Evidently, they were quite close."

It had to be true, thought Gabriel. There was no way Alexei Rozanov could have known about Tariq.

"Does Quinn know I'm still alive?"

"He was told earlier today."

"So you *do* know where he is?"

Rozanov said nothing. Gabriel pressed the barrel of the Glock against the inside the Russian's knee.

"Where is he, Alexei?"

"He's back in England."

"Where in England?"

"I don't know."

Gabriel ground the barrel of the gun painfully into the Russian's knee.

"I swear to you, Allon. I don't know where he is."

"Why is he back in England?"

"The second phase of the operation."

"Where will it happen?"

"Guy's Hospital in London."

"When?"

"Three p.m. tomorrow."

"And the target?"

"It's the prime minister. Quinn and Katerina are going to kill Jonathan Lancaster tomorrow afternoon in London."

59

NORTHERN GERMANY

THE RUSSIAN WAS WEAKENING, losing blood, losing the will to live. Even so, Gabriel walked him through it all, step by step, deal by deal, betrayal by betrayal, from the operation's sorry beginning to the e-mail that had arrived at Moscow Center earlier that evening. The e-mail that had been sent from an insecure device because the SVR-issue mobile phone belonging to one Katerina Akulova had transmitted its final watery signal from the bottom of the North Sea. Quinn, said Rozanov, had taken matters into his own hands. Quinn was outside Moscow Center's control. Quinn had gone rogue.

"Where were they when they sent the e-mail?"

"We were never able to trace it back to the source."

Gabriel stamped hard on Rozanov's shattered right foot. The Russian, when he regained the ability to speak, said the e-mail had been sent from an Internet café in the town of Fleetwood.

"Do they have a car?" asked Gabriel.

"A Renault."

"Model?"

"I believe it's a Scénic."

"What kind of attack is it going to be?"

"We're talking about Eamon Quinn. What do you think?"

"Vehicle borne?"

"That's his specialty."

"Car or truck?"

"Van."

"Where is it?"

"A garage in East London."

"Where in East London?"

Rozanov recited an address on Thames Road in Barking before his chin fell to his chest in exhaustion. With a glance, Gabriel instructed Keller and Mikhail to release their grip on him. When they did, the Russian toppled forward like a tree and landed on the damp floor of the forest. Gabriel rolled him over and pointed the gun at his face.

"What are you waiting for?" asked Rozanov.

Gabriel stared at the Russian down the barrel of the gun but said nothing.

"Perhaps it's true what they say about you."

"What's that?"

"That you're too old. That you don't have the stomach for it anymore."

Gabriel smiled. "I have one more question for you, Alexei."

"I've told you everything I know."

"Except for how you discovered I was still alive."

"We learned it through a communications intercept."

"What kind of intercept?"

"Voice," said Rozanov. "We heard your voice—"

Gabriel pointed the gun at Rozanov's knee and fired. The Russian seized up in agony.

"We . . . had . . . a . . . source."

"Where?"

"Inside . . . the . . . Office."

Gabriel fired a second shot into the same knee. "You'd better tell me the truth, Alexei. Otherwise, I'm going to waste all my bullets turning your knee to mush."

"Source," whispered Rozanov.

"Yes, I know. You had a source. But who was it?"

"He works . . ."

"Where does he work, Alexei?"

"MI6."

"In what department?"

"Personnel and . . ."

"Personnel and Security?"

"Yes."

"His name, Alexei. Tell me his name."

"I can't . . ."

"Tell me who he is, Alexei. Tell me so I can stop the pain."

PART THREE

BANDIT COUNTRY

60

VAUXHALL CROSS, LONDON

APPROXIMATELY ONE HOUR after the death of Alexei Rozanov, Graham Seymour received the first communication from his newest clandestine officer. It stated that the life of Prime Minister Jonathan Lancaster was in mortal peril and intimated that Russian intelligence had recruited a spy inside MI6. It was, Seymour would later say, a rather auspicious way to begin a career.

Given the circumstances, Seymour thought it best to send a private plane. It collected Gabriel and Keller at Le Bourget in Paris and delivered them to London City Airport in the Docklands. An MI6 car then ferried them at high speed to Vauxhall Cross, where Seymour waited in a windowless room on the top floor, a phone to his ear. He hung up as Gabriel and Keller entered and scrutinized them for a moment with expressionless gray eyes.

"Is there audio?" he asked finally.

Gabriel drew his BlackBerry, cued the recording to the relevant passage, and pressed the PLAY icon.

"Where will it happen?"

"Guy's Hospital in London."

"*When?*"

"*Three p.m. tomorrow.*"

"*And the target?*"

"*It's the prime minister. Quinn and Katerina are going to kill Jonathan Lancaster tomorrow afternoon in London.*"

Gabriel clicked PAUSE. Seymour stared at the phone.

"Alexei Rozanov?"

Gabriel nodded.

"Perhaps you should play it from the beginning."

"Actually, I think we should start at the end."

Gabriel recued the file and clicked PLAY a second time.

"*His name, Alexei. Tell me his name.*"

"*Grrrrr . . .*"

"*Sorry, Alexei, but I didn't catch that.*"

"*Grimes . . .*"

"*Is that his last name?*"

"*Yes.*"

"*And his first name, Alexei? Tell me his first name?*"

"*Arthur.*"

"*Arthur Grimes—is that his name?*"

"*Yes.*"

"*Arthur Grimes of the Personnel and Security department of MI6 is a paid agent of Russian intelligence?*"

"*Yes.*"

Next there was something that sounded very much like a gunshot. Gabriel tapped the PAUSE icon. Seymour closed his eyes.

At nine that morning a team from the A1A Branch of MI5 broke into the warehouse at 22 Thames Road in the Barking section of East London. They found no vehicles of any kind and no visible evidence to suggest a bomb had been constructed on the premises. Simultaneously, a second MI5 team entered the Internet café on Lord Street in Fleetwood. In a small stroke of good fortune, one of the employees on duty had worked the previous evening and recalled seeing a man and woman matching the descriptions of Quinn and Katerina. The employee also recalled which computer the couple had used. The MI5 team impounded the machine and loaded it onto a Royal Navy helicopter. It was expected to arrive in London no later than noon. Amanda Wallace had insisted that MI5's computer lab handle the forensic search. Graham Seymour, for political reasons, had agreed to her demand.

"Where's Grimes?" asked Gabriel.

"He entered the building a few minutes ago. A team is tearing apart his flat as we speak. It's a rather tricky business. Grimes is their immediate superior."

"How deep is his knowledge?"

"He's involved in the vetting process for current and prospective MI6 officers." Seymour glanced at Keller. "In fact, I spoke to him a few days ago about a special project that we would be undertaking soon."

"Me?" asked Keller.

Seymour nodded. "Grimes also investigates allegations of security breaches, which means he's in a perfect position to protect other Russian moles or spies. If he's really on the SVR's payroll, it's going to be the biggest scandal for Western intelligence since Aldrich Ames."

"Which is why you didn't mention any of this to Amanda Wallace."

Seymour said nothing.

"Would Grimes have known that Keller and I were staying at Wormwood Cottage?"

"He generally doesn't deal with safe houses, but he certainly knows when someone important is staying in one of them. In any case," Seymour added, "we'll know in a few minutes whether he was the source of the leak."

"How?"

"Yuri Volkov is going to tell us."

"Who's Volkov?"

"He's the deputy SVR *rezident* at the Russian Embassy. MI5 is convinced he met with an asset yesterday afternoon on the Underground. One of my men is at Thames House reviewing the footage now. In fact—"

The phone interrupted Seymour. He lifted the receiver and listened in silence for a few seconds. Then he killed the connection and placed a call of his own.

"Don't let him out of your sight. Not for a minute. If he goes to the gents, you go, too."

Seymour hung up the phone and looked at Gabriel and Keller.

"I should have retired when I had the chance."

"That would have been a big mistake," said Keller.

"Why?"

"Because you would have lost your chance to get Quinn."

"I'm not sure I want another chance. After all," Seymour added, "I haven't fared well against him. In fact, the score is two games to nil in his favor."

A heavy silence fell over the windowless room. Seymour and Keller were both staring at the phone. Gabriel was staring at the clock.

"How long do you intend to wait, Graham?"

"Before what?"

"Before you let me have a quiet word with Arthur Grimes."

"You're not going anywhere near him. No one is," Seymour added. "Not for a long time. It might be months before we're ready to start interrogating him."

"We don't have months, Graham. We have until three o'clock."

"There was no bomb in that warehouse in Barking."

"Not exactly encouraging news."

Seymour studied the clock. "We'll give the MI5 computer lab until two p.m. to locate that e-mail exchange. If they haven't found it by then, we'll confront Grimes."

"What do you intend to ask him?"

"I'll start with his train ride with Yuri Volkov."

"And do you know what he'll say to you?"

"No."

"Yuri who."

"You're a fatalistic bastard."

"I know," said Gabriel. "It prevents me from being disappointed later."

61

BRISTOL, ENGLAND

A T NINE O'CLOCK that morning, BBC Radio 4 broadcast its first account of the incident in Hamburg. The report was brief and fragmentary. Two men had been shot to death, two others were missing. The dead men were both Russians; of the missing men little was known. The German chancellor was said to be deeply concerned. The Kremlin was said to be outraged. These days, it usually was.

Quinn and Katerina heard the report while driving along the M5 north of Birmingham. An hour later they listened to an update while sitting outside Marks & Spencer at the Cribbs Causeway Retail Park in Bristol. The ten o'clock version contained a single new piece of information. According to the German police, the dead men were both carrying diplomatic passports. Katerina switched off the radio as a BBC foreign policy specialist was explaining how the incident threatened to spiral into a full-fledged crisis.

"Now we know why Allon faked his own death," she said.

"Why would Alexei have been in Hamburg last night?"

"Maybe he was deceived into going there."

"By whom?"

"Allon, of course. He's probably interrogating Alexei right now. Or maybe Alexei's already dead. Either way, we have to assume that Allon knows where we are. Which means we have to leave England immediately."

Quinn made no reply.

"What if I can prove Alexei was in that car?" asked Katerina.

"Another e-mail to Moscow Center?"

She nodded.

"Not a chance."

She glanced around at the other vehicles in the car park. "They could be watching us right now."

"They aren't."

"You're sure?"

"I've been fighting them for a long time, Katerina. I'm sure."

She didn't appear convinced. "I'm not a jihadist, Eamon. I didn't come here to die. Get me out of England. We'll make contact with the Center and arrange a payment for my safe return."

"That's exactly what we're going to do," said Quinn. "But we have to take care of one piece of business first."

Katerina watched a pair of women walking toward the entrance of Marks & Spencer.

"Why are we here?" she asked.

"We're going to do some shopping."

"And then?"

"We're going to take a walk."

62

10 DOWNING STREET

GRAHAM SEYMOUR LEFT Vauxhall Cross shortly after noon to brief Prime Minister Jonathan Lancaster at 10 Downing Street. He told Lancaster that Eamon Quinn was almost certainly back in the country and plotting another attack—perhaps on Guy's Hospital during the prime minister's appearance, perhaps on another target. They would know more, explained Seymour, once MI5's lab completed its assault on the computer from Fleetwood. He made no mention of Arthur Grimes and his covert encounter with Yuri Volkov of the Russian Embassy. He believed in doling out bad news in small portions.

"You just missed Amanda," the prime minister said. "She advised me to cancel my visit to Guy's Hospital. She also thought it might be a good idea for me to remain locked inside Number Ten until Quinn is captured."

"Amanda is a wise woman."

"When she agrees with you." The prime minister smiled. "It's good to see you two are playing nicely together." He paused, then asked, "You *are* playing nicely, aren't you, Graham?"

"Yes, Prime Minister."

"Then I'll tell you the same thing I told her," Lancaster continued. "I'm not going to change my schedule because of some IRA terrorist."

"This has nothing to do with the IRA. It's strictly business."

"All the more reason." The prime minister rose and escorted Seymour to the door. "One more thing, Graham."

"Yes, Prime Minister?"

"No arrests on this one."

"I'm sorry, sir?"

"You heard me. No arrests." He put his hand on Seymour's shoulder. "You know, Graham, sometimes revenge is good for the soul."

"I don't want revenge, Prime Minister."

"Then I suggest you find someone who does and put him very close to Eamon Quinn."

"I believe I have just the man. Two men, actually."

Seymour's car was waiting outside Downing Street's famous black door. It ferried him back to Vauxhall Cross, where he found Gabriel and Keller in the windowless room on the top floor. It looked as though they hadn't moved a muscle since he'd left.

"How was he?" asked Gabriel.

"Resolute to the point of stubbornness."

404   DANIEL SILVA

"What time does his motorcade leave Downing Street?"

"Two forty-five."

Gabriel looked at the clock. It was five minutes to two.

"I know we said two o'clock, Graham, but—"

"We wait until two."

The three men sat motionless and silent while the final five minutes slipped away. At the stroke of two, Seymour rang Amanda Wallace across the river at Thames House and asked about the status of the computer search.

"They're close," said Amanda.

"How close?"

"Within the hour."

"That's not good enough."

"What do you want me to do?"

"Call me the minute you have something."

Seymour hung up and looked at Gabriel. "It might be better if you weren't here for this."

"It might be," said Gabriel, "but I wouldn't miss it for the world."

Seymour picked up the phone again and dialed.

"Arthur," he said genially. "It's Graham. So glad I caught you."

Seven floors beneath Graham Seymour's feet, a man in a gray cubicle slowly hung up his phone. Like all the cubicles in Vauxhall Cross, it had no nameplate, only a series of numbers broken by a slash. It was odd that Graham Seymour had spoken his name because most people at Vauxhall Cross referred to him by his job title, which was Personnel. *Go and fetch Personnel. Run and hide, here comes Personnel.* His name was a slur, an insult. He was loathed and resented. Mostly, he was feared. He was the exposer of other men's secrets, the chronicler of their shortcomings and lies. He knew about their affairs, their problems with money, their weakness for alcohol. He had the power to ruin careers or, if so inclined, to save them. He was judge, jury, and executioner—a god in a gray box. And yet he, too, had harbored a secret. Somehow, the Russians had found it. They had given him a young girl, a Lolita, and in return they had taken his last shred of dignity.

It's Graham. So glad I caught you . . .

Interesting choice of words, thought Grimes. Perhaps it had been a Freudian slip, but he suspected otherwise. The timing of Seymour's summons— one day after Grimes had made a wireless dead drop on the Underground—was ominous. It had been a reckless encounter, a crash meeting. And in the process, it seemed he had exposed himself.

So glad I caught you . . .

His suit jacket was hanging from a hook in the wall, next to a photo of his family, the last one taken before the divorce. Outside in the corridor, Nick Rowe was flirting with a pretty girl from Registry— Rowe, who had been hovering around Grimes all day. He slipped past the pair without a word and went to the elevators. A car appeared the instant he pressed the call button. Surely, he thought, it was no accident.

The car rose so smoothly that Grimes had no

sense of movement. When the doors hissed open he saw Ed Marlowe, another man from his department, standing in the vestibule. "Arthur!" he called out, as though Grimes were suddenly hard of hearing. "Buy you a drink later? A couple of small matters to discuss."

Without waiting for a reply, Marlowe ducked between the closing elevator doors and was gone. Grimes stepped from the vestibule into the dazzling light of the atrium. It was the Valhalla of spydom, the Promised Land. The room where Graham Seymour waited was to the right. To the left was a doorway that led to the terrace. Grimes went to the left and stepped outside. The cold air hit him like a slap. Beneath him flowed the Thames, dark, leaden, and somehow reassuring. Grimes drew a deep breath and calmly collected his thoughts. He had the advantage of knowing their techniques. His cubicle was in order. So was his flat, his bank accounts, his computers, and his phones. They had nothing on him, nothing but a ride on the Tube with Yuri Volkov. He would beat them. He was above reproach, he thought. He was Personnel.

Just then, he heard a sound at his back, a door opening and closing. He rotated slowly and saw Graham Seymour standing on the terrace. His gray hair was moving in the wind and he was smiling— the same smile, thought Grimes, that had greased his way up the ladder of promotion while better men were left to toil in the boiler rooms of intelligence. Seymour was not alone. Standing behind him was a smaller man with unusually green eyes and temples the color of ash. Grimes recognized him. His bowels turned to water.

"Arthur," said Seymour with the same false geniality he had used on the telephone a moment earlier. "What are you doing? We're all waiting for you inside."

"Sorry, Graham. It's not often I have a reason to come up here."

Grimes offered a smile in return, though it was nothing like Seymour's. Gums and teeth, he thought, and more than a trace of guilt. Turning, he faced the river again, and suddenly he was running. A hand reached for him as he hurled himself over the balustrade, and as he plummeted toward the next terrace he imagined he was flying. Then the ground came rushing up to receive him and he landed with a thud that sounded like splitting fruit.

It was a fall of several floors, enough to kill a man, but not instantly. For a moment or two he was aware of familiar faces hovering over him. They were faces from files, faces of MI6 officers whose lives he had ransacked at will. And yet even in his suffering, no one referred to him by his given name. Personnel had fallen from the roof terrace, they said. Personnel was dead.

CORNWALL, ENGLAND

A T THE MARKS & SPENCER in Bristol, Quinn and Katerina purchased two pairs of hiking boots, two rucksacks, binoculars, walking sticks, and a guidebook for Devon and Cornwall. They loaded the bags into the back of the Renault and drove westward to the Cornish town of Helston. Its neighbor was the Royal Naval Air Station Culdrose, Europe's largest helicopter base. Quinn felt his chest tighten as he drove along the station's tall chain-link fence topped with swirls of concertina wire. Then a Sea King floated over the road and he was suddenly back in the Bandit Country of South Armagh. His war was over, he told himself. Today his war was here.

Three miles south of the airfield lay the village of Mullion. Quinn followed the signs to the Old Inn and found a car park directly across the lane, next to the Atlantic Forge beach shop. They pulled on the hiking boots and the oilskin coats; then Quinn stuffed the map, guidebook, and binoculars into the canvas rucksack. He left the bag of weapons in the car and carried only the Makarov. Katerina was unarmed.

"What's our cover story?" she asked as she finished dressing.

"Holidaymakers."

"In winter?"

"I've always been fond of sea resorts in winter."

"Where are we staying?"

"Your choice."

"How about the Godolphin Arms in Marazion?"

Quinn smiled. "You're very good, you know."

"Better than you."

"Can you pull off a British accent?"

She hesitated, then said, "Yes, I think I can."

"You're a banker from London. And I'm your Panamanian boyfriend."

"Lucky me."

They set out from the village along the Poldhu Road, Quinn at the edge of the asphalt, Katerina safely in the verge. After a half mile, a break appeared in the hedgerow and a small sign pointed them toward a public pathway. They negotiated a cattle grid and crossed a farmer's field to the South West Coast Path. They followed it north along the cliff tops to Poldhu Beach, then along the edge of Mullion Golf Club to the ancient church of St. Winwaloe. After paying a brief visit to the church for the sake of their cover, they continued north to Gunwalloe Cove. The cottage stood alone atop the cliffs at the southern end, nestled in a natural garden of thrift and fescue. Two cars were parked in the drive.

"That's it," said Quinn.

He dropped the rucksack, removed the binoculars, and swept the cliff tops, as though admiring the view. Then he took direct aim at the cottage.

One of the cars was unoccupied, but in the other sat two men. Quinn scanned the windows of the cottage. The shades were tightly drawn.

"We have company," said Katerina.

"I see him," said Quinn, lowering the binoculars.

"What do we do?"

"We walk."

Quinn returned the binoculars to the rucksack and the rucksack to his shoulder. Then he and Katerina set off again in the same direction. A hundred yards ahead, a man was walking toward them along the cliff tops. He was no ordinary hiker, thought Quinn. Disciplined movements, light on his feet, a gun beneath his dark blue windcheater. He was ex-military, perhaps even ex-SAS. Quinn felt the Makarov pistol pressing against the base of his spine. He wished it were more readily available, but it was too late to make a change now.

"Start talking," murmured Quinn.

"About what?"

"About how much fun you had with Bill and Mary last weekend and how you wish you could afford a place in the countryside. Maybe a little cottage in the Cotswolds."

"I hate the Cotswolds."

Nevertheless, Katerina spoke with passionate enthusiasm about Bill and Mary and their farm near Chipping Campden. And how Bill became flirty when he drank and how Mary was secretly besotted with Thomas, a good-looking colleague from the office whom Katerina always thought was gay. It was then that the ex-soldier came upon them. Quinn fell in behind Katerina to give the man room to pass. She slowed long enough to wish him a pleasant morning, but Quinn kept his eyes on the ground and said nothing.

"Did you see the way he was looking at us?" asked Katerina when they were alone again.

"Keep walking," said Quinn. "And whatever you do, don't look over your shoulder."

The cottage was now directly ahead of them. The coastal path ran behind it, along the edge of a green field. A slight differential in elevation allowed Quinn to peer innocently over a protective hedge and glimpse the faces of the two men sitting in the parked car. Katerina was speaking rather judgmentally about Mary, and Quinn was nodding slowly, as though he found her remarks unusually perceptive. Then, approximately fifty yards past the cottage, he stopped at the cliff's edge and gazed down into the cove. A man was casting a line into the heavy surf. Behind him a woman walked along a stretch of golden sand, trailed by another man whose windcheater was the same color as the one worn by the ex-soldier on the cliffs. The woman was walking away from them, slowly, aimlessly, like a prisoner taking her allotted exercise in the yard. Quinn waited until she turned before lifting the binoculars to his eyes. Then he offered them to Katerina.

"I don't need them," she said.

"Is that her?"

Katerina stared at the woman walking toward her along the water's edge.

"Yes," she answered finally. "It's her."

IN THE MINUTES following the suicide of Arthur Grimes, Graham Seymour once again appealed to Jonathan Lancaster to cancel his visit to Guy's Hospital. The prime minister held firm, though he did agree to add two men to his security detail. Two men who shared his opinion that revenge could be good for the soul. Two men who wanted Eamon Quinn dead. The head of SO1, the division of the Metropolitan Police that protects the prime minister and his family, was predictably appalled by the notion of adding two outsiders to his detail, one an officer of a foreign intelligence service, the other a man of violence with a dubious past. Nevertheless, he gave them radios and credentials that would open any door at the hospital. He also gave each a Glock 17 9mm pistol. It was a breach of every known protection protocol, but one that had been ordered by the prime minister himself.

There wasn't time for Gabriel and Keller to go to Downing Street, so a Metropolitan Police BMW scooped them up outside Vauxhall Cross and shot them up Kennington Lane toward Southwark. The historic Guy's Hospital, one of London's tallest structures, rose above a tangle of streets near the Thames, not far from London Bridge. The MPS unit dropped them off outside the futuristic skyscraper known as the Shard. Parking was forbidden on the street under normal circumstances and now, with the prime minister's arrival imminent, it was empty of traffic. There were several vehicles parked on Weston Street, though, including a white commercial van that was sitting low on its axles. On Gabriel's order, the Metropolitan Police tracked down the owner. He was a contractor, a veteran of the Royal Navy, who was doing renovation work in a nearby building. The van was loaded with limestone flooring tiles.

The last street adjoining the complex was Snowfields, a narrow urban gully with no parking, and on that day no cars other than police units. Gabriel and Keller followed it to Gate 3, the hospital's primary entrance, and passed through a cordon of security. The secretary of state for health waited outside in the forecourt, along with a team from the National Health Service and a large delegation from the hospital staff, many in white coats and scrubs. Gabriel moved silently among them, searching for the face he had sketched at the cottage in County Galway, searching for the woman he had seen for the first time in a quiet street in Lisbon. Then he rang Graham Seymour in the operations room at Vauxhall Cross.

"How far out is the prime minister?"

"Two minutes."

"Any news on the Fleetwood computer?"

"They're close."

"That's what they said an hour ago."

"I'll call you the minute they have something."

The connection went dead. Gabriel dropped the phone into his pocket and stared at Gate 3. A moment later two motorcycle outriders appeared, followed by a customized Jaguar limousine. Jonathan Lancaster bounded from the backseat and began shaking hands.

"Does he really have to do that?" asked Keller.

"I'm afraid it's congenital."

"Let's hope Quinn isn't in the neighborhood. Otherwise, it might be fatal."

The prime minister shook the last proffered hand. Then he looked toward Gabriel and Keller, nodded once, and went inside. It was three o'clock on the dot.

65

GUNWALLOE COVE, CORNWALL

A T THE INSTANT Jonathan Lancaster disappeared through the doors of Guy's Hospital, rain began to fall on central London, but in the deepest reaches of West Cornwall, a low sun shone through a slit in the stratified layers of cloud. The clear weather was an operational asset, for it lent credence to Katerina's presence on the beach at Gunwalloe Cove. She had arrived there at 2:50 p.m., five minutes after dropping Quinn near the ancient church. The Renault was in the car park above the cove, and in the rucksack at her side was a Samsung disposable phone and a Skorpion submachine gun with an ACC Evolution–9 sound suppressor screwed into the barrel.

You always liked the Skorpion, didn't you, Katerina?

During the drive from the church to the cove, she had briefly considered fleeing England and leaving Quinn to his fate. Instead, she had chosen to stay and see her mission to its end. She was all but certain Alexei was now dead. Even so, she knew it would be unwise to return to Russia having failed to carry out her assignment. It was the tsar who had sent her back to England, not Alexei. And like all Russians, Katerina knew better than to disappoint the tsar.

She checked the time. It was five minutes past three. Quinn would be nearing the cottage. Perhaps one of the security guards would approach him, the way the ex-soldier had done that morning. If that happened, Quinn would kill him, and then there would only be three men protecting the target— the two outside the cottage and the one now fishing in the cove. Katerina was certain of his identity. She could see the outline of a weapon beneath his jacket, and the miniature radio he had used to alert his colleagues to the presence of a visitor in the cove. In short order, the guard's radio would undoubtedly crackle with some sort of emergency signal. Or perhaps there wouldn't be time for a radio alert. Either way, the guard's destiny was the same. He was viewing his last sunset.

He hauled a fish from the sea, placed it in a yellow bucket at the tide line, and baited his hook. Then, after acknowledging Katerina with a nod, he waded into the breakers again and cast his line. Smiling, Katerina lifted the flap of the rucksack, exposing the stock of the Skorpion. It was set to full automatic mode, which meant it would be capable of firing twenty rounds in less than a second with minimal muzzle climb. Quinn was identically armed.

Just then, the Samsung mobile vibrated and a text message appeared on the screen: THE BRICKS ARE IN THE WALL . . . He had to do it, she thought. He had to let the British know it was him. She dropped the mobile phone into the rucksack, wrapped her hand

around the grip of the Skorpion, and stared at the
man in the breakers. Suddenly, his head snapped
sharply upward and to the left, toward the cliff
tops. Too late, he turned, only to find Katerina advancing toward him across the sand, the Skorpion
in her outstretched hands.

*Twenty rounds in less than a second, minimal muzzle
climb . . .*

The next waves that broke across the sand were
red with the blood of the dead MI6 security man.
Katerina calmly reloaded the Skorpion and climbed
the steep path to the car park. It was deserted except
for the Renault. She slid behind the wheel, started
the engine, and headed down the drive toward the
cottage.

66

THAMES HOUSE, LONDON

NOTHING IN THE language of the exchange was outwardly suspicious, but to the experienced eye of the MI5 tech it stank of inauthenticity. So did the addresses of the two participants. He showed the printout to his superior, and the superior in turn brought it to the attention of Miles Kent. Kent was most intrigued by a street address that appeared in the final e-mail. The address seemed familiar, so he quickly ran it through an MI5 database and there discovered an alarming match. His next stop was the operations room where Amanda Wallace was monitoring the prime minister's visit to Guy's Hospital. He placed the printout in front of her. Amanda read it and frowned.

"What does it mean?"

"Look at the address carefully."

Amanda did. "Isn't that the cottage where Allon used to live?"

Kent nodded.

"Who lives there now?"

"You should probably ask Graham Seymour."

Amanda reached for the phone.

Five seconds later, on the opposite bank of the Thames, in yet another operations room, Graham Seymour picked up the call.

"What do you have?"

"A problem."

"What's wrong?"

"Is anyone staying at Allon's cottage in West Cornwall?"

Seymour hesitated, then said, "I'm sorry, Amanda, but it's not something I can talk about."

"My God," she whispered gravely. "I was afraid you were going to say that."

The cottage was officially designated an MI6 safe facility, so it contained no active telephone line. Nor had its current occupant been entrusted with a mobile, lest she say something in an unguarded moment to divulge her whereabouts to her enemies. All attempts to contact her guardians proved unsuccessful. Their phones rang unanswered. Their radios crackled with no response.

One call, however, was answered without delay. It was the call that Graham Seymour placed to Gabriel's mobile at 3:17 p.m. Gabriel was in the auditorium at Guy's Hospital, where the prime minister was about to offer a remedy to the ills facing Britain's sacred government-run health care system. Seymour was watching a live feed of the event on the video screens in the operations room. He spoke with more calm than he would have thought possible, given the circumstances.

"I'm afraid the prime minister wasn't the target. There's a helicopter waiting for you and Keller on the pad in Battersea. The Metropolitan Police will give you a ride over."

The call went dead. Seymour replaced the receiver and stared at the screen as two men rushed from the auditorium.

67

WEST CORNWALL

MADELINE HART NEVER heard the gunshots, only the sharp crack of splintering wood. And then she had seen the man rushing through the broken front door of the cottage, an ugly-looking submachine gun in his hands. He had driven his fist into her abdomen—a brutal blow that had left her incapable of uttering a sound or drawing a breath—and as she lay writhing he had bound her hands and mouth with tape and covered her head in a hood of black serge cloth. Even so, she became aware of the presence of a second intruder, smaller than the first, lighter in step. Together they wrenched her to her feet and marched her gasping across her room with a view. Outside, a phone rang unanswered—the phone, she assumed, of one of her security guards. The intruders forced her into the trunk of a car and slammed the hatch with a coffin finality. She heard tires crunching over gravel and, faintly, waves breaking in the cove. Then the sea abandoned her and there was only the rush of rubber over asphalt. And voices. Two voices, one a man, the other a woman. The man was almost certainly from Ireland, but the woman's muddled accent did not betray her homeland. Madeline was certain of only one thing. She had heard the voice somewhere before.

She could not fathom the direction they were driving, only that the road was of moderate quality. It was a B road, she thought. Not that it mattered much; her knowledge of Cornwall's geography was limited by the fact that she had remained a virtual prisoner of Gabriel's cottage. Yes, there was the occasional ride down to Lizard Point for tea and scones at the café atop the cliffs, but for the most part she ventured no farther than the beach in Gunwalloe Cove. A man from MI6 headquarters in London came out to Cornwall regularly to brief her about her security situation—or, as he put it, to read her the riot act. His presentation rarely varied. Her defection, he said, had been a grave embarrassment to the Kremlin. It was only a matter of time before the Russians attempted to correct the situation.

Apparently that time had come. Madeline supposed her abduction was linked to the attempt on Gabriel's life. The man with the Irish accent was undoubtedly Eamon Quinn. *And the woman?* Madeline listened now to the low murmur of her voice and the peculiar blend of German, British, and Russian accents. Then she closed her eyes and saw two girls sitting in a park in a movie-set English village. Two girls who had been taken from their mothers and raised by wolves. Two girls who one day would be sent into the world to spy for a country they had never truly known. Now it seemed that someone at

Moscow Center had dispatched one of the girls to kill the other. Only a Russian could be so cruel.

Madeline had only the thinnest grasp on time, but she reckoned that twenty minutes elapsed before the car stopped. The engine died, the hatch rose, and two pairs of hands lifted her upright—one male, the other discernibly female. The air was sharp and iodized, the ground beneath her feet rocky and unstable. She could hear the sea and, overhead, the cry of circling gulls. As they moved closer to the water's edge, an engine fired and she smelled smoke. They splashed her through a foot of water and forced her aboard a small craft. Instantly, the craft came about and, rising on an approaching wave, headed out to sea. Hooded and bound, Madeline listened to the rotor churning beneath the surface of the water. You're going to die, it seemed to be saying. You're already dead.

68

GUNWALLOE COVE, CORNWALL

THE HELICOPTER WAITING on the pad at Battersea was a Westland Sea King transport with Rolls-Royce Gnome turboshaft engines. It bore Gabriel and Keller across the width of southern England at 110 knots, just shy of its top speed. They reached Plymouth at six, and a few minutes later Gabriel spotted the lighthouse at Lizard Point. The pilot wanted to set down at Culdrose, but Gabriel prevailed upon him to go straight to Gunwalloe instead. As they passed over the cottage, the rotating blue lights of police cruisers flashed in the drive and along the road from the Lamb and Flag. Light shone in the cove, too. It was crime-scene white. Gabriel felt suddenly ill. His beloved Cornish sanctuary, the place where he had found peace and restoration after some of his most difficult operations, was now a place of death.

The pilot dropped Gabriel and Keller at the northern end of the cove. They came down the tide line at a sprint and stopped at the crime-scene lamps. In their harsh downward glow lay the corpse of a man. He had been shot repeatedly in the chest.

The tight dispersal suggested the gunman had been well trained. Or perhaps, thought Gabriel, the killer had been a woman. He looked up at the four men standing over the body. Two were wearing the uniform of the Devon and Cornwall Police. The other two were plainclothes detectives from the Major Crime Branch. Gabriel wondered how long they'd been present. Long enough, he thought, to light up the cove like a football stadium at night.

"Do you really have to use those arc lamps? It's not as if he's going anywhere."

"Who's asking?" replied one of the detectives.

"MI6," said Keller quietly. It was the first time he had identified himself as an employee of Her Majesty's Secret Service, and the effect on his audience was instantaneous.

"I'll need to see some identification," said the detective.

Keller pointed toward the Sea King at the end of the cove and said, "That's my identification. Now do what the man says and turn off the damn lights."

One of the uniformed officers turned off the arc lamps.

"Now tell the cruisers to kill their flashers."

The same officer gave the order over his radio. Gabriel looked up toward the cottage and saw the blue lights go dark. Then he stared down at the corpse lying at his feet.

"Where did you find him?"

"Are you MI6, too?" asked the plainclothes detective.

"Answer his question," snapped Keller.

"He was at the water's edge."

"He'd been fishing?" asked Gabriel.

"How did you know?"

"Lucky guess."

The detective turned and pointed toward the cliffs. "The shooter was over there. We found twenty shell casings." He looked down at the body. "Obviously, most of them found their target. He was probably dead before he hit the water."

"Any witnesses?"

"None that have come forward."

"What about footprints near the shell casings."

The detective nodded. "Whoever did the shooting was wearing hiking boots."

"What size?"

"Small."

"Was it a woman?"

"Could have been."

Without another word, Gabriel led Keller up the footpath to the cottage. They entered through the French doors off the terrace. Gabriel's living room had been converted into a field command post. The broken front door hung ajar on one hinge, and through the opening he observed two more bodies lying in the drive. A tall detective approached and introduced himself as DI Frazier. Gabriel accepted the detective's hand, but did not identify himself. Neither did Keller.

"Which one of you is MI6?" asked the DI.

Gabriel looked at Keller.

"And you?" the detective asked Gabriel.

"He's a friend of the service," said Keller.

The detective's disdain for irregulars was written clearly on his face. "We've got four fatalities that we know of," he said. "One in the cove, two outside the cottage, and a fourth on the coastal path. He was hit once in the chest and once in the head. Never had a chance to draw his sidearm. The ones in the drive were hit multiple times, like the bloke in the cove."

"And the woman who lives here?" asked Gabriel.

"She's unaccounted for."

The detective walked over to Gabriel's easel, upon which he had hung a map of West Cornwall. "We have two witnesses from the village who noticed a Renault driving at high speed shortly after three this afternoon. The car was headed north. We've established roadblocks here, here, and here," he added, touching the map in three places. "Neither witness managed to see the driver, but both said the passenger was a woman."

"Your witnesses are correct," said Gabriel.

The detective turned away from the map. "Who is she?"

"An assassin from Russian intelligence."

"And the man driving the car?"

"He used to be the Real IRA's best bomb maker, which means you're wasting time with those roadblocks. You need to be concentrating your resources on the west coast. You should also be checking the trunk of every car rolling onto the Irish ferries tonight."

"Does the Real IRA man have a name?"

"Eamon Quinn."

"And the Russian?"

"Her name is Katerina. But in all likelihood, she's posing as a German. Don't be fooled by her appearance," added Gabriel. "She put twenty rounds through the heart of that security guard in the cove."

"And the woman they kidnapped?"

"It's not important who she is. She'll be the one with a bag over her head."

The detective turned again and studied the map. "Do you know how long the Cornish coast is?"

"More than four hundred miles," answered Gabriel, "with dozens of small coves. Which is why it was a smuggler's paradise."

"Is there anything else you can tell me?"

"There's tea in the pantry," said Gabriel. "And a sleeve of McVitie's, too."

69

GUNWALLOE COVE, CORNWALL

A T EIGHT THAT evening they brought the body up from the cove by torchlight and laid it out in the drive next to the others. The dead did not remain there long; within an hour a procession of vans arrived to transport them to the medical examiner's office in Exeter. There a highly trained professional would declare the obvious, that four men of secret employment had perished of bullet wounds to their vital organs. Or perhaps, thought Gabriel, the medical examiner would never see the bodies. Perhaps Graham Seymour and Amanda Wallace would manage to sweep the whole bloody mess under the rug. Quinn had managed to deliver yet another scandal to the doorstep of British intelligence—a scandal that would have been avoided if the MI5 computer lab had found an e-mail exchange a few minutes earlier than it had. Gabriel couldn't help but feel he bore some of the responsibility. None of it would have happened, he thought, if he hadn't laid a copy of *A Room with a View* on the lap of a beautiful young woman in the Hermitage Museum in St. Petersburg.

I believe this belongs to you . . .

There would be time for recriminations later. For now, finding Madeline was Gabriel's only concern. The Devon and Cornwall Police were watching every beach and cove in the region—anywhere a small craft might put ashore. In addition, Graham Seymour had quietly asked the Coast Guard to step up patrols along the southwest of England. All prudent steps, thought Gabriel, but probably too little too late. Quinn was gone. And so was Madeline. But why kidnap her? Why not leave her dead with her guardians as a warning to any other Russian spies pondering defection?

Gabriel couldn't bear to be inside the cottage—not with the police making a mess of the place, not with the bullet holes in the door and the memories stalking him at every turn—so he and Keller sat outside on the terrace, bundled in their coats. Gabriel watched the lights of a big freighter far out in the Atlantic and wondered whether Madeline was on it. Keller smoked a cigarette and stared down at the Sea King. No one intruded on their silence until shortly after ten, when the detective informed them a Renault Scénic had been found at the edge of a remote cove near West Pentire, on Cornwall's northern coast. The vehicle had been empty except for a shopping bag from Marks & Spencer.

"I don't suppose there was a receipt?" asked Gabriel.

"Afraid not." The detective was silent for a moment. "My DCI has been in touch with the Home Office," he said finally. "I know who you are."

"Then you'll accept our apologies for the way we spoke to your men earlier."

"None necessary. But you may want to remove any valuables from the cottage before you leave. Apparently, MI6 is sending a team to clean out the place."

"Ask them to handle my easel with care," said Gabriel. "It has sentimental value."

The detective withdrew, leaving Gabriel and Keller alone. The lights of the freighter had disappeared into the night.

"Where do you suppose he took her?" asked Keller.

"Somewhere he feels comfortable. Somewhere he knows the terrain and the players." Gabriel looked at Keller. "Know any place like that?"

"Unfortunately, only one."

"Bandit Country?"

Keller nodded. "And if he manages to get her there, he'll have a distinct home-field advantage."

"We have an advantage, too, Christopher."

"What's that?"

"Number Eight Stratford Gardens."

Keller was staring at the Sea King again. "Have you considered the possibility that this is exactly what Quinn wants?"

"Another shot at us?"

"Yes."

"Does it make a difference?"

"No," said Keller. "But it might not be something you should be getting involved in. After all . . ."

Keller left the thought unfinished because it

was obvious that Gabriel was no longer listening. He had pulled his BlackBerry from his pocket and was in the process of dialing Graham Seymour at Vauxhall Cross. Their conversation was brief, two minutes, no more. Then Gabriel returned the phone to his pocket and pointed toward the cove, where thirty seconds later the turboshaft engine of the Sea King began to whine. Slowly, he rose to his feet and followed Keller numbly down the path to the beach. He saw the cottage for the last time as he had seen it for the first, from a mile out to sea, knowing he would never set foot there again. Quinn had destroyed it for him, as surely as he had helped Tariq destroy Leah and Dani. It was personal now, he thought. And it was going to be very messy.

70

COUNTY DOWN, NORTHERN IRELAND

A T THAT SAME MOMENT the *Catherine May*, a Vigilante 33 commercial fishing vessel, was making twenty-six knots through St. George's Channel. Jack Delaney, a former member of the IRA who specialized in weapons smuggling and the movement of explosive devices, was at the helm. Delaney's younger brother Connor was leaning in the companionway, smoking a cigarette. By three in the morning they were due east of Dublin, and by five they had reached the mouth of Carlingford Lough, the glacial inlet that forms the border between the Republic of Ireland and Ulster. The ancient fishing port of Ardglass was approximately twenty miles to the north. Quinn waited until he could see the first flash of the Ardglass lighthouse before firing up his mobile. He composed a brief text message and with considerable reluctance fired it insecurely into the ether. Ten seconds later came the reply.

"Shit," said Quinn.

"What's the problem?" asked Jack Delaney.

"Ardglass is too hot for us to put in there."

"What about Kilkeel?"

Kilkeel was a fishing port located about thirty miles to the south of Ardglass. It was a majority Protestant town where loyalist sentiment ran deep. Quinn suggested it in a second text. When the reply came a few seconds later, he looked at Delaney and shook his head.

"Where does he want us to go?"

"He says Shore Road is quiet."

"Where?"

"Just north of the castle."

"It's not one of my favorite spots."

"Can you get in and out before sunrise?"

"No problem."

Jack Delaney increased the speed and set a course for the southern tip of the Ards Peninsula. Quinn peered into the forward cabin and saw Madeline lying bound and hooded on one of the two berths. She had passed the journey quietly. Katerina, who had made several emergency visits to the head to be sick, was smoking a cigarette at the galley table.

"How are you feeling?" asked Quinn.

"Do you care?"

"Not really."

She nodded toward the Ardglass lighthouse and said, "Looks as though we missed our exit."

"Change in plan," said Quinn.

"Police?"

Quinn nodded.

"What did you expect?"

"Get ready," he said. "We have one more boat ride."

"Lucky me."

Quinn slipped through the companionway and went onto the deck. The weather was clear and cold, and a spray of stars shone brightly in the black sky. The coastline north of Ardglass was mainly farmland, with a few scattered cottages overlooking the sea. Quinn swept the landscape with his binoculars, but it was still too dark to see anything. They churned past Guns Island, an uninhabited lump of green two hundred yards off the village of Ballyhornan, and a few minutes later rounded the rocky headland that guarded the mouth of Strangford Lough. Channel markers pointed the route north. The first lights were starting to come on in the cottages along Shore Road, enough so that Quinn could discern the silhouette of Kilclief Castle. Then he saw three bursts of light a little farther up the shoreline. He sent a text message that consisted only of a question mark. The reply said the front door was wide open.

Quinn readied the Zodiac and returned to the cabin. He pointed toward the spot where he had seen the flashes of light and instructed Jack Delaney to make for it. Then he ducked down the steps into the forward cabin and snatched the hood from Madeline's head. A pair of eyes glared at him in the semidarkness.

"Time to go ashore," said Quinn. "Be a good lass. Otherwise, I'll put a bullet through your brain. Are we clear?"

The two eyes stared coldly back at him. No fear there, thought Quinn, only anger. He had to admit he admired her courage. He pulled the black hood over her head and lifted her to her feet.

Connor Delaney took them in straight and fast. Quinn climbed out into a foot of water. Then, with Katerina's help, he lifted Madeline from the Zodiac and marched her toward the car parked along the edge of the road. The car was a Peugeot 508, dark gray. The boot was open. Quinn forced Madeline inside and slammed the lid. Then he and Katerina climbed into the car, Katerina in the front passenger seat, Quinn stretched across the backseat, the Makarov pointed at her spine. Behind the wheel, wearing a reefer coat and a woolen watch cap, was Billy Conway. "Welcome home," he said. Then he started the engine and pulled onto the road.

They headed west toward Downpatrick. Quinn turned his face away instinctively as a unit from the PSNI approached from the opposite direction, lights flashing.

"Where do you suppose he's going so early on a lovely Saturday morning?"

"It's like that all across the six counties." Billy Conway glanced into the rearview mirror. "I suppose you're the cause of it."

"I suppose I am."

"Who's the girl in the trunk?"

Quinn hesitated, then answered truthfully.

"The Russian girl who was sleeping with the prime minister?"

"One and the same."

"Christ, Eamon." Billy Conway drove in silence

for a moment. "You never told me you were bringing out a hostage."

"The facts on the ground changed."

"What facts?"

Quinn said nothing more.

"What do you intend to do with her?"

"Sit on her."

"Where?"

"Somewhere no one will find her."

"South Armagh?"

Quinn was silent.

"We'd better let them know we're coming."

"No," said Quinn. "No phones."

"We can't just show up on their doorstep."

"Yes, we can."

"Why?"

"Because I'm Eamon Quinn."

Another PSNI unit was speeding toward them out of Downpatrick. Quinn lowered his face. Billy Conway clutched the wheel tightly in both hands.

"Why did you bring that girl back here, Eamon?"

"Breadcrumbs," replied Quinn.

"For what?"

"Just drive, Billy. I'll tell you the rest when we get to Bandit Country."

71

THE ARDOYNE, WEST BELFAST

THE SEA KING had set down at JHFS Alder-grove, the Joint Helicopter Command flying station adjacent to Belfast Airport. Amanda Wallace of MI5 had arranged for a car, a five-year-old Ford Escort with faded blue paint and nearly a hundred thousand surveillance miles on the odometer. She had also opened the doors of an MI5 safe house in a Protestant section of North Belfast. Two officers from T Branch, MI5's Irish terrorism division, were waiting inside when Gabriel and Keller arrived shortly after midnight. Neither knew Keller's name or face, though Gabriel's identity proved harder to conceal. They passed a sleepless night together monitoring the search for the craft that had taken Madeline Hart from the isolated cove on the northern coast of Cornwall. By six in the morning it had become clear that the boat would not be found, at least not with Madeline still on board. The British public, however, knew nothing of her abduction. Nor did it know that an SIS officer had leapt to his death from a terrace of Vauxhall Cross. The lead story on the BBC's *Breakfast* program concerned the prime minister's controversial plan to reform the National Health Service. The reaction was universally hostile.

At half past six Gabriel and Keller left the safe house and climbed into the Ford. They spent the next thirty minutes driving in circles through the northern and eastern sections of the city to make certain they were not being followed by MI5 or any other entity of British intelligence. Then, at seven o'clock, they turned onto Crumlin Road and headed into the Catholic Ardoyne. Keller parked at one end of Stratford Gardens and killed the engine. Lights burned in a few windows along the terraces, but otherwise the street was in darkness.

"How long before your friends show up?" asked Gabriel.

"It's early," said Keller vaguely.

"That doesn't sound encouraging."

"We're in West Belfast. It's hard to be optimistic."

For several minutes Stratford Gardens did not stir. Keller scanned the street for evidence of trouble, but Gabriel had eyes only for the door of Number 8. It opened at 7:45 and two figures emerged, Maggie and Catherine Donahue, the wife and daughter of a man who could make a ball of fire travel a thousand feet per second. The wife and daughter of the man who had helped Tariq al-Hourani solve the problems he was having with his timers and detonators. Catherine Donahue was wearing a field hockey uniform beneath a gray coat. Her mother was wearing a tracksuit and trainers. They passed through the metal gate at the end of the garden walk and turned right, toward Ardoyne Road.

"Where's her game?" asked Gabriel.

"Lisburn. Bus leaves at eight thirty."

"Can't she find her way alone?"

"They have to pass through a Protestant area to get up to Our Lady of Mercy. There's been a lot of trouble over the years."

"Or maybe they're making a run for it."

"Dressed like that?"

"Follow them," said Gabriel.

"What if my friends show up?"

"I think I can look after myself."

Gabriel stepped out of the car without another word. The gate of Number 8 emitted a sharp squeak as he pushed it open, but the front door yielded soundlessly. Entering, he quickly drew a gun from the small of his back—the Glock 17 that he had been given by SO1, the prime minister's protection detail. A television blared unwatched in the sitting room; Gabriel left it on and stole up the stairs, the gun in his outstretched hands. He found both bedrooms in disarray but unoccupied. Then he went downstairs and entered the kitchen. There were a few breakfast dishes in the basin, and on the counter was a pot of tea. He took a mug from the cabinet, poured himself a cup, and sat down at the kitchen table to wait.

It took fifteen minutes for Maggie Donahue to walk her daughter to the gates of Our Lady of Mercy secondary school for girls. Her return trip was not without incident, for on the Ardoyne Road she became ensnared in a confrontation with two Protestant women from the Glenbryn housing estates who were angry that she, a Catholic, would dare to walk along a loyalist street. As a result, she was red-faced with anger when she turned into Stratford Gardens. She shoved her key into her lock and slammed the door so hard it rattled the windows of her little house. Someone on the television was complaining about the price of milk. She silenced it before coming into the kitchen to see to the breakfast dishes. Several seconds elapsed before she noticed the man drinking tea at her table.

"Jesus Christ!" she shouted, startled.

Gabriel merely frowned, as though he did not approve of those who took the Lord's name in vain.

"Who are you?" she asked.

"I was about to ask you the same thing," replied Gabriel calmly.

His accent puzzled her. Then a look of recognition flashed across her face.

"You're the one who—"

"Yes," he said, cutting her off. "I'm the one."

"What are you doing in my house?"

"I misplaced something the last time I was here. I was hoping you might help me find it."

"What's that?"

"Your husband."

She dug a mobile phone from the pocket of her tracksuit and started to dial. Gabriel leveled the Glock at her head.

"Stop," he said.

She froze.

"Give me that phone."

She handed it over. Gabriel looked at the screen. The number she had been attempting to dial was eight digits in length.

"The emergency number for the Police Service of Northern Ireland is one-zero-one, isn't it?"

She was silent.

"So who are you dialing?" Greeted by more silence, Gabriel tucked the phone into his coat pocket.

"That's mine," she said.

"Not anymore."

"What the hell do you want?"

"For the moment," said Gabriel, "I'd like you to sit down."

She glared at him, more contempt than fear. She was from the Ardoyne, thought Gabriel. She didn't frighten easily.

"Sit," he said again, and finally she sat.

"How did you get in here?" she asked.

"You left the front door unlocked."

"Bullshit."

Gabriel laid a photograph on the tabletop and turned it so she could see the image clearly. It showed her daughter standing on a street in Lisbon at the side of Eamon Quinn.

"Where did you get that?" she asked.

Gabriel lifted his gaze to the ceiling.

"From my daughter's room?" she asked.

He nodded.

"What were you doing in there?"

"I was trying to prevent your husband from carrying out yet another act of mass murder."

"I don't have a husband." She paused, then added, "Not anymore."

"This is your husband," said Gabriel, tapping the photograph with the barrel of the Glock. "His name is Eamon Quinn. He bombed Bishopsgate and Canary Wharf. He bombed Omagh, and he bombed Brompton Road. I found his clothing in your closet. I found his money, too. Which means you're going to spend the rest of your life in a cage unless you tell me what I want to know."

She stared at the photograph for a moment in silence. There was something else on her face now, thought Gabriel. It wasn't contempt. It was shame.

"He's not my husband," she said finally. "My husband has been dead for more than ten years."

"Then why is your daughter standing on a street in Lisbon with Eamon Quinn?"

"I can't tell you that."

"Why not?"

"Because he'll kill me if I do."

"Quinn?"

"No," she said, shaking her head. "Billy Conway."

72

CROSSMAGLEN, COUNTY ARMAGH

T HE SMALL FARM that lay just to the west of Crossmaglen had been in the Fagan clan for generations. Its current occupant, Jimmy Fagan, had never cared much for farming, and in the late 1980s he opened a factory in Newry that manufactured aluminum doors and windows for South Armagh's thriving building industry. His primary occupation, however, was Irish republicanism. A veteran of the IRA's notorious South Armagh Brigade, he had participated in some of the bloodiest bombings and ambushes of the conflict, including an attack on a British patrol near Warrenpoint that left eighteen British soldiers dead. In all, the South Armagh Brigade was responsible for the deaths of 123 British military personnel and 42 officers of the Royal Ulster Constabulary. For a time, the small area of farms and rolling hills was the most dangerous place in the world to be a soldier—so dangerous, in fact, that the British Army was forced to abandon the roads to the IRA and travel only by helicopter. Eventually, the South Armagh Brigade began attacking the helicopters, too. Four were brought down, including a Lynx that was hit by a mortar near Crossmaglen. Jimmy Fagan had fired the device. Eamon Quinn had designed and built it.

During the worst of the Troubles, an observation tower had loomed over the center of Crossmaglen. Now the tower was gone and in the heart of the village was a green park with a stark memorial to fallen IRA volunteers. Billy Conway dropped Quinn in front of the Cross Square Hotel; he walked around the corner to the Emerald bar on Newry Street. The colors of the Crossmaglen Rangers fluttered over the entrance. It seemed that football had replaced rebellion as the town's primary pastime.

Quinn opened the door and went inside. Instantly, several heads swiveled toward him. The war might have been over, but in Crossmaglen suspicion of outsiders was as strong as ever. Quinn knew several of the men in the room. They, on the other hand, didn't appear to know him. He ordered a Guinness at the bar and carried it over to the table where Jimmy Fagan sat with two other former members of the South Armagh Brigade. Fagan's salt-and-pepper hair was cropped short, and his black eyes had been turned to slits by the passing of the years. They scrutinized Quinn carefully, with no trace of recognition.

"Can I help you, friend?" Fagan asked finally.

"Mind if I join you?"

Fagan nodded toward an empty table at the other end of the room and suggested Quinn might be more comfortable there.

"But I'd rather sit with you."

"Take a walk, friend," Fagan said quietly. "Otherwise, you're going to get hurt."

Quinn sat. The man sitting to his left seized hold of his wrist.

"Take it easy," Quinn murmured. Then he looked at Fagan and said, "It's me, Jimmy. It's Eamon."

Fagan stared hard at Quinn's face. Then he realized the stranger seated across the table was telling the truth. "Christ," he whispered. "What are you doing back here?"

"Business," said Quinn.

"That would explain why the RUC is so jumpy all of a sudden."

"They're called the PSNI now, Jimmy. Haven't you heard?"

"The Good Friday accords forgave many sins," Fagan said after a moment, "but not yours. It would be better for all of us if you finished your beer and left."

"Can't, Jimmy."

"Why not?"

"Business."

Quinn drank the foam off his Guinness and looked around the room. The smell of wood polish and beer, the soft murmur of Armagh-accented voices: after all the years in hiding, all the years of selling his services to the highest bidder, he was finally home again.

"Why are you here?" Fagan asked.

"I was wondering whether you might be interested in a little action."

"What's in it for me?"

"Money."

"No more bombs, Eamon."

"No," said Quinn. "No bombs."

"So what kind of job is it?"

"Ambush," said Quinn. "Just like the old days."

"Who's the target?"

"The one who got away."

"Keller?"

Quinn nodded. Jimmy Fagan smiled.

The farm was two hundred acres—or two hundred and forty, depending on which member of the Fagan clan you asked. It was rolling pastureland mainly, divided into smaller plots by low stone fences, some of which had been erected long before the first Protestant had set foot on the land, or so the legend went. Ireland was just over the next hill. On none of the roads was there even a suggestion of a border.

On the highest part of the land stood a two-story brick house where Fagan, a widower, lived with his two sons, both veterans of the IRA and the rejectionist Real IRA. There was a large barn of corrugated aluminum and a second structure, deep within the property, where Fagan had hidden weapons and explosives during the war. It was there, in the winter of 1989, that a younger version of Christopher Keller underwent a brutal interrogation at the hands of Eamon Quinn. Now Madeline and Katerina took Keller's place. Quinn left enough food, water, and blankets to see them through the cold December afternoon and sealed the door with a pair of heavy padlocks. Then he walked with

Billy Conway along the dirt track leading back to the main house. Conway was staring at the ground, hands shoved into the front pockets of his coat. He looked on edge. He usually did.

"How long do we have?" he asked.

"If I had to guess," replied Quinn, "he's already here. Allon, too."

"Looking for me, no doubt."

"We can only hope."

"And if Keller asks to see me? What then?"

"You play the double game, Billy—just like you always did. Tell him they're wasting their time looking for me in the north. Tell him you heard a rumor I'm down in the Republic."

"What happens if he doesn't believe me?"

"Why wouldn't he believe you, Billy?" Quinn placed his hand on Conway's shoulder and smiled. "You were his best agent."

73

THE ARDOYNE, WEST BELFAST

KELLER PARKED THE car directly opposite the house and hurried up the garden walk. The door opened to his touch; he followed the sound of voices into the kitchen. There he found Gabriel and Maggie Donahue seated at the table, each with a mug of tea before them. There was also a large stack of used bills, a few articles of male clothing, an assortment of toiletries, a photograph, and a Glock 17 firearm. The Glock was a few inches beyond Maggie Donahue's reach. She was seated ramrod straight, with one arm lying protectively across her waist and a cigarette burning between the fingers of an uplifted hand. Keller reckoned she had been crying a few minutes earlier. Now her hard features had settled into a Belfast mask of reserve and mistrust. Gabriel was expressionless, a priest with a gun and a leather jacket. For a few seconds he seemed unaware of Keller's presence. Then he looked up and smiled. "Mr. Merchant," he said cordially. "So good of you to join us. I'd like you to meet my new friend Maggie Donahue. Maggie was just telling me how Billy Conway forced her to put these things in her house." He paused, then added, "Maggie is going to help us find Eamon Quinn."

74

CROSSMAGLEN, COUNTY ARMAGH

THE CORRUGATED METAL structure at the center of the Fagan farm was twenty feet by forty, with bales of hay at one end and an assortment of rusted tools and implements at the other. It had been designed to Jimmy Fagan's exacting specifications and assembled at his factory in Newry. The outer door was unusually heavy, and the raised flooring contained a well-concealed trapdoor that led to one of the largest caches of weapons and explosives in Northern Ireland. Madeline Hart knew none of this. She knew only that she was not alone; the smell of stale tobacco and cheap hotel shampoo told her so. Finally, a hand plucked the hood from her head and gently removed the duct tape from her mouth. Still, she had no sense of her surroundings, for the darkness was absolute. She sat silently for a moment, her back to the hay bales, her legs stretched before her. Then she asked, "Who's there?"

A cigarette lighter flared, a face leaned into the flame.

"You," whispered Madeline.

The lighter was extinguished, the darkness returned. Then a voice addressed her in Russian.

"I'm sorry," said Madeline, "but I don't understand you."

"I said you must be thirsty."

"Terribly," replied Madeline.

A water bottle opened with a snap. Madeline placed her lips against grooves of plastic and drank.

"Thank—"

She stopped herself. She didn't want to show a captive's helpless gratitude toward the captor. Then she realized Katerina was a captive, too.

"Let me see your face again."

The lighter flared a second time.

"I can't see you clearly," said Madeline.

Katerina moved the lighter closer to her face. "How do I look?" she asked.

"Exactly the way you looked in Lisbon."

"How do you know about Lisbon?"

"A friend of mine was watching you from across the street. He took your picture."

"Allon?"

Madeline said nothing.

"It's a shame you ever met him. You'd still be living like a princess in St. Petersburg. Now you're here."

"Where is *here*?"

"Even I'm not sure." Katerina extracted a cigarette from her packet and then inclined it toward Madeline. "Smoke?"

"God, no."

"You were always the good girl, weren't you?"

Katerina touched the end of her cigarette to the flame and allowed it to die.

"Please," said Madeline. "I've been in the dark for so long."

Katerina reignited the lighter.

"Walk around," said Madeline. "Let me see where we are."

Katerina moved with the lighter along the perimeter of the shed, stopping at the door.

"Try opening it."

"It can't be opened from the inside."

"Try."

Katerina leaned against the door but it didn't budge. "Any other bright ideas?"

"I suppose we could light the hay on fire."

"At this point," said Katerina, "I'm sure he'd be more than happy to let us burn to death."

"Who?"

"Eamon Quinn."

"The Irishman?"

Katerina nodded.

"What's he going to do?"

"First, he's going to kill Gabriel Allon and Christopher Keller. Then he's going to ransom me back to Moscow Center for twenty million dollars."

"Will they pay?"

"Perhaps." Katerina paused, then added, "Especially if the deal includes you."

The lighter went dark. Katerina sat.

"What should I call you?" she asked.

"Madeline, of course."

"It's not your real name."

"It's the only name I have."

"No, it isn't. We used to call you Natalya at the camp. Don't you remember?"

"Natalya?"

"Yes," she said. "Little Natalya, daughter of the KGB general. So pretty. And that English accent they gave you. You were like a doll." She was silent for a moment. "I adored you. You were all I had in that place."

"So why did you kidnap me?"

"Actually, I was supposed to kill you. Quinn, too."

"Why didn't you?"

"Quinn changed the plan."

"But you would have killed me if you'd had the chance?"

"I didn't want to," Katerina answered after a moment. "But, yes, I suppose I would have done it."

"Why?"

"Better me than someone else. Besides," she added, "you betrayed your country. You defected."

"It wasn't my country. I didn't belong there."

"And here, Natalya? Do you belong here?"

"My name is Madeline." She said nothing for a moment. "What will happen if I go back to Russia?"

"I suppose they'll spend several months wringing every drop of knowledge out of your brain that they can."

"And then?"

"*Vysshaya mera.*"

"The highest measure of punishment?"

"I thought you didn't speak Russian."

"A friend told me about that expression."

"Where's your friend now?"

"He'll find me."

"And then Quinn will kill him." Katerina struck her lighter again. "Are you hungry?"

"Famished."

"I think they left us some meat pies."

"I adore meat pies."

"God, but you're so English." Katerina unwrapped one of the pies and placed it carefully in Madeline's hands.

"It would be easier if you cut away the duct tape."

Katerina smoked contemplatively in the darkness. "How much do you remember?" she asked.

"About the camp?"

"Yes."

"Nothing," said Madeline. "And everything."

"I have no photographs of myself when I was young."

"Nor do I."

"Do you remember what I looked like?"

"You were beautiful," said Madeline. "I wanted to be exactly like you."

"That's funny," replied Katerina, "because I wanted to be like you."

"I was an annoying little child."

"But you were a good girl, Natalya. And I was something else entirely."

Katerina said nothing more. Madeline raised her bound hands and tried to eat more of the meat pie.

"Won't you please cut away the tape?" she asked.

"I'd like to, but I can't."

"Why not?"

"Because you're a good girl," she said, crushing out her cigarette on the floor of the shed. "And you'll only get in my way."

75

UNION STREET, BELFAST

I T WAS A few minutes after noon by the time Billy Conway came through the door of Tommy O'Boyle's on Union Street. An ex-IRA man named Rory Gallagher was polishing pint glasses behind the bar.

"I was about to send out a search party," he said.

"Long night," answered Conway. "Longer than I expected."

"Problems?"

"Complications."

"More to come, I'm afraid."

"What are you talking about?"

Gallagher glanced toward the stairs. "You have company."

Keller's feet were propped on Billy Conway's desk when the office door opened with a groan. Conway stood motionless in the breach. He looked as though he had just seen a ghost. In a way, thought Keller, he had.

"Hello, Billy. Good to see you again."

"I thought—"

"That I was dead?"

Conway said nothing. Keller rose to his feet.

"Take a walk with me, Billy. We need to talk."

The occasion of Christopher Keller's return to Northern Ireland had precipitated one of the largest reunions of the Provisional IRA's South Armagh Brigade since the signing of the Good Friday Agreement. In all, twelve members of the unit were at that same moment gathered around Eamon Quinn and Jimmy Fagan in the kitchen of the farmhouse in Crossmaglen. Eight of those present had served long sentences in the H-Blocks of the Maze prison, only to be freed under the terms of the peace accord. Four others had worked with Quinn in the Real IRA, including Frank Maguire, whose brother Seamus had died at the hands of Keller at Crossmaglen in 1989.

As usual at such gatherings, the air was thick with cigarette smoke. Spread across the center of the table was an Ordnance Survey map, faded and tattered along the edges, of the South Armagh region. It was the same map Fagan had used during the planning of the Warrenpoint massacre. In fact, some of his original markings and notations were still visible. Next to the map was a mobile, which at twelve fifteen pulsed with life. It was a text message from Rory Gallagher. Quinn smiled. Keller and Allon would soon be heading their way.

Keller and Billy Conway did indeed take a walk, but only as far as York Lane. It was a quiet street, no retail businesses or restaurants, just a church at one end and a row of redbrick industrial buildings at the other. Gabriel was parked in a gap in the security cameras. Keller shoved Billy Conway into the front passenger seat and climbed in back. Gabriel, staring straight ahead, calmly started the engine.

"Where's Eamon Quinn?" he asked of Billy Conway.

"I haven't seen Eamon Quinn in twenty-five years."

"Wrong answer."

Gabriel broke Conway's nose with a lightning strike of a blow. Then he slipped the car into gear and eased away from the curb.

The Ford Escort beneath Gabriel and Keller was fitted with a satellite beacon, a fact that Amanda Wallace had neglected to mention to them. As a result, MI5 had been tracking the car all morning as it moved from Aldergrove to the safe house, and then to Stratford Gardens and York Lane. In addition, MI5 was monitoring the car's movements with the aid of Belfast's CCTV network. A camera on Frederick Street captured a clear shot of the man in the front passenger seat—a man who appeared to be bleeding heavily from his nose. An MI5 tech enlarged the image and fed it into one of the video display screens in the ops center at Thames House.

Graham Seymour was seeing the same picture at Vauxhall Cross.

"Recognize him?" asked Amanda Wallace.

"It's been a long time," replied Seymour, "but I believe that's Billy Conway."

"*The* Billy Conway."

"In the flesh."

"He was one of ours, wasn't he?"

"No," said Seymour. "He was mine. And Keller helped to run him."

"So why is he bleeding?"

"Maybe he was never really ours, Amanda. Maybe he was Quinn's all along."

Seymour watched as the car turned onto the M2 motorway and headed north. That's the wonderful thing about our business, he thought. Our mistakes always come back to haunt us. And eventually all debts come due.

76

CREGGAN FOREST, COUNTY ANTRIM

THEY ASKED NO further questions of Billy Conway, and he asked none of them. Blood flowed freely from his broken nose during the ride north to Larne, but by the time they reached Glenarm a crust of black had formed around the rims of his nostrils. Keller directed Gabriel inland along the Carnlough Road, then north on Killy-carn. They followed it until it turned to gravel and shed its name. Then they followed it a little farther, until the last farm had fallen away and the Creggan Forest rose from the land. Keller told Gabriel to stop and kill the engine. Then he looked at Billy Conway.

"Remember this place, Billy? We used to come up here in the old days when you had something important to tell me. We'd drive up here in that old Granada and have a few beers while we listened to the guns over at the Creggan Lodge. Remember, Billy?"

Keller's voice had taken on a West Belfast accent, Falls Road with a touch of Ballymurphy. Billy Conway said nothing. He was staring straight ahead. A thousand-yard stare, thought Gabriel. A dead man's stare.

"We always took good care of you, didn't we, Billy? We paid you well. We protected you. But you didn't need protection, did you, Billy? You were working for the IRA the whole time. Working for Eamon Quinn. You're a tout, Billy. You're a lousy fucking tout." Keller placed the barrel of the Glock to the back of his head. "Aren't you going to deny it, Billy?"

"It was a long time ago."

"Not so long," said Keller. "Isn't that what you told me the day we renewed our friendship in Belfast? The day you found Maggie Donahue for me. The day you set me up." Keller pressed the barrel of the gun hard against Conway's skull. "Aren't you going to deny it, Billy?"

Billy Conway was silent.

"You were always honest, Billy."

"You should have never come back here."

"Thanks to Quinn, we didn't have much choice. Quinn led me back here. And you made sure I found the things he wanted me to find. A wife and a daughter. A pile of money. A torn tram ticket. A photograph of a Lisbon Street. Maggie Donahue wanted no part of it. She was too busy trying to survive in a shithole like the Ardoyne without a husband. But you threatened her into doing it. You told her you'd kill her if she went to the police. Her daughter, too. And she believed you, Billy, because she knows what happens to touts in West Belfast." Keller laid the barrel of the gun along Billy Conway's cheek. "Deny it, Billy."

"What do you want?"

"I want you to swear that you'll never go any-where near that woman or her child again."

"I swear it."

"Wise boy, Billy. Now get out of the car."

Conway sat motionless. Keller slammed the gun into his broken nose.

"I said get out!"

Conway pulled the latch and staggered from the car. Keller followed after him. "Start walking," he said. "And while you're walking, tell me where I can find Eamon Quinn."

"I don't know where he is."

"Sure you do, Billy. You know everything."

Keller shoved Conway along the track and fell in behind him. From the trees of the Creggan Forest came the crack of a hunter's twelve-gauge. Conway froze. With a jab from the barrel of the Glock, Keller prodded him forward.

"How did Quinn get out of England?"

"The Delaneys."

"Jack and Connor?"

"Aye."

"He wasn't alone, was he, Billy?"

"He had two women with him."

"Where did the Delaneys drop them?"

"Shore Road, near the castle."

"You were there?"

"I picked them up."

"What kind of car did you have?"

"Peugeot."

"Stolen, borrowed, or rented?"

"Stolen. False plates."

"Quinn's favorite."

Two more shotgun blasts, closer. A brace of pheasants took flight from a field. Smart birds, thought Keller.

"Where is he, Billy? Where's Quinn?"

"He's in South Armagh," said Conway after a moment.

"Where?"

"Crossmaglen."

"Jimmy Fagan's farm?"

Conway nodded. "The same place we took you that night. Quinn says he wants to nail you to the Cross for your sins."

"We?" asked Keller.

There was silence.

"You were there, Billy?"

"For part of it," admitted Conway. "The two women are in the same building where Quinn strapped you to that chair."

"You're sure?"

"I put them there myself."

They had reached the edge of the trees. Billy Conway stumbled to a stop.

"Turn around, Billy. I have one more question."

Billy Conway stood motionless for a long moment. Then slowly he turned to face Keller.

"What do you want to know?" he asked.

"I want a name, Billy—the name of the man who told Eamon Quinn that I was in love with a girl from Ballymurphy."

"I don't know who did it."

"Sure you do, Billy. You know everything."

Conway said nothing.

"His name," said Keller, pointing the gun at Conway's face. "Tell me his name."

Conway lifted his face to the gray sky and spoke his own name. Keller's vision blurred with rage and he felt his legs begin to buckle. The gun provided him a sense of balance. He never remembered pulling the trigger, only the controlled recoil of the weapon in his hand and a flash of pink vapor. He knelt with Billy Conway until he was certain he was dead. Then he rose to his feet and headed back to the car.

77

RANDALSTOWN, COUNTY ANTRIM

ON THE OUTSKIRTS of Randalstown, Keller's MI6 mobile phone vibrated. He drew it from his coat pocket and frowned at the screen.

"Graham Seymour."

"What does he want?"

"He's wondering why Billy Conway is no longer in the car."

"They're watching us."

"Obviously."

"What are you going to tell him?"

"I'm not sure. This is uncharted territory for me." Keller held up the phone and asked, "Do you think this is acting as a transmitter?"

"Could be."

"Maybe I should throw it out the window."

"MI6 will dock your pay. Besides," added Gabriel, "it might come in handy in Bandit Country."

Keller placed the phone in the center console.

"What's it like?" asked Gabriel.

"Bandit Country?"

"Crossmaglen."

"It's the kind of place they wrote songs about." Keller stared out the window for a moment before continuing. "South Armagh was totally under the control of the Provos during the war, a de facto IRA state, and Crossmaglen was its holy city." He glanced at Gabriel and added, "Its Jerusalem. The IRA never had to adopt a cell structure there. It operated as a battalion. An *army*," added Keller. "They would spend their days plowing their fields and at night they would kill British soldiers. Before every patrol we were reminded that beneath every gorse bush or pile of stones there was probably a bomb or a sniper. South Armagh was a shooting gallery. And we were the targets."

"Go on."

"We referred to Crossmaglen as XMG," Keller continued after a moment. "We had a watchtower in the main square called Golf Five Zero. You took your life in your hands every time you entered. The barracks were windowless and mortarproof. It was like serving on a submarine. When I escaped from Jimmy Fagan's farm that night, I didn't even try to get to XMG. I knew I would never make it alive. I went north to Newtownhamilton instead. We called it NTH." Keller smiled and said, "We used to joke that it stood for 'No Terrorists Here.' "

"Do you remember Fagan's farm?"

"It's not something I'll ever forget," replied Keller. "It's on the Castleblayney Road. A portion of his land runs along the border. During the war it was a major smuggling route between the South Armagh Brigade and IRA elements in the Republic."

"And the shed?"

"It's situated at the edge of a large pasture, sur-rounded by stone walls and watchdogs. If the PSNI goes anywhere near that farm, Fagan and Quinn will know about it."

"You're assuming Madeline's there."

Keller said nothing.

"What if Conway was lying again? Or what if Quinn has already moved her?"

"He hasn't."

"How can you be sure?"

"Because it's Quinn's way. The question is," said Keller, "do we tell our friends at Vauxhall Cross and Thames House what we know?"

Gabriel glanced at the MI6 mobile and said, "Maybe we just did."

They passed beneath a nest of CCTV cameras keeping watch on the M22. Keller removed a ciga-rette from his packet and twirled it unlit between his fingertips.

"There's no way we can set foot in South Armagh without someone spotting us."

"So we'll go through the back door."

"We have no night-vision capability or sound suppressors."

"Or radios," added Gabriel.

"How much ammunition do you have?"

"One full magazine and one spare."

"I'm down a round," said Keller.

"Pity."

Keller's MI6 phone vibrated a second time.

"What does he want?" asked Gabriel.

"He's wondering where we're going."

"I guess they're not listening after all."

"What shall I tell him?"

"He's your boss, not mine."

Keller keyed in a message and returned the phone to the console.

"What did you say?"

"That we're developing a piece of potentially vital intelligence."

"You're going to make a good MI6 officer, Christopher."

"MI6 officers don't operate in South Armagh without backup." Keller paused, then added, "And neither does a man who's about to be the chief of Israeli intelligence, not to mention a father of two."

The motorway dwindled into a two-lane highway. It was half past two in the afternoon. Sunset was just ninety minutes away. Keller lit the cigarette and watched as Gabriel reflexively lowered his window to vent the smoke.

"You know," said Keller, "none of this would have happened if you'd told Graham Seymour to take a hike when he came to see you in Rome. You'd be working on your Caravaggio, and I'd be drinking a glass of wine on my terrace in Corsica."

"Any other pearls of wisdom, Christopher?"

"Just a question."

"What's that?"

"Who is Tariq al-Hourani?"

In London the same video image flickered in the op centers of Thames House and Vauxhall Cross—a winking blue light moving westward across Ulster on the A6. When the light reached Castledawson, it turned south toward Cookstown. Graham Seymour sent a third text to Keller's mobile, but this time there was no reply, a fact he reluctantly shared with Amanda Wallace across the river at Thames House.

"Where do you think they're going?" she asked.

"If I had to guess, they're going back to the place where this all started."

"Bandit Country?"

"Jimmy Fagan's farm, to be precise."

"They can't go in there alone."

"I'm not sure there's much we can do to stop them at this point."

"At least light up Keller's mobile so we can hear what they're saying."

Seymour made eye contact with one of the techs and gave the order. A moment later he heard Gabriel explaining how Eamon Quinn, in a terrorist training camp in Libya, had made the acquaintance of a man named Tariq al-Hourani. No, thought Seymour. There was no stopping them now.

THEY STOPPED IN Cookstown long enough to purchase an Ordnance Survey map, a tin of black shoe polish, and two heavy-duty kitchen knives before driving into the setting sun to Omagh. A light rain fell as they moved south, enough so that Keller had to keep the wipers working all the way to Castleblayney on the Republic side of the border. Just outside the town was Lough Muckno. Keller followed a ribbon of a road around the southern shore of the lake, into a valley dotted with small farmhouses. Each of the houses represented a potential tripwire. Border or no border, they were now in Bandit Country.

Finally, Keller turned the car into a dense patch of blackthorn along the banks of the Clarebane River and killed the lights and the engine. The MI6 mobile lay on the center console, aglow with unread text messages from Vauxhall Cross. Gabriel handed it to Keller and said, "It might be time to let Graham know where we are."

"Something tells me he already knows."

Keller dialed Seymour's number in London. Seymour came on the line instantly.

"It's about time," he snapped.

"Do you see where we are?"

"By my calculation, you're less than a kilometer from the border."

"Any chance you can give us a little covering fire?"

"It's already in the works."

"I haven't told you what we need."

"Yes, you have. And one more thing," said Seymour. "I'll need a receipt for those knives. The map and the shoe polish, too."

By two that afternoon it had become apparent to Eamon Quinn that Billy Conway was in serious trouble. By four Quinn assumed that Conway was in British custody or, more likely, lying somewhere in the province with a bullet in his head. Surely, his death had not been a pleasant one. Before it, he would have divulged two pieces of information: the exact location of Madeline Hart and the truth about his role in the death of Elizabeth Conlin twenty-five years earlier. Quinn had no doubts as to how his old adversary would react. Keller was an SAS veteran turned professional assassin. He would come back to Jimmy Fagan's farm. And Quinn would be waiting.

At half past four, as the sun was dropping into the hills, Quinn dispatched twelve men into the two hundred acres of the Fagan clan's farm. Twelve veterans of the legendary South Armagh Brigade. Twelve hardened snipers with much British blood on their hands. Twelve men who wanted Christopher Keller dead as badly as Quinn did. In addition, Jimmy Fagan deployed another eight men at various spots around South Armagh to serve as scouts—including Francis McShane, who was sitting behind the wheel of a parked car outside the PSNI base in Crossmaglen.

Quinn and Fagan sat in the kitchen of the farmhouse, smoking, waiting. Quinn's Makarov lay on the table, a suppressor screwed into the barrel. Next to it was the phone, and next to the phone lay the faded old map of what had once been the most dangerous two hundred square miles in the world. Quinn's eyes traveled across it from east to west: JONESBOROUGH, FORKHILL, SILVERBRIDGE, CROSSMAGLEN . . . Places of glory, he thought. Places of death. Tonight he would write one more chapter in the legend.

Quinn looked down at his wristwatch, the watch that had been given to him by a man named Tariq al-Hourani, in a camp by the sea. It was seven fifteen. He removed the watch and read the inscription on the back.

No more timer failures . . .

After blackening their faces with the shoe polish, Gabriel and Keller struck out along the bank of the Clarebane River, Keller leading the way, Gabriel a step behind. The clouds obscured the moon and stars; the smack of the rain covered their footfalls. Keller flowed like water over the land, swiftly, without a sound. Gabriel, the secret soldier of the street, did his best to emulate his friend's movements. Keller held his weapon in both hands and at eye level. Gabriel, behind him, pointed the barrel downward and to the right.

Five minutes after leaving the car, Keller paused and with the barrel of his Glock made a straight-line gesture toward the ground. It meant they had reached the Ulster border. He turned to the north and led Gabriel across a series of pastures, each divided by hedgerows of blackthorn. The border was a few yards to their right. Once, there would have been watchtowers manned by Grenadier Guards and Hussars, but now only grain silos and barns marked the horizon. Keller, the bloodstained survivor of South Armagh's dirtiest fighting, moved slowly, planting each step as though a mine were beneath his foot, breaching each hedgerow as if his killer waited on the other side.

After moving about a kilometer in this laborious manner, Keller led Gabriel across a rocky patch of ground between a pair of ponds. Before them rose a stand of trees, and beyond the trees was Jimmy Fagan's farm in Northern Ireland. Keller crept forward, tree to tree, and then froze. About thirty feet away, shrouded in darkness, stood a man with an AK-47 at the ready. The gun was fitted with a carbon-fiber over-barrel suppressor, a serious weapon for a serious predator. Keller carefully removed his MI6 mobile and sent a pre-typed text message to Vauxhall Cross. Then he drew the knife from his pocket and he waited.

Because it was a domestic matter, Graham Seymour allowed Amanda Wallace to make the actual call. It arrived at the Crossmaglen base of the PSNI at 7:27 p.m., and within a minute several units were rolling into Newry Street, lights blazing. By seven thirty Jimmy Fagan's phone was buzzing with text messages from his scouts.

"How many units?" asked Quinn.

"Six at least, including some tactical boys."

"Where are they headed?"

"Down the Dundalk Road."

"The wrong way," said Quinn.

"Not even close."

Another text hit Fagan's phone.

"What does it say?"

"They're turning right on Foxfield."

"Still the wrong way."

"What do you think it means?"

"It means you should tell your boys to be on their toes, Jimmy."

"Why?"

Quinn smiled. "Because they're here."

At 7:31 the man standing thirty feet from Christopher Keller removed his right hand from the AK-47 and used it to remove a mobile phone from his pocket. The phone flared briefly, and in the glow of its screen Keller glimpsed the face of the man who would soon be dead. He was Keller's age, Keller's height and build. He might have been a farmer. He might have driven a lorry or done odd jobs. In another lifetime he had been Keller's enemy. Now he was his enemy again.

Like all veterans of the South Armagh Brigade, the man standing thirty feet from Keller knew every inch of the blood-soaked land. He knew every ditch, every patch of bramble, every hole where a gun was hidden or a booby-trap bomb was buried. He knew, too, the difference between the sound of an animal and the sound of a man. Too late, he looked up from his phone and saw Keller bearing down on him, a knife in one hand, a gun in the other. Keller forced the man to the ground. Then he drove the knife into his throat and held it until the man's hands released their grip on the phone and the AK-47. Keller seized the gun; Gabriel, the phone. Then they moved silently forward across the field, toward the shed of corrugated metal, twenty feet by forty, where Keller should have died a long time ago.

"Everyone check in?" asked Quinn.

"Everyone but Brendan Magill."

"Where's he posted?"

"West side of the property, against the border."

"Hit him again."

Jimmy Fagan sent Magill a direct text. After ninety seconds there was still no response.

"Looks like we found them," said Quinn.

"What now?"

"Kill the bait. And then bring me Keller and Allon alive."

Fagan typed the message and hit SEND. Quinn carried the Makarov outside to watch the fireworks.

Thirty yards beyond the spot where Brendan Magill lay dead was a rock wall running on a north-south axis. Gabriel took cover behind it after a 7.62x39mm round shredded the air a few inches from his right ear. Keller hit the ground next to him as rounds exploded against the stones of the wall, sending sparks and fragments flying. The source of the fire was silenced, so Gabriel had only a vague idea of the direction from which it was coming. He poked his head above the wall to search for a muzzle flash, but another burst of rounds drove him downward. Keller was now crawling northward along the base of the wall. Gabriel followed after him, but stopped when Keller suddenly opened up with the dead man's AK-47. A distant scream indicated that Keller's rounds had found their mark, but in an instant they were taking fire from several directions. Gabriel flattened himself on the ground at Keller's side, the Glock in one hand, the dead man's phone in the other. After a few seconds he realized it was pulsing with an incoming text. The text was apparently from Eamon Quinn. It read KILL THE GIRL . . .

79

CROSSMAGLEN, SOUTH ARMAGH

AMID THE HEAP of broken and dismembered farm implements in Jimmy Fagan's shed, Katerina had found a scythe, rusted and caked in mud, a museum piece, perhaps the last scythe in the whole of Ireland, north or south. She held it tightly in her hands and listened to the sound of men pounding up the track at a sprint. Two men, she thought, perhaps three. She positioned herself against the shed's sliding door. Madeline was at the opposite end of the space, hooded, hands bound, her back to the bales of hay. She was the first and only thing the men would see upon entry.

The latch gave way, the door slid open, a gun intruded. Katerina recognized its silhouette: an AK-47 with a suppressor attached to the barrel. She knew it well. It was the first weapon she had ever fired at the camp. *The great AK-47! Liberator of the oppressed!* The gun was pointed upward at a forty-five-degree angle. Katerina had no choice but to wait until the barrel sank toward Madeline. Then she raised the scythe and swung it with every ounce of strength she had left in her body.

Two hundred yards away, crouched behind a stone wall at the western edge of Jimmy Fagan's property, Gabriel showed the text message to Christopher Keller. Keller immediately poked his head above the wall and saw muzzle flashes in the doorway of the shed. Four flashes, four shots, more than enough to obliterate two lives. A burst of AK-47 fire drove him downward again. Eyes wild, he grabbed Gabriel savagely by the front of his coat and shouted, "Stay here!"

Keller hauled himself over the wall and vanished from sight. Gabriel lay there for a few seconds as the rounds rained down on his position. Then suddenly he was on his feet and running across the darkened pasture. Running toward a car in a snowy square in Vienna. Running toward death.

The blow that Katerina delivered to the neck of the man holding the AK-47 resulted in a partial decapitation. Even so, he had managed to squeeze off a shot before she wrenched the gun from his grasp—a shot that struck the hay bales a few inches from Madeline's head. Katerina shoved the dying man aside and quickly fired two shots into the chest of the second man. The fourth shot she fired into the partially decapitated creature twitching at her feet. In the lexicon of the SVR, it was a control shot. It was also a shot of mercy.

When the gunfire ended, Madeline tore away the serge-cloth hood. Her hands were still bound. Katerina cut away the duct tape and helped her to her feet. Outside, a battle raged. From their vantage point at the center of the rolling property, the lines were clearly drawn in streaks of white tracer fire. Two figures were working their way across the pastures from the west, under heavy fire from several positions. Another man stood motionless on the porch of the distant farmhouse, watching the spectacle as though it had been arranged for his private amusement. Katerina suspected the two men approaching from the west were Gabriel Allon and Christopher Keller. And the man on the porch was Quinn.

Katerina forced Madeline to the ground. Then she dropped to one knee and fired four rounds toward one of Quinn's men. Instantly, the tracer fire from that position ceased. Four more rounds eliminated a second member of Quinn's team, and a single well-placed shot eradicated a third. Quinn's pose was no longer so dispassionate. Katerina fired several shots at him, driving him back into the farmhouse. Then she turned for Madeline, but Madeline was gone.

She was stumbling down the slope of the hill toward Allon and Keller, weary and unbalanced, like a ragdoll come to life. Katerina shouted at her to get down, but it was no use; fear and gravity held Madeline in an unbreakable grip. Katerina turned to look for Quinn, and it was then the shot hit her. A perfect shot, square in the breastbone, through and through. Katerina scarcely felt its impact, nor did she feel pain. She dropped to her knees, her hands hanging limply at her sides, her face tilted toward the black sky. As she fell to the damp earth of South Armagh, she imagined she was drowning in a lake of blood. A hand tried to pull her to the surface. Then the hand released her and she was dead.

The gunfire had ended by the time Madeline collapsed into Gabriel's arms. Keller left behind the AK-47 and, armed only with the Glock, sprinted down the pasture toward Jimmy Fagan's house. Bullet holes pocked the rear facade, and a curtain billowed from the open door. Keller pressed his cheek against the bricks, listening for any sound from within, and then pivoted inside with the gun in his outstretched hands. He was about to fire upon Jimmy Fagan, but stopped when he noticed the lifeless stare in his eyes and the neat bullet hole in the center of his forehead. Keller quickly searched the house, but Quinn was nowhere present. Once again, Quinn had wisely fled the field of battle. Quinn, thought Keller, would die another day.

PART FOUR

HOME

80

SOUTH ARMAGH–LONDON

T WAS THE kind of night they used to write songs about. Eight men dead in the green hills of South Armagh, six by the gun, two by the sword. Their names were an honor roll of the IRA's most notorious unit: Maguire, Magill, Callahan, O'Donnell, Ryan, Kelly, Collins, Fagan . . . Eight men dead in the green hills of South Armagh, six by the gun, two by the sword. It was the kind of night they used to write songs about.

In the immediate aftermath, however, there were no ballads, only questions. Among the facts never firmly established, for example, was who had telephoned the police or why. Even the commissioner of the PSNI, when pressed by reporters, could not produce a log that showed the time or origin of the emergency call. As for the motive behind the bloodletting in Crossmaglen, he could only speculate. The most likely explanation, he said, was that it was the result of a long-simmering dispute between rival dissident factions of the republican movement—though he could not rule out the possibility that illegal drugs had played a role. He even suggested there might be a link between the massacre in Crossmaglen and the unsolved disappearance of Liam Walsh, a drug dealer with known ties to the Real IRA. And though he did not know it, on that point the commissioner was entirely and unquestionably correct.

His theories as to the origin of the massacre played reasonably well in the wider world, but not in the clannish communities of South Armagh. In the bars where they did their drinking, and in the black boxes where they confessed their sins, all was known. The killings had had nothing to do with feuds or drugs. It was Quinn's doing. They knew other things as well, things the commissioner never mentioned to the press. They knew that two women had been present that night. So had a former SAS man named Christopher Keller. One of the women had been killed, shot through the heart at nearly a hundred yards by none other than Quinn himself. Afterward, Quinn had vanished without a trace. They were going to find him and give him the bullet he so richly deserved, the bullet they should have given him after Omagh. And then they were going to find the SAS man named Keller and kill him, too.

They kept this to themselves, as they kept most things, and went about their business. Eight names were added to the IRA memorial in Cross Square, eight graves were dug in St. Patrick's cemetery. At the funeral mass the priest spoke of resurrection, but afterward, in the dark corners of the Emerald bar, they spoke only of revenge. Eight men dead in the green hills of South Armagh, six by the gun, two by the sword. It was Quinn's doing. And Quinn was going to pay.

On that same day in London, the director-general of Her Majesty's Secret Intelligence Service, Graham Seymour, announced that four MI6 security officers had been killed at a cottage in a remote section of West Cornwall. Additionally, said Seymour, an employee of MI6's personnel department had committed suicide by jumping from the upper terrace of Vauxhall Cross. Seymour refused to say whether the two events were linked, but the press saw the timing of his announcement as proof they were. It was one of the blackest days in the proud history of the service, and the fallout soon overwhelmed developments across the Irish Sea. The British press barely noticed when the body of a Belfast publican named Billy Conway was found at the edge of a forest in County Antrim—or, three days after that, when a hiker stumbled on the partially decomposed corpse of Liam Walsh across the border in County Mayo. Nine-millimeter slugs were recovered from both victims, though ballistics analysis determined they had been fired by two different weapons. The Garda Síochána and the PSNI investigated the killings as separate incidents. No link was ever found.

In Germany the police had made a troubling discovery of their own: another body, another 9mm bullet. The body belonged to a man who would later be identified as a Russian intelligence officer named Alexei Rozanov. Who had fired the bullet was anyone's guess. Presumably he was linked to the team

of operatives who had killed the Russian's driver
and bodyguard in Hamburg. Among the more dis-
turbing aspects of the discovery was the fact that
the Russian's passport was found shoved into his
mouth. Clearly, someone had wanted to send a message. And by all accounts, the message had been
received. The BfV, Germany's domestic security
service, detected a distinct increase in the level of
Russian activity. The BfV's British counterpart,
MI5, noticed a similar change in the Russian profile
in London. In Moscow the Kremlin made no secret
about its feelings. The Russian president vowed
that the killers of Alexei Rozanov would receive the
"highest measure" of punishment possible. Students
of Russian intelligence knew what that meant. In all
likelihood, another body would soon be turning up.

But was there a link between the events in Germany, Britain, and the thirty-two counties of Ireland and Ulster? An uncharted star around which
they moved in a finely grooved orbit? A few of the
lesser news outlets thought so, and before long
some of the more reputable organizations came to
the same conclusion. Germany's *Der Spiegel*, long
a beacon of investigative journalism, linked Israel
to the killing of Alexei Rozanov and his security
team—a link the Israeli prime minister's office, in a
rare comment on intelligence matters, flatly denied.
Soon after, the *Irish Times* suggested a British hand
in the abduction and murder of Liam Walsh, while
RTÉ explored Walsh's alleged role in the bombing of Omagh in August 1998. The *Daily Mail* then
weighed in with a rumor-filled exclusive that the

MI6 employee who had leapt to his death was in fact a spy for Russia.

The British Foreign Office denied the report unequivocally, though its credibility was called into question two days later when Prime Minister Jonathan Lancaster announced a draconian set of economic and diplomatic sanctions aimed at Russia and the cabal of former KGB officers who controlled the Kremlin. His stated reason was "a pattern of Russian behavior on British soil and elsewhere." Included in the sanctions were a freeze on the London-based assets of several pro-Kremlin oligarchs and restrictions on their travel to Britain. With great fanfare, the Russian president announced a package of retaliatory sanctions. Russian stocks plummeted on the news. The ruble sank to an all-time low against major Western currencies.

But why had the British prime minister acted so harshly? And why now? The chattering classes found his initial explanation wanting. Surely, they said, there had to be more to it than bad Russian behavior. After all, the Russians had been behaving badly for years. And so the reporters dug, and the columnists opined, and the television analysts speculated and spun theories, some plausible, others not so. A few managed to land a glancing blow on the truth, but not one would ever find the faint pencil line, partially erased, that ran from a killing by the shore of a frozen Russian lake, to the murder of a princess, to the bloodletting in the green hills of South Armagh. Nor would they link the seemingly unconnected series of events to the legendary Israeli

488   DANIEL SILVA

intelligence officer who had died in the car bombing on London's Brompton Road.

But he was not dead, of course. In fact, with a bit of luck, the British press might have caught a glimpse of him in London during the tense forty-eight hours immediately following the killings in Crossmaglen. His movements were swift and his time was tightly budgeted, for he had pressing personal matters to attend to at home. He cleared up a few outstanding affairs at Vauxhall Cross and mended fences across the river at Thames House. He had a working dinner with the staff of the Office's London Station, and late the next morning he appeared unannounced at an art gallery in St. James's to tell a trusted old friend he was still very much among the living. The old friend was relieved to see him alive but angry that he had been among those deceived. It was, thought Gabriel remorsefully, a heartless thing to have done.

From St. James's he traveled to a redbrick Victorian manor house in rural Hertfordshire. It had once served as a training facility for new MI6 recruits. Now Madeline Hart was its only occupant. Gabriel walked with her across the fog-shrouded grounds, trailed by a team of bodyguards. They were four in number—the same number who had died at the hands of Quinn and Katerina in Cornwall.

"Will you ever go back there again?" she asked.

"To Cornwall?"

Madeline nodded slowly.

"No," said Gabriel. "I don't think I will."

"I'm sorry," she said. "It seems I've ruined everything. None of this would have happened if you'd left me in St. Petersburg."

"If you want to blame someone," said Gabriel, "blame the Russian president. He sent your friend to kill you."

"Where's her body?"

"Graham Seymour has offered it to the SVR *rezident* in London."

"And?"

"It seems the SVR isn't interested. They claim not to know who she is."

"Where will she end up?"

"An unmarked grave in a potter's field."

"A typically Russian ending," said Madeline darkly.

"Better her than you."

"She saved my life." Madeline glanced at Gabriel and added, "Yours, too."

He left Madeline in midafternoon and traveled to Highgate, where he repaid an outstanding debt to one of London's most prominent political reporters. By the time the meeting concluded, it was approaching five o'clock. His flight home was at ten thirty. He hurried down the front walk and climbed into the back of his embassy car. He had one more errand to run. One last restoration.

81

VICTORIA ROAD, SOUTH KENSINGTON

IT WAS A STOUT little house, with a wrought-iron gate and a fine flight of steps rising to a white door. Potted flowers bloomed in the tiny fore-court, and in the drawing room window a light burned. The curtain was parted a few inches; through the gap Gabriel could see a man, Dr. Robert Keller, upright in a wing chair. He was reading a broadsheet newspaper. Gabriel could not discern which one because rain streaked the car windows and a pall of cigarette smoke clouded the interior. Keller had been smoking without a break since Gabriel had collected him from a street corner in Holborn, his temporary London address. Now he was staring at his father's house as though it were the target of a close-observation surveillance operation. Gabriel realized suddenly that it was the first time he had ever seen Keller nervous.

"He's old," he said finally. "Older than I imagined he'd be."

"It's been a long time."

"Then I suppose it won't matter if we just sit here for a minute or two."

"Take as much time as you need."

"What time is your flight?"

"It's not important."

Gabriel cast a discreet glance at his wristwatch.

"I saw that," said Keller.

In the window across the street, an elderly woman was placing a cup and saucer at the elbow of the man reading the newspaper. Keller turned away—in shame or anguish, Gabriel could not tell.

"What's she doing now?" asked Keller.

"She's looking out the window."

"Did she make us?"

"I don't think so."

"Is she gone?"

"She's gone."

Keller looked up again.

"What kind of tea does he drink?" asked Gabriel.

"It's a special blend he gets from a man in New Bond Street."

"Maybe you should join him."

"In a minute." Keller crushed out his cigarette and immediately lit another.

"Must you?"

"At this moment," said Keller, "I most definitely must."

Gabriel lowered the window a few inches to vent the smoke. The night wind blew rain against his cheek.

"What are you going to say to them?"

"I was wondering whether you had any suggestions."

"You might start with the truth."

"They're old," said Keller. "The truth might kill them."

"Then give it in small doses."

"Like medicine," said Keller. He was still staring at the house. "He wanted me to be a doctor. Did you know that?"

"I think you mentioned it once."

"Can you imagine me as a doctor?"

"No," said Gabriel. "I cannot."

"You didn't have to say it like that."

Gabriel listened to the rain drumming on the roof.

"What if they won't take me back?" asked Keller after a moment. "What if they send me away?"

"Is that what you're afraid of?"

"Yes."

"They're your parents, Christopher."

"You're obviously not English." Keller rubbed a porthole in his fogged window and frowned at the rain. "I've been wet since the day I got back to this godforsaken country."

"It rains in Corsica, too."

"Not like this."

"Have you decided where you're going to live?"

"Somewhere close to them," Keller replied. "Unfortunately, they'll have to carry on as though I'm still dead. That's part of my deal with MI6."

"When do you start?"

"Tomorrow."

"What's your first assignment?"

"Find Quinn." Keller glanced at Gabriel and said,

"I would appreciate any help your service can provide. Apparently, I have to play by MI6 rules."

"Too bad."

Keller's mother appeared in the window again.

"What's she looking for?" he asked.

"Could be anything," said Gabriel.

"Do you think she'll be proud?"

"Of what?"

"Of the fact that I work for MI6 now."

"I know she will."

Keller reached for the latch, then stopped. "I've gone into a lot of dangerous situations before . . . " His voice trailed off. "Can I sit here a little longer?"

"Take as much time as you need."

"What time is your flight?"

"I'll put a hold on it if I have to."

Keller smiled. "I'm going to miss working with you."

"Who says it has to stop?"

"You'll be the chief soon. And chiefs don't associate with plebes like me." Keller placed his hand on the latch and raised his eyes toward the window of the house. "I know that look," he said.

"What look?"

"The look on my mother's face. She always looked like that when I was running late."

"You *are* running late, Christopher."

Keller turned sharply. "What have you done?"

"Go," said Gabriel, offering his hand. "You've kept them waiting long enough."

Keller climbed out of the car and hurried across the wet street. He fumbled for a moment with the garden gate, then bounded up the steps as the front door swung open. His parents stood in the entrance hall, leaning on each other for support, disbelieving of their eyes. Keller raised a finger to his lips and gathered them into his powerful arms before quickly closing the door. Gabriel saw him one last time as he passed before the window of the drawing room. Then a shade fell and he was gone.

82

NARKISS STREET, JERUSALEM

THAT SAME EVENING a cease-fire between Israel and Hamas collapsed and war resumed in the Gaza Strip. As Gabriel's flight approached Tel Aviv, flares and tracer fire lit the southern horizon. One Hamas rocket streaked dangerously close to Ben-Gurion Airport but was blown from the sky by an Iron Dome antimissile battery. Inside the terminal all appeared normal except for a group of Christian package tourists who huddled transfixed around a television monitor. No one noticed the deceased future chief of Israeli intelligence as he moved though the concourse, an overnight bag over his shoulder. At passport control he bypassed the long line and slipped through a door reserved for Office field personnel returning from missions abroad. Four Office security agents were drinking coffee in the waiting room on the other side. They led him along a brightly lit corridor to a secure door, beyond which two American-made SUVs idled in the predawn dark. Gabriel slid into the back of one. The closing of the armor-plated door made his ears pop.

On the opposite seat lay a copy of the overnight intelligence digest, courtesy of Uzi Navot. Gabriel opened the cover as the motorcade turned onto Highway 1 and started up the Bab al-Wad, the staircase-like gorge separating the Coastal Plain from Jerusalem. Its pages read like a catalogue of horrors from a world gone mad. The Arab Spring had turned into the Arab Calamity. Radical Islam now controlled a swath of territory that stretched from Afghanistan to Nigeria, an accomplishment that even Bin Laden would have never dreamed possible. It might have been funny were it not so dangerous—and so utterly predictable. The American president had allowed the old order to topple without a viable alternative in place, a reckless act with no precedent in modern statecraft. And for some reason he had chosen this moment in time to throw Israel to the wolves. Uzi was lucky, thought Gabriel, as he closed the digest. Uzi had managed to keep his finger in the dike. Now it would be left to Gabriel to build the ark. For the flood was coming, and there was nothing that could be done to stop it.

By the time they reached the fringes of Jerusalem, the stars were melting and the skies above the West Bank were beginning to lighten. Morning traffic moved along the Jaffa Road, but Narkiss Street slept on under the watch of an Office security detail. Eli Lavon had not been exaggerating about its size. There were teams at either end of the street and another outside the little limestone apartment house at Number 16. As Gabriel moved up the garden walk, he realized he had no key in his possession. It was no matter; Chiara had left the door unlocked. He set his bag on the floor in the entrance foyer. Then, after noticing the immaculate condition of the sitting room, he picked it up again and carried it down the hall.

The door to the spare bedroom hung slightly ajar. Gabriel opened it the rest of the way and peered inside. It had once been his studio. Now there were two cribs, one with pink bedding, the other with blue. Giraffes and elephants marched across the carpet. Plump clouds scudded across the walls. Gabriel felt a stab of guilt; in his absence Chiara must have done the work herself. As he ran his hand over the surface of the changing table a memory overtook him. It was the evening of April 18, 1988. Gabriel had returned home from the assassination of Abu Jihad in Tunis to find Dani suffering from a ferocious fever. He held the burning child in his arms that night while images of fire and death played ceaselessly in his thoughts. Three years later the child was dead.

Apparently, it had something to do with a man named Tariq . . .

Gabriel closed the door and entered the master bedroom. His life-size portrait, painted by Leah after Operation Wrath of God, hung upon the wall. Beneath it slept Chiara. He placed his bag on the floor in the closet, removed his shoes and clothing, and eased into bed next to her. She lay motionless, apparently unaware of his presence. Then suddenly she asked, "Do you like it, darling?"

"The nursery?"

"Yes."

"It's beautiful, Chiara. I only wish you would have let me paint the clouds."

"I wanted to," she answered. "But I was afraid it might be true."

"What's that?"

She said nothing more. Gabriel closed his eyes. And for the first time in three days he slept.

When finally he woke it was late afternoon and the shadows were long and thin upon the bed. He swung his feet to the floor and ambled into the kitchen for coffee. Chiara was watching the war on television. An Israeli bomb had just landed on a Palestinian school filled exclusively with women and young children—or so claimed Hamas. It seemed nothing had changed.

"Do we have to watch that?"

Chiara lowered the volume. She was wearing a pair of loose-fitting silk pants, gold sandals, and a maternity blouse that hung elegantly over her swollen breasts and abdomen. Her face was unchanged. If anything, she was more radiantly beautiful than Gabriel remembered. Suddenly, he regretted the month of time he had lost with her.

"There's coffee in the thermos."

Gabriel poured a cup and asked Chiara how she was feeling.

"Like I'm about to pop."

"Are you?"

"The doctor says they can come at any time."

"Any complications?"

"I'm starting to run a bit low on amniotic fluid, and one child is slightly smaller than the other."

"Which one?"

"The girl. The boy is fine." She looked at him for a moment. "You know, darling, we're going to have to choose a name for him at some point."

"I know."

"It would be better if we did it before they were born."

"I suppose."

"Moshe is a fine name."

"Yes."

"I've always loved Yaakov."

"Me, too. He's a fine officer. But there's a certain Iranian who'll be happy never to lay eyes on him again."

"Reza Nazari?"

Gabriel looked up from his coffee. "How do you know his name?"

"I received regular briefings during your absence."

"Who briefed you?"

"Who do you think?" Chiara smiled. "They're coming to dinner, by the way."

"Can't we do it another night? I just got home."

"Why don't you tell him you're too tired? I'm sure he'll understand."

"It would be easier," said Gabriel wearily, "to convince Hamas to stop shooting rockets at us."

At sunset Gabriel showered and dressed. Then he rode in his motorcade to the Mahane Yehuda Market where, trailed by bodyguards, he secured the necessary provisions for that evening's meal. Chiara had given him a list, which he left crumpled in his coat pocket. Instead, he shopped by instinct, his preferred method, and indulged his every whim and desire: nuts, dried fruits, hummus, baba ghanoush, bread, Israeli salad with feta cheese, prepared rice and meat, and several bottles of wine from the Galilee and Golan. A few heads turned to watch him pass, but otherwise his presence in the crowded souk went undetected.

When Gabriel's motorcade returned to Narkiss Street, a Peugeot limousine was parked curbside. Upstairs, he found Chiara and Gilah Shamron in the sitting room, surrounded by bags of clothing and other supplies. Shamron had already retired to the terrace to smoke. Gabriel plated the salads and laid them buffet-style on the kitchen counter. Then he placed the rice and the meat in a warm oven and poured two glasses of his favorite Israeli sauvignon blanc, which he carried onto the terrace. It was dark, and a cold wind was beginning to swirl. The smell of Shamron's Turkish tobacco mingled with the sharp tang of the eucalyptus tree that rose from the building's front garden. It was, thought Gabriel, an oddly comforting aroma. He handed Shamron a glass of wine and sat next to him.

"Future chiefs of the Office," said Shamron in a tone of mild rebuke, "don't go shopping in the Mahane Yehuda Market."

"They do if their wife is the size of a zeppelin."

"I'd keep thoughts like that to myself if I were you." Shamron smiled, inclined his glass in Gabriel's direction, and said, "Welcome home, my son."

Gabriel drank of the wine but said nothing. He was staring at the southern sky, waiting for the streak of a rocket, the flash of an Iron Dome missile strike. *Welcome home . . .*

"I had coffee with the prime minister this morning," Shamron was saying. "He sends his best. He'd also like to know when you intend to take your oath."

"Doesn't he know I'm dead?"

"Nice try."

"I'm going to need some time with my children, Ari."

"How much time?"

"Assuming they're healthy," said Gabriel thoughtfully, "I would think three months."

"Three months is a long time to be without a chief."

"We won't be without a chief. We have Uzi."

Shamron deliberately crushed out his cigarette. "Is it still your intention to keep him on?"

"By force if necessary."

"What shall we call him?"

"Let's call him Uzi. It's a very cool name."

Gabriel looked down at the young bodyguards milling in the quiet street. Never again would he set foot in public without them. And neither would his wife and children. Shamron started to light a cigarette but stopped himself.

"I can't say the prime minister is going to be pleased about a three-month paternity leave. In fact," he added, "he was wondering whether you would be willing to undertake a diplomatic mission on his behalf."

"Where?"

"Washington," said Shamron. "Our relationship with the Americans could use a bit of restoration. You've always got on well with the Americans. Even the president seems to like you."

"I wouldn't go that far."

"Will you make the trip?"

"Some paintings are beyond repair, Ari. And so are some relationships."

"You're going to need the Americans when you become chief."

"You always told me to keep my distance from them."

"The world has changed, my son."

"That's true," said Gabriel. "The American president writes love letters to the ayatollah. And us . . ." He gave an indifferent shrug of his shoulders but said nothing more.

"American presidents come and go, but we spies endure."

"So do Persians," remarked Gabriel.

"At least Reza Nazari won't be feeding the Office any more *taqiyya*. For the record," Shamron added, "I never thought much of him."

"Why didn't you say anything?"

"I did." Shamron finally lit another cigarette. "He's back in Tehran, by the way. He'd better stay there. Otherwise, the Russians are likely to kill him." Shamron smiled. "Your operation managed to plant a seed of mistrust between two of our adversaries."

"May it grow into a very large tree."

"How long before the next shoe drops?"

"Her article will appear in the Sunday edition."

"The Russians will deny it, of course."

"But no one will believe them," said Gabriel. "And they'll think twice about ever taking another shot at me."

"You underestimate them."

"Never."

A silence fell between them. Gabriel listened to the wind moving in the eucalyptus tree and the sound of Chiara's gentle voice drifting from the sitting room. It seemed a lifetime ago that he was in South Armagh. Even Quinn was slipping from his grasp. Quinn who could make a ball of fire travel a thousand feet per second. Quinn who had made the acquaintance in Libya of a Palestinian named Tariq al-Hourani.

"Is this how you imagined it would be?" asked Shamron quietly.

"Coming home?" Gabriel lifted his gaze to the south sky and waited for a flash of fire. "Yes," he said after a moment. "This is exactly how I imagined it would be."

83

NARKISS STREET, JERUSALEM

As with most noteworthy occasions in his life, Gabriel prepared for the birth of his children as though it were an operation. He planned the escape route, prepared a backup plan, and then devised backups for his backups. It was a model of economy and timing, with few moving parts, save for the star of the show. Shamron gave it a thorough review, as did Uzi Navot and the rest of Gabriel's fabled team. Without exception, all declared it a masterpiece.

It was not as if Gabriel had much else to do. For the first time in years he had no work and no prospect of work. He had managed to put the Office on hold, and there were no paintings to restore. Chiara was his only project now. The dinner with the Shamrons turned out to be her last public appearance. She was too uncomfortable to receive visitors, and even brief phone calls fatigued her. Gabriel hovered over her like a headwaiter, ever eager to fill an empty glass or send an unsatisfactory meal back to the kitchen. He was flawless in his demeanor and unfailingly considerate of her demands, be they physical or emotional. Even Chiara came to resent the perfection of his conduct.

Owing to her age and a complicated reproductive history, Chiara's pregnancy was considered high-risk. Consequently, her doctor insisted on seeing her every few days for a sonogram. In Gabriel's absence, she had traveled to Hadassah Medical Center accompanied by her bodyguards and, on occasion, Gilah Shamron. Now Gabriel came with her, with all the attendant madness of his official motorcade. In the examination room he would stand proprietarily over Chiara as the doctor ran the probe across her lubricated belly. Early in the pregnancy, the ultrasound had rendered the two children complete and distinct. Now it was difficult to tell where one child left off and the other began, though occasionally the machine would offer a shockingly clear glimpse of a face or hand that made Gabriel's heart beat with operational swiftness. The ghostly images looked like X-rays depicting the underdrawing of a painting. The dwindling supply of amniotic fluid appeared as islands of solid black.

"How long does she have?" asked Gabriel, with the gravity of a man who conducted most of his conversations in safe flats and over secure phones.

"Three days," said the doctor. "Four at most."

"Any chance they could come before that?"

"There's a *chance*," replied the doctor, "that she could go into labor on the way home today. But that's not likely to happen. She'll run out of fluid long before she goes into labor."

"What then?"

"A caesarean delivery is safest."

The doctor seemed to sense his unease. "Your wife will be fine," he said. Then, with a smile, he added, "I'm glad you're not dead. We need you. And so do your children."

The visits to the hospital were their only break from the long monotonous hours of bed rest and waiting. Restless with inactivity, Gabriel longed for a project. Chiara allowed him to pack her suitcase for the hospital, which consumed all of five minutes. Afterward, he went in search of something else to do. His quest led him into the nursery, where he stood for a long time before Chiara's clouds, a hand pressed to his chin, his head tilted slightly to one side.

"Would you mind terribly," he asked Chiara, "if I retouch them a bit?"

"What's wrong with them?"

"They're beautiful," he said too hastily.

"But?"

"They're a bit childlike."

"They're for children."

"That's not what I meant."

Grudgingly, she approved the commission, provided he use only child-safe paints and that the work be done within twenty-four hours. Gabriel hurried off to a nearby paint store with his bodyguards in tow and returned in short order with the necessary supplies. With a few strokes of a roller—an instrument he had never used before—he obliterated Chiara's work beneath a fresh layer of pale blue paint. It remained too wet to work more that evening, so he rose early the next morning and swiftly decorated the wall in a bank of glowing Titianesque clouds. Lastly, he added a small child angel, a boy, who was peering downward over the edge of the highest cloud on the scene below. The figure was borrowed from Veronese's *Virgin and Child in Glory with Saints*. With tears in his eyes and a trembling hand, Gabriel gave the angel the face of his son as it appeared on the night of his death. Then he signed his name and the date, and it was done.

Later that day the London *Sunday Telegraph* published an exclusive exposé linking Russia and its foreign intelligence service to the murder of the princess, the bombing on Brompton Road, the killing of four MI6 security personnel in West Cornwall, and the bloodbath in Crossmaglen, Northern Ireland. The operation, said the paper, was in reprisal for the revocation of lucrative Russian drilling rights in the North Sea and the defection of Madeline Hart, the Russian sleeper agent who had briefly shared Prime Minister Lancaster's bed. Russia's president had ordered it; Alexei Rozanov, the SVR officer recently found dead in Germany, had overseen its implementation. His primary operative had been Eamon Quinn, the Omagh bomber turned international mercenary. Quinn was now missing and was the target of a global manhunt.

The reaction to the report was swift and explosive. Prime Minister Lancaster denounced the Kremlin's actions as "barbaric," a sentiment echoed across the Atlantic in Washington, where politicians from both sides of the political divide called for Russia's expulsion from the G8 and the other economic clubs of the West. In Moscow a Kremlin spokesman dismissed the *Telegraph*'s story as a piece of anti-Russian propaganda, and he called on the reporter, Samantha Cooke, to reveal the identities of her sources—something she steadfastly refused to do during a round of television interviews. Those in the know suggested the Israelis had surely been of assistance. After all, they pointed out, the Russian operation had claimed the life of a legend. If anyone wanted Russian blood, it was the Israelis.

No one in Israeli officialdom agreed to speak about the *Telegraph*'s piece—not in the prime minister's office, not at the Ministry of Foreign Affairs, and surely not at King Saul Boulevard, where outside lines rang unanswered. A small piece on a gossipy Israeli Web site did provoke a comment, however. It stated that the same legendary Israeli operative who had died in the Brompton Road bombing had been spotted recently in the Mahane Yehuda Market looking none the worse for wear. An unidentified aide in an unnamed ministry dismissed the report as "hogwash."

But his neighbors in Narkiss Street, were they not protective of him to a fault, would have told a different story. So, too, would the staff at Hadassah Medical Center, and the pair of rabbis who spotted him late that same afternoon placing a stone atop a grave on the Mount of Olives. They did not attempt to speak to him, for they could see he was grieving. He left the cemetery in twilight and traveled across Jerusalem to Mount Herzl. There was a woman there who needed to know he was still among the living, even if she would not remember him when he was gone.

84

MOUNT HERZL, JERUSALEM

D URING THE DRIVE from the Mount of Olives, a gentle snow began to fall upon God's fractured city on a hill. It coated the tiny circular drive of the Mount Herzl Psychiatric Hospital and whitened the limbs of the stone pine in the walled garden. Inside the clinic, Leah watched the snow vacantly from the windows of the common room. She was seated in her wheelchair. Her hair was gray and cut institutionally short; her hands were twisted and white with scar tissue. Her doctor, a rabbinical-looking man with a round face and a wondrous beard of many colors, had cleared the room of other patients. He seemed not entirely surprised to learn that Gabriel was still alive. He had been caring for Leah for more than ten years. He knew things about the legend others did not.

"You should have alerted me that it was all a ruse," the doctor said. "We could have done something to shield her. As you might expect, your death caused quite a stir."

"There wasn't time."

"I'm sure you had good reason," the doctor said reproachfully.

"I did." Gabriel allowed a few seconds to pass to take the sharp edge off the conversation. "I never know how much she understands."

"She knows more than you realize. We had a rough few days."

"And now?"

"She's better, but you have to be careful with her." He shook Gabriel's hand. "Take as much time as you want. I'll be in my office if you need anything."

When the doctor was gone, Gabriel moved quietly across the limestone tiles of the common room. A chair had been placed at Leah's side. She was still watching the snow. But upon what city was it falling? Was she in Jerusalem at that moment? Or was she trapped in the past? Leah suffered from a particularly acute combination of post-traumatic stress disorder and psychotic depression. In her watery memory, time was elusive. Gabriel never quite knew which Leah he would encounter. One minute she could be the stunningly gifted painter he had fallen in love with at the Bezalel Academy of Art and Design in Jerusalem. The next she could present herself as the mature mother of a beautiful young boy who had insisted on accompanying her husband on a work trip to Vienna.

For several minutes she watched the snow, unblinking. Perhaps she was unaware of his presence. Or perhaps she was punishing him for allowing her to think that he was dead. Finally, her head turned and her eyes traveled over him, as though she were searching for a lost object in the cluttered closets of her memory.

"Gabriel?" she asked.

"Yes, Leah."

"Are you real, my love? Or am I hallucinating?"

"I'm real."

"Where are we?"

"Jerusalem."

Her head turned and she watched the snow. "Isn't it beautiful?"

"Yes, Leah."

"The snow absolves Vienna of its sins. Snow falls on Vienna while the missiles rain on Tel Aviv." She came back to him. "I hear them at night," she said.

"What's that?"

"The missiles."

"You're safe here, Leah."

"I want to talk to my mother. I want to hear the sound of my mother's voice."

"We'll call her."

"Make sure Dani is buckled into his seat. The streets are slippery."

"He's fine, Leah."

She looked down at his hands and noticed smudges of paint. It seemed to wrench her back to the present. "You've been working?" she asked.

"A little."

"Something important?"

He swallowed hard and said, "A nursery, Leah."

"For your children?"

He nodded.

"Have they been born yet?"

"Soon," he said.

"A boy and a girl?"

"Yes, Leah."

"What are you going to call the girl?"

"She'll be called Irene."

"Irene is your mother's name."

"That's right."

"She's dead, your mother?"

"A long time ago."

"And the boy? What will you name the boy?"

Gabriel hesitated, then said, "The boy will be named Raphael."

"The angel of healing." She smiled and asked, "Are you healed, Gabriel?"

"Not quite."

"Nor am I."

She looked up at the television, puzzlement on her face. Gabriel held her hand. The scar tissue made it feel cold and firm. It was like a patch of bare canvas. He longed to retouch it but could not. Leah was the one thing in the world he could not restore.

"Are you dead?" she asked suddenly.

"No, Leah. I'm here with you."

"The television said you were killed in London."

"It was something we had to say."

"Why?"

"It's not important."

"You always say that, my love."

"Do I?"

"Only when it really is." Her eyes settled on him. "Where were you?"

"I was looking for the man who helped Tariq build the bomb."

"Did you find him?"

"Almost."

She gave his hand a reassuring squeeze. "It was a long time ago, Gabriel. And it won't change a thing. I'll still be the way I am. And you'll still be married to another woman."

Gabriel couldn't bear her accusatory stare any longer, so he watched the snow instead. After a few seconds she joined him.

"You'll let me see them, won't you, Gabriel?"

"As soon as I can."

"And you'll take good care of them, especially the boy?"

"Of course."

Her eyes widened suddenly. "I want to hear the sound of my mother's voice."

"So do I."

"Make sure Dani is buckled into his car seat tightly."

"I will," said Gabriel. "The streets are slippery."

During the drive back to Narkiss Street, Gabriel received a text message from Chiara requesting his estimated time of arrival. He didn't bother to respond because he was just around the corner. He hurried up the garden walk, leaving a trail of telltale size-ten footprints in the undisturbed layer of snow, and climbed the stairs to his apartment. Entering, he saw the suitcase he had so carefully packed standing in the entrance hall. Chiara was seated on the couch, dressed and coated, singing softly to herself as she leafed through a glossy magazine.

"Why didn't you tell me earlier?" Gabriel asked.

"I thought it would be a nice surprise."

"I hate surprises."

"I know." She smiled beautifully.

"What happened?"

"I wasn't feeling well this afternoon, so I called the doctor. He thought we should get it over with."

"When?"

"Tonight, darling. We need to get to the hospital."

Gabriel stood with the stillness of a bronze statue.

"This is the part where you help me to my feet," said Chiara.

"Oh, yes, of course."

"And don't forget the bag."

"Wait . . . what?"

"The suitcase, darling. I'll need my things at the hospital."

"Yes, the hospital."

Gabriel helped Chiara down the stairs and across the front walk, all the while flogging himself for having neglected to factor the possibility of snow into his planning. In the back of the SUV, she leaned her head against his shoulder and closed her eyes to rest. Gabriel inhaled the intoxicating scent of vanilla and watched the snow dancing against the glass. It was beautiful, he thought. It was the most beautiful thing he had ever seen.

T WASN'T AS if they had nothing better to do that spring. After all, even the most casual observer— the historically brain-dead, as Graham Seymour often described them in his darker moments— realized the world was wobbling dangerously out of control. Strapped for resources, Seymour assigned only one officer to the task. It didn't matter; one officer was all he needed. He gave the man a briefcase full of cash and considerable operational leeway. The briefcase came from a shop in Jermyn Street. The money was American, for in the nether regions of the espionage world, dollars remained the reserve currency.

He traveled under many names that spring, none of them his own. In fact, at that particular point of his life and career, he really didn't have a name. His parents, with whom he had recently been reunited, referred to him by the name they had given him at birth. At work, however, he was known only by a four-digit numeric cipher. His flat in Chelsea was officially owned by a company that did not exist. He had set foot there only once.

His search took him to many dangerous places, which was of no consequence, for he was a dangerous man himself. He spent several days in Dublin at the perilous intersection of drugs and rebellion, and then popped into Lisbon on the off chance his quarry's connection to the city was more than merely cosmetic. A nasty rumor took him to a godforsaken village in Belarus; an intercepted e-mail, to Istanbul. There he met a source who claimed to have seen the target in an ISIS-controlled region of Syria. With London's reluctant blessing, he crossed the border on foot and, disguised as an Arab, made his way to the house where the target was said to be living. The house was empty, save for a few snippets of wiring and a notebook that contained several diagrams for bombs. He pocketed the notebook and returned to Turkey. Along the way he saw images of brutality that he would not soon forget.

Late February saw him in Mexico City, where a bribe produced a lead that sent him to Panama. He spent a week there watching an empty condominium on the Playa Farallón. Then, on a hunch, he flew to Rio de Janeiro, where a plastic surgeon with a dubious clientele admitted he had recently altered the target's appearance. According to the doctor, the patient claimed he was living in Bogotá, but a visit there turned up nothing but a distraught woman who might or might not have been carrying his child. The woman suggested he look in Buenos Aires, which he did. And it was there, on a cool afternoon in mid-April, that an old debt came due.

He was cooking at a restaurant called Brasserie Petanque, in the southern barrio of San Telmo. His apartment was around the corner, on the third floor of a building that looked as though it had been plucked from the boulevard Saint-Germain. Across the street was a café where Keller sat drinking coffee at a table on the pavement. He wore a brimmed hat and sunglasses; his hair had the healthy sheen of a man gone prematurely gray. He appeared to be reading a Spanish-language literary magazine. He was not.

He left a few pesos on the table, crossed the street, and entered the foyer of the apartment building. A tabby cat circled his feet while he read the name on the mailbox for Apartment 309. Upstairs, he found the door to the apartment locked. It was no matter; Keller had acquired a copy of the key from the building's maintenance man for a bribe of five hundred dollars.

He drew his gun as he entered and closed the door. The apartment was small and sparsely furnished. Next to the bed was a pile of books and a shortwave radio. The books were thick, weighty, and learned. The radio was of a quality rarely seen any longer. Keller powered it on and raised the volume to a whisper. "My Funny Valentine" by Miles Davis. He smiled. He had come to the right place.

Keller switched off the radio and moved aside the curtain that shaded Quinn's last remaining window on the world. And there he stood with the discipline of a close-observation specialist for the remainder of the afternoon. Finally, a man appeared at the café and sat at the same table Keller had vacated. He drank local beer and was dressed in local clothing. Even so, it was clear he was not a native of Argentina. Keller raised a miniature monocular telescope to his eye and studied the man's face. The Brazilian had done a fine job, he thought. The man at the table was unrecognizable. The only thing that betrayed him was the way he handled his knife when the proprietor brought his steak. Quinn was a master technician, but he always did his best work with a knife.

Keller remained at the edge of the window with the miniature telescope pressed to his eye, watching, waiting, while Quinn consumed the last meal he would ever eat. When he was finished, he paid the proprietor and, rising, crossed the street. Keller slipped the miniature telescope into his pocket and stood in the entrance hall, the gun in his outstretched hands. After a moment he heard footfalls in the corridor and the crunch of a key entering the lock. Quinn never saw Keller's face and never felt the two bullets—one for Elizabeth Conlin, the other for Dani Allon—that ended his life. For that much at least, Keller was sorry.

*T*HE *ENGLISH* *SPY* is a work of entertainment and should be read as nothing more. The names, characters, places, and incidents portrayed in the story are the product of the author's imagination or have been used fictitiously. Any resemblance to actual persons, living or dead, businesses, companies, events, or locales is entirely coincidental.

There is indeed a lovely cottage at the southern end of the Gunwalloe fishing cove that has always reminded the author of Monet's *Customs Officer's Cabin at Pourville,* but to the best of my knowledge neither Gabriel Allon nor Madeline Hart have ever resided there. Nor should readers go searching for Gabriel at 16 Narkiss Street, as he and Chiara have their hands full at the moment. Reports from Jerusalem indicate that mother and children are doing fine. Father is another matter altogether. More on that in the next installment of the series.

Visitors to the northern English town of Fleetwood will search in vain for an Internet café opposite the chippy. There is no pub in Gunwalloe called Lamb and Flag, nor is there a bar in Crossmaglen called the Emerald, though there are several like it. Apologies to the management of Le Piment restaurant on the island of Saint Barthélemy for placing an IRA bomb maker in their small but glorious kitchen. Apologies as well to Die Bank restaurant in Hamburg, the InterContinental Hotel in Vienna, and, especially, the Kempinski Hotel in Berlin. Room 518 must have been quite a mess.

For the record, I am aware that the headquarters of Israel's secret intelligence service is no longer located on King Saul Boulevard in Tel Aviv. My fictitious service continues to reside there, in part because I like the name better than that of the current location, which I will not mention in print. Also, I have been asked many times whether Don Anton Orsati is based on a real individual. He is not. The don, his valley, and his unique business enterprise were all invented by the author.

The English Spy is the fourth Gabriel Allon adventure to feature the don's best assassin: former SAS commando Christopher Keller. The novel ends in the place where Keller's story began, in the dangerous green hills of South Armagh. During the worst of the long and bloody war for Northern Ireland, the region truly was the most dangerous place in the world to wear the uniform of a soldier or police officer. The largest single loss of life occurred on August 27, 1979, when two large roadside bombs killed eighteen British soldiers at Warrenpoint. The attack occurred just hours after Lord Mountbatten, a British statesman and relative of Queen Elizabeth II, was killed by an IRA bomb concealed aboard his fishing boat—an incident that suggested the open-